THE MIDNIGHT LINE

www.**penguin**.co.uk

Also by Lee Child

KILLING FLOOR
DIE TRYING
TRIPWIRE
THE VISITOR
ECHO BURNING
WITHOUT FAIL
PERSUADER
THE ENEMY
ONE SHOT
THE HARD WAY
BAD LUCK AND TROUBLE
NOTHING TO LOSE
GONE TOMORROW
61 HOURS
WORTH DYING FOR
THE AFFAIR
A WANTED MAN
NEVER GO BACK
PERSONAL
MAKE ME
NIGHT SCHOOL
NO MIDDLE NAME

For more information on Lee Child and his books,
see his website at www.leechild.com

THE MIDNIGHT LINE

Lee Child

BANTAM PRESS

LONDON • TORONTO • SYDNEY • AUCKLAND • JOHANNESBURG

TRANSWORLD PUBLISHERS
61–63 Uxbridge Road, London W5 5SA
www.penguin.co.uk

Transworld is part of the Penguin Random House group of companies
whose addresses can be found at global.penguinrandomhouse.com

Penguin
Random House
UK

First published in Great Britain in 2017 by Bantam Press
an imprint of Transworld Publishers

A CIP catalogue record for this book
is available from the British Library.

ISBNs 9780593078181 (cased)
9780593078174 (tpb)

Typeset in 11/15½pt Century Old Style by Falcon Oast Graphic Art Ltd.
Printed and bound by Clays Ltd, Bungay, Suffolk.

Penguin Random House is committed to a sustainable
future for our business, our readers and our planet. This book
is made from Forest Stewardship Council® certified paper.

MIX
Paper from
responsible sources
FSC® C018179

3 5 7 9 10 8 6 4 2

So far in American history nearly two million Purple Hearts have been awarded. This book is respectfully dedicated to each and every recipient.

ONE

Jack Reacher and Michelle Chang spent three days in Milwaukee. On the fourth morning she was gone. Reacher came back to the room with coffee and found a note on his pillow. He had seen such notes before. They all said the same thing. Either directly or indirectly. Chang's note was indirect. And more elegant than most. Not in terms of presentation. It was a ballpoint scrawl on motel notepaper gone wavy with damp. But elegant in terms of expression. She had used a simile, to explain and flatter and apologize all at once. She had written, *You're like New York City. I love to visit, but I could never live there.*

He did what he always did. He let her go. He understood. No apology required. He couldn't live anywhere. His whole life was a visit. Who could put up with that? He drank his coffee, and then hers, and took his toothbrush from the bathroom glass, and walked away, through a knot of streets, left and right, towards the bus depot. She would be in a taxi, he guessed. To the airport. She had a gold card and a cell phone.

At the depot he did what he always did. He bought a ticket for

1

the first bus out, no matter where it was going. Which turned out to be an end-of-the-line place way north and west, on the shore of Lake Superior. Fundamentally the wrong direction. Colder, not warmer. But rules were rules, so he climbed aboard. He sat and watched out the window. Wisconsin flashed by, its hayfields baled and stubbly, its pastures worn, its trees dark and heavy. It was the end of summer.

It was the end of several things. She had asked the usual questions. Which were really statements in disguise. She could understand a year. Absolutely. A kid who grew up on bases overseas, and was then deployed to bases overseas, with nothing in between except four years at West Point, which wasn't exactly known as a leisure-heavy institution, then obviously such a guy was going to take a year to travel and see the sights before he settled down. Maybe two years. But not more. And not permanently. Face it. The pathology meter was twitching.

All said with concern, and no judgement. No big deal. Just a two-minute conversation. But the message was clear. As clear as such messages could be. Something about denial. He asked, denial of what? He didn't secretly think his life was a problem.

That proves it, she said.

So he got on the bus to the end-of-the-line place, and he would have ridden it all the way, because rules were rules, except he took a stroll at the second comfort stop, and he saw a ring in a pawn shop window.

The second comfort stop came late in the day, and it was on the sad side of a small town. Possibly a seat of county government. Or some minor part of it. Maybe the county police department was headquartered there. There was a jail in town. That was clear. Reacher could see bail bond offices, and a pawn shop. Full service, right there, side by side on a run-down street beyond the restroom block.

2

He was stiff from sitting. He scanned the street beyond the restroom block. He started walking towards it. No real reason. Just strolling. Just loosening up. As he got closer he counted the guitars in the pawn shop window. Seven. Sad stories, all of them. Like the songs on country radio. Dreams, unfulfilled. Lower down in the window were glass shelves loaded with smaller stuff. All kinds of jewellery. Including rings. Including class rings. All kinds of high schools. Except one of them wasn't. One of them was West Point 2005.

It was a handsome ring. It was a conventional shape, and a conventional style, with intricate gold filigree, and a black stone, maybe semi-precious, maybe glass, surrounded by an oval hoop that had *West Point* around the top, and *2005* around the bottom. Old-style letters. A classic approach. Either respect for bygone days, or a lack of imagination. West Pointers designed their own rings. Whatever they wanted. An old tradition. Or an old entitlement, perhaps, because West Point class rings had been the first class rings of all.

It was a very small ring.

Reacher wouldn't have gotten it on any of his fingers. Not even his left-hand pinky, not even past the nail. Certainly not past the first knuckle. It was tiny. It was a woman's ring. Possibly a replica for a girlfriend or a fiancée. That happened. Like a tribute or a souvenir.

But possibly not.

Reacher opened the pawn shop door. He stepped inside. A guy at the register looked up. He was a big bear of a man, scruffy and unkempt. Maybe in his middle thirties, dark, with plenty of fat over a big frame anyway. With some kind of cunning in his eyes. Certainly enough to perfect his response to his sudden six-five two-fifty visitor. Driven purely by instinct. The guy wasn't afraid. He had a loaded gun under the counter. Unless he was an idiot. Which he didn't look. All the same, the guy didn't want to risk

3

sounding aggressive. But he didn't want to sound obsequious, either. A matter of pride.

So he said, 'How's it going?'

Not well, Reacher thought. *To be honest*. Chang would be back in Seattle by then. Back in her life.

But he said, 'Can't complain.'

'Can I help you?'

'Show me your class rings.'

The guy threaded the tray backward off the shelf. He put it on the counter. The West Point ring had rolled over, like a tiny golf ball. Reacher picked it up. It was engraved inside. Which meant it wasn't a replica. Not for a fiancée or a girlfriend. Replicas were never engraved. An old tradition. No one knew why.

Not a tribute, not a souvenir. It was the real deal. A cadet's own ring, earned over four hard years. Worn with pride. Obviously. If you weren't proud of the place, you didn't buy a ring. It wasn't compulsory.

The engraving said *S.R.S. 2005*.

The bus blew its horn three times. It was ready to go, but it was a passenger short. Reacher put the ring down and said, 'Thank you,' and walked out of the store. He hustled back past the restroom block and leaned in the door of the bus and said to the driver, 'I'm staying here.'

'No refunds.'

'Not looking for one.'

'You got a bag in the hold?'

'No bag.'

'Have a nice day.'

The guy pulled a lever and the door sucked shut in Reacher's face. The engine roared and the bus moved off without him. He turned away from the diesel smoke and walked back towards the pawn shop.

TWO

The guy in the pawn shop was a little disgruntled to have to get the ring tray out again so soon after he had put it away. But he did, and he placed it in the same spot on the counter. The West Point ring had rolled over again. Reacher picked it up.

He said, 'Do you remember the woman who pawned this?'

'How would I?' the guy said. 'I got a million things in here.'

'You got records?'

'You a cop?'

'No,' Reacher said.

'Everything in here is legal.'

'I don't care. All I want is the name of the woman who brought you this ring.'

'Why?'

'We went to the same school.'

'Where is that? Upstate?'

'East of here,' Reacher said.

'You can't be a classmate. Not from 2005. No offence.'

'None taken. I was from an earlier generation. But the place doesn't change much. Which means I know how hard she worked for this ring. So now I'm wondering what kind of unlucky circumstance made her give it up.'

The guy said, 'What kind of a school was it?'

'They teach you practical things.'

'Like a trade school?'

'More or less.'

'Maybe she died in an accident.'

'Maybe she did,' Reacher said. *Or not in an accident,* he thought. There had been Iraq, and there had been Afghanistan. 2005 had been a tough year to graduate. He said, 'But I would like to know for sure.'

'Why?' the guy said again.

'I can't tell you exactly.'

'Is it an honour thing?'

'I guess it could be.'

'Trade schools have that?'

'Some of them.'

'There was no woman. I bought that ring. With a lot of other stuff.'

'When?'

'About a month ago.'

'From who?'

'I'm not going to tell you my business. Why should I? It's all legal. It's all perfectly legitimate. The state says so. I have a licence and I pass all kinds of inspections.'

'Then why be shy about it?'

'It's private information.'

Reacher said, 'Suppose I buy the ring?'

'It's fifty bucks.'

'Thirty.'

'Forty.'

6

'Deal,' Reacher said. 'So now I'm entitled to know its provenance.'

'This ain't Sotheby's auction house.'

'Even so.'

The guy paused a beat.

Then he said, 'It was from a guy who helps out with a charity. People donate things and take the deduction. Mostly old cars and boats. But other things too. The guy gives them an inflated receipt for their tax returns, and then he sells the things he gets wherever he can, for whatever he can, and then he cuts a cheque to the charity. I buy the small stuff from him. I get what I get, and I hope to turn a profit.'

'So you think someone donated this ring to a charity and took a deduction on their income taxes?'

'Makes sense, if the original person died. From 2005. Part of the estate.'

'I don't think so,' Reacher said. 'I think a relative would have kept it.'

'Depends if the relative was eating well.'

'You got tough times here?'

'I'm OK. But I own the pawn shop.'

'Yet people still donate to good causes.'

'In exchange for phony receipts. In the end the government eats the tax relief. Welfare by another name.'

Reacher said, 'Who is the charity guy?'

'I won't tell you that.'

'Why not?'

'It's none of your business. I mean, who the hell are you?'

'Just a guy already having a pretty bad day. Not your fault, of course, but if asked to offer advice I would have to say it might prove a dumb idea to make my day worse. You might be the straw that breaks the camel's back.'

'You threatening me now?'

'More like the weather report. A public service. Like a tornado warning. Prepare to take cover.'

'Get out of my store.'

'Fortunately I no longer have a headache. I got hit in the head, but that's all better now. A doctor said so. A friend made me go. Two times. She was worried about me.'

The pawn shop guy paused another beat.

Then he said, 'Exactly what kind of a school was that ring from?'

Reacher said, 'It was a military academy.'

'Those are for, excuse me, problem kids. Or disturbed. No offence.'

'Don't blame the kids,' Reacher said. 'Look at the families. Tell the truth, at our school there were a lot of parents who had killed people.'

'Really?'

'More than the average.'

'So you stick together for ever?'

'We don't leave anyone behind.'

'The guy won't talk to a stranger.'

'Does he have a licence and does he pass inspections by the state?'

'What I'm doing here is legal. My lawyer says so. As long as I honestly believe it. And I do. It's from a charity. I've seen the paperwork. All kinds of people do it. They even have commercials on TV. Cars, mostly. Sometimes boats.'

'But this particular guy won't talk to me?'

'I would be surprised.'

'Does he have no manners?'

'I wouldn't ask him over to a picnic.'

'What's his name?'

'Jimmy Rat.'

'For real?'

8

'That's what he goes by.'

'Where would I find Mr Rat?'

'Look for a minimum six Harley-Davidsons. Jimmy will be in whatever bar they're outside of.'

THREE

The town was relatively small. Beyond the sad side was a side maybe five years from going sad. Maybe more. Maybe ten. There was hope. There were some boarded-up enterprises, but not many. Most stores were still doing business, at a leisurely rural pace. Big pick-up trucks rolled through, slowly. There was a billiard hall. Not many street lights. It was getting dark. Something about the architecture made it clear it was dairy country. The shape of the stores looked like old-fashioned milking barns. The same DNA was in there somewhere.

There was a bar in a stand-alone wooden building, with a patch of weedy gravel for parking, and on the gravel were seven Harley-Davidsons, all in a neat line. Possibly not actual Hell's Angels as such. Possibly one of many other parallel denominations. Bikers were as split as Baptists. All the same, but different. Apparently these particular guys liked black leather tassels and chromium plating. They liked to lay back and ride with their legs spread wide and their feet sticking out in front of them. Possibly a cooling effect. Perhaps necessary. Generally they wore heavy leather vests. And pants, and boots. All black. Hot, in late summer.

The bikes were all painted dark shiny colours, four with orange flames, three with rune-like symbols outlined in silver. The bar was dull with age, and some shingles had slipped. There was an air conditioner in one of the windows, straining to keep up, dripping water in a puddle below. A cop car rolled past, slowly, its tyres hissing on the blacktop. County Police. Probably spent the first half of its watch ginning up municipal revenue with a radar gun out on the highway, now prowling the back streets of the towns in its jurisdiction. Showing the flag. Paying attention to the trouble spots. The cop inside turned his head and gazed at Reacher. The guy was nothing like the pawnbroker. He was all squared away. His face was lean, and his eyes were wise. He was sitting behind the wheel with a ramrod posture, and his haircut was fresh. A whitewall buzz cut. Maybe just a day old. Not more than two.

Reacher stood still and watched him roll away. He heard a motorcycle exhaust in the distance, coming closer, getting louder, heavy as a hammer. An eighth Harley came around the corner, as slow as gravity would allow, a big heavy machine, blatting and popping, the rider laying back with his feet on pegs way out in front. He leaned into a turn and slowed on the gravel. He was wearing a black leather vest over a black T-shirt. He parked last in line. His bike idled like a blacksmith hitting an anvil. Then he shut it down and hauled it up on its stand. Silence came back.

Reacher said, 'I'm looking for Jimmy Rat.'

The guy glanced at one of the other bikes. Couldn't help himself. But he said, 'Don't know him,' and walked away, stiff and bow-legged, to the door of the bar. He was pear-shaped, and maybe forty years old. Maybe five-ten, and bulky. He had a sallow tan, like his skin was rubbed with motor oil. He pulled the door and stepped inside.

Reacher stayed where he was. The bike the new guy had glanced at was one of the three with silver runes. It was as huge as all the others, but the footrests and the handlebars were set a little closer to the seat than most. About two inches closer than the new guy's, for example. Which made Jimmy Rat about five-eight, possibly. Maybe skinny, to go with his name. Maybe armed, with a knife or a gun. Maybe vicious.

Reacher walked to the door of the bar. He pulled it open and stepped inside. The air was dark and hot and smelled of spilled beer. The room was rectangular, with a full-length copper bar on the left, and tables on the right. There was an arch in the rear wall, with a narrow corridor beyond. Restrooms and a pay phone and a fire door. Four windows. A total of six potential exits. The first thing an ex-MP counted.

The eight bikers were packed in around two four-tops shoved together by a window. They had beers on the go, in heavy glasses wet with humidity. The new guy was shoehorned in, pear-shaped on a chair, with the fullest glass. Six of the others were in a similar category, in terms of size and shape and general visual appeal. One was worse. About five-eight, stringy, with a narrow face and restless eyes.

Reacher stopped at the bar and asked for coffee.

'Don't have any,' the barman said. 'Sorry.'

'Is that Jimmy Rat over there? The small guy?'

'You got a beef with him, you take it outside, OK?'

The barman moved away. Reacher waited. One of the bikers drained his glass and stood up and headed for the restroom corridor. Reacher crossed the room and sat down in his vacant chair. The wood felt hot. The eighth guy made the connection. He stared at Reacher, and then he glanced at Jimmy Rat.

Who said, 'This is a private party, bud. You ain't invited.'

Reacher said, 'I need some information.'

'About what?'

'Charitable donations.'

Jimmy Rat looked blank. Then he remembered. He glanced at the door, somewhere beyond which lay the pawn shop, where he had made assurances. He said, 'Get lost, bud.'

Reacher put his left fist on the table. The size of a supermarket chicken. Long thick fingers with knuckles like walnuts. Old nicks and scars healed white against his summer tan. He said, 'I don't care what scam you're running. Or who you're stealing from. Or who you're fencing for. I got no interest in any of that. All I want to know is where you got this ring.'

He opened his fist. The ring lay in his palm. *West Point 2005*. The gold filigree, the black stone. The tiny size. Jimmy Rat said nothing, but something in his eyes made Reacher believe he recognized the item.

Reacher said, 'Another name for West Point is the United States Military Academy. There's a clue right there, in the first two words. This is a federal case.'

'You a cop?'

'No, but I got a quarter for the phone.'

The missing guy got back from the restroom. He stood behind Reacher's chair, arms spread wide in exaggerated perplexity. As if to say, what the hell is going on here? Who is this guy? Reacher kept one eye on Jimmy Rat, and one on the window alongside him, where he could see a faint ghostly reflection of what was happening behind his shoulder.

Jimmy Rat said, 'That's someone's chair.'

'Yeah, mine,' Reacher said.

'You've got five seconds.'

'I've got as long as it takes for you to answer my question.'

'You feeling lucky tonight?'

'I won't need to be.'

Reacher put his right hand on the table. It was a little larger than his left. Normal for right-handed people. It had a few more nicks and scars, including a white V-shaped blemish that looked like a snakebite, but had been made by a nail.

Jimmy Rat shrugged, like the whole conversation was really no big deal.

He said, 'I'm part of a supply chain. I get stuff from other people who get it from other people. That ring was donated or sold or pawned and not redeemed. I don't know anything more than that.'

'What other people did you get it from?'

Jimmy Rat said nothing. Reacher watched the window with his left eye. With his right he saw Jimmy Rat nod. The reflection in the glass showed the guy behind winding up a big roundhouse right. Clearly the plan was to smack Reacher on the ear. Maybe topple him off the chair. At least soften him up a little.

Didn't work.

Reacher chose the path of least resistance. He ducked his head, and let the punch scythe through the empty air above it. Then he bounced back up, and launched from his feet, and twisted, and used his falling-backward momentum to jerk his elbow into the guy's kidney, which was rotating around into position just in time. It was a good solid hit. The guy went down hard. Reacher fell back in his chair and sat there like absolutely nothing had happened.

Jimmy Rat stared.

The barman called, 'Take it outside, pal. Like I told you.'

He sounded like he meant it.

Jimmy Rat said, 'Now you've got trouble.'

He sounded like he meant it too.

Right then Chang would be shopping for dinner. Maybe a small grocery close to her home. Wholesome ingredients. But simple. She was probably tired.

A bad day.

Reacher said, 'I've got six fat guys and a runt. That's a walk in the park.'

14

He stood up. He turned and stepped on the guy on the floor and walked over him. Onward to the door. Out to the gravel, and the line of shiny bikes. He turned and saw the others come out after him. The not-very-magnificent seven. Generally stiff and bow-legged, and variously contorted due to beer guts and bad posture. But still, a lot of weight. In the aggregate. Plus fourteen fists, and fourteen boots.

Possibly steel-capped.

Maybe a very bad day.

But who cared, really?

The seven guys fanned out in a semicircle, three on Jimmy Rat's left, and three on his right. Reacher kept moving, rotating them the way he wanted, his back to the street. He didn't want to get trapped against someone's rear fence. He didn't want to get jammed in a corner. He didn't plan on running, but an option was always a fine thing to have.

The seven guys tightened their semicircle, but not enough. They stayed about ten feet away, with better than a yard between each one of them. Which made the first two plays obvious. They would come shuffling in, slowly, maybe grunting and glaring, whereupon Reacher would move fast and punch his way through the line, after which everyone would turn around, Reacher now facing a new inverted semicircle, now only six in number. Then rinse and repeat, which would reduce them to five. They wouldn't fall for it a third time, so at that point they would swarm, all except Jimmy Rat, who Reacher figured wouldn't fight at all. Too smart. Which in the end would make it a close-quarters four-on-one brawl.

A bad day.

For someone.

'Last chance,' Reacher said. 'Tell the little guy to answer my question, and you can all go back to your suds.'

No one spoke. They tightened some more and hunched down

into crouches and started shuffling forward, hands apart and ready. Reacher picked out his first target and waited. He wanted him five feet away. One pace, not two. Better to save the extra energy for later.

Then he heard tyres on the road again, behind him, and in front of him the seven guys straightened up and looked around, with exaggerated wide-eyed innocence all over their faces. Reacher turned and saw the cop car again. The same guy. County Police. The car coasted to a stop and the guy took a good long look. He buzzed his passenger window down, and leaned across inside, and caught Reacher's eye, and said, 'Sir, please approach the vehicle.'

Which Reacher did, but not on the passenger side. He didn't want to turn his back. Instead he tracked around the trunk to the driver's window. Which buzzed down, while the passenger side buzzed back up. The cop had his gun in his hand. Relaxed, held low in his lap.

The cop said, 'Want to tell me what's going on here?'

Reacher said, 'Were you army or Marine Corps?'

'Why would I be either?'

'Most of you are, in a place like this. Especially the ones who hike all the way to the nearest PX to get their hair cut.'

'I was army.'

'Me too. There's nothing going on here.'

'I need to hear the whole story. Lots of guys were in the army. I don't know you.'

'Jack Reacher, 110th MP. Terminal at major. Pleased to meet you.'

The cop said, 'I heard of the 110th MP.'

'In a good way, I hope.'

'Your HQ was in the Pentagon, right?'

'No, our HQ was in Rock Creek, Virginia. Some ways north and west of the Pentagon. I had the best office there for a couple of years. Was that your security question?'

'You passed the test. Rock Creek it was. Now tell me what's going on. You looked like you were fixing to fight these guys.'

'So far we're just talking,' Reacher said. 'I asked them something. They told me they would prefer to answer me outside in the open air. I don't know why. Maybe they were worried about eavesdroppers.'

'What did you ask them?'

'Where they got this ring.'

Reacher rested his wrist on the door and opened his hand.

'West Point,' the cop said.

'Sold to the pawn shop by these guys. I want to know who they got it from.'

'Why?'

'I don't know exactly. I guess I want to know the story.'

'These guys won't tell you.'

'You know them?'

'Nothing we can prove.'

'But?'

'They bring stuff in from South Dakota through Minnesota. Two states away. But never enough to get the Feds interested in an interstate kind of thing. And never enough to put a South Dakota police detective on an airplane. So it's pretty much risk-free for them.'

'Where in South Dakota?'

'We don't know.'

Reacher said nothing.

The cop said, 'You should get in the car. There are seven of them.'

'I'll be OK,' Reacher said.

'I'll arrest you, if you like. To make it look good. But you need to be gone. Because I need to be gone. I can't stay here my whole watch.'

'Don't worry about me.'

'Maybe I should arrest you anyway.'

'For what? Something that hasn't happened yet?'

'For your own safety.'

'I could take offence,' Reacher said. 'You don't seem very worried about their safety. You talk like it's a foregone conclusion.'

'Get in the car. Call it a tactical retreat. You can find out about the ring some other way.'

'What other way?'

'Then forget all about it. A buck gets ten there's no story at all. Probably the guy came back all sad and bitter and sold the damn ring as fast as he could. To pay the rent on his trailer.'

'Is that how it is around here?'

'Often enough.'

'You're doing OK.'

'It's a spectrum.'

'It wasn't a guy. The ring is too small. It was a woman.'

'Women live in trailers too.'

Reacher nodded. He said, 'I agree, a buck gets ten it's nothing. But I want to know for sure. Just in case.'

Silence for a moment. Just the engine's whispered idle, and a breeze in the telephone wires.

'Last chance,' the cop said. 'Play it smart. Get in the car.'

'I'll be OK,' Reacher said again. He stepped back and straightened up. The cop shook his head in exasperation, and waited a beat, and then gave up and drove away, slowly, tyres hissing on the blacktop, exhaust fumes trailing. Reacher watched him all the way to the corner, and then he stepped back up on the sidewalk, where the black-clad semicircle re-formed around him.

FOUR

The seven bikers resumed their previous positions, and they hunched down into their combat stances again, feet apart, hands held wide and ready. But they didn't move. They didn't want to. Not right away. From their point of view a new factor had been introduced. Their opponent was completely batshit crazy. He had proved it. He had been offered a graceful exit by the county cops, and he had turned it down. He had stayed to fight it out.

Why?

They didn't know.

Reacher waited. At that point he figured Chang would be hauling her packages home. Dumping them on the kitchen counter. Assembling her ingredients. Taking a knife from a drawer. Maybe heating the stove. Dinner for one. A quiet evening. A relief, perhaps.

Still the bikers didn't move.

Reacher said, 'You guys having second thoughts now?'

No response.

Reacher said, 'Answer my question and I'll let you walk away.'

No movement.

Reacher waited.

Then eventually he said, 'A person less patient than me might think it's time to shit or get off the pot.'

Still no response.

Reacher smiled.

He said, 'Then I guess I was just born lucky. This is like winning the slots in Vegas. Ding, ding, ding. I got seven big girls all in a line.'

Which got a reaction, like he wanted it to. Like he needed it to. Motion was his friend. He wanted moving mass and momentum. He wanted them raging and blundering. Which he got. They glanced among themselves, outraged, but not wanting to be the first to move, or the last, and then on some kind of unspoken signal they all jerked forward, suddenly mad as hell, all pumped up and vulnerable. Reacher put his original plan in action. It was still good. Still the obvious play. He waited until they were five feet away, and then he launched hard and smashed through the line with a horizontal elbow in his first target's face, and then he turned immediately and launched again, no delay at all, stamping his foot to kill the old momentum and get some new, scything his elbow at the guy to the right of the sudden new gap, who turned straight into it, facing front with all kinds of urgency, meeting the blow like a head-on wreck on the highway.

Two down.

Reacher turned again and stood still. The five survivors formed up in a new semicircle. Reacher took a long step back. Simply to gauge their intentions. Which were exactly as predicted. Jimmy Rat faded backward, and the other four came on forward.

Reacher had graduated most of the specialist combat schools the army had to offer, most of them on posts inside the old Confederacy, all of them staffed by grizzled old veterans who had done things no normal person could imagine. Such schools concluded with secret notes in secret files and a lot of bruises and maybe even broken bones. The rule of thumb in such establishments, when faced with four opponents, was to make it three opponents pretty damn quickly. And then to make it two opponents just as fast, which was the win right there, the whole ball game, because obviously any graduate of any such school could not possibly have the slightest problem going one-on-two, because if he did, it would mean the instructors had done a poor job of instructing, which was of course logically impossible in the army.

Reacher called it getting his retaliation in first. The four guys were all hunched again, arms wide, bow-legged and feet apart. Maybe they thought such poses looked threatening. To Reacher they looked like a target-rich environment. He darted in and picked off the end guy on the left with a kick in the balls, and then danced away at right-angles, in line with them, where the back three couldn't get to him without detouring around the end guy, who by that point was doubled over, retching and puking and gasping.

Reacher stepped back again. The back three came after him, making the detour, the first guy going right, the second left, the third right again. All of which gave Reacher time to slip around behind the line of bikes, to the other side. Which gave the three guys a decision to make. Obviously two would follow one way and one the other, but which one and which way? Obviously the lone guy carried the greatest risk. He was the weak point and would get hit first, and maybe hardest. Who wanted that duty?

Reacher saw Jimmy Rat watching from the sidewalk.

The three guys split up two and one, the two coming around to Reacher's right, the lone guy from the left. Reacher moved to meet him, fast, his mind on the invisible geometry unspooling behind him, figuring he would get just shy of three seconds

21

of pure one-on-one, before the other two arrived behind him.

Three seconds was plenty. The lone guy thought he was ready, but he wasn't. He was thinking all wrong. His subconscious mind was telling him his best play was to hang back a little. Human nature. Millions of years of evolution. Then the front part of his brain was telling him no, if a confrontation was inevitable, then logically his interests would be best served by staging it as close to reinforcements as he could get. Therefore he should move towards the other two. Not away from them.

The stop-start impulses in the guy's head produced a sudden forward lurch, which brought him too close too soon. His mental bandwidth was all taken up with locomotion issues. Time and space. He wasn't thinking about how to defend himself. Until too late. And even then he showed no imagination. He had seen elbows and feet, and he improvised a kind of all-purpose defensive posture against either, but Reacher ignored both and took the last unexpected stride at full speed, and seamlessly head-butted the guy full on the bridge of the nose. Moving mass and momentum. You bet your ass. Game over, right there. A second and a half.

Reacher turned fast and found the last two guys already around behind the line of motorcycles, twelve feet away, coming on at a medium speed, somewhere between eager and obligated. Reacher stepped backward over his head-butted victim and looped back around to the street side of the bikes. He watched the last two follow. Watched them realize. They were on an oval racetrack. They could go around and around all night long.

They split up, one and one. They glanced and paused and coordinated. They waited, one behind the last bike on the left, one behind the last bike on the right. The survivors. The pick of the litter. The smartest, certainly. Always better to go fifth and sixth than first or second.

Then on a silent count of three they stepped forward. Not the worst Reacher had ever seen. Their speed was right, and their angles were right. The textbooks would say it was very likely Reacher would get hit. From one direction or another. It was almost unavoidable. They would arrive together. He would be the turkey in the sandwich.

Probably Chang was sitting down and eating by that point. Whatever she had made. At her kitchen table. With a glass of wine. A small celebration, maybe. Home safe.

Getting hit was a rare event for Reacher. And he intended to keep it rare. Not just vanity. Getting hit was inefficient. It degraded future performance.

He stepped forward, just as the two guys were rounding the ends of the line of bikes. Now the angle was flatter. More of a straight line than a triangle. He took a breath. The two guys got closer. One from his left, and one from his right. They were mincing along, pace for pace, always glancing ahead at the relative distances. Aiming to arrive together.

Human nature. Millions of years of evolution.

Reacher darted left, and two things happened. The left-hand guy reared up backward, because he was surprised, and the right-hand guy speeded up forward, to close the gap, because he was in full-on hunting mode, and his prey was getting away.

So Reacher spun back instantly, and the right-hand guy ran full speed straight into his scything elbow, whereupon Reacher turned once more, and found he had half a second to spare, because the left-hand guy was taking some major amount of time to get his rearing-up-backward momentum converted into forward motion again. Which gave Reacher space to pick his spot. He kicked the guy in the knee, which dropped him face down on the gravel, *bang*, and then Reacher kicked him in the head, but left-footed, which was his weaker side. Normal for right-handed people. And appropriate. No need to go too far. Being dumb wasn't a capital crime. Wasn't a crime at all, in fact. Merely a handicap.

He breathed out.

Undefeated.

From the sidewalk Jimmy Rat said, 'Feel better now?'

Reacher said, 'A little.'

'You could work for me, if you want.'

'I don't want.'

'Is it woman trouble?'

Reacher didn't answer. Instead he squeezed between adjacent handlebars, and he swung his leg over, and he sat down on Jimmy Rat's bike. He pushed back in the saddle and got comfortable and put his foot up on a peg.

'Hey,' Jimmy Rat said. 'You can't do that. You can't sit on another rider's motorcycle. It's disrespectful. It's a thing, man.'

'How big of a thing?'

'It's rule one.'

'So what are you going to do about it?'

Jimmy Rat said nothing.

Reacher said, 'Answer my question and I'm out of here.'

'What question?'

'I want a place and a name in South Dakota, where you got that ring.'

No answer.

Reacher said, 'I'm happy to sit here all night. Right now there are no witnesses. But sooner or later someone will come along. They'll see me sitting on your bike. With you doing nothing about it. Like a pussy, not a rat. You'll be finished.'

Jimmy Rat glanced all around.

He said, 'This is not a guy you want to meet.'

'Neither were you,' Reacher said. 'But here I am anyway.'

There was the sound of traffic, one block over. Maybe a pick-up truck, rolling slow. Jimmy Rat watched the corner. Would it turn in? It didn't. It hissed away into the distance, and silence came back.

24

Reacher waited.

There was the sound of another car, a block the other way.

Jimmy Rat said, 'He operates out of a laundromat in Rapid City. His name is Arthur Scorpio.'

The car on the parallel block was slowing. Preparing to turn towards them. It was thirty seconds from the corner. Reacher got off the bike, and squeezed back between the handlebars again, to the sidewalk. Jimmy Rat went the other way, around the bikes, into the shadows behind the building. Maybe in through the rear door.

The car showed up at the corner, right on time. It was the county cop. Back again.

FIVE

The cop paused a beat, with his foot on the brake, and then he hauled on the wheel and stopped on the same kerb he had used before. He buzzed his window down and surveyed the scene. Six men, all horizontal, some of them moving. Plus Reacher on the sidewalk, standing straight.

The cop said, 'Sir, please approach the vehicle.'

Reacher stepped over.

The cop said, 'Congratulations.'

'On what?'

'What you did here.'

'No, this was all self-inflicted. I was just a spectator. They had some kind of a big falling out. I think someone sat on the wrong motorcycle.'

'That's your story?'

'You don't believe it?'

'Just theoretically, would I be expected to?'

'The pawnbroker's lawyer says it would be better for us all if you did.'

'I want you out of the county.'

'Works for me. I'm planning on the first bus.'

'Not fast enough.'

'Want me to steal a motorbike?'

'I'll drive you.'

'You want me gone that bad?'

'It would save a lot of paperwork. For both of us.'

'Where would you drive me?'

'I'm guessing they answered your question. So now you're headed west. The county line out there is a straight shot to the I-90 on-ramp. Plenty of friendly folks. You'll get a ride.'

So Reacher climbed in, and forty uneventful minutes later he climbed out again, in the middle of nowhere, on a dark two-lane road, next to a sign that said he was leaving one county and entering the next. He waved goodbye to the cop, and walked forward, a hundred yards, two hundred, and then he stopped and looked back. The cop flashed his lights and backed up and turned and drove away. Reacher watched his tail lights disappear, and then he moved on, to a spot where the shoulder widened a little. He waited there. Ahead of him was about sixty miles of two-lane, and then I-90. Which led west through Minnesota, into South Dakota, through Sioux Falls, and all the way to Rapid City.

And onward. All the way to Seattle, if he wanted.

At that moment, more than fifteen hundred miles away, Michelle Chang was eating a delivery pizza at her kitchen table. With a glass of water, not wine. Not a celebration. Just calories. She had been busy all afternoon, catching up on a week's worth of missed chores. She was tired, and partly happy to be on her own, and partly not. She figured Reacher would have gone to Chicago next. Plenty of options from there. She missed him. But it wouldn't have worked. She knew that. She knew it as clearly as she had ever known anything.

Also at that moment, nearly seven hundred miles away, a phone was ringing on a desk in the Rapid City Police Department's Crimes Against Property unit. It was answered by a detective named Gloria Nakamura. She was small and dark and three years in. No longer a rookie, but not yet a veteran. She was an hour away from the end of her watch. She said, 'Property, Nakamura.'

It was a tech from Computer Crimes, doing her a favour. He said, 'My guy at the phone company called me. Someone named Jimmy on a Wisconsin number just left a voice mail for Arthur Scorpio. On his personal cell. Some kind of warning.'

Nakamura said, 'What kind?'

'I'll email it to you.'

'Owe you,' Nakamura said, and hung up. Her email dinged. She clicked on the message, and clicked on a file, and dabbed her volume button. She heard what sounded like a bar room, and then a nervous voice speaking fast. It said, 'Arthur, this is Jimmy. I just had a guy enquiring about an item I got from you. He seems set on working his way along the chain of supply. I didn't tell him anything, but he already found me somehow, so what I'm thinking is maybe he'll somehow find you too. If he does, take him seriously. That's my advice. This guy is like Bigfoot come out of the forest. Heads up, OK?'

Then there was a plastic rattle as a big old receiver was fumbled back in its cradle. Maybe a pay phone on a wall. In a bar in Wisconsin. The Arthur Scorpio file was already three inches thick. Nothing ever stuck. But Rapid City's CID never quit. Every scrap of intelligence was logged. Sooner or later something would click. Nakamura wrote it up. After the narrative summary she added her notes. *No smoking gun, but persuasive about the existence of a supply chain.* Then she opened a search engine and typed *Bigfoot.* She got the gist. A mythic ape-man, hairy, seven feet tall, from the Northwest woods. She reopened her document and added: *Maybe Bigfoot will shake something loose!* She emailed a copy to her lieutenant.

Afterwards she felt bad about the exclamation point. It looked girlish. But it had to. Really she meant for her boss to read her note and order an immediate resumption of surveillance. Just in case Scorpio's incoming visitor proved significant. A no-brainer, surely. Obviously Jimmy from Wisconsin was lying when he said he didn't tell the guy anything. That claim wasn't logical. A guy scary enough to warrant a heads-up voice mail was scary enough to elicit the answer to just about any question he wanted to ask. So obviously the guy was already on his way. Time was therefore of the essence. But her boss claimed all executive authority as his own. Nudging was counterproductive. Hence the giggly deflection, to take the sting away. To make the guy think it was his own idea all along.

Then the night shift came in, and Nakamura went home. She decided she would swing by Scorpio's laundromat in the morning. On her way back to work. Thirty minutes or an hour. Just to take a look. It was possible Bigfoot might have arrived by then.

Reacher had no reason to doubt the county cop when he said western Wisconsin was populated by friendly folks. The problem was quantity, not quality. It was a lonely rural road, in the middle of nowhere, and by that point it was late in the evening. There was no traffic. Or almost none, to be exact. A Dodge pick-up truck had blasted by in a howl of warm wind, and five minutes after that a Ford F-150 had slowed down to take a look, before speeding up again and driving on without stopping. Now the eastern horizon was stubbornly dark and silent. But Reacher remained optimistic. It only took one. And there was plenty of time. There was no big strategic hurry. The ring had been in the pawn shop for a month. There was no red-hot trail to follow.

A buck gets ten there's no story at all.

Reacher waited, and eventually he saw distant headlights in the east, just dim twinkles like faraway stars. For a whole minute they seemed to get no closer, because of the head-on perspective, but then the picture sharpened. A pick-up truck, he thought, or an SUV. Because of the height and the spacing of the lights. He stood a yard inside the traffic lane and stuck out his thumb. He turned half sideways, like a Hollywood pose, so his profile was presented at an angle, so visually his bulk was minimized. Nothing he could do about his height. But the less threatening the better. He was an experienced hitchhiker. He knew he was subject to snap decisions.

It was a pick-up truck. A big one. A crew cab. Japanese. Lots of chrome and lots of shiny paint. It slowed down. Came close. The driver's face was lit up red, from the instrument panel. *Not going to happen*, Reacher thought. The driver was a woman. She'd have to be nuts.

The truck stopped.

It was a Honda. Dark red metallic. The window buzzed down. There was a dog on the back seat. Like a German shepherd, but bigger. About the size of a pony. Maybe a freak mutation. It had teeth the size of rifle ammunition. The woman leaned across the console. She had dark hair up in a knot. She was wearing a dark red shirt. She was about forty-five years old.

She said, 'Where are you headed?'

Reacher said, 'I need to get on I-90.'

'Hop right in. That's near where I'm going.'

'You sure?'

'About where I'm going?'

'About me hopping in. From the safety point of view. You don't know me. As a matter of fact I'm not a threat, but I would say that anyway, right?'

'I have a savage dog in here.'

'I might be armed. The obvious play would be shoot the dog first. Or cut its throat. And then start on you. That's what I would be worried about. Professionally speaking, I mean.'

'You a cop?'

'I was in the military police.'

'You armed?'

'No.'

'Then hop in.'

She was a farmer, she said, with a lot of dairy cattle on a lot of acres. Doing well, Reacher figured, judging by her car. It felt about as wide as a Humvee inside. It was upholstered in quilted leather. It was as silent as a limousine. They talked. He asked if she had always been a farmer, and she said yes, four generations. She asked him what he did for a living, and he said he was between jobs. The giant dog followed the conversation from the back seat, turning its wicked head one way, and then the other.

An hour later she stopped and let him out at the I-90 cloverleaf. He thanked her and waved her away. She was a nice person. One of the random encounters that made his life what it was.

Then he walked to the westbound ramp and started over, standing at an angle, one foot on the rumble strip, the other in the traffic lane, with his thumb out wide.

Nearly seven hundred miles away, in his office behind his laundromat in Rapid City, Arthur Scorpio was clearing the last of the day's texts and emails and voice mails off his phone. He got to Jimmy Rat's message, and heard *I didn't tell him anything, but he already found me somehow, so what I'm thinking is maybe he'll somehow find you too.* Which, translated into plain English, meant *I snitched on you and a guy is definitely on his way.* So, in the long term, no more business for Jimmy Rat, and in the short term, defensive measures might have to be considered.

31

Scorpio called his secretary at home. She was on her way to bed. He asked her, 'Who or what is Bigfoot?'

She said, 'He's a giant ape-man who lives in the woods. On the slopes in the Northwest. About seven feet tall and covered in hair. Eats bears and cattle. One rancher lost a thousand head, over the years.'

'Where was this?'

'Nowhere,' the secretary said. 'It's imaginary. Like a fairy tale.'

Scorpio said, 'Huh.'

Then he disconnected, and made two more calls, both to reliable guys he knew, and then he locked up his laundromat and drove himself home.

SIX

Close to midnight Reacher got a ride in a shiny stainless steel truck carrying five thousand gallons of organic milk in a tank shaped like a boat-tail bullet. It was headed to Sioux Falls, which was the western limit of that particular dairy's distribution area. But which was still more than 350 miles short of Rapid City. Don't worry, the driver said. Onward rides would be easy to get. There was a truck stop with all kinds of traffic, night and day. A real big place, like the crossroads of the world.

Reacher kept the guy talking all the way through Minnesota, which he figured was his job, like human amphetamine. Anything to keep the guy awake. Anything to avoid the old joke: *I want to die peacefully in my sleep like Grandpa. Not screaming in terror like his passengers.* The resulting conversation spiralled off in all kinds of different directions. Institutional injustices in the milk business were exposed. Grievances were aired. Then the guy wanted to hear war stories, so Reacher made some up. The big truck stop came along soon enough. The guy had not been exaggerating. There was an acres-wide fuel stop, and a spreading two-storey motel a hundred yards long, and a warehouse-sized family restaurant, blazing with neon outside and fluorescence inside. There were back-to-back eighteen-wheelers wheezing in and out, and all kinds of cars and trucks and panel vans.

Reacher climbed out of the milk tanker and headed straight for the motel office, where he took a room, even though it was already close to dawn. No point arriving in Rapid City all tired and exhausted. No point arriving exactly when expected, either. Obviously Jimmy Rat would have called Arthur Scorpio. Some kind of a get-in-first cover-your-ass play, as in *It wasn't me, honest, but I think someone dimed you out.* Which wouldn't necessarily be believed in every particular, but which would certainly be acted upon, as a distant early warning. *There's something out there.* The oldest fear in human history. Scorpio would post sentries right away. And so in turn Reacher would make them stare at a whole lot of nothing for the first day. To dull them down, to sap their enthusiasm, to make them yawn and blink. Always better to engage at a time of your own choosing. So he ate breakfast in the bustling restaurant, and then he headed back to his room, and took a shower, and went to bed just as the sun rose, with the tiny West Point ring on the night table beside him.

At that point, more than 350 miles away to the west, in Rapid City, Detective Gloria Nakamura was already up and about. She had woken before dawn, and showered and dressed and eaten breakfast. Now she was heading out, a whole hour early. To work, but not yet.

She commuted in her own car, which was a mid-size Chevy sedan. It was pale blue, and as anonymous as a rental. She drove through downtown, and turned off the main drag towards Arthur Scorpio's territory. He owned a whole city block. His laundromat

34

was in the centre building. Like a flagship operation. The block fronted on a cracked concrete cross street with a narrow sidewalk featuring a dead tree in a bone-dry pit. Running down the back of the block was a service alley, for deliveries and trash collection.

She tried the alley first. It was patched and narrow. Overhead a skein of power lines and phone wires looped left and right from tilted poles. There was a guy outside the laundromat's back door. He was leaning on the wall, with his arms folded. He was in a short black coat against the dawn chill. A black sweater under it. Black pants, black shoes. He was more than six feet tall, and heavy. About twice Nakamura's size. He was wide awake and watchful.

She wanted to take a cell phone picture. For the endless file. But she couldn't be obvious about it. She had heard nothing from her boss. Surveillance had not been officially reauthorized. So she swiped through to camera, and put the phone to her ear, next to her window, as if she was taking a call, and she drove slowly by, eyes front, furtively dabbing with her thumb, *click click click*, until the sentry was well behind her. Then she turned left out of the alley, and left again, and drove past the front of the building.

There was another guy at the front door. Same deal. Leaning on the wall, watchful, arms crossed. Dressed in black. Like a nightclub bouncer. No velvet rope. Nakamura put her phone to her ear. *Click click click*. She turned right at the end of the block and parked on the street where the guy couldn't see her.

She checked her pictures. Both sets were tilted and blurry and neither had the subject anywhere near the centre of the frame. But the building was recognizable. The overall context was clear. The narrative told a story. Scorpio had gotten word from Wisconsin, and had immediately hired security. Local muscle. Two guys. One in front, one in back.

Because Scorpio was at least somewhat worried about Bigfoot.

Who was where?

Incoming, Nakamura thought. Had to be. *He seems set on working his way along the chain of supply.* She got out of her car. She walked back the same way she had come, and turned in on Scorpio's street. She stayed on the opposite sidewalk. The guy at the laundromat's door saw her. She felt his eyes on her. He didn't move. Just watched. She kept walking. There was a breakfast place almost opposite the laundromat. Not Scorpio's. His neighbour's. It had an undersized front window, but if you took the first table and craned up in your chair you got a pretty good view. Nakamura had spent hours in there.

She pushed in the door.

Her table was taken. By a guy with the ruins of a bacon and egg breakfast pushed away from him, and a half-full cup of coffee cradled in its place. He was a neat, compact man, in a collar and tie, and a dark conventional suit made of sensible hardwearing fibres. His hair was neatly brushed. He was somewhere over fifty, but how much over was hard to say. His hair was still brown. He had a lean and ageless face. He could have been sixty. He could have been seventy.

He was watching the laundromat through the window.

Had to be. Nakamura knew the signs. He wasn't craning up in his chair, because although not tall he was taller than she was. But even so, his back was unnaturally straight. Had to be, to get his eye line up over the sill. And his gaze was unwavering. He never looked down. He found his cup by feel, and raised it blind, and watched over the rim while sipping.

Was this Bigfoot?

Take him seriously, the voice from Wisconsin had said. And certainly the guy at the table looked like he should be taken seriously. Deep down there was something hard and competent about him. Not immediately obvious. His expression was amiable. But he had limited patience. He wasn't to be messed with. That was clear. Theoretically it was possible to imagine him as a quiet and deadly foe of some sort. It was possible to imagine him as the kind of man who might merit a whispered heads-up voice mail. With an urgent warning and a pithy description. But the description would not have been *like Bigfoot come out of the forest*. Not for this man. It would have been a reference to a spy movie perhaps, about a faceless KGB killer blending in with the crowd. It would have been about how neat he was. How physically unobtrusive. He was almost dapper. He was the opposite of Bigfoot.

So who was he?

One sure way to find out.

She sat down across from him, and took her badge from her purse. It was in a department-issued vinyl wallet, opposite a photo ID behind a plastic window. *Nakamura, Gloria, Detective*, and her signature and her picture.

The guy took a pair of tortoiseshell reading glasses from an inside pocket, and put them on. He glanced at the ID, and glanced away. He took a small notebook from another inside pocket. He opened it with his thumb. He glanced at it, changed pages, and glanced away.

He said, 'You're with Property Crimes.'

'You got us all listed in there?'

'Yes,' he said.

'Why?'

'I like to know who does what in a place.'

'What are you doing here?'

'My job.'

'What's your name?'

'Bramall,' the guy said. 'First name Terrence, but you can call me Terry.'

'And what's your job, Mr Bramall?'

'I'm a private investigator.'

'From where?'

'Chicago.'

'What brings you to Rapid City?'

'A private investigation.'

'Of Arthur Scorpio?'

'I'm afraid I'm bound by a certain degree of confidentiality. Unless and until I believe a crime has been or is about to be committed. Which I don't at this moment.'

Nakamura said, 'I need to know whether you're for him or against him.'

'Like that, is it?'

'He won't be voted citizen of the year.'

'He's not my client, if that's what you mean.'

'Who is?'

'Can't say.'

Nakamura asked, 'Do you have a partner?'

'Romantically?' Bramall said. 'Or professionally?'

'Professionally.'

'No.'

'Are you part of an agency?'

'Why do you ask?'

'We heard someone was on his way here. Not you. Someone else. He was in Wisconsin yesterday. I wondered if he was an associate.'

'Not mine,' Bramall said. 'I'm a one-man band.'

Nakamura took a business card from her purse. She put it on the table, near Bramall's coffee cup. She said, 'Call me if you need me. Or if you decide to take the confidentiality stick out of your ass. Or if you need advice. Scorpio is a dangerous man. Never forget that.'

'Thank you,' Bramall said, his eyes on the window.

Nakamura walked back to her car, with the guy at the laundromat door watching her all the way. She drove to work, and got there early. She woke her computer and opened a search engine. She typed *Bramall, Terrence, private investigator, Chicago*. She got a bunch of hits. The guy was sixty-seven years old. He was retired FBI. A long and distinguished career. Many successful cases. Senior rank. Multiple medals and awards. Now he was in business on his own account. He was high end. He didn't advertise. He was hard to get. He was expensive. He was a true specialist. He offered only one service. All he did was find missing persons.

SEVEN

Reacher woke himself up when he figured the lunch rush would be over. He felt OK, after his exertions the previous evening. No real aches or pains. He checked the mirror. He had a light bruise on his forehead, from head-butting the fourth guy. And his right forearm was tender. It had dispatched three of them all by itself. Fully fifty per cent. Along the bone there was nothing to bruise, but the skin looked about twice as thick as normal. And red, with tiny puncture wounds here and there. Even through his shirtsleeve. Which happened. Teeth, usually, or chips of bone from broken noses, or eye sockets. Collateral damage. But really nothing to worry about. He was in good shape. Same old same old, on another lonely day.

He showered and dressed and walked over to the emptying restaurant and ate off the all-day breakfast menu. He asked for quarters in his change and stopped at a pay phone near the door. He dialled an ancient number from memory.

It rang twice and was answered.

'West Point,' a woman's voice said. 'Superintendent's office. How may I help you?'

'Good afternoon, ma'am,' Reacher said. 'I'm a graduate of the academy, and I have an enquiry I'm sure will end up in your office anyway, so I figured I might as well start there.'

'May I have your name, sir?'

Reacher gave it, and his date of birth, and his service number, and his graduation year. He heard the woman write it all down.

She said, 'What is the nature of your enquiry?'

'I need to identify a female cadet from the class of 2005. Her initials were S.R.S. and she was small. That's all I've got so far.'

He heard her write it down.

She said, 'Are you a journalist?'

'No, ma'am.'

'Do you work in law enforcement?'

'Not currently.'

'Then why do you need to make this identification?'

'I have lost property to return.'

'You can send it here. We can forward it.'

'I know you can,' Reacher said. 'And I know why you're suggesting we do it that way. You have all kinds of security issues to worry about now. Privacy rights too. Not like it was when I was there. I understand that completely. You really shouldn't tell me anything. Which is fine. I don't want to put you on the spot, believe me.'

'Then we seem to understand each other.'

'Just do me one favour. Look her up, and then look me up. Consider all the possible circumstances. Either you'll be kind of happy you didn't give me a name, or you'll be kind of sorry. I'll call you back sometime and you can tell me which it was. Purely out of interest.'

'Why would I be sorry I followed procedure?'

'Because in the end you'll realize that right now was the first faint whisper you ever heard that a West Pointer with the initials S.R.S was in some kind of trouble somewhere. Maybe alone and in need of help. Afterwards you'll wish you'd taken it seriously from the beginning. You'll be sorry you didn't tell me sooner.'

'Who are you exactly?'

'Look me up,' Reacher said.

The voice said, 'Call me back.'

Reacher walked the length of the motel to an area near the fuel pumps, where a kind of unofficial hitchhiking market was being run, by a homeless-looking guy wearing a coat tied up with rope. He would collect the desired destination from each new arriving hitch-hiker, and then he would walk around shouting it out to the drivers in line for the pumps, and sooner or later one or another would wave and agree to some particular destination, and the lucky hitchhiker would tip the shouting guy a dollar and climb up in the cab.

Good business. Reacher was happy to pay a buck. Not that he would need help or luck. Every single driver was going to Rapid City. It was 350 miles away, but it was the first stop. There wasn't much before it. After it there were choices. Wyoming, Montana, Idaho. But everyone had to pass through Rapid City first.

He got a ride inside about a minute and a half, in a huge red truck pulling a white boxed-in trailer. The cab had a quadruple sleeper pod behind the seats, bigger than some accommodations Reacher had been raised in. For cross-country house-moving jobs, the driver said. The whole crew could sleep in the vehicle. Saved on motels.

The guy was old, like a lot of drivers. Maybe it was a fading profession. Maybe it had gotten too hard. Reacher thought the last of the frontier would die with it. Those guys were the final generation. The end of the DNA. Now people wanted to be home every night.

The guy said it would be five hours and five minutes to Rapid

City. He said it with the kind of confidence that comes from having done it a thousand times before. They rolled out, sitting way up high, with a clear view to the horizon, and they ground up through the gears, and up, and up, until they were bowling along at more than seventy on the flat, and faster still on the down grades. The mile markers flashed past. Five hours and five minutes seemed dead-on plausible.

As always the driver wanted to know where his temporary passenger was travelling to, and why. As if in payment. A long story, for a long distance. For some reason Reacher told him the truth. The pawn shop, the ring, his compulsion to find out what connected the two. Which he said he couldn't entirely explain.

The driver chewed on it all for ten whole miles.

Then he said, 'My wife would say you feel guilty about something.'

Reacher didn't answer.

'She reads books,' the driver said. 'She thinks about things.'

'I don't even know who this woman is. I don't know her name. I never met her. How could I feel guilty about her? All I know is she sold her ring.'

'Doesn't have to be about her. There's a word. Transference, I think. Or projection, although that might be something different. My wife would say you feel guilty about a separate issue.'

'Would it have to be related?'

'Broadly, I suppose. Not necessarily that you made some other woman sell her jewellery too. Doesn't have to be obvious. My wife would say it might be some other failure or injustice.'

Reacher said nothing.

'My wife would ask if you had a wife or girlfriend to talk things over with.'

Chang would be halfway through her first full day back to work. Maybe she had new cases. Maybe she was already back at the airport.

43

'Tell your wife to keep on reading,' Reacher said. 'She sounds like a very smart woman.'

As so often, getting from the highway to the city was the hardest part of the trip. The red truck was too big for downtown. Reacher got out at the cloverleaf, at ten to eight in the evening, after five hours and five minutes exactly. He stretched and breathed and set out looking for a local ride. There was plenty of traffic. Plenty of pick-up trucks, and SUVs, and regular cars. But there was the wrong frame of mind. They were all coming off the highway. They were all on their last lap. All almost home. Almost there. Almost to the bar. Almost to the girlfriend's house. Almost to wherever. They all speeded past. No one was in the mood to offer a ride. Not then. Did not compute. Rides were offered at the start of a journey. Not at the end.

Best hope in such a situation would always be a guy who had shaken his head three hundred miles ago, and then regretted it all the way since. Mostly a self-image thing. Such a guy was cooler than that. Such a guy would stop in his last few miles, maybe secretly hoping his limited offer would get a rueful refusal, thereby salving his conscience at zero personal cost, but also weirdly happy to actually go ahead and pick a guy up and drive him five or ten miles. In Reacher's experience, given the traffic density, such a guy would come along about every twenty or twenty-five minutes. Visibility was key. The earlier they saw you, the better your chances. More time for the cool-guy thing to kick back in. Enough space to glide to a casual stop, and lean across with a smile.

In the end it took forty minutes. At eight-thirty exactly a Dodge crew cab pulled over. The driver put on a generous but apologetic expression and said he was going only as far as downtown. Reacher said that was great. He said he needed the part with the cheap motels. The guy said he would be passing by that general area, about two streets over, and would be happy to point the way.

The cheap part of downtown was dark. Daylight was long gone. There were lights on some street corners, and some of them worked, but not enough. Reacher got out of the Dodge and walked a long block west, mostly by feel, with visibility about a yard, and then another block just the same, and then he turned left and as promised he found two side-by-side motels, on a strip that also featured a diner and a gas station and a tyre shop, which likely meant it was a popular route in and out of town. The right-hand motel had a tall lit-up sign, with come-on offers stacked up vertically, like logs in a pile: *Free Breakfast, Free Cable, Free Wi-Fi, Free Upgrades.*

The left-hand motel had: *Free Everything.*

Which Reacher doubted. Not the actual accommodation itself, surely. But nothing ventured, nothing gained. There was an old lady at the desk. She was slender and refined. She had blue hair, spun as fine as cotton candy. She was maybe eighty. Maybe she was the original owner, from way back long ago. Reacher asked his question, and she smiled and said no, he had to pay for his room, but everything else was included. She said it with a half-amused look in her eye, up and then down, and he sensed she meant *Free Everything* partly as a response to her neighbour's boasting, whether good-humoured or teasing or edgy all in the eye of the beholder, but also partly she meant it as a despairing lament that these days, whatever you did, there was always some-one in the world prepared to do it cheaper. Where could she go after free?

Reacher paid for a room.

He asked her, 'Where could I wash my clothes around here?'

'What clothes?' she said. 'You don't have a bag.'

'Theoretically. Suppose I got a bag.'

'You would go to a laundromat.'

'How many do you have?'

'How many do you need?'

'Some might be better than others.'

'Are you worried about bedbugs? You shouldn't be. That's what laundromats are for. Turn the dryer on high, and you kill them stone dead. That's what I do here. With the sheets.'

'Good to know,' Reacher said. 'How many laundromats are there in Rapid City? I'm curious, is all. I like to know things.'

She thought about it and almost answered, but then she stopped herself, too naturally meticulous to rely on memory alone. She wanted corroboration. She took a thin Yellow Pages from a drawer. She checked under L, and again under C, for coin-operated.

'Three,' she said.

'Do you know the owners?'

Again she thought about it, at first looking sceptical, as if the question was odd and such acquaintances unlikely, but then her face changed, as if she was recalling old trade associations, and local business campaigns, and rubber chicken, and cocktail parties.

She said, 'Actually I do know two of the three.'

'What are their names?'

'Does it matter?'

'I'm looking for a man named Arthur Scorpio.'

'He's the third of the three,' she said. 'I don't know him at all.'

'But you know the name.'

'This is a small town. We gossip.'

'And?'

'He's not well spoken of.'

'In what way?'

'Just gossip. I shouldn't repeat it. But a friend with a great-nephew in the police department says they have a file on Mr Scorpio three inches thick.'

46

'He buys and sells stolen property,' Reacher said. 'That's the story I got.'

'Are you a policeman?'

'No. Just a regular guy.'

'What do you want from Arthur Scorpio?'

'I want to ask him a question.'

'You should proceed with great caution. Mr Scorpio has a reputation for hostility.'

'I'll ask politely,' Reacher said.

There was a Rapid City street plan in the front of the Yellow Pages. The old lady tore it out, very carefully, and she marked where the motel was, and where Scorpio's laundromat was. She folded the page in quarters and gave it to Reacher. For the morning, no doubt she assumed, but he went straight there. Nearly ten o'clock in the evening. He walked long pitch-dark blocks, checking the old lady's map wherever he found a bulb that worked, and then up ahead he saw the glow of neon. A late-night convenience store, on a corner. According to the old lady's map, Scorpio's laundromat was across the street and halfway down the block.

Reacher found it right where it should be. Just beyond a dead tree. It was in the middle of the block, in the centre unit of a larger structure that ran from corner to corner. It was currently closed for business. The lights were off. The door was locked, and it had a padlocked chain wrapped through the handles. The door was glass, with a wider window next to it. Inside was gloom, with a row of stacked machines on one wall, ghostly white and bulky, and a row of plastic lawn chairs on the other, below dispensers for change and soap and fabric conditioner and dryer sheets. Everything seemed to cost a dollar.

Across the street was the lit-up convenience store way on the left, and then a shoe outlet, and then a couple of empty units

47

dead ahead, and then a little right of centre was a breakfast place. A real greasy spoon. Its front window was small, but its line of sight would be good. Its food too, probably. And its coffee. Reacher made a mental note.

Then he walked around the block, and located the laundromat's rear door, in an alley. It was a blank fireproof slab, made of metal. A standard industrial product. Nothing special. A zoning requirement, maybe, or insurance. It was locked.

He walked back. He paced out the depth of the building, from the alley to the street. Too much. It was about twice the depth he could see through the laundromat's window. Which meant there was another room in back, about equal in size. A storeroom, maybe, or offices. Where business was done that gave rise to gossip.

He stood in the dark a minute more, and then headed back the way he had come. On the opposite corner he stopped in at the convenience store. He figured a cup of coffee would be a good idea. Maybe a sandwich. He was hungry. There was another guy in there on the same mission. He was standing at the deli counter sipping from a go cup. He was a small man, neat and compact, in a dark suit and a necktie. Apparently he had ordered an elaborate construction involving a fried egg and a large quantity of grated cheese. Clearly not worried about cholesterol. The counterman finished his work and wrapped the sloppy result first in paper, and then in aluminium foil. He handed it over and the guy in the suit turned and stepped around Reacher and headed for the door.

Reacher ordered his go-to, which was roast beef and Swiss cheese, with mayo and mustard, on white bread. Plus coffee. The counterman turned away and spun up the slicing machine. Reacher asked him, 'What do you know about the laundromat down the block?'

The guy turned back. The blade hissed and sang behind him.

He looked puzzled at first, and then a little hostile, as if he suspected someone was making fun of him. Then he looked pre-occupied, as if he was struggling with a difficult arithmetic calculation, and coming out with an answer he liked but didn't trust.

He said, 'That's what the other guy just asked.'

Reacher said, 'The guy with the fried egg sandwich?'

'But what does that kind of guy need with a laundromat? The suits go to the dry cleaner, and the shirts get starched for a buck and a half. Am I right?'

'I'll be back in a second,' Reacher said.

He stepped to the door, and out to the sidewalk.

No sign of the guy in the suit and the tie.

No echo of lonely night-time footsteps.

Reacher came back in and stepped back to the counter, and the guy making his sandwich said, 'He would need to wash his underwear, maybe. And socks. But all the hotels have laundry bags in the closet. A guy like that wouldn't sit and watch the soap suds go around and around.'

'You think he's staying in a hotel?'

'He's not local. Did you get a look at him? He's some kind of a professional person. I would say a lawyer, in town to try a big case, but he didn't look rich enough. So now I'm thinking IRS or something. A government worker. And then you asked the same question. About the laundromat. I don't think you're IRS, but you could be a cop. So now I'm thinking Arthur Scorpio has got trouble coming.'

'How do you feel about that?'

'Depends.'

'On what?'

'Whether it works. Mr Scorpio has been in trouble before. Nothing ever sticks.'

EIGHT

The next morning Reacher left his not-free room just as the sun was coming up. He retraced his steps from the night before, until the last couple of blocks, which he looped around at a distance, until he was beyond them. Then he doubled back, towards Scorpio's alley from the far side, and he peeked in.

There was a sentry posted at the laundromat's rear door. Leaning on the wall, arms folded, short black coat, black sweater, black pants and shoes. Maybe forty years old, maybe six-two, maybe two-ten.

Reacher backed away, and looped around again at the same distance he had used before, two blocks over, two blocks down, so he could approach the breakfast place unseen, from the rear. He figured it would have an alley of its own behind it. Like Scorpio's place. A necessary amenity. Greasy spoons generated a lot of trash. Eggshells, coffee grounds, packaging, leftovers. Drums of used grease. And where there was an alley would be a kitchen door. It would be open. Almost certainly a legal requirement. *This door must remain unlocked during business hours.* To act as a fire escape for the cook. Another necessary amenity. Greasy spoon kitchens burned like napalm.

Reacher found the alley. Found the door. He went in through the kitchen. Into the dining room. He focused on the window, and stepped left for a better view.

There was a second sentry at the laundromat's front door. Same kind of guy. Same kind of pose. Leaning on the wall, impassive, dressed in black.

Arthur Scorpio was taking precautions.

There's something out there.

Reacher looked away, and looked around the room. And saw the guy he had seen the night before. In the convenience store. In the dark suit and the necktie. He was at the table under the window, looking out.

Detective Gloria Nakamura repeated her routine from the previous day. Up before dawn, showered, dressed, breakfasted, and out the door a whole hour early. To work, but not yet. She parked where she had before, and turned in on Scorpio's street, and felt the guy at the laundromat door watching her all the way. She walked to the breakfast place and went in.

Her table was taken. Again. By the same guy as the day before. *Bramall, Terrence, private investigator, Chicago.* The same dark suit, a fresh shirt, a different tie.

And standing in the middle of the room was Bigfoot.

No doubt about it. The guy was huge. Not quite seven feet, but close. Almost to the ceiling. And he was wide. From shoulder to shoulder he looked like four basketballs in a rack in her high school gym. He had fists like Thanksgiving turkeys. He was wearing canvas work pants and a huge black T-shirt. His forearms were battered and sculpted. His hair was a mess. Like he had towelled it dry but not combed it. Like he didn't even own a

51

comb. He hadn't shaved in days. His face was all bone and stubble. His eyes were pale blue, like her car, and he was looking straight at her.

Reacher saw a petite Asian woman, wearing a black skirt suit like a uniform. Five feet nothing, maybe 95 pounds soaking wet. Maybe thirty years old. Long black hair, big dark eyes, cute as a button. But no smile. A severe expression instead, as if she was in charge of something important. As if looking severe was the only way to stay in charge of it. Which was possibly true, when you were starting out from five feet nothing and 95 pounds. But whatever, she certainly wasn't shy. She was looking straight back at him, openly, examining him, top to bottom and side to side. With some kind of dawning recognition in her eyes. Which he didn't understand. Not at first. He was pretty sure he had never seen her before. He felt he would remember. Then he figured Jimmy Rat would have included a description. In the cover-your-ass phone call he must have made. *A big guy in a black T-shirt is coming.* Maybe the Asian woman worked for Arthur Scorpio. Maybe she had been briefed about the emergency.

Or maybe she was just an office worker, grumpy about her early start.

He looked away.

The guy in the necktie was still staring out the window. His expression was patient and contained. And equable. He looked like the type of guy who would give a polite answer to a reasonable question. But maybe only as a professional veneer. As if he held a place in a hierarchy where old-fashioned courtesy oiled the wheels. He reminded Reacher of army colonels he had known. Squared away, buttoned up, a little grey and dusty, but driven by some kind of quiet internal vigour and confidence.

Reacher took a table against the wall, at a distance, where he could see out the window over the other guy's head. Nothing was happening out there. The sentry was still leaning on the laundro-mat wall. Not moving. The lights were on inside. There were no customers yet.

A waitress came by and Reacher ordered his go-to breakfast, which was coffee plus a short stack of pancakes with eggs, bacon and maple syrup. The coffee arrived first. Black, fresh, hot and strong. Pretty good.

The Asian woman sat down at his table.

She took a small vinyl wallet from her purse. She opened it up and held it out for inspection. On the left was a gold-coloured shield. On the right was a photo ID behind a plastic window. It said *Nakamura, Gloria, Detective, Rapid City Police Department.* It had a picture of her face. Dark eyes, a severe expression.

She said, 'Were you in Wisconsin yesterday?'

Which told Reacher that Jimmy Rat had indeed made a phone call. And that the Rapid City PD was tapping Scorpio's line. Which meant there was an active and ongoing investigation. Probably the typed transcript of Jimmy Rat's call was already the new top sheet in the three-inch file.

But out loud he said, 'Are you entitled to ask that question, even as a cop? I have the right to privacy, and the right to go where I want. It's a First Amendment thing. And a Fourth.'

'Are you declining to answer my question?'

'No choice, I'm afraid. I was in the army. I swore an oath to uphold the Constitution. Can't stop now.'

'What's your name?'

'Reacher. First name Jack. No middle initial.'

'What did you do in the army, Mr Reacher?'

'I was a military cop. A detective, just like you.'

'And now you're a private investigator?'

She glanced at the guy in the necktie as she said it.

Reacher asked her, 'Is that guy a private investigator?'

She said, 'I decline to answer your question.'

He smiled.

He said, 'I'm not a private investigator. Just a private citizen. What did you hear from Wisconsin?'

'I'm not sure I should tell you.'

'Cop to cop. Because that's what we are.'

'Are we?'

'If you want to be.'

She put her ID wallet back in her purse and took out her phone. She swiped through to a section with audio recordings. She chose one and touched an on-screen symbol. Reacher heard a plastic and distorted version of bar-room noise, and then Jimmy Rat's voice. He recognized it right away. It sounded fast and nervous. It said, 'Arthur, this is Jimmy. I just had a guy enquiring about an item I got from you. He seems set on working his way along the chain of supply. I didn't tell him anything, but he already found me somehow, so what I'm thinking is maybe he'll some-how find you too.'

Nakamura touched the pause symbol.

Reacher said, 'Why would that be me?'

She pressed play again.

Jimmy Rat said, 'If he does, take him seriously. That's my advice. This guy is like Bigfoot come out of the forest. Heads up, OK?'

Nakamura pressed stop.

'Bigfoot?' Reacher said. 'That's not very nice.'

She said, 'What item?'

'Does it matter? All I want to do is ask Scorpio a question. Then I'll be gone.'

'Suppose he doesn't answer?'

'Jimmy in Wisconsin did.'

'Scorpio has protection.'

'So did Jimmy in Wisconsin.'

'What item?' Nakamura said again.

54

Reacher dug in his pocket and came out with the ring. *West Point 2005*. The gold filigree, the black stone, the tiny size. He put it on the table. Nakamura picked it up. She tried it on. Third finger, right hand. It fit easily. Even loosely. But then, she was five feet nothing and weighed 95 pounds. Her fingers were about as thin as pencils.

She took the ring off again. She weighed it in her palm. She looked at the inside, at the engraving. She asked, 'Who is S.R.S.?'

'I don't know,' Reacher said.

'So what's the story?'

'I found it in a pawn shop in a small town in Wisconsin. It's not the kind of thing you would give up easily. This woman suffered four hard years to get it. Every day they tried to break her and make her quit. That's how West Point works. And 9/11 had just happened. Those were serious years. And what came afterwards was worse. Iraq, and Afghanistan. She might have sold her car, or the watch she got from her aunt for Christmas, but she wouldn't have sold her ring.'

'Does this guy Jimmy own the pawn shop?'

Reacher shook his head. 'He's a local biker. Goes by the name Jimmy Rat. He wholesaled the ring along with a bunch of other trinkets. He told me he got it from Arthur Scorpio, here in Rapid City. So now I want to know who Arthur Scorpio got it from. That's the only question I want to ask him.'

'He won't tell you.'

'That's what the guy in the pawn shop said about Jimmy Rat.'

Nakamura didn't reply. Nothing was happening out the window. The waitress came back with Reacher's meal. Pancakes, eggs, bacon, maple syrup. It looked good. He asked for more coffee. Nakamura ordered hot tea and a bran muffin.

Reacher put the ring back in his pocket.

The guy in the necktie got up and left.

Still nothing happening out the window.

Reacher asked, 'What kind of private investigator is he?'

Nakamura said, 'I didn't say he was.'

'I told you stuff. Now you can tell me stuff.'

The waitress brought Nakamura's muffin. It was about as big as her head. She broke off a pea-sized crumb and ate it.

She said, 'He's from Chicago. His name is Terry Bramall. He's retired FBI. He finds missing persons.'

'Who is he looking for here?'

'I don't know.'

'Is Scorpio a kidnapper too?'

'We don't think so.'

'Yet Mr Bramall from Chicago is watching his place. Not just this morning. He was in the neighbourhood last night. I saw him in the convenience store.'

'You got in last night?'

Reacher nodded. 'Pretty late.'

'You came straight here from Wisconsin. This is important to you.'

'I could have gotten here sooner. I took a nap in Sioux Falls.'

'Exactly how did you get Arthur Scorpio's name from Jimmy Rat?'

'I asked him nicely.'

She didn't reply. He carried on eating his breakfast. She sipped her tea. There was a long silence.

Then she said, 'Arthur Scorpio is not well liked within the police department.'

'Understood,' Reacher said.

'Nevertheless I am officially required to warn you against committing any kind of crime inside our jurisdiction.'

'Don't worry,' Reacher said. 'All I'm going to do is ask him a question. No law against that.'

'What if he doesn't answer?'

'I suppose that's always a theoretical possibility,' Reacher said.

She took a business card from her purse. She put it on the table, near his coffee cup. She said, 'Those are my numbers. Office and cell. Call me if you need to talk. Scorpio is a dangerous man. Never forget that.'

She put five bucks on the table. For her tea and her muffin. Then she got up and left. Out the door, along the sidewalk, and out of sight.

Still nothing happening out the window.

She had left her muffin. Whole and untouched, apart from the pea-sized crumb she had eaten. So Reacher ate the rest of it, with another mug of coffee. Then he called for his check, and asked for quarters in his change. He stopped in the restroom corridor, where there was a pay phone on the wall. Just like there was in the bar in Wisconsin. Which was where Jimmy Rat had made his call to Arthur Scorpio. The background noise proved it. Reacher had seen the guy loop around the line of bikes, to the rear of the building, where he must have gone in the back door, where he must have seen the phone on the wall, where he must have decided upon an immediate warning. Right there and then. While Reacher was still outside, still talking to the county cop.

Some kind of urgency.

Reacher leaned on the wall, where he could still watch the front window, and he dialled the same ancient number from memory.

The same woman answered.

'West Point,' she said. 'Superintendent's office. How may I help you?'

'This is Reacher,' he said.

'Wait one, major.'

She knew his rank. She had read his file. There was a click, and a long silence, and then another click, and a man's voice said, 'This is the supe.'

The superintendent. The big boss. What any other college would call the president.

Reacher said, 'Good morning, general,' politely but vaguely, because he didn't know the guy's name. He didn't keep up with alumni affairs. But the supe was always a general. Usually smart and accomplished, sometimes progressive, never a pushover.

The guy said, 'Your enquiry yesterday was most irregular.'

'Yes, sir,' Reacher said, purely out of habit. In such situations there were only three permissible responses at West Point: yes sir, no sir, no excuse, sir.

The guy said, 'I would like an explanation.'

So Reacher told the same story he had just gotten through telling Nakamura, about the pawn shop, and the ring, and his nagging sense of disquiet.

The supe said, 'So this is about a ring.'

'It seemed significant.'

'Yesterday you implied the former cadet was in danger.'

'She might be.'

'But you don't know for sure.'

'She pawned the ring, or sold it, or had it stolen. Any of which would suggest some kind of misfortune. I think we should find out.'

'We?'

'She's one of ours, general.'

The guy said, 'I read your file. You did well. Not well enough to get a statue on campus, which you wouldn't get anyway, mostly because of the corners you cut.'

'No excuse, sir,' Reacher said, purely out of habit.

'I have one obvious question. What are you doing now?'

'Nothing.'

'What does that mean?'

'It's a long story, general. We shouldn't take the time.'

'Major, I'm sure you understand that supplying personal details about current or former military personnel is strictly prohibited about nineteen different ways. The only possible chance it could happen would be a top-secret off-the-record whisper from one West Pointer to another. Purely as a courtesy. Exactly the kind of oak-panelled bullshit we're always being accused of. Therefore naturally you and I face a question of mutual trust. Possibly less important to you than to me. You could put my mind at rest by letting me take your measure.'

Reacher was quiet a beat.

'I get uneasy,' he said. 'I can't stay in one place. I'm sure if you gave the VA enough time, they could come up with a name for it. Maybe I could get a cheque from the government.'

'It's a medical condition?'

'Some would say.'

'Does it bother you?'

'Turns out I don't want to stay in one place anyway.'

'How frequently do you move around?'

'Constantly.'

'Do you think that's a fitting way for a West Pointer to live?'

'I think it's perfectly fitting.'

'In what sense?'

'We fought for freedom. This is what freedom looks like.'

The guy said, 'There are a hundred reasons for selling a ring. Or pawning it. Or losing it, or getting it stolen somehow. Not all the reasons are bad. This could be completely innocent.'

'Could be? That's a little lukewarm, general. Sounds like you don't know for sure. Even after reading her file. Which therefore can't have reassured you completely. So now you're hinting about a whisper. Because now you're worried. I think deep down you want to tell me her name. So let me guess. She took off the green suit and now she's under the radar.'

'Three years ago.'

'After what?'

'Five hard tours in Iraq and Afghanistan.'

'Doing what?'

'Unpleasant things, I imagine.'

'Is she small?'

'Like a bird.'

'That's her,' Reacher said. 'Now it's decision time, general. What are you going to do?'

The supe didn't answer.

Out the window Reacher saw a black sedan slow up. It stopped on the kerb across the street. Outside the laundromat. The driver's door opened. A guy climbed out. He was tall and bony. Maybe fifty years old. He had grey hair cut short. He was wearing a black suit with a white shirt buttoned to the neck, but without a tie. He stood on the sidewalk for a second, and looked a question at the sentry at the door. Who shook his head, as if to say, *No trouble, boss.*

Arthur Scorpio.

Who nodded back at the sentry, and then stepped past him, in through the door.

The sentry stepped across the sidewalk in the other direction and got in Scorpio's car. He drove it away. To park it, presumably. On a side street, or in the alley. Maybe a five-minute absence. The first of two such absences, presumably. He would go retrieve the car at close of business. Two five-minute windows every day.

Good to know.

In Reacher's ear the West Point supe said, 'She might not want to be found. Did you consider that? No one comes back whole. Not from five tours.'

'I'm not trying to sell her a timeshare in Mexico. If she looks OK from a distance I'll walk away and leave her alone.'

'How will you even find her? She's under the radar. Will her name even help?'

'It won't hurt,' Reacher said. 'Especially not at the end. I'll follow the ring until I find someone who heard of her.'

The supe said, 'Her name is Serena Rose Sanderson.'

NINE

O ut the window the front sentry walked back into view, after parking Scorpio's car. He resumed his position, leaning on the wall to the left of the laundromat door, arms folded, impassive.

He had been gone just over five minutes.

Still no customers inside.

Into the phone Reacher said, 'Where is Serena Rose Sanderson from?'

'As a cadet her home state was listed as Wyoming,' the supe said. 'That's all we've got. You think she went back there?'

'Depends,' Reacher said. 'For some people, home is the first place they go. For others, it's the last. What was she like?'

'She was before my time,' the supe said. 'But her file is very solid. She was pretty close to outstanding, without ever quite getting there. Never in the top five, always in the top ten. That kind of person. She branched infantry, which was considered a smart choice for a woman, back in '05. She knew she wouldn't see combat, but she guessed the chaos would push her pretty damn near to it. Which I'm sure is what happened. Close support units were always busy. A lot of driving for resupply, which meant a lot of roadside IEDs. Plus vehicle recovery, which would have exposed her out in the open. Off post she would have been armed at all times. I'm sure she was in firefights. Those units took plenty of casualties, same as anyone else. She has a Bronze Star and a Purple Heart. So she was wounded herself at some point.'

'Rank?'

'Terminal at major,' the guy said. 'Like you. On her last tour she was doing a pretty big job. She led her soldiers well. On paper she's a credit to the school.'

'OK,' Reacher said. 'Thank you, general.'

'So proceed, but with caution.'

'Don't worry.'

'I do.'

'Why?'

'I read your file,' the guy said again. 'If you tilt it right and hold it in a sunbeam you can see the invisible writing. You were effective, but reckless.'

'Was I?'

'You know you were. You got away with things time after time.'

'Did I?'

'One damn thing after another. But you always came up smelling of roses.'

'Then draw the appropriate conclusion, general. I wasn't reckless. I was relying on methods I knew had worked before, and would likely work again. I felt I was the opposite of reckless. There's a clue in the word. Reck comes from reckon, and I felt I did more reckoning than most folks. Not less.'

'Call me back,' the guy said. 'Let me know about Sanderson.'

*

63

For the second day running Gloria Nakamura was early to work. She parked her car and walked up the stairs. The mother hen at the gate to the detectives' pen told her the lieutenant wanted to see her. First thing. Urgent but not critical. The mother hen said his voice on the phone had sounded OK. Not particularly angry.

Nakamura dropped her bag at her desk and headed off down the corridor. The lieutenant's office was a corner suite at the far end of the floor. He was a cancer survivor, worn down to nothing but lacy bone and sinew, but lit up through his papery skin by some kind of crazed internal energy. He had gotten some bonus years, and he was going to slap the shit out of them. He was going to get big things done. Privately Nakamura felt his brush with death had produced an epiphany. He was afraid of being forgotten.

He was at his desk, reading email.

He said, 'You sent me a thing about Arthur Scorpio.'

She said, 'The voice mail from Wisconsin. Yes, boss. There have been developments.'

'Has Bigfoot arrived?'

'Yes, boss, I believe he has. But first there was a private eye from Chicago.'

'What did he want?'

'He wouldn't say. But I checked him out. He's a missing persons specialist. Very expensive.'

'Who's missing?'

'About a million people nationwide.'

'Any reason to believe one of them is washing his shorts in Scorpio's place?'

'There's nothing on the wires.'

'Tell me about Bigfoot.'

'He's a military veteran named Reacher. He found a West Point class ring in a pawn shop and he's tracing its provenance.'

'Like a hobby?'

'No, like a matter of military honour. Like a moral obligation. Verging on the sentimental, in my opinion.'

'How is Scorpio involved?'

'The likelihood is the ring was stolen property fenced by Scorpio to a Wisconsin biker named Jimmy Rat, who then sold it onward to the pawn shop, where Bigfoot found it. Bigfoot says the pawn shop owner told him Jimmy Rat's name, who told him Arthur Scorpio's name. Now he wants Scorpio to name the next name. Whoever he got the ring from. And so on, all the way down the line. Bigfoot wants to return the ring to its rightful owner. That's my assessment.'

'Scorpio won't tell him shit.'

'I think he might. I'm not sure Bigfoot was telling the whole truth about what happened in Wisconsin. I don't think a biker with a lucrative trade in stolen property would tell anyone anything. Least of all the name of a supplier. Not voluntarily. You should listen to the audio. Jimmy Rat sounds scared.'

'Of Bigfoot?'

'I saw him, boss. You could put him in a zoo.'

'You think Scorpio will be scared too?'

'Either way I think a serious crime is about to be committed. Either Bigfoot will squeeze too hard, or Scorpio will push back too hard.'

Then she waited.

The lieutenant said, 'I think we should get the surveillance going again.'

She said, 'Yes, boss,' and breathed out.

'Just you. Eyes on at all times. Nothing subtle. Get right up in his grille.'

'I might need back-up. I might need to intervene.'

'No,' the guy said. 'Don't intervene. Let nature take its course. It's a win-win. If Scorpio hurts the guy, that's great, because then we've got something on him at last. We've got you as an actual

65

eyewitness to a felony assault. On the other hand, if the guy hurts Scorpio, that's good news anyway. The worse the better. Plus you could always arrest the guy afterwards. If you wanted to. For a felony assault of his own. If you need to boost your quarterly numbers, I mean.'

Reacher left the breakfast place through the kitchen door and slipped away through the alley. He didn't want the front sentry to see him. Not yet. The Bigfoot description would leave the guy in no doubt. Word would pass instantly to Scorpio inside. Better not to get them too excited too soon.

So he skirted around at a safe radius, and then headed downtown, and started looking for better hotels than his own. The kind of place a retired-FBI gumshoe might choose. No fleapits, but nothing fancy, either. Probably a mid-market national chain. The guy probably had a loyalty card.

Reacher found four possibilities. At the first he went in and asked the clerk for a guest named Terrence Bramall, small guy, neat, in a suit and tie. If he was in a car, it might have Illinois plates. The woman pattered at her keyboard and stared at her screen, and then she said she was sorry, but currently the hotel had no guests with that name.

At the second possibility Reacher was told Terrence Bramall had checked out just thirty minutes before.

Or maybe even less, the clerk said. Maybe only twenty. She called up the closed account, to calibrate her memory. It was twenty-seven minutes ago. The guy had stopped at the desk, in his suit and tie, with a leather travelling bag in one hand, and a leather briefcase in the other. He paid his bill, and headed out to his car, which was in the covered lot. It was a black SUV, with Illinois plates. Bramall loaded his bags, and then got in and drove off, towards the Interstate, but whether he then turned east or west was anyone's guess.

'Do you have his cell phone number?' Reacher asked.

The woman glanced at her screen. Left-hand column, Reacher thought, maybe two-thirds of the way up.

The woman said, 'I really can't give it out.'

Reacher pointed at the base of the wall behind her.

'Is that a cockroach?' he said.

Not a word hotel keepers liked to hear.

She turned to look. He leaned over the desk and bent his neck. Left-hand column, two-thirds of the way up. Ten digits. Not a prodigious feat of memory.

He straightened up.

She turned back.

'I didn't see anything,' she said.

'False alarm,' Reacher said. 'Sorry. Maybe just a shadow.'

Reacher found a pay phone in the lobby of an all-day Chinese restaurant. It was a chromium instrument mounted on a wall of red velvet. Not as glamorous as it looked from a distance. The chrome was pitted and the velvet was threadbare and tacky with grease.

Reacher dialled Bramall's cell number. It rang and rang. It wasn't picked up. No big surprise. The guy was probably on the Interstate. Probably a safety first type of person. Probably had to be, to survive a lifetime in the FBI.

No answer.

A recorded voice came on, inviting Reacher to leave a message.

He said, 'Mr Bramall, my name is Reacher. We waited in line together last night for sandwiches and we were briefly in the breakfast place at the same time this morning. I infer you were watching Arthur Scorpio's place in connection with a missing persons inquiry. I was watching it in connection with trying to trace the source of a piece of stolen property. I think we should put our heads together, to figure out exactly what we both know. Just in case there's more here than meets the eye. Could be useful for one of us, if not both. You can't call me back because I don't have a phone, so I'll try you again at a later time. Thank you. Goodbye.'

He hung up.

He stepped out from the velvet lobby to the concrete sidewalk.

Arthur Scorpio's black sedan stopped at the kerb.

Right next to him, level with his hip.

The window buzzed down.

The front-door sentry said, 'Get in the car.'

TEN

The guy had a gun. A revolver. It looked like a worn-out Chief's Special. A .38 five-shooter by Smith & Wesson. Short barrel. It looked small in the guy's hand. His right hand. He was half-twisted behind the wheel, aiming half-sideways through the open passenger window, with a bent arm and a cramped right shoulder.

'In the car,' he said again.

Reacher stood still. He had choices. Life was full of them. Easiest thing would be just walk away. Straight ahead along the sidewalk, in the same direction the car had been driving. A right-handed shooter in a left-hand-drive car would have a practical problem with that kind of geometry. His windshield was in the way. Couldn't shoot through it. The bullet would deflect and miss. And afterwards there would be a hole in the windshield. Not a smart thing to have. Rapid City was no doubt a tough old town, but it wasn't South-Central LA. Morning gunfire would get called in. Especially downtown, near the hotels and the restaurants. Police cruisers would show up fast. Questions about a bullet hole in a windshield would be hard to answer.

So the guy would have to move. He would have to shift the transmission, and take his foot off the brake, and shrug off his seatbelt, and flip up the armrests, and shuffle his ass across the front bench, and hang his right arm out the passenger window. All of which would take a small but finite amount of time. During which Reacher would be walking farther and farther away. And all the guy had was a worn-out .38 with a two-and-a-half-inch barrel. Not an accurate weapon. More or less a guaranteed miss, with the speed Reacher could walk.

So the better bet would be hang out the driver's window. Much quicker. It was right there. But how? The guy would have to kneel up sideways on the driver's seat, and stick his whole upper body out, and wriggle his right arm free, like putting on a tight sweater, bringing him all the way out of the car up to his waist, and then he would have to twist, and aim, and fire. Except at that point he would also be overbalancing and about to fall out the window. An inaccurate weapon, and a preoccupied shooter clinging to the door mirror. Not a whole lot to worry about.

Which meant the guy's best bet would be step out and brace behind the open door. Like a cop. Except as soon as Reacher heard the creak of the hinge he would duck out of sight into the nearest store or alley. Same thing if he heard the car move off the kerb and roll towards him. Stalemate. The whole get-in-the-car thing looked pretty good in the movies, but on the street it was basically optional. Plenty of choices. Keep calm and walk away. Live to fight another day.

But Reacher stayed where he was.

He said, 'You want me to get in the car?'

The guy said, 'Right now.'

'Then put the gun away.'

'Or?'

'Or I won't get in the car.'

'I could shoot you first and get you in bleeding.'

'No,' Reacher said. 'You really couldn't.'

All he had to do was take one fast pace left. Then the guy would be shooting through glass again, or the B-pillar, or the C-pillar, plus anyway his shoulder was tight against the upholstery and wouldn't rotate. Plus again, the cops would come. Lights and sirens. Questions. The guy was stuck.

He was an amateur.

Which was encouraging.

'Put the gun away,' Reacher said again.

'How do I know you'll get in?'

'I'm happy to visit with Mr Scorpio. He has information for me. I was planning to call on him later today, but since you're here, I guess this is as good a time as any.'

'How do you know I'm working for Scorpio?'

'Magic,' Reacher said.

The guy held still for a second, and then he put the gun back in his coat pocket. Reacher opened the passenger door. The sedan was an ancient Lincoln Town Car. The old square style. The kind that got crashed and burned on the TV shows, because they were cheaper than dirt. The upholstery was red velvet, no better or worse than the restaurant lobby's walls. A little crushed and greasy. Reacher crammed himself in the seat. He put his elbow on the armrest. His left hand hung loose, the size of a dinner plate. The guy stared at it for a second. Long thick fingers, with knuckles like walnuts. Old nicks and scars healed white. The guy looked away. No longer top dog. Uncharted territory, for a man who made his living leaning on walls and scaring people.

'Drive,' Reacher said. 'I haven't got all day.'

They took off, left and right through the downtown blocks, back to the low-rent district. They parked outside the laundromat. The guy took out his gun again. Saving face, in front of Scorpio. Reacher let him. Why not? It cost him nothing. He

71

waited until the guy came around and opened his door, and then he got out, and the guy nodded towards the laundromat entrance. Reacher went in first, to the smell of drains and cold soap, and the back-door sentry leaning on a washing machine, and Arthur Scorpio himself sitting in a plastic lawn chair, as if he was a customer hypnotized by the churning drums.

Up close he had pitted skin on his face, unnaturally white, as if it had been treated with chemicals. The pallor made his eyes look dark. He was tall and thin. Maybe six feet two. Maybe 160 pounds. But only if he had a dollar's worth of pennies in his pocket. All skin and bone, and awkward as a stepladder.

The back-door sentry pushed himself off the washing machine and came over to stand close. The guy who had driven the car stepped up from behind.

Scorpio said, 'What do you want?'

'You fenced a ring to Jimmy Rat,' Reacher said. 'I want to know who fenced it to you.'

'You got the wrong person altogether. I run a laundromat. I don't know any Jimmy Rat.'

'Is the laundromat doing well?'

'I'm comfortable.'

'And modest. You're doing better than comfortable. Your cash flow is so big you had to hire two guys to watch over it. Except I don't see how. You got no customers.'

'You accusing me of something?'

Out the window a pale blue car stopped on the opposite kerb. A domestic product. A Chevrolet, possibly. Nothing fancy. A plain specification. In it was a small Asian woman. Black hair, dark eyes. A severe expression. Nakamura. She just sat there, engine off, head turned, watching. A level gaze, over the hood of Scorpio's parked Lincoln. Her eyes were locked on Reacher's, through two layers of glass and thirty feet of air.

Reacher turned back to Scorpio and said, 'Jimmy Rat left you a voice mail, which is why you hired these guys. He told you I was coming. And here I am. It's up to you how long I stay.'

Scorpio said, 'Firstly I don't know what you're talking about, and secondly do you know who that is, in the blue car across the street?'

'She's a cop. Detective Nakamura.'

'Who harasses me on a regular basis. As you can see. For completely invented reasons. But this time she can make herself useful for once. You're trespassing, and she can come remove you herself. My tax dollars at work.'

'You pay taxes?'

'You accusing me of something?'

'I'm not trespassing. You invited me here. Kind of insisted.'

'My point is you can stick your little threats where the sun don't shine. Up to me how long you stay? What are you going to do, with a cop watching?'

'I know her name because we talked. She told me you're not well liked within the police department.'

'Mutual.'

'It's a code. In plain English it means I could rip your arm off and beat you to death with it, and they wouldn't stop me. They'd sell tickets instead.'

'What code? You a cop too? From somewhere?'

'You expecting one? Not me. I'm just a guy with a question. Tell me the answer, and I'm gone.'

Scorpio said, 'You never asked how I found you.'

Reacher said, 'Didn't need to. I already figured it out. From where your boy showed up. Restaurant staff. You slip them a few bucks. They all talk to each other. They all have cell phones. They text. A nice little network. Underpaid and under-appreciated. You put the word out. Based on Jimmy Rat's voice mail. Watch out for Bigfoot come out of the forest. That's what Jimmy said, right?'

'I don't know any Jimmy. Which is my point. I'm going to sit here and deny it all day long. Nothing you can do about it with a cop watching.'

'Maybe she'll leave.'

'She won't. She sits there all day. We'll be gone before she is. Then what are you going to do? Run after us? Which is my other point. Good luck with your night in town. You won't get a meal anywhere. You won't get a drink. You won't get a bed. I got more than one network running.'

'I'm sure you're a regular Al Capone,' Reacher said. 'Except you got the worst piece-of-shit car in the world.'

'Get lost. You're wasting everyone's time. Nothing you can do. Not with a cop watching. Code or no code. Which is bullshit anyway. This is America.'

'We could run a test,' Reacher said. 'I could punch you in the mouth, and we could time how long she took to get in here.'

The two sentries stepped in closer. No guns. No pushing or shoving. They couldn't. Nakamura was watching. They put themselves one each side of Scorpio's lawn chair, a step ahead of it, overlapping it a little. Closing it off. Reacher was facing them, not more than an arm's length away, in a flat little triangle.

He said, 'Is she still watching?'

Scorpio said, 'Harder than ever.'

'Are you going to answer my question?'

'You got the wrong person altogether.'

'OK,' Reacher said. 'I get it.' He patted the air, a placatory gesture, as if defeated, as if requesting a time out, or a reset, or a reboot, or whatever else might help him. He said, 'What if,' in a speculative way, but he didn't finish the question. Instead he cupped his hand on his brow, and rubbed, as if easing a headache or searching for a word, and then he raised his other hand too, and ran his fingers through his hair, back and forth fast, like a mental rinse, and then he moved his hands down and put his fingers flat over his mouth, almost steepled, over pursed lips, a meditative gesture, and then he rubbed his eyes, and then he pressed his fingers hard on his temples, like a person just one thought away from a solution.

All of which got his hands up at eye level, with no one suspecting a thing.

He flicked his right hand out and back real fast, a blur, like a snake's tongue, his fingers closing into a fist as it went, and he hit the right-hand guy in the face. Not much force behind it. A busted nose, maybe. Nothing more. But nothing more was required. The idea was to freeze the guy for a split second. That was all. While the same right hand on its way back pivoted into a full-blown right hook, with a violent twist at the waist and the shoulders, which hit the left-hand guy smack in the throat. Better than the face. No bones.

The left-hand guy went down like a slammed door.

Meanwhile Reacher was unwinding the twist and turning it into an equal and opposite left hook, and hitting the right-hand guy also in the throat.

Perfectly symmetrical.

Less than three seconds, beginning to end.

Plus style points.

The right-hand guy went down late and slowly, like a street light in an auto wreck. Reacher heard the slap of linoleum, and the thump of bone.

He stood there like nothing had happened.

He said, 'Just you and me now.'

Scorpio said nothing.

Reacher said, 'Is the cop getting out of her car?'

Scorpio didn't answer.

Reacher ducked down, left and right, and took guns out of pockets. Both the same. Smith & Wesson Chief's Specials, both looking older than he was. He put them in his own pockets.

He said, 'Is she out of her car yet?'

Scorpio said, 'No.'

'Is she on the phone?'

'No.'

'The radio?'

'No.'

'So what's she doing?'

'Just watching.'

'Remember what I said about running a test?'

Scorpio didn't answer.

Nakamura saw the sentries close ranks in front of Scorpio, who was leaning back in his lawn chair, like some kind of emperor on a throne. Reacher was facing the three of them. Up close. An arm's length away. There was some verbal back and forth. Two questions, two answers. Short sentences. Brief and to the point. Then Reacher scratched his head. Then he seemed to have some kind of violent physical spasm, and for no apparent reason the sentries fell over.

He had hit them.

She scrabbled for her door release.

She stopped.

That's good news anyway.

Don't intervene.

She took a deep breath, and watched.

Reacher sat down in the lawn chair next to Scorpio's. He stretched out and got comfortable and stared straight ahead at an inert Maytag. Scorpio was silent beside him. They looked like two old men at a ball game. The sentries stayed on the floor, breathing, but not easily.

Reacher took the West Point ring from his pocket. He balanced it on his palm. He said, 'I need to know who you got this from.'

76

'I never saw that before,' Scorpio said. 'I run a laundromat.'

'What have you got in your pockets?'

'Why?'

'You need to take it all out. I'm going to put you in the tumble dryer. Keys or coins might damage the mechanism.'

Scorpio glanced at a tumble dryer.

Couldn't help himself.

He said, 'I wouldn't fit.'

'You would,' Reacher said.

'I never saw that ring before.'

'You sold it to Jimmy Rat.'

'Never heard of him.'

'Where I set the temperature dial is up to you. We'll start on delicates. Then we'll turn it up. Someone told me it goes all the way to where it can kill a bedbug.'

Scorpio said nothing.

'I understand,' Reacher said. 'You're Mr Rapid City. You're the man. You got a bunch of networks running. Which is your problem. Maybe they're all interconnected. In which case, one question might lead to another. The whole thing might unravel. You can't afford for that to happen. Hence the stone wall. I get it. Perfectly understandable. Except you need to remember two very important things. Firstly, I don't care. I'm not a cop. I don't have another question. And secondly, I'll put you in the tumble dryer. So you're between a rock and a hard place here. You need to get creative. You ever read a book?'

'Sure.'

'What kind?'

'About the moon landings.'

'That's called non-fiction. There's another kind, called fiction. You make stuff up, perhaps to illuminate a greater central truth. In your case, maybe you could tell me a story about a poor home-less man, maybe from out of town, who came in to launder his clothes, except he had no money, nothing at all except a ring, which you reluctantly traded for a couple of hot-wash cycles and a couple of dryer loads, plus enough left over for a square meal and a bed for the night. All out of the kindness of your generous heart. Detective Nakamura couldn't argue with that. It would be a fine story.'

'I would have to admit selling the ring to Jimmy Rat.'

'Which was perfectly legal. You run a laundromat. You carry quarters to the bank. You don't know what to do with a ring. Fortunately a guy passing by on his motorcycle offered to buy it from you. Not your fault he turned out to be a bad guy. You're not your brother's keeper.'

'You think that's a good enough story?'

'I think it's a fine story,' Reacher said again. 'Just as long as you happen to remember the out-of-towner's name.'

'Out of state,' Scorpio said. 'That's exactly what happened. More or less. Some broke guy came in from Wyoming. I helped him out.'

'When?'

'Six weeks ago, maybe.'

'From where in Wyoming?'

'I believe a small town called Mule Crossing.'

'What was his name?'

'I believe it was Seymour Porterfield. I believe he told me people call him Sy.'

ELEVEN

Across the street Nakamura was still watching. Reacher stood up and stepped over the left-hand sentry. He looked at a tumble dryer. Bigger than people had in their homes. Good for comforters and other large items. He might have gotten Scorpio in there.

He said, 'You want me to leave through the back door?'

Scorpio shook his head.

'No,' he said. 'Go out the front.'

So Reacher stepped over the right-hand sentry and pushed out to the sidewalk. The air smelled warm and fresh. He turned right and started walking. He heard Nakamura's car start up. He heard the wheeze of its steering, and grit under its tyres, and then it pulled alongside him and stopped. The same as Scorpio's, except lower and bluer.

The window came down.

Black hair, dark eyes, a severe expression.

She said, 'Get in the car.'

'You mad at me now?'

'I told you not to commit a crime inside my jurisdiction.'

'We were in the laundromat. Does that even count?'

'That's not fair. We're trying.'

Reacher opened the passenger door and slid inside. He racked the seat backward, for leg room. He said, 'I apologize. I know you're trying. Scorpio is a tough nut to crack.'

'What did he tell you?'

'The ring came in from a guy in Wyoming named Sy Porterfield. About six weeks ago. Scorpio as good as admitted an onward connection to Jimmy Rat in Wisconsin. So he's part of a chain, flowing west to east along the I-90 corridor.'

'Can't prove it.'

'Also he pays off restaurant workers for information. Which he claims is only one of many networks he's running. Maybe he's the neighbourhood bookie. Maybe he lends money.'

'Can't prove any of it.'

'But I'm not sure how successful he is. His personal vehicle is a piece of crap worth about a hundred dollars, and his goons had guns older than you.'

'Did the car work?'

'I guess so.'

'Would the guns have worked?'

'Probably. Revolvers are usually pretty reliable.'

'This is South Dakota. People are thrifty. I think Arthur Scorpio is plenty successful.'

'OK.'

'Where are the guns now?'

Reacher took them out of his pockets and dropped them on her rear seat.

She said, 'Thank you.'

He said, 'Also there's something wrong with his back room. It would have made more sense to talk to me in there. Certainly it would have made more sense for me to leave that way. He must have known you would stop me and ask me questions. Better if I went out through the alley. You wouldn't have seen me. But he wouldn't let me. You should check it out.'

'We'd need a warrant.'

'You've got the tap on his phone. He might say something stupid. A buck gets ten he's calling Porterfield in Wyoming right now.'

'Is that where you're going?'

'As soon as I find a map. The town is called Mule Crossing. I never heard of it.'

Nakamura took out her phone. She swiped and typed and waited, and then she said, 'It's down near Laramie. A wide spot in the road.'

She held out the phone to show him.

She said, 'That's the I-80 corridor, not I-90.'

He said, 'Population density drops to nothing west of here. A supply chain would need to branch out, literally. Maybe there are many Porterfields, all over Wyoming and Montana and Idaho. All feeding Scorpio, like a river system. Do you monitor his visitors?'

'We try, from time to time. We've seen cars and bikes in the alley. Some with out-of-state plates. People go in and out his back door.'

'You need to get a look in his back room. It ain't full of drums of spare detergent. That's for damn sure. The guy has no customers.'

Nakamura was quiet a beat.

Then she said, 'Thanks for the report.'

He said, 'You're welcome.'

'Can I give you a ride somewhere?'

'The bus depot, I guess. I'll take whatever heads west on I-90. I'll get out in Buffalo and go south to Laramie.'

'That would be the Seattle bus.'

'Yes,' Reacher said. 'I thought it might be.'

He got out of Nakamura's car at the depot and said goodbye and wished her luck. He didn't expect to see her again. He bought a ticket as far as Buffalo, and sat down to wait, with about twenty other people. They were the usual mixture. The room had pale inoffensive walls, and fluorescent squares in the ceiling. Out the picture window was an empty asphalt space, where sooner or later the Seattle bus would show up. It was on its way from Sioux Falls.

Nakamura called her friend the tech, and asked him to check with his pal at the phone company, to see who Scorpio had called in the last hour, with special focus on outgoing attempts to the 307 area code, which was Wyoming.

No need to check, the guy told her. The lieutenant had re-upped electronic surveillance too. Everything on Scorpio's land line and personal cell was going straight to a hard drive, accessible from her desktop computer.

Only one problem, the guy said.

Scorpio had made no calls at all.

Reacher saw South Dakota change to Wyoming through the bus window. He was in his favourite spot, on the left, over the rear axle. Most people avoided that location, because they feared a bumpy ride. It was everyone else's last choice. Which made it his first.

He liked Wyoming. For its heroic geography, and its heroic climate. And its emptiness. It was the size of the United Kingdom, but it had fewer people in it than Louisville, Kentucky. The Census Bureau called most of it uninhabited. What people there were tended to be straightforward and pleasant. They were happy to leave a person alone.

Reacher country.

The first part of the state was high plains. Fall had already started. He gazed across the immense tawny distances, to the spectre of the mountains beyond. The highway was a dark black-top ribbon, mostly empty. From time to time trucks would pass the bus, slowly, sometimes spending a whole minute alongside, edging ahead imperceptibly. Reacher was eye to eye with their drivers, across their empty cabs. Old men, all of them.

My wife would say you feel guilty about something.

He looked the other way, across the aisle, at the other horizon.

Nakamura walked the length of the corridor to her lieutenant's corner suite. He looked up, all glittering eyes and restlessness.

'Bigfoot left,' she said. 'Scorpio answered his question. Next stop Wyoming.'

'What's in Wyoming?'

'The ring was supplied to Scorpio by a man named Porterfield from a town named Mule Crossing. About six weeks ago.'

'How did Bigfoot make Scorpio tell him all that?'

'He decked the muscle. I suppose Scorpio knew he was next.'

'Did you see it happen?'

'Not really,' Nakamura said. 'It was over very fast. I couldn't swear to exactly what took place. Not precisely enough for a courtroom.'

'So we're nowhere,' the lieutenant said. 'In fact we're back a step. Scorpio's phones have gone quiet. Which means he went to the pharmacy and bought a burner and some pre-paid minutes. Which means from now on we have no idea who or where he's calling.'

The lieutenant said nothing more. He returned to his email. Nakamura walked back to her desk, quiet and alone.

More than eight hundred miles east, in an expensive kitchen in a big Tudor house on the Gold Coast north of Chicago, a woman named Tiffany Jane Mackenzie dialled Terry Bramall's cell number. It rang and rang and wasn't picked up. A recorded voice came on and asked her to leave a message.

She said, 'Mr Bramall, this is Mrs Mackenzie. I'm wondering if you've made any progress. So far, I mean. Or not, I suppose. I would like to hear either way, so please call me back as soon as you can. Thank you. Goodbye.'

Then Mrs Mackenzie used her phone to check her email, and her bookmarked web pages, and her chat rooms, and her message boards.

Nothing.

Reacher got out of the bus at the Buffalo stop. His onward options were limited. There was no direct service to Laramie. There was a departure to nearby Cheyenne, but not until the next day. So he set out walking, following signs to the highway south, with his thumb out, hoping to get a ride before he hit the on-ramp. About fifty-fifty, he figured. Heads or tails. In his favour was a friendly population not given to irrational fears. Against him was almost no traffic at all. The friendly population was thinly spread. Wyoming. Mostly uninhabited.

But even so, he came up heads within half a mile. A dusty pick-up stopped alongside him, and the driver leaned across and said he was going to Casper, which was about halfway to both Cheyenne and Laramie, straight south on I-25. Reacher climbed in and got comfortable. The truck was a Toyota. It was raised up on its suspension and tricked out with all kinds of heavy-duty components. It looked fit for service on the back side of the moon. Certainly it handled I-25 with no trouble at all. It droned along pretty fast. The driver was a rangy guy in work boots and off-brand jeans. A carpenter, he said, busy fixing roof beams before the winter. Also a rock crawler, he said, on the weekends. If he got weekends. Reacher asked him what a rock crawler was.

Turned out to mean driving off-road vehicles over extreme boulder-strewn terrain, or along rocky rapids in dried-up mountain streams. Reacher was at best a reluctant driver, so any assessment was necessarily theoretical, but he was inclined to admit it sounded fun, if pointless.

Nakamura drove her Chevy back to Scorpio's block, but on a hunch she stopped short of the laundromat and parked outside the convenience store instead. She went in and looked around. An inventory check. She saw all kinds of canned and packaged foods, and coolers full of soda and juice and beer in bottles, and rolls of paper towel, and potato chips and candy, and a deli counter, and behind the register a wall of small stuff, including over-the-counter medications, and vitamin pills, and batteries, and phone chargers.

And phones.

She saw no-contract cell phones, in plastic bubble packs. Lots of them, in two rows, on two pegs, left and right, next to a faded sign saying pregnant women shouldn't drink too much.

She pointed and asked, 'Did Arthur Scorpio just buy one of those?'

The counterman said, 'Oh, Jesus.'

'No big deal if he did. You're not in trouble. Information is all I need.'

The counterman said, 'Yes, he bought one. And some painkillers.'

'Which one?'

'Which painkiller?'

'Which phone? Left peg or right peg?'

The counterman thought about it. He pointed.

'Right peg,' he said. 'More convenient for me.'

'Give me the next two.'

The guy took down two more bubble packs and Nakamura

85

handed over her credit card. When she was back in her car she called her friend in Computer Crimes. She said, 'Scorpio bought a burner in the convenience store. I got the next two off the rack. I'm going to bring them to you. I need you to figure out if the numbers run in some kind of predictable sequence. If they do, maybe we can put Scorpio back on the radar.'

'I'll try my best,' her friend said.

Terry Bramall let himself into his motel room, and hung his suit coat in the closet. He took his phone from his briefcase and set about answering his messages. The first was from some guy he had never heard of named Reacher. *We waited in line together last night for sandwiches and we were briefly in the breakfast place at the same time this morning.* And then something to do with Arthur Scorpio and stolen property.

He hit delete, because he was done with Scorpio.

The second message was from his client Mrs Mackenzie. Anxious about progress, understandably. *I would like to hear either way, so please call me back as soon as you can.* He didn't. He didn't like talking on the phone, especially with anxious clients. So he texted back instead, slowly and methodically, using only his right forefinger: *Dear Mrs Mackenzie, progress remains very satisfactory, and I hope to have definitive news very soon. Best wishes, T. Bramall.*

He pressed send.

In Casper, Reacher had a choice. He could stick with I-25 and head south and east to Cheyenne, whereupon Laramie would be a short hop west again on I-80. Or he could go direct on a state road. Two fast sides of a triangle versus one slow side. The hitch-hiker's eternal dilemma.

He chose the state road. He was sick of the highway. And he had plenty of time. There was no big hurry. The ring had been out of Wyoming for six weeks. No red-hot trail to follow. He walked west out of town, more than a mile, until the commercial lots left and right petered out into high desert scrub. A hundred yards later he found a head-high sign that said *Laramie 152 miles*. He set up next to it. He felt it told the story. He watched the horizon for oncoming traffic. There wasn't much.

Scorpio gave his sentries twenty bucks and a bottle of Tylenol each, and then sent them home. They went out the front, and he went in the back room. He sat down at a long counter loaded with humming equipment. He tore apart the bubble pack and took out his new phone. He dialled the activation number, and then he dialed a 307 number.

Wyoming.

Ring tone.

No answer.

A voice invited him to leave a message.

He said, 'Billy, this is Arthur. We got some weird shit going on. Nothing real serious. Just a strange piece of bad luck. Some guy showed up chasing a ring. He wasn't a cop. He knew nothing at all. He was just a random passer-by, interested in the wrong thing at the wrong time. Turned out he was kind of tough to get rid of, so in the end I gave him Sy Porterfield's name. Which means sooner or later he's likely to arrive in your neck of the woods. Don't mess with him. Use a deer rifle from behind a tree. I'm not kidding about that. He's like the Incredible Hulk. Don't even let him see you. But get on it, OK? He's got to go, because he's a random loose end. Easier for you to deal with out there than it would be for me here. So get it done.'

Then he added, 'Your privileges are suspended till I hear back from you.'

He clicked off and dropped the phone in the trash basket.

TWELVE

Reacher arrived in downtown Laramie at six o'clock in the evening, after 152 miles in the passenger seat of an ancient Ford Bronco, driven by a guy who made his living turning logs into sculptures with a chainsaw. He let Reacher out on the corner of Third Street and Grand Avenue, which the guy seemed to regard as some kind of an exact geographic centre. Which it might have been. But it was quiet. Everything had closed at five, except the bars and the restaurants, and it was still early for them.

Reacher turned a full circle and got his bearings. The railroad tracks lay to the west. The university was east. South was a straight shot to Colorado, and north was back towards Casper. He headed west for the tracks and stopped in at the first bar he liked the look of. It had a mirror on the wall with a bullet hole in it. As if some old desperado had come in mad about something. Maybe faked, maybe real. It was all the same to the mirror.

The room was quiet and the crowd was thin, and the barman had time on his hands. Reacher asked him directions to Mule Crossing. The guy said he had never heard of it.

'Where are you looking for?' some other guy called out. He had foam on his lip, from a long hard pull on a long-neck bottle. Maybe a helpful guy, maybe a busybody into everyone's business, maybe a local expert eager to show off his specialist knowledge.

Or a mixture of all three.

'Mule Crossing,' Reacher said.

'Nothing there,' the guy said. 'Except a firework store.'

'I heard it was a small town.'

'This is a small town. Mule Crossing is a wide spot in the road. There was a post office, but it closed twenty years ago. I think there's a flea market in there now. Maybe you can get soda and potato chips. No gas, that's for sure.'

'How many people live there?'

The guy took another pull on his bottle.

He said, 'Five or six, maybe.'

'That all?'

'The flea market guy, for sure. Probably not the firework guy. Who would live above a firework store? Probably wouldn't sleep a wink. I bet he drives in from somewhere else. But there's a dirt road into the hills. People have cabins. Maybe four or five of them. According to the postal service it's all officially Mule Crossing. Which is why they had a post office there, I guess. The zip code is about the size of Chicago. With five people. But hey, welcome to Wyoming.'

'Where is it exactly?'

'Forty minutes south. Take the state road out towards Colorado. Look for a billboard about bottle rockets.'

Reacher walked back to the corner of Third and Grand. He was optimistic about getting a ride. To his left was a university and straight ahead an hour away was legal weed. But it was getting dark. Might not be much to see. Clearly Mule Crossing was no kind of a bustling metropolis.

89

On the other hand, the flea market guy lived there.

He probably had a doorbell.

No time like the present.

Reacher walked south on Third Street, in the gutter, with his thumb out.

Gloria Nakamura rode the elevator two floors down to Computer Crimes, where she found her friend in his cubicle. He had torn her two phones out of their packaging. Now they were side by side on his desk above his keyboard. Their screens were blank.

'Sleep mode,' he said. 'All is well.'

'You got the number?'

'You have to act it out. Pretend you're a Chinese assembly worker. In fact don't, because your job was just automated and now you're not there at all. Pretend you're a machine instead. The phone numbers are carried on the SIM cards, bought in bulk from the service providers, and installed fairly late in the process, I would think. Then the heat-sealed packaging goes on, with the cardboard insert, and the packages slide off the line one after the other into shipping cartons, which are taken away by another conveyor belt. How many in a box, do you think?'

Nakamura thought about it, and said, 'Ten, probably. A place like that convenience store wouldn't want more than ten at a time. Mom-and-pop pharmacies would be the same. The manufacturers must know their market. So it's a small box. Bigger than a shoebox, but not by much.'

'And are the phone numbers sequential?'

'It would help.'

'Let's assume they are. Why wouldn't they be? There are plenty of new numbers to go around. So they fall off the line and go into the box in numerical order, one, two, three, all the way up to ten. So far so good. But we don't know what happens when they're unpacked. This is where you need to act it out. You slit the tape and you rest the box on the counter, and then you hang the contents on two pegs on a board behind the register. Talk me through it.'

Nakamura glanced at an imaginary counter, and then over her shoulder at a pair of imaginary pegs. She said, 'First I would rotate the box so the plastic blisters were facing towards me. So that I could pick them up, and turn a 180, and place them on the pegs face-out. Any other way would be a contortion.'

The tech said, 'And presumably they rode the conveyor belt with the blister upward and the flat side down, for stability. So if you have the blisters towards you, number one is nearest and number ten is farthest away. How many would you pick up at once?'

'I would do them one at a time. Those pegs are awkward.'

'Starting where? Front or back of the box?'

'Front,' she said.

'Which peg first?'

'The farther one. More satisfying to fill that first. The nearer one is easier. Like a reward.'

'So what do you get on the right-hand peg?'

'Numbers six through ten, in reverse order. Number ten will get bought first. Then nine, then eight, and so on. What were my numbers?'

'They weren't sequential,' the tech said. 'There was a two-digit gap. You gave me a seven and a four, essentially. Or a four and a seven. I don't know which came off the peg first.'

'I'm sorry,' Nakamura said. 'I should have marked the order.'

'Don't worry. Let's make another assumption. Let's say the convenience store guy gets his satisfaction a different way than you. Maybe he fills the pegs left, right, left, right. Perhaps he likes that better.'

'Then numbers four and seven couldn't be together on the same peg.'

91

'So let's make another assumption, based on the fact that you have the smallest hands in the world, and the convenience store guy is reasonably dexterous, working as he does with knives and what-not, so perhaps he hung them two at a time.'

'Yes,' she said. 'That would put three and four on the right, immediately behind seven and eight. If I bought seven and four, then Scorpio bought eight. His phone number is one higher than mine.'

'And listen to what my buddy at the phone company found,' her friend said. He shuffled his mouse and his screen lit up. He clicked on an email, and then on an audio file, and jagged green bandwidth spiked on the screen, and Scorpio said, 'Billy, this is Arthur. We got some weird shit going on.'

Reacher got a ride from two kids pulling out of a gas station on the southern edge of town. A boy and a girl. Grad students, probably, or undergrads with great ID. They said they were headed to Fort Collins, across the state line. Shopping, they said, but not for what. Their car was a tidy little sedan. Unlikely to attract a trooper's attention. Safe enough, for the return leg of their journey.

They said they knew the bottle rocket billboard. And sure enough, after forty minutes on a gentle two-lane road, there it was, on the right shoulder, caught square in the high beams. It was bright yellow, half urgent, and half quaint. The students pulled over, and Reacher got out. The students drove away, and Reacher stood alone in the silence. The firework store itself was dark and closed up tight. Beyond it fifty yards south was a ramshackle building with a light in a small square upstairs window. The flea market, presumably. The former post office.

Reacher walked towards it.

*

Nakamura carried her laptop to her lieutenant's office, and played him the voice mail. *Use a deer rifle from behind a tree. Your privileges are suspended till I hear back from you.*

'He's ordering a homicide,' she said.

Her lieutenant said, 'His lawyer will say talk is cheap. And he'll point out we don't have a warrant. Not for the new number.'

Nakamura said nothing.

Her lieutenant said, 'Anything else?'

'Scorpio mentioned privileges. I don't know what that means.'

'A business relationship of some kind, I suppose. Discount, priority, or access.'

'To what? Soap powder?'

'Surveillance should tell us.'

'We've never seen anything that looks like privileged access to something. Never. Nothing goes in or out.'

'Billy might not agree. Whoever Billy is.'

'Bigfoot is going to walk right into trouble. We should call someone.'

Her lieutenant said, 'Play the voice mail again.'

She did. *He's got to go, because he's a random loose end. Easier for you to deal with out there than it would be for me here. So get it done.*

'He's ordering a homicide,' she said again.

Her lieutenant said, 'Can we ID Billy from his phone number?'

Nakamura shook her head. 'Another drugstore burner.'

'Where is Mule Crossing exactly?'

'In a county measuring seven thousand square miles. Which is run by a sheriff's department likely no bigger than two men and a dog.'

'You think we should play the Good Samaritan?'

'I think we have a duty.'

'OK, call them in the morning. Fingers crossed the men answer, not the dog. Tell them the story. Ask them if they know a guy named Billy, with a deer rifle and a tree.'

The ramshackle building looked like a post office. Something about the shape, and the size. It was plain and bureaucratic, but also prideful. As if it was saying the mails could be carried anywhere, even into empty and inhospitable regions. *Neither snow nor rain nor heat nor gloom of night stays these couriers from the swift completion of their appointed rounds.* All that good stuff. But not any more. A car passed by on the road and in the wash of its lights Reacher saw less-faded wood where twenty years before stern metal letters had been prised out of the siding: *United States Post Office, Mule Crossing, Wyo.* Below that was a replacement message, hand-painted in gaudy multicoloured foot-high letters: *Flea Market.*

The market itself had a sign in the window saying it was closed. It was dark inside. The door was locked. No knocker, no bell. Reacher walked back to where he could see the lit-up window. Below it in the end wall of the building was a door, with a shallow stoop, which had a boot scraper on one side and a garbage can on the other. All very domestic. The entrance to the residence, presumably. To the foot of a staircase direct to the second floor. Where the lit window was. Living above the store, literally.

There was no doorbell.

Reacher knocked, hard and loud. Then waited. No response. He knocked again, harder and louder. He heard a voice.

It roared, 'What?'

A man, not young, not delighted at being disturbed.

'I want to talk to you,' Reacher called back.

'What?'

'I need to ask you a question.'

'What?'

Reacher said nothing. He just waited. He knew the guy would come down. He had been an MP for thirteen years. He had knocked on a lot of doors.

The guy came down. He opened the door. He was a white man, maybe seventy years old, tall but stooping, with not much flesh over a solid frame.

He said, 'What?'

Reacher said, 'I was told only five or six people live here. I'm looking for one of them. Which makes it about an eighteen per cent chance that person is you.'

'Who are you looking for?'

'Tell me your name first.'

'Why?'

'Because if you're the guy, you'll deny it. You'll pretend you're someone else and send me on a wild goose chase.'

'You think I would do that?'

'If you're the guy,' Reacher said again. 'It's been known to happen.'

'You a cop?'

'Once upon a time. In the army.'

The guy went quiet.

He said, 'My son was in the army.'

'What branch?'

'Rangers. He was killed in Afghanistan.'

'I'm sorry.'

'Not as much as I am. So remind me again, how may I help the army tonight?'

'I'm not here for the army,' Reacher said. 'I've been out a long time. This is a purely private matter. Purely personal. I'm looking for a man I was told was from Mule Crossing, Wyoming.'

'But you won't tell me his name till I tell you mine. Because if I'm him, I'll lie about it. Have I got that straight?'

'Hope for the best, plan for the worst.'

'If I was the sort of guy other guys came looking for, wouldn't I lie anyway?'

Reacher nodded.

He said, 'This whole thing would go better if I saw ID.'

'You got some nerve, you know that?'

'Nothing ventured, nothing gained.'

The guy stood still for a second, deciding, and then he shook his head and smiled and hauled a wallet out of his back pants pocket. He flipped it open and held it out. There was a Wyoming driver's licence behind a scratched plastic window. The photograph was right. The address was right. The name was John Ryan Headley.

Reacher said, 'Thank you, Mr Headley. My name is Reacher. I'm pleased to meet you.'

The guy clapped his wallet shut and put it back in his pocket.

He said, 'Am I the man you're looking for, Mr Reacher?'

'No,' Reacher said.

'I thought not. Why would anyone look for me?'

'I'm looking for a guy named Seymour Porterfield. Apparently people call him Sy.'

'You're a little late for Sy, I'm afraid.'

'Why's that?'

'He's dead.'

'Since when?'

'About eighteen months ago, I guess. Around the start of spring last year.'

'Someone told me he was seen in South Dakota six weeks ago.'

'Then someone was lying to you. There's no doubt about it. It was a big sensation. He was found in the hills, mostly eaten up. Killed by a bear, they thought. Maybe waking up after hibernation. They're hungry then. Other folks thought a mountain lion. His guts were all ripped out, which is what mountain lions do. Then the ravens came, and the crows, and the raccoons. He was scattered all over the place. They made the ID with his teeth. And the keys in his pocket. April, I think. April last year.'

'How old was he?'

'He could have been forty.'

'What did he do for a living?'

'Come on in,' Headley said. 'I've got coffee brewing.'

Reacher followed him up a narrow stair, to a long A-shaped attic that had been panelled with pine boards, and boxed off into separate rooms. There was an aluminium percolator thumping away on the stove. All the furniture was small. No sofas. The staircase was too narrow and the turns too tight to get them in. Headley poured two cups and handed one over. The coffee was thick and inky and smelled a little scorched.

'What did Porterfield do for a living?' Reacher asked again.

'No one knew for sure,' Headley said. 'But he always had money in his pocket. Not a whole lot, but a little more than made any kind of sense.'

'Where did he live?'

'He had a log house up in the hills,' Headley said. 'Twenty miles away, maybe, on one of the old ranches. All by himself. He was pretty much a loner.'

'West of here?'

Headley nodded. 'Follow the dirt road. I guess his place is empty now.'

'Who else lives out in that direction?'

'Not sure. I see folks driving by. I don't necessarily know who they are. This ain't the post office any more.'

'Were you here when it was?'

'Man and boy.'

'How many folks do you see driving by?'

'Could be ten or twenty total.'

'I was told four or five.'

'Who pay their taxes and sign their names. But there are plenty of abandoned places. Plenty of unofficial residents.'

Reacher said, 'You know a woman, also ex-army, very small, name of Serena Sanderson?'

97

Headley said, 'No.'

'You sure?'

'Pretty much.'

'Maybe she got married. You know any kind of a Serena?'

'No.'

'What about Rose? Maybe she goes by her middle name.'

'No.'

'OK,' Reacher said.

'What is this about exactly?'

Reacher took the ring out of his pocket. The gold filigree, the black stone, the tiny size. *West Point 2005*. He said, 'This is hers. I want to return it. I was told Sy Porterfield sold it in Rapid City six weeks ago.'

'He didn't.'

'Evidently.'

'What's the big deal?'

'Would your boy have given up his Ranger tab?'

'Not after what he went through to get it.'

'Exactly.'

'I can't help you,' Headley said. 'Except I can promise you Sy Porterfield didn't sell that ring in Rapid City six weeks ago, on account of getting ate up by a bear or a mountain lion more than a year before in another state entirely.'

'So someone else sold it.'

'From here?'

'Possibly. Fifty-fifty maybe. Mule Crossing was mentioned. Either true or false.'

'I see folks drive by. I don't know who they are.'

'Who would?'

Headley squirmed around in his chair, as if gazing west through the wall, as if picturing the dirt road rolling away into the darkness. He turned back and said, 'The guy who runs the snowplough in the winter lives in the first place on the left. About two miles in. I guess he knows who lives where, from seeing their tyre tracks, and maybe towing them out from time to time.'

'Two real miles in, or two Wyoming miles?'

'It's about a five minute drive.'

Which even on a dirt road could be more than two real miles. At an average speed of thirty, it would be two and a half. At forty, it would be more than three. And then back again.

'You got a car?' Reacher asked.

'I got a truck.'

'Can I borrow it?'

'No, you can't.'

'OK,' Reacher said. 'What's the guy's name, with the snowplough?'

'I don't know his second name. Not sure I ever heard it. But I know his first name is Billy.'

THIRTEEN

Reacher let himself out and walked down to where the dirt road met the two-lane. In the pitch dark there was nothing to see. No lights in the distance. Underfoot the surface felt like sand and fine gravel. Not hard to walk on. Except for the darkness. There was no clue at all as to direction, or curves, or turns, or camber, or gradient, or anything. He would be like a blind man, staggering slowly, blundering into fences, falling into ditches. Two miles was too far, in the gloom of night. He would have been a severe disappointment as a mail carrier.

He turned around. He crossed the two-lane and waited on the shoulder going north. Back to Laramie. Too soon to get the same students coming home again. But there would be others. Earlier birds, or regular folk coming back from shopping or a blue-plate special. He waited. The first two cars blew by without slowing, five minutes apart. The third stopped. It was a battered sedan with the hubcaps missing. The driver was a guy about forty, wearing a denim jacket. He said he was going to Laramie. Reacher asked him what he knew about motels in town. The guy said there were three types of place. Chain hotels south of the highway, or the same thing near the university, where people stayed for the football games, or dumpy mom-and-pop fleapits on the main drag north of the centre. All Reacher wanted was a bed and a pay phone, so he said the guy should let him out wherever was the most convenient. Which turned out to be the chains south of the highway. They were right there, on a service road parallel with the two-lane, across a grassy strip.

He paid for a room, and found a phone in an alcove off the lobby. He dug in his pocket and took out Nakamura's business card. *Those are my numbers. Office and cell. Call me if you need to talk. Scorpio is a dangerous man.*

He dialled her cell.

She answered.

He said, 'This is Reacher.'

She said, 'Are you OK?'

She sounded worried.

'I'm fine,' he said. 'Why?'

'Where are you?'

'Laramie, Wyoming.'

'Don't go to Mule Crossing.'

'I just did.'

'Scorpio made a call. He set you up.'

'I already know he lied to me about Seymour Porterfield. The guy died a year and a half ago. So I want you to give Scorpio a message. If you get the chance. Tell him one day I'm going to come back to Rapid City and pay him a visit.'

'I'm serious, Reacher.'

'So am I.'

'He told a man named Billy to shoot you on sight. From behind a tree with a deer rifle.'

'A man named what?'

'Billy.'

Reacher said, 'I just heard that name.'

'Don't go to Mule Crossing,' Nakamura said again. 'No point going there anyway, if he lied about it.'

'He lied about Porterfield. I don't know if he lied about Mule Crossing too. Depends how fast he was thinking. He was under pressure at the time. I was going to put him in a tumble dryer. How would he even know the name Mule Crossing? It's not a famous place. It's nothing but a flea market and a firework store on a two-lane road in the middle of nowhere. It's possible Scorpio told me the wrong person but the right place. Maybe Porterfield used to be in business with him. Maybe this guy Billy took over.'

'Scorpio's call implied Billy gets privileges of some kind. So they might be in business together.'

'What sort of business?'

'I don't know. But the threat to you was very clear. In my opinion he was ordering a homicide. I'm going to call the local sheriff in the morning.'

'Don't,' Reacher said. 'That would only complicate things.'

'I'm a police officer. I have to.'

'What exactly did Scorpio say on the phone?'

'It was a voice mail again. He called it weird shit going on. He said you were a strange piece of bad luck. The implication was there was something taking place on an ongoing basis, but you knew nothing about it, because you were just a random passer-by. He said he gave you Porterfield's name to get rid of you. Then he told Billy to kill you. He said not to mess with you, because you're like the Incredible Hulk. He said to use a deer rifle from behind a tree. He was ordering a homicide, Reacher. Clear as day. I have to put it in the system.'

'The Incredible Hulk? I thought I was Bigfoot. These guys need to make up their minds.'

'This isn't funny.'

'Did he mention Mule Crossing?'

'Not in the voice mail. Not specifically.'

'Was it a Mule Crossing number he called?'

'No, it was another drugstore burner. We can't trace it.'

'Then wait a day, OK? Wouldn't mean much to the sheriff without an exact location. Wyoming is a big state. I wouldn't want to waste anyone's time.'

'What are you going to do?'

'Nothing,' Reacher said. 'I want to know where the ring came from. That's all.'

Nakamura didn't reply to that, and they hung up. Room service was nothing more than a Xeroxed sheet of paper with a phone number for pizza delivery, so Reacher dialled again and ordered a large pie with extra pepperoni and anchovies. He waited for it in the lobby. An old habit. He didn't like people to know which room was his.

He woke the next morning with the sunrise, and went out in search of coffee. Which meant walking through the hotel's parking lot to get back to the two-lane. There was a black SUV parked near the door. It was a Toyota Land Cruiser. A serious vehicle. He had seen them in dusty and rugged parts of the world. The United Nations used them. This particular example was fairly new, and basically clean, but a little travel-stained.

It had Illinois plates.

He ducked back to the phone in the lobby and dialled Terry Bramall's cell number from memory. The private eye from Chicago. Last seen leaving Rapid City in a black SUV with Illinois plates. There was ring tone, but no answer. A voice came on and invited him to leave a message. He didn't. He just shrugged and set out again for coffee.

He found coffee along with breakfast in a diner on Third Street. He asked the waitress where the county sheriff was based. She said right there in town, about half a mile away. Not hard to find. The sky was blue and the sun was shining but the air was cool. He stopped in at a clothing store. In his experience the West was better than the East for tall guys. He found jeans the right length, and a flannel shirt, and a thin canvas jacket. As always he changed in the cubicle and had the clerk dump his old stuff in the trash. Then he walked onward to the spot the waitress had told him, and found the sheriff's office. It was a single-width storefront, with the bottom part of the window painted over. Above that was a gold pinstripe, and above that was a gold star about two feet wide and two feet high, with the county's name in a curve above, and *Sheriff's Department* in a curve below. The design looked a little bit like the West Point ring.

He went in. There was a woman in civilian clothes at the reception desk. He asked to see the sheriff, and she asked why he wanted to. He said he had a question about an old case. She asked his name, and he told her. She asked if his visit was in some way official. Whether he worked in law enforcement. He said not currently, but he had been an MP in the army for thirteen years. She told him to go ahead upstairs to the sheriff's office, which was the last door on the left. No hesitation. In his experience the West was better than the East for veterans.

He went upstairs. According to gold writing on the last door on the left the sheriff's name was Connelly. Reacher knocked and entered. The office was a dusty wood-framed room gone a golden hue with age, and Sheriff Connelly himself turned out to be a solid leathery guy of about fifty. He was wearing blue jeans and a tan shirt and a Stetson hat. Clearly the woman at the desk had called ahead, because Connelly already knew his name. He said, 'How can I help you, Mr Reacher?'

Reacher said, 'I came to Wyoming to look up a guy named Seymour Porterfield, but I'm told he got eaten up by a bear a year and a half ago. I was hoping you could tell me what you know about that.'

Connelly said, 'Take a seat, Mr Reacher.'

Reacher sat down, on an old-fashioned wooden visitor chair polished to a high shine by a thousand pairs of pants. Connelly looked at him without speaking. A level gaze, equal parts suspicion and the benefit of the doubt. He said, 'What was your connection with Seymour Porterfield?'

'None at all,' Reacher said. 'I'm looking for someone else, and I was told Porterfield might be able to point me in the right direction.'

'Who told you that?'

'A guy in South Dakota.'

'Who is the someone else you're looking for?'

Reacher took the ring out of his new pants pocket, and said, 'I want to return this to its rightful owner.'

'A woman,' Connelly said.

'Name of Serena Rose Sanderson. You know her?'

The guy shook his head. 'She a friend of yours?'

'Never met her. But we look after our own.'

'You a West Pointer too?'

'A long time ago.'

'Where did you find the ring?'

'In a pawn shop in Wisconsin. I traced it back to Rapid City, South Dakota. I was told it was brought there from Wyoming by Porterfield.'

'When?'

'After he was dead.'

'So how can I help you?'

'You can't,' Reacher said. 'But I'm curious. Getting eaten by a bear seems a little extreme.'

'Could have been a mountain lion.'

'How likely is that?'

'Not very,' Connelly said. 'Either thing would be rare.'

'So what do you think happened?'

'A practical man would say the guy was gut-shot or knifed in the stomach and then dumped in the woods. It was the end of winter. Bears or mountain lions might have been hungry enough to scavenge the corpse. Birds would have, for sure. Also raccoons and what-not. But there was zero evidence either way. We confirmed all the parts were Porterfield, but he was real torn up. We didn't find a bullet. Didn't find a knife. There were marks on the bones, but they were all animal teeth. I had folks at the university take a good long look. All inconclusive. We called it an accident, and maybe it was.'

Reacher said, 'What do you know about the guy himself?'

'Very little. This is Wyoming. We leave people alone. No one enquires into other people's business. He lived by himself. He had a fairly new car with a lot of miles on it. So he got around some. He had cash in a shoebox in the back of his closet. That's all we found out.'

'How much cash?'

'Nearly ten grand.'

'Not bad.'

'I agree. I wish I had ten grand in the back of my closet. But it wasn't enough to get all excited about.'

'Except you formed the impression he was the type of guy who could get gut-shot or knifed in the stomach.'

'I try to keep an open mind, both ways around.'

'No friends or relatives showing up asking questions?'

'Not a peep.'

'OK,' Reacher said. 'Thanks.'

'You're welcome,' Connelly said. 'I hope you find who you're looking for.'

'I plan to,' Reacher said.

FOURTEEN

Reacher walked east the best part of a mile, to where the university buildings started. He stopped in at what looked like a general office and asked for the geography department. The kid at the desk looked like a student. He was half asleep. But eventually he understood the question. He said, 'What do you need there?'

'I want to look at a map,' Reacher said.

'Use your phone, man.'

'I don't have a phone.'

'Really?'

'And I want to see detail.'

'Use satellite view.'

'All I would see is trees. Plus like I told you, I don't have a phone.'

'Really?'

'Where's the geography department?'

The kid pointed and said further on down the road, so Reacher went back to walking. Five minutes later he was in the right place, in front of another kid at another desk. This one was a girl, and she was wider awake. Reacher told her what he needed, and she went away and then came back labouring under the weight of a hardbound Wyoming topographical atlas about the size of a sidewalk paving slab. Reacher took it from her and hefted it to a table under a window. He opened it up and found the southeast corner of the state. Found Laramie, and the two-lane south towards Colorado, and the dirt-road turnoff at Mule Crossing.

Reacher had been at West Point when reading paper maps was still taught as a serious lifesaving skill. Terrain was important to an army. Understanding it was the difference between winning and getting wiped out. What he saw west of the old post office was an unimproved road of reasonable width, never quite straight, following the gentle contours of the surrounding land, flanked on both sides by empty plains, which broke up after a mile or so into the faintest first foothills of the Snowy Range mountains fifty miles further on. There were fence lines here and there, engraved as fine as the detail on a hundred-dollar bill. There were thin streams coloured blue, and forests coloured green, and orange contour lines rising and falling. Left and right along a twenty-mile distance were occasional ranch roads, leading to faraway buildings drawn as tiny brown squares. The first such track on the left was almost exactly two and a half miles from the old post office. It ran south for a spell, through patchy conifer woods, and then it curved west, and then snaked east, and then west again, up a shallow rise on to a knoll cradled by a higher U-shaped ridge to the south. On the knoll were shown two tiny brown squares. A house and a barn, maybe.

Billy's place.

The next track on the left was almost three miles further west. Same kind of situation. A meandering dirt track, squirming right and left through the early hills and the thickening forest, leading to some kind of an inhabited dwelling. Obviously Reacher could use that second track and loop back to Billy's place through the trees on the blind side. Which would be an advantage. Except that to get there in the first place he would have to walk the unimproved road all the way from the old post office. He would be visible from Billy's house for the best part of forty minutes. The knoll was at least a hundred feet higher than the road. He would be a speck in the far distance, for sure, but the guy had been warned. Maybe he had binoculars. Or a scope on his deer rifle.

A problem.

The girl at the desk said, 'You OK, sir?'

'Doing well,' Reacher said.

He turned the page.

Much more interesting was what lay farther to the south. The next right off the two-lane after Mule Crossing came three miles later. It was a forest service track into a nature preserve labelled *Roosevelt National* something. It was right at the bottom of the map. Right on the state line. The third word would be on the first Colorado sheet. *Forest*, presumably. Teddy Roosevelt, Reacher supposed, not Franklin. The great naturalist, except for when he was shooting things like tigers and elephants. People were complicated. The service track fed a spider web of more service tracks, one of which curved around north and came out on the back slope of the U-shaped ridge right behind Billy's house. The contour lines showed the ridge was more than a hundred feet higher than the knoll. A person could get within fifty yards completely unobserved, no matter how many binoculars or rifle scopes the guy was using.

Map reading. The difference between winning and getting wiped out.

Reacher heaved the giant book shut, like closing a heavy door. The girl at the desk told him to leave it right there on the table. Maybe she felt she had done enough bicep curls for one day. He thanked her and stepped out to the sidewalk and headed back west to town, in the right-side gutter, with his left thumb out. He got a ride within a minute, with a friendly wild-haired bearded character, maybe an eccentric professor, but the guy was going only as far as the supermarket, so Reacher got out on the corner of Third Street and started over, walking south like he had the night before. A ratty old pick-up truck stopped before he got to the edge of town, and he climbed in and asked for a spot three miles south of the bottle rocket billboard. The driver looked a little puzzled, as if wondering what the hell was there, but he didn't ask. He just drove. *This is Wyoming. No one enquires into other people's business.* They passed under the highway bridge and Reacher glanced left, across the grassy strip, at the lot in front of his hotel. The black SUV was gone.

FIFTEEN

Forty minutes later Reacher was alone on the two-lane's shoulder, watching the pick-up truck drive away. The mouth of the forest road was overgrown with sagebrush, and it had a heavy chain slung across it, dipping low between two weathered posts. He stepped over it and set out hiking. The altitude was more than eight thousand feet above sea level, and the air was thin. The effort made him breathe hard, and left him light-headed. The forest was mostly fir and pine, dappled with sun, blazing here and there with bright yellow groves of aspen. His normal rule of thumb for walking north through a wood was to look for moss on the tree trunks. Less of it would be facing east, south and west. Regular daylight would see to that. But the mountain air was bone dry and there was no moss at all. So he navigated by the sun. It was mid-morning, so he kept it forty-five degrees behind his right shoulder. He kept his shadow ahead and to the left. He angled west where he could, and felt the ground rise under his feet. An hour or less, he figured, before he got to the back side of the U-shaped ridge. He pictured

Billy, watching the wrong horizon. He trudged on, panting.

Nakamura walked the corridor to her lieutenant's corner suite, and said, 'Reacher called me last night.'

Her lieutenant said, 'Who?'

'Bigfoot,' she said. 'The Incredible Hulk.'

'And?'

'He asked me to hold off a day before calling the sheriff in Wyoming.'

'Why would he?'

'He pointed out there was no specific location mentioned in Scorpio's voice mail, and therefore he felt a warning wouldn't mean much to law enforcement out there. He didn't want to waste anyone's time.'

'That's very scrupulous of him.'

'I got the impression he wants freedom of action.'

'Do you think he should have it?'

'That's not for me to say. Or him, either.'

'We work for the people of Rapid City, and no one else. Certainly not a bunch of cowboys out west.'

'Yes, sir.'

'Therefore, on that basis, what helps Rapid City most?'

Nakamura said nothing.

'Well?'

'I checked him out,' Nakamura said. 'I made some calls. He was an elite MP. He has medals. He's possibly better prepared than the average person.'

'Can he help us with Scorpio?'

You could put him in a zoo.

She said, 'I really don't see how he could hurt.'

'OK then,' the lieutenant said. 'Wait a day.'

Then he said, 'No, wait two days.'

*

112

Reacher found what had to be the lower back slope of the U-shaped ridge after fifty minutes of hiking. The dirt underfoot was thin and gritty. There were pine cones everywhere, some of them the size of softballs. He climbed slowly, with short choppy steps, kicking his toes into the dirt for grip. He got close to the top and found what might have been a fox trail that led him the rest of the way to the summit. He dropped to his knees and took a look.

He was a couple hundred yards east of where he needed to be. He dropped back to the fox trail and went west, three minutes at a slow pace, arms out for balance.

He took another look.

Now Billy's place was directly below him, fifty yards away.

It was a log house, stained dull brown, with a log barn, both structures surrounded by beaten-down brush and dusty red dirt. A rutted driveway ran away through the woods, appearing and reappearing in the gaps between the trees. On the right the land fell away and flattened into wide empty plains. The old post office was visible in the far distance, and the firework store, and the two-lane road. There was a grazing herd of pronghorns about a mile away. The dirt road was vivid ochre, neatly scraped, nicely cambered. On the left the land rose into low jagged peaks, like miniature mountain ranges, like premonitions of what would come for real a hundred miles farther west. The air was still and unnaturally clear. The sky was deep blue. There was absolute silence.

Billy's house had a green metal roof, and small windows with no light inside. Not a trophy cabin. Not a weekend place. But not a mess, either. No junk in the yard. No rusted washing machines. No cars up on blocks. No pit bull on a chain. Just a workaday house.

No people.

Reacher eased down the near slope, slowly, from tree to tree.

Forty yards away. Thirty. A pine cone rolled ahead of him and hit a bump and kicked up in the air.

He froze.

No reaction.

He kept on going, stepping sideways for grip, staying where the trees were thickest. Twenty yards away. Ten. He could see Billy's back door. Footsteps had beaten a path from it to a similar door in the back of the barn.

He stopped five yards inside the tree line. Safe enough. All was quiet. He waited. He figured Billy wouldn't have taken Scorpio's voice mail literally. The guy wouldn't be hiding behind an actual tree with his rifle at his shoulder. He was more likely sitting in a chair on his front porch. With his rifle on the boards beside him. He could see twenty miles. He would figure he would get plenty of early warning.

Reacher moved east through the trees and lined up with the back of the barn. His first port of call. He took a breath and stepped out.

No reaction.

He crossed the open space, controlled, not fast, not slow, with tiny slaps and crunches from his feet on the grit and the gravel.

No reaction.

He pressed up against the back of the barn. There were no windows. The personnel door was ten feet to his left. He crabbed sideways and tried the handle. Locked. Which was a pity. Barns were usually good for useful stuff. Hammers, hatchets, wrenches, knives. He crabbed back to where he started, and onward to the corner. The house was twenty feet away. Still quiet. The side facing him was made of heavy logs, and it had two small windows on the first floor and two on the second. All four were backed by half-closed sun-faded drapes.

He took another breath and crossed the open space. He pressed his back hard against the logs. The first-floor window sills were about level with his shoulder. He inched closer and risked a one-eyed look inside. He saw a powder room, with a closed door. He moved on. Checked the second window. Saw a small alcove at the foot of a staircase. Beyond it was the front half of a living room. Two more windows, a front door, a stone fireplace, well-worn armchairs. Log walls, stained dark.

No people.

The front door would lead to a front porch.

Which would be around the next exterior corner.

He moved on, slow and cautious. He stopped a foot short of the corner and listened hard. Heard nothing except silence, and the tiniest eddy of breeze through the trees, and the caw of a rook far in the distance. No breathing, no movement, no creak of wood. Nothing at all.

One more half-step.

He peered around the corner. Saw a covered porch, with a railing, and two heavy wooden chairs, and a swing seat hanging motionless on four thick chains.

No people.

No rifle resting on the boards.

No Billy.

Reacher shuffled sideways to the rear corner of the house. He paused a beat, and slid around, and moved along the back wall. He checked the first window he came to. A kitchen. Still and quiet and no one in it. Next to the kitchen window was a kitchen door. Solid wood. No glass. He passed it by and checked a second window. A small back parlour. A desk, a chair. Still and quiet and no one in it.

Silence.

He crept back to the kitchen door. Now logic said Billy was upstairs. He had been warned. His view would be marginally better from a second-floor window. He would see a mile or more of the two-lane beyond the old post office. He would get six or seven minutes, even if an incoming vehicle was driving fast.

Reacher tried the door handle.

It turned.

The door opened.

He pushed it gently, with spread fingers. The kitchen air smelled still and stale. There were dark wood cabinets and a cold stove. Yesterday's dishes were in the sink. There was tile on the floor. The inside door was open to the living room. No people. Last winter's ash was still in the fireplace. A poker and a brush and a long-handled shovel were propped together in a stand on the hearth stones.

Slowly, carefully, he eased the poker out of the stand. It was iron, about a yard long, and it had a vicious hook at the end, jutting out like a hitchhiker's thumb.

Better than nothing.

He crept to the foot of the stairs. Listened hard. The log construction was massive and solid. No sound. Nothing at all.

He started up the stairs. The moment of maximum vulnerability. Nothing to be done if Billy showed up shooting in the upstairs hallway. Short of swinging the poker at the bullet like a slugger going after a high fastball. Unlikely to work. But, nothing ventured, nothing gained. The stairs were sawn half-logs about ten inches thick. No danger of creaking. He held his breath.

He made it to the top. Directly ahead of him was a half-open door to a bathroom, directly above the kitchen. No one in it. Ahead and to his right was a half-open door to a back bedroom, above the back parlour. No one in it. He turned in the hallway and faced two front bedrooms. One had a wide-open door. No one in it.

One had a closed door.

Reacher held the poker across his body, at port arms.

You and me, Billy, he thought.

There was a rag rug in the upstairs corridor. He stepped on to

116

it and walked slowly, carefully, silently. He stopped four feet short of the door. He was a big believer in shock and awe and surprise and overwhelming force. What used to be called common sense, before the Pentagon pointy-heads started dreaming up fancy names for simple concepts. He set his feet and rocked back and forth, back and forth, like a high-jumper going for a record, and then he smashed through the door with the sole of his boot and exploded into the room with the poker scything through the air in front him.

The room was empty.

No Billy.

Just an unmade bed, and the sour smell of sleep, and a three-pane window with a perfect view to the horizon. Nothing out there except the herd of pronghorns, grazing unconcerned a mile away.

Reacher had searched a lot of houses, and he found the barn keys in the first place he looked, on a nail in the wall near the kitchen door. The barn was a big one-storey space that smelled of dust and wood stain and cold motor oil. There were bald tyres and all kinds of mechanical junk and a detached snowplough blade stacked on the floor. No actual vehicles. Nothing else of interest. He went back to the house and stood on the front porch and checked the view. He traced the route, along the driveway, along the dirt road, bit by bit, his eyes moving like a finger on a map, all the way out past the old post office and the firework store.

Nothing coming.

No dust on the dirt road.

He started downstairs and searched the house methodically, running a clock in his head, returning to the porch every sixty seconds to check the horizon. There was nothing of significance in the kitchen. Nothing in the living room. Billy seemed to be a guy with neat but not obsessive habits. The place was reasonably tidy and reasonably clean. The stuff in it was neither obviously expensive nor obviously cheap. It was clear he lived alone.

The back parlour was set up as an office. A desk, a chair, a file cabinet. On the desk was a cell phone. A simple thing. Old-fashioned but not old. It was plugged in to a charger. The battery icon said a hundred per cent. The screen said *New Message.*

Sixty seconds. Reacher slipped out to the porch and checked the view. Nothing coming. He went back to the office. He had never owned a cell phone, but he had used one from time to time. He knew how they worked. At the bottom of the screen were the words *Menu* and *Play,* and below them were two slim bar-shaped buttons. He pressed the bar below *Play.*

He heard a nervous breath and a throat being cleared.

Then he heard Scorpio's voice.

It said, 'Billy, this is Arthur. We got some weird shit going on. Nothing real serious. Just a strange piece of bad luck. Some guy showed up chasing a ring.'

Sixty seconds. Reacher stepped out to the front porch again and checked the view. Still nothing coming. He went back in and up the stairs to the slept-in bedroom. First thing he looked at was the closet. Just for fun. Against the back wall behind a rail of hanging pants he found four shoeboxes. They were neatly stacked two on two. The top two held shoes. White athletic sneakers on the left, and rubber-soled black leather dress items on the right. The kind of thing a country boy might wear to a wedding or a funeral or a visit with the loan officer at the bank. Both pairs had been worn, but not often. Both pairs were size eight and a half. The hanging pants were all thirty-two waist and thirty leg.

Billy was a small guy.

Sixty seconds. He checked out the window.

118

There was a long dust plume on the dirt road.

A hanging ochre cloud, long, spiralling and drifting. A vehicle, coming on fast. Still just a tiny dot in the distance. Too far away to see what it was.

Six minutes, maybe.

He went back in the closet. Checked the bottom pair of boxes.

One was full of money.

Tens and twenties and fifties, used and creased, sour and greasy, done up in inch-thick bricks with rubber bands. Maybe ten grand in total. Maybe more.

The other box was full of trinkets. Mostly gold. Gold crosses on thin tangled chains, gold earrings, gold bracelets, gold charms, gold chokers.

And gold rings.

Some were wedding rings.

Some were class rings.

Reacher stepped back to the window and watched. The dust plume was a mile long, hanging in the motionless air. At the head of it was a tiny dark dot, quivering, bobbing, bouncing. The pronghorn herd rippled, uneasy.

The tiny dot looked black.

It was hammering and juddering right to left in front of him. It was doing maybe forty miles an hour. Maybe more. Some kind of familiarity with the terrain, or some kind of urgency, or some kind of both.

He waited.

It slowed.

The dust cloud caught up with it.

It turned in at the driveway.

Billy's ride would be a pick-up truck, Reacher figured. Snowploughs usually were. Winter tyres, chains, a hydraulic

119

mechanism for the blade, extra spotlights mounted high. All detached in the summer, leaving a familiar silhouette. Hood, cab, bed.

Which Reacher didn't see.

It wasn't a pick-up truck.

It was big and square and boxy. An SUV. A black SUV. Travel-stained and dusty. It flashed in and out of sight through the trees. Then it pulled clear and drove the last hundred yards over the beaten red dirt.

It slowed and turned and came to a stop.

It was a Toyota Land Cruiser.

It had Illinois plates.

SIXTEEN

Reacher watched from the upstairs window. The black SUV parked a respectful distance from the house. The driver's door opened. A man stepped down. A small guy, neat and compact, in a dark suit and a shirt and a tie. Terry Bramall. From Chicago. Retired FBI. The missing persons specialist. Last seen the day before, in Rapid City, in the breakfast place opposite Arthur Scorpio's laundromat.

The guy stood still for a long moment, and then he set out walking towards the house, with a purposeful stride.

Reacher went down the stairs. He made it to the bottom and heard a knock on the door. He opened up. Bramall was standing on the porch. He had taken a polite step back. His hair was brushed. His suit was the same, but his shirt and his tie were different. He had the kind of look on his face that Reacher recognized. The kind of look he had used himself, many times. Open, inquisitive, inoffensive, faintly apologetic for the interruption, but no-nonsense all the same. An experienced investigator's look. Which changed for a split second, first to surprise, then to puzzlement, and then finally it came back the same as before.

'Mr Bramall,' Reacher said.

'Mr Reacher,' Bramall said. 'I saw you yesterday in the coffee shop in Rapid City. And the night before in the convenience store. You called me and left a message.'

'Correct.'

'I assume your first name isn't Billy.'

'You assume right.'

'Then may I ask what you're doing here?'

'I could ask you the same question.'

'May I come in?'

'Not my house. Not for me to say.'

'Yet you seem to be making yourself at home.'

Reacher looked beyond Bramall's shoulder at the view. The dust cloud over the dirt road had settled. The pronghorn herd had gone back to placid grazing. Nothing was moving. No one was coming.

He said, 'What do you want from Billy?'

'Information,' Bramall said.

'He's not here. Probably been gone about twenty-four hours. Or more. Scorpio left him a voice mail around this time yesterday and it was still showing on his phone as a new message. It hadn't been picked up yet.'

'He went out without his phone?'

'It was charging. Maybe it's not his main phone. It looks like a burner. Maybe it's for special purposes only.'

'Did you listen to the message?'

'Yes.'

'What did it say?'

'Scorpio asked Billy to shoot me with a deer rifle from behind a tree.'

'To shoot you?'

'He included a description.'

'That's not very nice.'

'I agree.'

Bramall said, 'We should talk.'

'On the porch,' Reacher said. 'In case Billy comes back.'

Four eyes were better than two. They sat side by side in Billy's wooden chairs, with Bramall gazing west of dead ahead, and Reacher gazing east. They talked into the void in front of them, not looking at each other, which made the conversation easier in some respects, and harder in others.

Bramall said, 'Tell me what you know.'

Reacher said, 'You're retired.'

'That's what you know? Hardly relevant. Or even true. I'm pursuing a second career.'

'I mean you're retired FBI. Which means you don't get to use FBI bullshit any more. As in, you don't get to ask all the questions and then walk away. You get to give as well as take.'

'How do you know I was FBI?'

'A police detective in Rapid City told me. Name of Nakamura.'

'She must have done some research.'

'That's what detectives do.'

'What do you want to know?'

'Who are you looking for?'

'I'm afraid I'm bound by a certain degree of confidentiality.'

Reacher said nothing.

Bramall said, 'I don't even know who you are.'

'Jack Reacher. No middle name. Retired military police. Some of your guys came to us for training.'

'And some of yours came to us.'

'So we're on an equal footing. Give and take, Mr Bramall.'

'Rank?'

'Does it matter?'

'You know it does.'

'Terminal at major.'

'Unit?'

'Mostly the 110th MP.'

'Which was?'

'Like the FBI, but with better haircuts.'

'Is the military connection why you're here?'

'Should it be?'

'I'm serious,' Bramall said. 'Clients like discretion. Most of the time I make my living by keeping things quiet. For all I know, you work for a website now.'

'I don't. Whatever that means.'

'Who do you work for?'

'I don't work.'

'Then why are you here?'

'Tell me about your client, Mr Bramall. Broad strokes, if you like. No names at this point. No identifying details.'

'You can call me Terry.'

'And you can call me Reacher. And you can quit stalling.'

'My client is someone in the Chicago area worried about a family member.'

'Worried why?'

'No contact for a year and a half.'

'What took you to Rapid City?'

'Landline calls in old phone records.'

'What brought you here?'

'The same.'

'Was the family with the missing member originally a Wyoming family?'

Bramall said nothing.

'There are hundreds of families in Wyoming,' Reacher said. 'Maybe even thousands. You won't be giving anything away.'

'Yes,' Bramall said. 'Originally it was a Wyoming family. From the other side of the Snowy Range. About sixty miles from here.

Maybe seventy. That's about two blocks away, by Wyoming standards.'

Reacher said, 'Had the family member in question spent time overseas?'

'Give and take, Mr Reacher. You're retired too.'

Reacher checked his part of the horizon, from the dirt road out past Mule Crossing's forlorn buildings, to the two-lane. No movement. Nothing coming. He checked Bramall's part too, tracing the dirt road west until it disappeared in the hills. No dust. No movement. Nothing coming.

He took the ring out of his pocket. He balanced it on his palm. He held out his hand. Bramall took the ring from him. He looked at it. He took out a pair of tortoiseshell reading glasses from an inside pocket. He read the engraving on the inner face.

S.R.S. 2005.

He said, 'Now we really need to talk.'

Reacher told him the story. The bus out of Milwaukee, and the comfort stop, and the pawn shop, and Jimmy Rat in the biker bar, and Arthur Scorpio in the Rapid City laundromat, and the tale about how a guy named Porterfield brought him the ring, which had proved to be a lie, because of the big sensation with either the bear or the mountain lion, or both.

Bramall said, 'That was a year and a half ago?'

Reacher nodded. 'The start of spring last year.'

'Which was when my client got worried.'

'If you say so.'

'And you're here in his house because you think Billy replaced Porterfield in the ring-transportation business?'

'I think it's likely.'

'Why?'

'I'll show you,' Reacher said. He checked the view again, both ways, and saw no one coming. He led Bramall into the house, and up the stairs, and to Billy's bedroom. To the closet. He showed him the shoeboxes, one crammed with cash, the other rattling and tinkling with cheap gold jewellery.

'Drug dealers,' Bramall said. 'Don't you think? Small-time. Home-cooked meth or cheap heroin up from Mexico. Twenty bucks sees you right, and if you can't pay you trade your rings and your necklaces. Or you steal someone else's.'

'I thought it was all pain pills now,' Reacher said.

'That boom is over,' Bramall said. 'Now it's back to how it used to be. Scorpio is the wholesaler, employing first Porterfield and now Billy as his local retailer, using the first guy as a decoy and secretly telling the second guy to get rid of you. He doesn't like scrutiny.'

'Possible,' Reacher said.

'You got another coherent explanation?'

'Who's your client?'

'A woman in Lake Forest named Tiffany Jane Mackenzie. Serena Rose Sanderson's twin sister. Married, hence the different name. They were close as children, but pretty soon went their separate ways. Mackenzie's living the dream. Big house, rich husband. She didn't altogether approve of her sister's career choice. But blood is thicker than water. There was occasional contact. Until the start of spring last year. How thorough was the investigation about the bear and the mountain lion?'

'Very,' Reacher said. 'By rural standards, anyway. The sheriff looks solid. There was only one body, and it was all Porterfield. They knew from his dental records and the keys in his pocket.'

'So you think Sanderson is still alive?'

'Probably. The ring showed up in Rapid City about six weeks ago, and in Wisconsin about two weeks later. I'm guessing they move stuff along pretty quickly. The sheriff said Porterfield's car had a lot of miles. He was probably running back and forth pretty regularly. I imagine Billy is too. What we've got here in the shoebox is probably just a few weeks' worth. The sheriff said Porterfield had cash in his closet too. A similar amount. Small-time, maybe, but it seems to add up.'

'So where is Billy now?'

Reacher stepped to the window and checked the view. No one coming, either east or west. He said, 'I have no idea where Billy is. There are dishes in the sink. Feels like he stepped out for a minute.'

'Show me the phone.'

Reacher led Bramall down the stairs, to the small parlour in back. To the phone on the desk. Bramall stabbed at buttons and played the message again. *He's like the Incredible Hulk. Don't even let him see you. But get on it, OK? He's got to go, because he's a random loose end.*

Bramall said, 'You took a risk coming here.'

'Getting up in the morning is a risk. Anything could happen.'

'Did you know Sanderson?'

'No,' Reacher said. 'I was already out eight years before 2005.'

'Then what's your interest?'

'You wouldn't understand.'

'Why not?'

'I'm not sure I understand.'

'Try me.'

'I felt sad when I saw the ring. Simple as that. It wasn't right.'

'You a West Pointer too?'

'Long time ago.'

'Where's your ring?'

'I didn't buy one.'

Bramall pressed more buttons. Checked the call log, looked for old voice mails. Didn't find any. He went to another menu and chose a keep-as-new option. The screen went back to announcing one new message, the way it was when Reacher found it. Deniability. Score one for the Bureau.

Bramall said, 'Leaving dishes in his sink doesn't mean much. Maybe he's just a slob. Leaving the phone at home doesn't necessarily mean much either. Probably doesn't work in the hills. No signal. Right here he's got a direct line of sight to the tower in Laramie. Maybe he never carries a phone with him.'

Reacher said, 'Scorpio seems to have expected some kind of an instant response.'

'Do you believe the story about the bears and the mountain lions?'

'The sheriff has his doubts. He thinks maybe Porterfield was stabbed or gut-shot and dumped in the woods to let nature take its course.'

'Maybe Billy did it. Maybe he took over from Porterfield by force. Like an armed coup. Now maybe someone else has done the same thing to Billy. Live by the sword, die by the sword. What goes around comes around.'

'I don't care,' Reacher said. 'I'm here to find Sanderson. That's all.'

'Might not be a happy ending. Not if she traded her ring to a two-bit dope dealer. You might not like what you find.'

'Someone else might have stolen it. You said so yourself.'

'I sure hope so,' Bramall said. 'Because sooner or later I'll have to give the sister the news. And then give her my invoice. Sometimes that doesn't go down so well.'

'How big of an invoice?'

'She has a house on the lake. She can afford it.'

'You worth it?'

'Usually.'

'So what's your next move?'

'I think she's close by. This feels like the end of the line. I think Billy is the final interface with the public. We're down to one degree of separation. Either she gave the ring to him herself or a neighbour stole it and gave it to him.'

'Not bad for the FBI,' Reacher said. 'Plus Billy drives the snow-plough. He knows all the local roads. Ideal cover for getting around and supplying his customers. Never held up by the weather, either. But his retail territory must be huge. Like you said, two blocks is seventy miles out here. All the way to Sanderson's childhood home, as a matter of fact. I assume you've already looked there?'

'The assumption is Sanderson won't go back. Her sister was sure of it.'

'Why?'

'She didn't explain. So knowing that, where would you start?'

'I could tell you, but then I'd have to bill you.'

Bramall said, 'Did you park your car in the barn?'

Reacher said, 'I don't have a car.'

'Then how did you get all the way out here?'

'Hitchhiked and walked.'

'Suppose I let you ride in my truck?'

'That would be nice.'

'Suppose you shut up about a bill?'

'Deal,' Reacher said.

'So where?'

'What other information did the sister give you? Any names or places?'

'She says Sanderson was always very cagey. Maybe embarrassed, maybe upset. She never mentioned locations. She never said what she was doing. They could go three months without talking.'

'Is that usual for twins?'

'Twins are siblings, same as anyone else.'

'She got nothing at all?'

'The last time they spoke she got the impression Sanderson had a friend called Cyrus. She heard her say that name.'

'Cyrus?'

'Well, Cy, at least. As if he was in the room with her. Like, shut up, Cy, I'm on the phone. Said in a friendly way. Like she was comfortable with him. The sister says for a second she sounded happy.'

'Was that rare?'

'Very.'

'When was this?'

'A couple of years ago, she thinks. Maybe a bit less.'

'Is that all she got?'

'She said their conversations were usually very stiff. Are you OK, yes I'm OK. That kind of thing.'

'Maybe it wasn't Cy for Cyrus,' Reacher said. 'Maybe it was Sy for Seymour. Which was Porterfield's first name. Scorpio told me he went by Sy. Let's go find where he lived. That would be my first move. There might still be something there. Or neighbours we can talk to.'

SEVENTEEN

The old guy in the old post office had said Porterfield had lived in a log house up in the hills, maybe twenty miles down the dirt road, on one of the old ranches Reacher had seen on the university's map, behind fence lines as fine as the engraving on a hundred-dollar bill. Bramall's Land Cruiser had a navigation screen that showed the dirt road, but not much else. So they watched the trip meter and drove west and counted the miles as they clicked by. The truck was as neat and competent as Bramall himself. It floated over the rough surface and felt like it could run for ever.

Reacher asked, 'What was the last time the sisters met face to face?'

Bramall said, 'Seven years ago. After Sanderson's third deployment. The visit didn't go so well. I guess they decided not to repeat it. After that it was all on the phone.'

'Sanderson was wounded at some point.'

'I didn't know that. Mrs Mackenzie never mentioned it.'

'She might not have known about it. Sanderson might not have told her.'

'Why wouldn't she?'

'It happens a lot. It's a complex dynamic. Maybe she didn't want to upset her family. Or appear diminished in any way. Or weak. Or to appear to be asking for sympathy. Or help. Or to avoid a told-you-so moment. Sounds like her sister didn't like the army.'

'Wounded how bad?'

'I don't know,' Reacher said. 'All I know is she got a Purple Heart. Which can be anything from a scratch to losing a limb. Or all of them. Some of those people came home in a hell of a mess.'

The mileage counter showed eight miles gone. Bramall was quiet for a long moment. Then he said, 'You sure you want to do this? I don't see how the outcome can be good. She's either all messed up or a junkie or both. She might not want to be found.'

'In which case I'll leave her alone. I'm not trying to save the world. I just want to know.'

Ten miles gone. Either side of the road the high plains were getting higher. The mountain foothills rippled and folded, and tongues of conifer forest came and went. The sky was huge and high and impossibly blue, like a sapphire on the horizon, shading to deep navy way overhead. Like a Kodak photograph. Like the edge of outer space. The wind was getting up. The dust plume behind them was pulling south off the road.

'PTSD too,' Bramall said. 'I guess they all have that.'

'I guess they do,' Reacher said.

Fourteen miles. Aspen groves blazed like flares on the slopes. Whole copses of hundreds of separate trees, but all joined together underground by a single root. An aspen wood was all one organism. The largest living thing on earth.

Bramall said, 'Did the guy mean twenty miles to the house itself, or twenty miles to the end of the driveway?'

'The driveway,' Reacher said. 'I guess. That's how it worked with Billy's place. Except the guy underestimated. He called it about twenty per cent short.'

'So his twenty miles could be twenty-five.'

'Unless sometimes he overestimates also. Maybe he's an all-around inaccurate guy, on a number of levels and a random basis. Which could make his twenty miles sixteen. Which would give us a nine-mile window.'

'Then logically we should take the next track we see. Unlikely to be two in a nine-mile distance. This is Wyoming. Therefore the first track is our track, however sooner or later it comes.'

'Not bad for the FBI,' Reacher said.

The track came bang in the middle of the nine-mile stretch, at twenty miles from the post office exactly. Score one for the old guy. It was a right turn off the dirt road, under a high ranch gate, which had a name on it, spelled out in letters so weathered Reacher couldn't read them. Then the track ran straight north for close to a mile, before rising and curving west through the trees, out of sight, towards an unseen destination.

Bramall stopped the truck.

He said, 'From my point of view this kind of thing is perfectly normal. I drive up to hundreds of houses. Sometimes there's yelling and sometimes there are dogs, but no one has ever discharged a weapon in my direction. We should talk about how you think those odds might change, with you in the car right next to me.'

'You want me to get out and walk?' Reacher said. 'Feel safer that way?'

'It's a tactical discussion. Worst case, Billy took over Porterfield's house as well as his business, and he's in there now. He wasn't in his other place, after all.'

'Why would he want two places?'

'Some people do.'

'Not twenty miles apart. They have a house on the lake.'

'There were no heirs or relatives. Why wouldn't Billy take it?'

'Doesn't matter if he did. Doesn't matter if he's in there now. He never got the phone message. He doesn't know me from Adam. He'll think we're Mormons.'

'You're not dressed like a Mormon.'

'So you go knock on the door. Just in case. If he's there, tell him you're a Mormon who is coincidentally also in the snow-plough business, and you want to talk to him about insurance against global warming.'

The truck moved on. The track ran through the wooded slopes five more miles, always rough, with deep baked ruts in places, and worn gravel, and flat rocks the size of tables. The Land Cruiser nodded from side to side, and soldiered on. All the way through a final curve, and up a sudden sharp rise, to a stadium-sized plateau, full of trees, except for a home site set about a third of the way in. It had a long low log house, with wide porches all around, all in the centre of a slightly tended acre, behind an informal fence made up of posts and rails twisted and greyed by the wind and the weather. Bramall drove in, and parked a respect-ful distance from the house. There were tatters of crime scene tape on the porch rails either side of the entrance. As if at one time the house was roped off.

'This wasn't the crime scene,' Bramall said. 'The guy died in the woods.'

'He was found in the woods,' Reacher said. 'Maybe the sheriff thought that was a whole different thing entirely. We know he searched here. He found a car with a lot of miles, and ten grand in the closet.'

'Where is Billy right now?'

'Why worry about him?'

'I'm not. But you should. Scorpio was ordering a homicide.'

'Billy's not here. What are the odds? Plus he didn't get the message. He doesn't know Scorpio gave me Porterfield's name. So why would he come here to Porterfield's house? What were the odds we would ever find it anyway? Who knew the old post office guy was so good at guessing distances? Billy is somewhere else and this place is empty.'

'OK,' Bramall said.

He got out of the car and went to knock on the door.

A purposeful stride.

Reacher saw him knock, and he heard the sound, loud and clear, a fraction delayed by the distance, like a mismatched movie soundtrack.

He saw Bramall step back politely.

No one came to the door.

No movement anywhere.

Bramall knocked again.

The same no reaction.

He walked back and got in the truck, and said, 'This place is empty.'

Reacher said, 'How do you feel about going in?'

'It's all closed up.'

'We could break a window.'

'Legally we have to ask ourselves if the county owns it now. Which it might, officially. Because of the unpaid taxes. Breaking into county property is a big step. You can't fight city hall.'

'Maybe you smelled a suspicious smell, or thought you heard something. Like a despairing cry. The kind of thing that would justify a warrantless search. Did you?'

'No,' Bramall said.

'You're retired,' Reacher said. 'You don't have to stick to FBI bullshit any more.'

'What would be the army approach? Set the place on fire?'

'No, that would be the Marine Corps approach. The army would conduct a careful survey of the exterior, and by great good fortune would discover a pane of glass previously broken by persons unknown, at a previous time, maybe long ago, or even just recently, which if true would reasonably suggest an ongoing emergency inside, which in turn would justify a good look around. I don't think the Supreme Court could argue with that.'

'Previously broken either recently or a long time ago?'

'Obviously any sounds you hear in real time will be me, accidently stepping on previously broken glass left lying on the porch ever since the unknown previous incident. That can sound very like a freshly breaking window. It's a common illusion.'

'That's a standard FBI trick too. We weren't all bullshit.'

'Some of you came to us for training.'

'And some of you came to us.'

'I'm going to conduct a careful survey,' Reacher said.

He got out of the car.

EIGHTEEN

It was a big house, but an easy survey, because the porch ran all the way around the structure, flat and level and true, and it served up all the first-floor doors and windows at a convenient height for inspection. Reacher started at the front, with the door Bramall had knocked on, which was a solid wooden affair, locked tight, and way too much effort to break down. So he moved on, to a hallway window, which would have taken no effort at all to get through, except it was on the front of the house, and even in the uninhabited middle of nowhere some ancient part of his brain sounded a warning. The front was never good. Not during, and not even afterwards. Why leave after-action evidence in plain view? Not that there would be much. A discreet punched-out hole in the glass, about the size of a big man's elbow, and a slit insect screen rippling in the breeze. That would be all. Not much. But maybe enough to catch a passer-by's eye. Always safer if that kind of thing happened later, not sooner, for all kinds of reasons.

The back was better.

Reacher walked down the side of the house, past five more windows all the same as the front. Which made it likely the windows in back would be all the same, too. Some kind of a unifying design theme. Or some kind of a big discount for a bulk purchase. But either way was good news. Windows like that were easy.

He turned the corner, and the first window he came to was broken.

It had a hole punched through it, about the size of a big man's elbow.

The insect screen was slit.

The broken glass was dirty, and the screen was mildewed. A year, maybe more. At least four seasons of wind and weather. Inside was a kitchen. Countertops that should have been shiny were dull with dust. Beyond the kitchen was a dining area, all gloom and shadows.

He walked the long way around the porches, and back to the car. Bramall had gotten out again. He was standing in a no-man's-land patch of dirt about thirty feet from the house.

Reacher said, 'I found a busted window.'

'Nicely done,' Bramall said. 'I didn't hear a thing.'

'For real. An actual busted window. Previously broken by persons unknown. A year or more ago, by the look of it. Exactly how we would have done it.'

'Show me,' Bramall said.

Reacher led him along the front porch, and the side porch, and around the corner to the back. Bramall took a good long look. He seemed impressed by the mildew. He said, 'A year at least. Let's say a year and a half. Why not? Let's say this happened right after Porterfield died. Was it the sheriff? You told me he searched the place.'

'The sheriff had the keys,' Reacher said. 'He found them in Porterfield's pocket. That's how they identified him, along with

his teeth. So the sheriff didn't need to break in. This was someone else, who didn't have the keys.'

'Squatters, maybe.'

'They wouldn't bust the kitchen window. The kitchen is a room
they would want to use. They would have bust a window somewhere else.'

'Ordinary burglars, then.'

'Possible. We'll know by how much mess they made.'

'We're still going inside?'

'We were before,' Reacher said. 'I don't see why we shouldn't
now. This is practically an open invitation. We have a duty as
citizens.'

'To call the sheriff, technically.'

'It's a grey area. The owner is dead. There are no heirs. It's a
different situation. People read whole books about this kind of
thing in law school. I'm sure the sheriff doesn't want to get in a
big long discussion. Plus this could be where she called her
sister. Right here. When she said, shut up, Sy, I'm on the phone.
Had to be his place or hers. Either way she spent time here. So
you know we're going in.'

'I know I am,' Bramall said. 'But you're under no obligation.'

'You looking out for me now?'

'I feel I ought to point out the legal downside.'

'I get it. You want me to go first. So you can say to yourself the
worst thing you ever did was get all swept up. You want me to be
the bad guy. Because you have scruples.'

'Not as such. What I have is a licence from the state of Illinois.
Which I would like to keep. Doesn't matter who goes first. What
matters is, it would count against me if I didn't explicitly caution
a junior partner against potential legal jeopardy.'

'Are we partners?'

'Effectively.'

'Junior and senior?'

139

'By age and experience.'

'Do you have to explicitly caution me every step of the way?'

'Technically, yes.'

'Let's not do that part, OK? Let's take it as read. More fun that way.'

'OK,' Bramall said. 'You want fun, you go first.'

Bramall's contribution was to stick his arm in through the hole in the glass and wind the window open with the inside handle. Reacher's jacket was new, and his shirt was new. He didn't want to smear either one of them with mildew, which he would if he pushed through the slit in the screen, like the original intruder or intruders must have, a year or more ago, back when the screen was clean. So he tore it out of its frame, all the way around, and folded it in a ragged square, and dropped it on the porch.

Best way into a kitchen was face down and feet first. Because of the countertop. You stood a chance of ending the manoeuvre standing on your feet, not your hands. But it was hard to set up. It required a contortion. Worse if there was a sink under the window, with a tap. Which could get to the wrong place at the wrong time. But Porterfield's sink was on a different wall. Which helped. A little.

Reacher felt his legs swim free, and he jack-knifed at the waist, and planted his feet, and pushed himself upright. Inside, looking out. The kitchen was a little weather-beaten, because of the hole in the glass, but it had started out expensive. That was clear. The wood was thick, and the granite was thicker. There were appliances made out of stainless steel. They all had clock screens, dark and blank. There was absolute silence. No subliminal hum, no rustle in the pipes. No power, no water. No one paying the bills. All closed up.

He moved on through the gloom, out of the kitchen, into the

140

dining area. From where he saw the living room, all open plan, with a complicated cathedral ceiling, and a full-height rock fireplace, made out of stones the size of tractor tyres.

A trophy cabin. Authentic designs didn't have fireplaces built with forklift trucks and hydraulic cranes. They used smaller rocks. And why make a weird ceiling, where a flat one would fit?

But it was a lived-in trophy cabin. Reacher didn't hate it. The log walls were stained a light honey shade. The furniture looked comfortable but unobtrusive. There were weird collections on shelves. Animal skulls, interesting stones, interesting pine cones. Almost a family feel. A rich-family feel.

He walked back to the kitchen. To the broken window. Bramall was looking in at him.

Reacher said, 'Nothing to worry about. It's like a time capsule. Which rules out a burglary. Because nothing is out of place. The dust is a uniform thickness everywhere. There's no mess at all. Which I guess rules out squatters too.'

'I'm coming in,' Bramall said.

He was stiffer in the joints than Reacher, but those joints started out much closer together, because he was smaller, so overall his manoeuvre was easier. He pushed himself upright, and looked around the same way Reacher had. Kitchen, dining area, living room.

Undisturbed.

Bramall said, 'Not what I expected.'

'In what way?' Reacher said.

'If I had a cabin it might look like this.'

'Dope dealers don't have taste?'

'Not usually.'

Reacher checked the hallway.

He said, 'There are bedrooms at both ends.'

Bramall said, 'If it wasn't burglars or squatters, who broke the window?'

'Not the sheriff,' Reacher said. 'But like the sheriff. A pro with a reason to search.'

'But where's the mess? Pro searchers tear a place apart.'

'Maybe they found what they wanted the first place they looked. Maybe that's what it means to be a pro. Or maybe they knew where it was all along. Maybe they came to get something back.'

'Get what back?'

'I don't care,' Reacher said. 'All I want to do is find Sanderson.'

'You think she was here. Back when she was dating a dope dealer worth getting gut-shot or stabbed in the stomach.'

'You're her older brother now?'

'I doubt the relationship would have happened. She would have done better for herself.'

'She said, shut up, Sy, I'm on the phone. Even the uptight twin called it friendly and comfortable and happy. Best case, they were real good friends.'

'Even worse,' Bramall said. 'You choose your friends.'

'Either way, they spent time together. Here, and her place. Wherever that is.'

'A year and a half ago.'

'Better than nothing.'

'If your Sy is the right Sy.'

'Fifty-fifty right or wrong. Not bad odds.'

Bramall took out his phone.

'Two bars,' he said. 'She could have called from here.'

'What did the cell records say?'

'You need three masts to triangulate. There's only one here. Omnidirectional. She was calling from somewhere inside a giant circular area about the size of New Jersey. That's all we know.'

'Could have been here. No reason why not.'

Bramall moved to the centre of the living room. He said, 'It was a year and a half ago and this place has been searched twice since then. And if you're right about someone getting something back, then the most important thing we could have found is already gone. So this is about looking for what two other parties missed. Which is slow work. How long have we got?'

'Out here, about a hundred years, I would think,' Reacher said. 'Pull your car around the back, and we could move in and live here for ever. No one would ever know.'

'OK, we'll search together. No look-out. Two heads are better than one.'

They found the first missed item in less than a minute.

NINETEEN

It was in a mud room near the back door. In a closet where snow clothes were kept. A pair of snow pants had slipped off a hanger. Some kind of stiff nylon. They had hit the floor like spears, and then half crumpled and half stayed rigid, like wobbly legs, like a cartoon picture of a guy who just received a nasty shock. They had toppled backward and had ended up half propped in the corner. Reacher moved them, purely out of habit, and behind them he found a pair of women's snow boots. A technical product, with hooks and loops. A woman's size six. Which was small.

He said, 'Boots in the closet is a thing, right? She spent quality time here.'

'If it was her. Could have been anybody.'

'I agree. But it's evidence a guy two separate people described as a loner living alone actually had a companion in his house. Which should have tilted the investigation a little, when such a guy shows up dead. Maybe we can forgive the sheriff. He had a preconceived notion. And I bet everyone in Wyoming has a closet like that. Hard to see what you always see. But whoever came along afterwards should have seen it. They should have had fresh eyes. Makes me wonder who they were. And what they were doing. Maybe they didn't really look at anything. Maybe it really was a fast in-and-out, to get something back. Has to be. Nothing else has been touched.'

Bramall said, 'We should check the other closets.'

They did, but there was nothing in them, except Porterfield's own stuff. Apparently he had been a guy who liked blue jeans, and saw no problem at all with laundering things until they went threadbare.

No women's clothing.

No dresses, no blouses, no pants.

Bramall said, 'Why would she leave only her boots behind?'

'She left at the start of spring. She hadn't used them for a month. She forgot them. Or maybe they were uncomfortable. Maybe she left them on purpose. Maybe she was fixing to buy new. But she was here. Or someone was. Porterfield didn't live alone. Not all the time.'

'That's a lot to read into a pair of boots.'

'I bet we find more.'

They did. But not much more. After two hours they had a very modest haul. More persuasive than conclusive. They saved time by ignoring what was on open view. Instead they looked inside things, and under things, and behind things.

They found a woman's comb between the sofa cushions. It was made of pink plastic. All the teeth were widely spaced. Not half and half, like a regular comb. In the master bathroom they found two sinks, each with a soap dish, one with a dried-out cake of scented soap, and one with a dried-out cake of plain. Also in the bathroom they found two sets of towels laid out. In the laundry room behind the dryer they found a pair of women's athletic socks. Some kind of miracle fibre, small in size, pink in colour, stuck all over with dust bunnies.

That was it.

Not enough for a courtroom. But suggestive. Reacher said, 'She was here. Or someone was. At least some of the time. Maybe just a casual on-again, off-again type of thing. But she was here long enough to get somewhat ingrained. When she left, she did it in style. She made a clean break. Some kind of statement. She scoured the place and packed up everything of hers she could see, leaving behind only the few things she couldn't. Like her lost comb. She couldn't take her soap anyway. At the time it was all wet and slimy. Couldn't just toss it in a bag with her clothes. She didn't count the towels. Who would? She forgot her snow boots. But it's the socks I like best.'

'Why?'

'They prove she still has two legs. The Purple Heart might not be as bad as it could be.'

'If it's her.'

'Suppose it was. Porterfield must have gone to her place from time to time. Where would that be? How far from here? Suppose you were a guy like Porterfield. How far would you drive to get laid?'

'Depends.'

'On what?'

'A number of things.'

'Look on the bright side. Maybe not Miss America exactly, but assume she's a nice-looking person.'

'This is Wyoming. They drive epic distances for a loaf of bread. For a girlfriend, two hours, maybe. A hundred miles.'

'Which doesn't help us,' Reacher said. 'That's too big of an area to contemplate.'

Bramall nodded. 'I was going to say our next move should be go talk to Porterfield's neighbours. But I don't know exactly what that means out here. Everyone lives twenty miles from everyone else. I bet they never see each other.'

'But I guess they depend on each other. Suppose they get a sudden emergency. Who are they going to call? The police department or the fire department two hours away? Or their nearest neighbour, who could be there in fifteen minutes? Maybe that's the country way. Maybe country neighbours are closer than you suspect. Maybe they're always into each other's business and have plenty to tell us.'

'You're very cheerful.'

Reacher didn't answer. He was alone in the kitchen, perhaps subconsciously needing to keep his exit in view. The open window, with the broken glass and the torn-out screen. A cool breeze came in. And borne on it, sounds. Most of them were inoffensive. Wind in the trees, the beat of a heavy bird's wing, a bee flying by, and pausing, and flying on.

One sound was different.

Very brief, and very distant. Barely audible. A fragment only. A tiny scratch, or a tiny crunch, or a tiny squelch. A small part of a familiar local sound. A Wyoming sound. Like all sounds, made from a mix of different components. Like DNA.

Grit was involved.

And rock.

And rubber.

'We need to get out,' he said. 'There's a car on the driveway.'

Bramall went first. Less likely to get stuck. Reacher followed him successfully, and Bramall put his arm back in and wound the handle to close the window. Then they hustled to the front.

Nothing yet.

'We should get in the car,' Bramall said. 'Just in case.'

Reacher said, 'If in doubt, run them over.'

They climbed in the Toyota and Bramall started the motor.

147

A truck came up over the final rise and started across the plateau.

It was a Ford pick-up truck, loaded with a police-department version of a camper shell. Its paint was clean and shiny. All white, except for the doors, which had gold stars about two feet wide and two feet high, with the county's name in a curve above, and *Sheriff's Department* in a curve below. A little like a West Point ring.

Sheriff Connelly.

Connelly parked close by the Toyota, at a casual angle, partly to look nonchalant and unworried and therefore unthreatening, but mostly, Reacher thought, to subtly block off the Toyota's forward path. The guy had judged it well. Not obvious, but the Toyota would have to back up and loop around.

Connelly buzzed his window down. He was wearing his hat in the car. Plenty of room. It was a tall truck.

Reacher buzzed his window down. He was closest.

Connelly said, 'You told me you had no connections to Porterfield.'

Reacher said, 'I don't.'

'Yet here you are at his house.'

'The woman I'm looking for was here, at least for a few months. I'm trying to figure out where she went next.'

'Porterfield lived alone.'

'Not always.'

Connelly said, 'Have you been inside the house?'

'Yes,' Reacher said.

'How?'

'There was a previous break-in here, a year or more ago. We went in the same hole.'

'What break-in?'

'You searched this place when he died. You found what you

148

found, and you locked up and drove away. Then someone else came by and went in the window.'

'Show me,' Connelly said.

They got out of their cars and trooped back to the far corner of the house. Connelly took a good long look. He unfolded the torn-out insect screen and held it in place, as if recreating the original scene. He rubbed the mildew between finger and thumb, and sniffed it.

He said, 'Could be a year and a half.'

Then he said, 'How are things inside?'

Reacher said, 'No mess, no damage, nothing pulled out or overturned. This wasn't a burglary, or squatters.'

Connelly said, 'Why do you think there was a woman living up here?'

They moved to the porch rail, facing the rear view, all lined up, looking straight ahead at trees and mountains. Bramall talked through the boots, and the comb, and the soap, and the towels, and the small pink socks.

Connelly said, 'The boots don't mean much, or the comb or the socks. They could be historic. Twenty years ago there could have been nieces and cousins here every summer and winter. That kind of stuff stays lost a long time.'

'But?' Reacher said.

'I'm prepared to admit when I make a mistake. I like the soap and the towels. Two sinks in use always means a couple, and if one soap is smelly, it's a man and a woman. And soap and towels is real-time evidence. That's exactly how the room looked the morning Porterfield died. I guess I missed it. But no one came forward at the time. No one ever has. All the evidence said Porterfield was a loner and no one else had barely even met him. So where was the woman then, and where is she now?'

'That's what we're trying to figure out.'

'If it's the same woman.'

149

'Nothing says it isn't.'

Connelly said, 'The ring you showed me was pretty small.'

'Yes, it was,' Reacher said.

'Are you judging this thing by the size of the socks? Because maybe they shrunk.'

'The boots didn't. They're small, too.'

'Where did she serve?'

'Iraq and Afghanistan, five times.'

'A tough character.'

'Like you wouldn't believe.'

'If it's the same woman.'

'It might be.'

'Would such a woman come home and use smelly soap and wear pink socks?'

'I'm sure she would do exactly that. Stuff like that is the whole point of coming home.'

Connelly turned around and looked back at the house.

At the broken window.

Reacher said, 'I know.'

'You know what?'

'We can't figure out who would have done that either. It's good clean professional work. A neat break-in, and nothing disturbed inside. Feels like training and experience were involved. Feels like government work. Except that's ridiculous.'

Connelly said, 'Mostly because what would the government want with Porterfield? Whatever he was, he was small-time. And a government agency would have called me first. As a courtesy, at least, and for practical assistance too. Which I could have given them in this case. I had the keys.'

'Then regular petty criminals are getting neater these days.'

'That hasn't been my experience.'

'Then who was it?'

'Fancy criminals, maybe. The kind who can afford the best.'

'What would they want with small-time Porterfield?'

Connelly didn't answer.

Bramall said, 'We apologize for trespassing. We intended no disrespect to the laws of the county.'

Connelly said, 'I can't help you with the woman. There's no evidence of a crime. I can't take soap and towels to a county board budget hearing. I'm sorry. I have no manpower.'

'Who could help us?' Bramall said. 'Neighbours?'

'They might. I'm their sheriff, but I don't know any of them. In fact this is only the second time I've ever been out here. It's a quiet corner. The squeaky wheels get all my attention.'

'We should get going,' Bramall said. 'Sheriff, thank you for your time.'

At that moment three hundred miles away in Rapid City, South Dakota, Gloria Nakamura was sitting in her blue car, on the cross street, artfully positioned, this time watching Scorpio's back door, not his front. She had been there close to two hours, and she had seen nothing of interest.

Until.

A Harley with a Montana plate pulled into the alley. The sound beat back off the walls. Then it shut down. The rider got off, and the back door opened, and the rider went in.

Nakamura made a note.

Four minutes on her watch later, the rider came out again. He got on his bike, and started the noise again, and rode away.

Nakamura made a note.

Then she drove back to the station.

Bramall and Reacher drove the ranch track back to the dirt road, and turned west, which was where they thought they would find the bulk of the local neighbourhood population, such as it was. Bramall watched the left-hand shoulder, and Reacher watched the right. They agreed they would take the first track they saw, whichever side of the road it was on, because by definition whatever dwelling lay at the end of it was Sy Porterfield's nearest next-door neighbour.

The first track came eleven miles later. On the left. They nearly missed it. It was a plain and inconspicuous entry. After which it twisted and rose through the trees, steep and tight in places, but better maintained than Porterfield's. The Land Cruiser rolled on, implacably, more than three miles, and then all of a sudden the trees opened up and gave out on a flat acre with a long view east. There was a one-storey house up on a stone foundation. It was made of brown boards, in places twisted and silvery. It had a front porch, with ancient millwork holding up the rail. On the porch was an old church pew, pressed into service as a place to sit and take the air in the morning sun.

Bramall parked a respectful distance from the house.

He checked his phone.

'Two bars,' he said. 'Coverage is actually pretty good here. She could have called from anywhere.'

They made to get out of the car, but before they could the house door opened and a woman stepped out. She must have heard their tyres. She looked lean and strong and tanned by wind and sun. She was wearing a faded red dress, over bare legs and cowboy boots. She was maybe forty, but it was hard to tell. Reacher would not have ventured an opinion. If forced, he would have said thirty, just to be safe, and wouldn't have been surprised if the truth was fifty. She stood there, hands on hips, just watching. Not hostile. Not yet.

Bramall said, 'She thinks we're Mormons.'

Reacher got out. He raised his hand. A universal gesture. Unarmed. Friendly. She moved her head, part responsive, part enquiring. Bramall got out. He and Reacher walked together and stopped a polite distance short of the porch.

Reacher said, 'Ma'am, we're looking for a missing woman, who we think once stayed a spell with your neighbour Sy Porterfield. We wonder if you could tell us about that.'

'You should come in,' the woman said. 'I have lemonade in a jug.'

TWENTY

Reacher and Bramall followed the woman inside. The walls were made of the same boards as the outside, but stained and polished, not weather-beaten. The kitchen was a low dark room. The woman poured lemonade into glasses. They sat down at her table.

'Are you private detectives?' she asked.

'I am,' Bramall said.

She looked at Reacher.

He said, 'Military investigator.'

Which was true, in a historic sense.

She said, 'Was it last year Sy died, or the year before?'

'Last year,' Reacher said. 'The start of spring.'

'I didn't know him very well. Never really met him, except for once or twice. Seemed to be a solitary type of guy, always coming and going.'

'What did he do for a living?'

'None of us knew.'

'Us? Did you talk about him with other people?'

'That's what neighbours do. You don't like it, mister, go live on the moon.'

'What was the consensus opinion?'

'We all thought he was a solitary guy, always coming and going.'

'No one saw any sign of a woman living there?'

'Never,' she said.

Which sounded definitive.

Reacher said, 'You ever heard the name Serena?'

'In my life?'

'Around here.'

'No,' she said.

'Or Rose?'

'No.'

'Or Sanderson?'

'No.'

Reacher said, 'We found stuff in Porterfield's house.'

'What kind?'

'Random items of women's apparel and toiletries. Not much. Like very faint clues.'

The woman said nothing.

Then she said, 'How faint?'

'We know the bathroom was used by two people,' Reacher said.

The woman said, 'Huh.'

'What does that mean?'

'It means I guess one time I wondered something. In the end I figured I made a mistake.'

'Wondered what?'

'I was on the dirt road, heading out to the turn at Mule Crossing. He was driving the other way. From the turn, heading home. It's rare to see another car. It kind of perks you up. It makes you get in your own lane, and so forth. You don't want to get in a collision.

So we passed each other by. We kind of waved, I guess. No big deal. Except I was sure he had someone in the passenger seat beside him. I thought it was a girl. Just a glimpse. She was hunched down low, turned away from him, kind of pressing herself into the side of the seat. I couldn't see her face.'

'How old?'

'Not young. Not a kid. But quite small, and agile, I guess. She was all twisted around, hiding her face from him.'

'Weird.'

'And silvery, somehow. That's what I remember. A silvery colour.'

'Also weird.'

'I thought so too. It stayed on my mind. So the next day I went over there. I took him a pie. Said I had one extra. But really to check. Back then there were all kinds of stories. Human trafficking, and custody disputes. Maybe he was into that kind of stuff. Or maybe she really was a genuine girlfriend. Who knew? Maybe they had been having a fight in the car. I figured they might be over it by then and he would introduce me.'

'What happened?'

'He acted weird. He was pleased about the pie. Very polite. But he wouldn't let me in the house. We talked on the porch. He pulled the door almost shut behind him and stood where I couldn't see through the gap. He didn't say much. I tried to introduce the subject. I said I was sorry the pie was too big for one. It was a natural opening. It gave him a chance to tell me he was planning to share it with his girlfriend. But he didn't. He said he would wrap the second slice in aluminium foil and eat it in a couple days.'

'What kind of pie was it?'

'Strawberry,' the woman said. 'They had some nice ones at the market. Where I was going when I passed him on the road.'

'What happened next?'

'Nothing. That was it. It was kind of awkward, just standing there, so I said, OK, I guess I'll get going, and he said thanks again for the pie, and then he practically rushed me off his property.'

'What was your conclusion?'

'It was in the way he was standing. He was screening me off from the house. He was hiding something in there. Or someone. Then I got to wondering about when I saw them in the car. Maybe she was hiding her face from me, not him. Maybe he told her to. Like she was his secret.'

'But you never found out for sure?'

'I never saw him again. He was dead a month later. No one ever said anything about a widow or a partner or a girlfriend. Or a sex slave or a hostage. So in the end I figured I must have been wrong. Then I guess I forgot all about it. Time passes.'

'How long had he lived there?'

'Five years, maybe.'

'Did any of the neighbours ever take a wild-ass guess about what he did for money?'

'That would enter the realm of gossip.'

'I guess it would, technically.'

'We figured he already had plenty. We figured he was a rich guy from out of state, come to find himself. We get those, from time to time. Maybe they're writing a novel.'

At that moment three hundred miles away in Rapid City, South Dakota, the clerk behind the deli counter in the convenience store was finishing up making change for a BLT and a diet soda, and then picking up the phone, and dialling the police department.

He said, 'Excuse me, I think you have a woman detective working for you. An Oriental person. Or Japanese-American. Or Asian, or whatever it's supposed to be now. I need to speak with her.'

The call was transferred, and a voice said, 'Property, Nakamura.'

'This is the guy from the convenience store. On the corner from Arthur Scorpio's laundromat. I got something I figure I need to tell you before you find out for yourself and get mad at me.'

'What kind of something?'

'Arthur Scorpio just came in.'

'And?'

'He bought another phone.'

'How long ago?'

'Five minutes.'

'Which phone?'

'First one off the left peg.'

Also at that moment, Arthur Scorpio was dialling Billy in Wyoming again. Again there was no answer. Just voice mail.

Scorpio said, 'Billy, this is Arthur. I need to hear from you. You're making me worried now. What's with not answering your phone all the time? And you got that guy coming. Plus maybe another guy. We just got a message from Montana. They sent a rider down especially. They have a Fed up there asking questions. He just left Billings. We don't know where he's headed next. Eyes open, OK? And call me back. Don't make me worried, Billy.'

He clicked off and dropped the phone in the trash basket.

Bramall's phone dinged. Reacher figured it was a text message. He was getting to where he could tell the difference. The woman in the faded red dress got up and started to gather the empty lemonade glasses.

Bramall read his message.

Twice.

He said, 'Ma'am, the lemonade was delicious, but I'm afraid we really have to get going now.'

Then he just stood up and hustled out the door. Reacher shrugged at the woman, palms up, as if in puzzlement. Another universal gesture. *Yeah, I know, but I better go with my crazy friend.* He followed Bramall outside, and across the dirt, to the car.

He said, 'What's up?'

Bramall said, 'Mrs Mackenzie is dissatisfied with progress so far, and informs me she's going to Wyoming to search certain places near the old family homestead herself. Apparently she's reconsidering her opinion her sister would never go back there.'

'Doesn't she know you're only sixty miles away?'

'No,' Bramall said. 'I never tell clients where I am.'

'Why not?'

'I like to build up the mystery.'

'You can take the boy out of the FBI.'

'We need to get there first.'

'When is she leaving Chicago?'

'She'll charter a plane. She has a card. We should go there now. We should have gone there first. But I was told Sanderson would never return. Now we're saying maybe she did? Terrific. Maybe she's been there all along. It's a two-hour drive. Nothing for Porterfield to complain about.'

Sheriff Connelly had said a government agency would call him first, before entering on his territory. At least as a courtesy. Which is exactly what happened. He got back from his impromptu trip out to the old Porterfield place, and two minutes later his phone rang with a field agent from the federal DEA. The guy said he was heading south from Montana, and sooner or later was going to be passing through the county, nothing much in mind, maybe stopping in one or two places, but overall nothing for anyone to get concerned about. He said he didn't require assistance or any other courtesies, but thank you very much for asking. Then he hung up.

There was a big difference between crows flying and cars driving. To get across the Snowy Range, first they had to go back to the dirt road, and then back to Mule Crossing itself, and past the old post office and the bottle rocket store, and all the way back to Laramie, all in order to pick up a different westward route, which started with a left turn about four blocks north of the bar with the bullet hole in the mirror. Then the trip started all over again at zero. Still seventy miles to go. Reacher told Bramall to look on the bright side. More hours on the invoice. Bramall told a joke about a lawyer who died and got to the pearly gates. Not fair, he said. I'm only 45. Saint Pete said no, we got a new system. Now we do it by billable hours. According to our records you're 153.

They passed a sign that said the road would close pretty soon for the winter. And then it started to rise, into the mountains, up over ten thousand feet, into thin and glittering air. The Toyota slowed a little, but it kept on going, winding through rocky gaps and around sparse copses of wind-stunted trees, across what already felt like the roof of the world. Then the road held level through a wide half-mile curve, and started to fall again, through the same type of gaps and around the same type of trees, and the Toyota started rolling faster and faster, under its own weight, with no gas at all.

Thirty miles later the navigation screen showed a thin tracery of ranch roads, two on the north side, and two on the south. Beyond them was blank.

'Is that it?' Reacher asked.

'I think so,' Bramall said. 'Apparently one of the ranches is bigger than the other three. That's the old homestead. The others came later.'

'Did the sisters inherit?'

'No, the place was sold when they were in college. The parents moved out. New owners moved in. And so on. The same with the other three places, I'm sure.'

'You think she's squatting in one of them?'

'I doubt a person who has to pawn her ring is paying rent.'

'Why would they be empty?'

'Rural real estate often is. Places shrivel and die. Especially when the neighbourhood royalty moves out.'

'Is that your description, or Mrs Mackenzie's?'

'A little of both. Their father was a judge, which back then in a place like this made him the most important man in the county. Everything came through the courts eventually. Mrs Mackenzie seems aware of that.'

'Why did the parents move out?'

'Mrs Mackenzie had a hard time explaining. I'm sure we could speculate. I'm sure as kids they both had ponies. On a judge's salary.'

'I'm sure all Wyoming kids have ponies. There are more ponies than kids.'

'It was a metaphor. For little arrangements that work great, until they don't. Then sometimes you need to get out of town and start over.'

'Is that how Mrs Mackenzie remembers it?'

'She was in college at the time. In the end she credits George W. Bush. She claims it was an entrepreneurial thing. The old man was moving from the public sector to the private.'

'To do what exactly?'

'No one knew exactly, except they noticed it stopped the day after the banks crashed.'

'Where is the old boy now?'

'Dead soon after.'

'Mom?'

'Also dead. But much more recently. Still raw.'

'Hence the sudden worry about her semi-estranged twin.'

'Exactly,' Bramall said. 'Now her semi-estranged twin is all she's got.'

They had no way of knowing which of the tracks led to the largest ranch, because they all ran far out of sight into the invisible distance, so they tried to judge by width or construction or other hint of architectural grandeur. In the end they agreed one track was wider than the others. Possibly the surface was better. There were piles of rocks that might once have been ceremonial gate-posts. Like the archaeological remains of a once-mighty palace.

The Toyota turned in, and started climbing.

TWENTY-ONE

The old homestead was both old and a homestead. It was a classic piece of western real estate, with wide tawny pastures, and dark green conifer trees, and outcrops of rock, and bubbling blue water in streams through the bottoms. Way in the distance were the Rocky Mountains, just hints in the mist. The main house was a spreading log construction with all kinds of extra wings built out. There were log barns and log garages. A lot of logs, Reacher thought, and all of them old-school, huge and heavy, hard as a rock, smoothed by axes and joined by pegs.

Like an old-time travel poster on an airport wall.

Except for a new-model rental sedan parked at an angle, and a woman standing next to it.

The sedan was a handsome item with a Chevrolet grille, basic red, with barcodes in all the back windows. The woman was small and slender. Maybe five-two and a hundred pounds. She was wearing boots, and boot-cut blue jeans, and a gauzy white shirt under an open leather jacket. She had a purse on her shoulder. She had long thick hair, heaped and wild and tangled, most of it pale red, some of it bleached by the sun. Her face was like a picture in a book. Pale flawless skin, perfect bones, delicate features. Green eyes, frank and open. A red mouth, confident, in control, almost smiling. Radiant. Composed. She had to be thirty-something. But she looked brand new.

Like a movie star.

'Shit,' Bramall said. 'That's Mrs Mackenzie.'

The twin sister. An exact replica. Army minimum for women was four-ten and 91 pounds. Sanderson would have gotten in comfortably. But everything else would have been twice as hard. From that point onward. Especially with the face. It was drop-dead spectacular.

Bramall got out of the car. He took a couple of steps, and stopped. So did she. Then Reacher got out. He heard Bramall say, 'Mrs Mackenzie, I didn't expect to see you so soon.'

She said, 'One of those things. The text didn't send till we landed. You thought I was leaving Chicago. Actually I was leaving the Hertz office in Laramie.'

'I was close by.'

'Of course you were. For which I apologize most sincerely. Fact and logic brought you to Wyoming, but I wouldn't let you get all the way here. I told you it was impossible she would come back.'

'What changed?'

'You should introduce me to your friend.'

Reacher stepped up and said his name and shook her hand. It felt like a dove's wing in a gorilla's paw.

'What changed?' Bramall said again.

'Now I'm afraid nothing has changed,' Mackenzie said. 'This place is empty. I think I made a mistake. I wasted a day. I apologize.'

'Why would she come back here?'

164

'Suddenly I thought familiarity might be important to her. I try to think like her. We had some good times here. Eighteen years of stability. Since then she's had none. I thought it might be something she's craving.'

Reacher looked up at the house.

He asked, 'How long has it been empty?'

She said, 'I think it's just someone's summer house now.'

'It's still summer.'

'They must have skipped this year.'

'Do you remember who bought it?'

Mackenzie shook her head. 'I'm not sure we ever knew. I was away in school, and Rose was at West Point.'

'You call her Rose?'

'We insisted. Jane and Rose.'

'How did you feel when you found out your folks had sold the place?'

'May I know the root of your interest in my family's affairs?'

So Reacher ran through the story one more time, from the bus out of Milwaukee all the way to the there and then across the Snowy Range. But some kind of instinct made him smooth it out as he went. He stayed strictly on the poignant pawned-ring track, and didn't mention either Scorpio or Billy, or speculate about anyone's specific occupation. He ended with the meagre trove of evidence from Sy Porterfield's hall closet, and his living room sofa, and his master bathroom, and his laundry room.

Mackenzie was quiet a beat.

Then she said, 'What size were the boots?'

'Six,' Reacher said.

'OK.'

He looked at her hair. Heaped, wild, tangled. Untamed was the word. Must take for ever to wash.

An exact replica.

He said, 'Show me your comb.'

She paused again.

Then she said, 'Yes, I see.'

She dug in her bag and came out with a pink plastic comb. All the teeth were widely spaced. Not half and half, like a regular comb.

Reacher said, 'Have you always used that brand?'

'It's the only kind that works.'

'It's the same.'

'The boots fit too.'

He took the ring from his pocket and balanced it on his palm. She picked it up, carefully, between delicate fingers.

West Point 2005.

The gold filigree, the black stone, the tiny size.

She read the engraving.

She selected a finger and pulled off a designer bauble as thick and gold as a false tooth. In its place she slipped her sister's trophy. Fourth finger, right hand. It sat there like it should. The perfect fit. The perfect size. Prominent, like it should be, and proud, like it should be, but not as big as a carnival prize. Reacher pictured the same hand, but maybe worn down a bit leaner, with a darker tan, and a couple of nicks and cuts healed white.

He pictured the same face, the same way.

Mackenzie said, 'You mentioned that you bought the ring.'

'Correct,' Reacher said.

'May I buy it back from you?'

'It's not for sale. It's a gift for your sister.'

'I could give it to her.'

'So could the lady at West Point. Eventually.'

'You feel a need to hand it over personally?'

'I need to know she's OK.'

'You never met her.'

'Makes no difference. Should it? I don't know. You tell me.'

Mackenzie took the ring off. She handed it back.

Some kind of look on her perfect face.

Reacher said, 'I know.'

'You know what?'

'I know what you're thinking. You're here because it's family, and Mr Bramall is here because he's getting paid. Why am I here? I'm giving you the impression I'm some kind of a weird obsessive. Maybe a couple soldiers short of a squad. I don't mean to. But I get it. I'm making you feel uncomfortable.'

'Not at all.'

'You're very polite.'

'I assume it's an honour thing. Rose was in a world I didn't understand.'

'What we need now is solid information. Are you confident this place is empty?'

'There are dust sheets everywhere and the water is off.'

'So where would Rose go, if not here?'

'This is ridiculous.'

'What is?' Reacher said.

'I should be on a psychiatrist's couch to answer these questions.'

'Why?'

'We participated in a fantasy. OK? We were required to. As if we were lords of the manor and owned the whole valley. As if when the neighbours built, we were practically giving them almshouses out of sheer benevolence. Obviously later on we discovered Father had to sell some acres. But it was like we still owned them. Like slave quarters. We lorded it over the poor people. We were in and out any time we wanted.'

'Which of the three would she go to now?'

'Any of them.'

'You want a ride? In the front, if you like. You're paying the bills, after all.'

*

167

Reacher got in the back, and got comfortable. Mackenzie took his place in the passenger seat. Bramall drove, but not back to the road. Mackenzie showed him different tracks. The ways they went as kids. Easy enough for a slip of a girl to skip along. Harder for the car. But it made it, bending saplings, all four tyres grabbing, like a ponderous cat. The nearest neighbour slid into view. Not a trophy cabin. Built before the word existed. The product of a more innocent age, when a vacation house could be a plain and simple thing. The view was a picture postcard.

Bramall and Mackenzie went to the door.

They knocked.

It opened.

A guy stood there. Same kind of age as the guy in the Mule Crossing post office. Same kind of tired-out stoop. Bramall said something to him, then Mackenzie, and the old guy nodded and made to let them in. Bramall turned and waved to Reacher, and Reacher got out of the car, and walked over to join them. They went inside, and the old guy said yes, all those years ago he had bought the land and built the house. For family vacations. Now he came alone. Which was borne out by the evidence. Reacher looked around and saw one of everything, and felt the quiet patient air of a lonely place.

The guy said he remembered the twins coming by. Way back they were wild-haired little girls in country dresses. They visited all the time, until they were ten or twelve, then not so much, until they were fifteen or so, and then hardly at all after that.

Mackenzie said, 'Have you seen Rose recently?'

The old guy said, 'Where would I see her?'

'Around here, maybe.'

'I guess it's a dumb question to ask what she looks like now.'

Mackenzie smiled. 'Maybe a bit more tan than me. Maybe a bit more toned. She would claim she's been working harder. She might have cut her hair. Or dyed it. She might have gotten

168

tattoos.' She looked a question at Bramall. 'Anything else we should consider?'

Bramall looked a question at Reacher.

Is this where we tell her she was wounded?

'No,' Reacher said. 'I'm sure the gentleman knows what she looks like.'

'I haven't seen her,' the old guy said.

They used the old guy's driveway, and crossed the road, and took the driveway opposite. It came out on another idyllic scene, but smaller, a quarter-sized version of the old homestead, with a newer house and no active stream.

The house was closed up and empty. Locked doors, shaded windows, no broken glass. No burglars, no squatters. No feral Rose Sanderson, going to earth in a place she remembered.

They moved off again, on another rough trail Mackenzie seemed half to know and half to imagine. The Toyota squeezed between trees, and rode up and down dips and hollows, and bucked and nodded. Bramall stayed calm behind the wheel. He drove most of the way one-handed.

The last house came into view.

It was the same kind of thing as before, an unpretentious A-framed cabin, with a lot of glass on a spectacular view. Bramall looped around to the driveway, as if he had been on it all along, and he parked a respectful distance from the house.

The front door opened.

A woman stood in the shadow.

She must have heard their tyres.

She took a hopeful step forward, into the sun.

She looked like Porterfield's neighbour, but wound up way tighter. Upset about something. She was staring all around, and then staring at the car.

Bramall got out.

She watched him.

Mackenzie got out.

She watched her.

Reacher got out.

She watched him.

No one else got out.

She staggered back, like she had been hit in the head. She leaned on the frame of the door.

She said, 'Have you guys seen Billy?'

Bramall didn't answer.

The woman said, 'I thought maybe you were him. Maybe he got a new car. He's supposed to be coming.'

'For what?' Reacher said.

'Have you seen him?'

Mackenzie said, 'Who is Billy?'

Reacher said, 'We'll get to that.'

To the woman in the doorway he said, 'I got a question for you first, and then I'll tell you about Billy.'

'What's the question?'

'Tell me about the other woman, who looks just like my friend here. Like her twin sister.'

'What other woman?'

'I just told you. Pay attention. Like my friend here. In this neighbourhood.'

'Never seen her.'

'She might be Billy's friend too.'

'Don't know her.'

'You sure?'

'A woman who looks like her? Never seen one.'

'You ever heard the name Rose?'

'Never ever. Now tell me about Billy.'

'I haven't met him yet,' Reacher said. 'But I hear his privileges were suspended. His cupboard is bare. Until he takes care of a local problem. Which he hasn't yet. I know that, because I'm the local problem. And here I still am. So if he happens to drop by, tell him I'm looking for him. The Incredible Hulk. Tell him I plan to stop by and pay him a visit. Give him a good description. That might be worth twenty bucks to him. You could get a freebie.'

'Billy never gives freebies,' the woman said.

'Who is Billy?' Mackenzie asked again.

They told her in the car. Not the whole story. Still they kept him separate. As if he was an accidental discovery, off to one side. They told her about the shoebox of cash, but not the shoebox of jewellery.

But Mackenzie was a smart woman.

She said, 'Then why were you in his home in the first place?'

Which under her critical gaze led to the whole soup-to-nuts narrative, involving Scorpio, and Porterfield, and Billy, and Bramall's old phone records, and Nakamura's overheard voice mails.

Mackenzie said, 'In other words for at least two years Rose has been involved with drug dealers and drug users. Meth and heroin. With all that entails. Such as shacking up with one who got eaten by a bear.'

They didn't answer.

Mackenzie asked, quietly, 'Is she an addict?'

They told her about the shoebox of jewellery.

She started to cry.

TWENTY-TWO

They drove back to the old homestead, where Mackenzie's rental was parked, at an angle, like a garish red blot on the old-timey landscape.

She said, 'Now I'm worried about the timescale. Her comb was lost at least a year and a half ago. We know that. Possibly months before. This is likely a two-year thing. Or more. But her ring left Wyoming just six weeks ago. Doesn't that feel like a final threshold? Like some kind of end stage?'

Reacher said, 'Did you call the army during your search?'

'They told me nothing. They had privacy concerns. Any other time, I would have been cheering them on.'

'I called a place I know. I pulled some strings. They didn't have much. They had a list of her West Point scores. She did very well.'

'I remember.'

'They had a list of her deployments. Iraq and Afghanistan. Five tours and out.'

'OK.'

'They had a list of her medals.'

'I didn't know she won any.'

'She won a Bronze Star.'

'For what?'

'The regulation says the Bronze Star medal is awarded to individuals who distinguish themselves in a combat theatre by heroism, outstanding achievement, or meritorious service.'

'I didn't know,' Mackenzie said again.

'She also won a Purple Heart.'

Mackenzie was quiet a long moment.

First she said, 'I didn't know.'

Then she said, 'What for?'

Last she said, 'Oh, no.'

Reacher didn't recite the regulation. Not happy listening. *Awarded to any member of the armed forces who has been wounded, killed, or who has died or may die of wounds.*

Mackenzie said, 'How bad?'

'Can't tell,' Reacher said. 'Right now it's just the name of a medal. Lots of people have them. As a matter of fact I have one. Truth is none of them come cheap. Most of them leave a mark. But you heal up and you walk away. Almost always. Certainly a big percentage. Doesn't have to be bad news.'

Mackenzie said, 'Iraq and Afghanistan was all bad news.'

She looked ahead at her sleek red car.

She said, 'I'm not going home. I'm staying here. She's close. You said so yourself. She's in trouble. Maybe she lost an arm. Maybe she's a disabled veteran with nowhere to live and nothing to eat.'

She told them to follow her back to the Hertz office, and then take her to see Billy's place.

Nakamura carried her laptop down the corridor to her lieutenant's corner suite. She played the captured voice mail. *We*

173

just got a message from Montana. They sent a rider down especially. They have a Fed up there asking questions. He just left Billings.

She said, 'I saw the rider from Montana. He was there four minutes.'

Her lieutenant said, 'Does this get us anywhere?'

'My friend in the lab is doing great work with predicting the phone numbers.'

'What does he want, the Medal of Honor?'

'A pat on the back would be good. You know, stick your head in, say hi.'

'What do you want?'

'It would be good to know what kind of Fed they had up there in Billings. And it would be good to know who sent the warning. Was it a subsidiary, an affiliate, a franchise, or just a friendly bunch of guys all loosely in the same boat?'

'What do you want me to do about it?'

'Call the Billings PD and ask them who was in town last night. They'll know, because they'll have gotten a courtesy call ahead of time.'

'And this guy is going to Wyoming next? Remind me again, why should I care?'

'Because Scorpio got one of his tentacles trodden on. If we knew exactly who he's scared of, maybe we could work out exactly what he's doing.'

The lieutenant called through a closed hutch to his secretary, and told her to get a number for whatever captain or commissioner or other fancy rank was top boy in the Billings PD, over in Montana. And then to dial it, and put it on line one.

They got to Billy's place in the late afternoon. The sun was over the distant mountains. The pronghorns were throwing shadows taller than they were. The colours were different.

The place was still empty.

They went in the kitchen door, and up to the slept-in bedroom. To the closet. Reacher put the shoeboxes on the bed. Mackenzie whirred her finger down the wadded cash, and then poked through the jewellery, pushing her nail through the inch of clinking metal, gathering necklace chains as fine as hair, tumbling high school rings aside, and brassy wise-guy pinkie-finger signet rings, with black onyx faces and tiny off-centre chips of diamond.

She said, 'Was the pawn shop window like this?'

'Exactly like that,' Reacher said.

'Poor Rose.'

'Do you know this area?'

'I know Laramie. Or I used to. Down here was all railroad land. Before the track was laid they used mules. Hence the name, probably.'

'No old friends or relatives?'

'Seven months of the year the road is closed. This was the other side of the world to us.'

'Nowhere she would remember?'

'From later on, probably bars and restaurants downtown. Some stores, possibly. Sometimes we went out to the university. For music, or whatever. But I don't think she would want to live out there now. We're thirty-five years old.'

'So where?'

'Forget what I said. Ignore familiarity. I was wrong. I was desperate. Every idea looked like a good idea. Maybe she chose unfamiliarity instead. Somewhere she didn't know at all.'

'She knows Wyoming.'

'Exactly. To have both is just right. Familiarity and unfamiliarity.'

Reacher checked the view from the bedroom window. There was dust on the dirt road. A long cloud, vivid red in the softening

175

light, spiralling and drifting. A tiny dot at its head, winking in the low sun.

Six minutes, maybe.

'Coming here?' Bramall said.

'Maybe,' Reacher said. 'Maybe not. But I hope so. I hope it's Billy. He knows where Rose lives. From ploughing her driveway, if nothing else.'

'He might have his deer rifle.'

'Has he listened to his voice mail yet?'

'We didn't check. I guess he could have snuck home at some point. A fast in and out. We've been gone for hours.'

'OK,' Reacher said.

'How do you want to do this?'

'Inside, obviously. Downstairs would be best. There's a poker on the fireplace. I'll head in that direction. You take the other side. Find what you can. Look for steak knives. Often in a side-board drawer.'

Mackenzie said, 'What should I do?'

'You go check if the phone is still there. On the desk in the back parlour. If it is, it should say one new message. That's how Mr Bramall left it. If it's there but it's showing a regular screen, that means Billy came back and listened to it, but left the phone home again for whatever reason. So check it out and tell us which. Shout it out good and loud. Then we'll know what we're dealing with here. We'll know how hard to hit the guy.'

'If it's Billy,' Bramall said.

'Hope for the best,' Reacher said.

They went down the stairs, Reacher first, heading left, then Bramall, heading right, and last Mackenzie, looping back toward the parlour. Reacher took a look out the front window. The dust was closer. It was lit up from within by the setting sun. Four minutes, maybe. He moved on to the fireplace and picked up the poker. The yard of iron, with the hook at the end, like a hitchhiker's thumb.

176

Mackenzie called out, 'The phone is still here and now it says two new messages.'

Reacher paused a beat.

Then he called back, 'Listen to the second one.'

He heard a static whisper from the distant earpiece as the first message was skipped, and then more as the second was played. He figured there might be some kind of urgency behind the faint breathy cadence.

Mackenzie called out, 'It's Arthur Scorpio leaving another voice mail for Billy. They got a warning about a federal agent leaving Montana for parts unknown. And Scorpio wants Billy to call him back. He sounds mad. He said, don't make me worried, Billy. Not in a nice way.'

Bramall said, 'Got to be either ATF or DEA in Montana. They both have western task forces.'

Reacher said, 'I don't care.'

They waited.

From the shadows deep in the room Reacher saw a truck nose through the trees and come out at the top of the driveway. Not a pick-up truck. It was a Chevy Suburban SUV, the large size. Black in colour, but caked red from the road. A basic specification. Cheap wheels, not much chrome. An aftermarket antenna, mounted in the centre of the roof.

It crunched over the dirt and came to a stop not far from Bramall's Toyota. A guy got out. He was broad but not tall, maybe fifty-something, with a lot of hard miles on his clock. He was dressed in grey flannel pants and a tweed sport coat. He moved with a certain amount of grace. Maybe once an athlete. Given his shape, probably field not track. Maybe he had put the shot, or thrown the discus.

Now he worked for the government.

The pants and the coat and the truck made that clear.

'Relax, guys,' Reacher called. 'Step down to Defcon Two.'

Mackenzie called back, 'What does that mean?'

'We'll try talking to this guy. Before we do anything else.'

'Is it Billy?'

'I'm pretty sure not,' Reacher said.

Out on the dirt the guy tweaked the tails of his coat and squared up his shoulders and headed for the porch. On the way he took out an ID wallet and held it ready. Reacher saw straps under his coat, for a shoulder holster.

They heard footsteps on the porch boards, and then a knock at the door.

TWENTY-THREE

Bramall opened up. Reacher and Mackenzie stood behind him. The guy from the government car held up a federal ID. A worn gold badge, with a shield and an eagle, and a plastic card like a driver's licence, except it said *United States Department of Justice, Drug Enforcement Administration*. The photograph was the right guy, a little younger, with his hair brushed better and his tie knotted tighter. The writing said his name was Kirk Noble, and his rank was Special Agent.

Reacher couldn't help it.

He said, 'Sounds like a comic book. Kirk Noble, Boy Detective.'

No response.

'I guess you never heard that before.'

Noble said, 'Who are you?'

They all introduced themselves, names only.

Noble said, 'What are you doing here?'

Reacher said, 'We're waiting for a guy named Billy. He lives here. We want to ask him a question.'

'What question?'

'We're looking for a missing woman. We think he knows where she is.'

'What woman?'

Reacher had no real sense that Noble could help. But he knew for sure he could hinder. If he wanted to. He worked for the government. He had a shield with an eagle. He had a thick book of rules.

So Reacher told the story fair and square. Maybe somewhat aware of his federal audience. Maybe nudging a little way towards a certain kind of circular argument, in which the participants' professional backgrounds not only justified but actually required their involvement, while simultaneously absolving them of any kind of blame. Because of their status. As in, a retired military major, with a Silver Star and a Purple Heart, joined a near-forty-year veteran of the FBI, now a properly licensed private investigator in a populous state, to search for another retired military major, this one with a Bronze Star and a Purple Heart all her own. Feds couldn't argue with stuff like that. Not without saying yeah, all our lives are bullshit.

And even if they did, there was the *twin sister*, right there, a connection so spectrally close it legitimized everything, in a blinding flash, like bleach thrown on a crime scene. Especially with the face and the hair. Noble was a guy. Deep down he wasn't thinking legal technicalities. He was thinking: *There are two like that?*

Reacher kept it as subtle as he could.

Eventually he finished up.

Noble said, 'You won't get an answer to your question.'

'Why not?'

'Because Billy ain't coming back.'

'Why not?'

'Long story.'

The guy moved in through the hallway and glanced up the stairs. He looked at the ceiling. He looked at the walls. He turned this way and that, craning his neck, like a contractor about to ballpark an estimate.

He said, 'Did you check the refrigerator?'

Reacher said, 'For what?'

'Food.'

'No.'

Noble moved to the kitchen. He looked at the dishes in the sink. He opened the refrigerator. He glanced back, as if counting heads.

He said, 'We could share bacon and eggs. There's beer to drink.'

Mackenzie said, 'You're going to eat Billy's food?'

'First of all, it ain't Billy's any more, and second of all, I have to. I can't claim expenses if there's food in the house.'

'Expenses from who?'

'You, in the end,' Noble said. 'The taxpayer. We're saving you money.'

'We make you eat dinner from the suspect's refrigerator?'

'It's your refrigerator. And mine. This place became federal property at two o'clock this afternoon. Seized by the government.'

'So where's Billy?'

'That's the long part of the story,' Noble said. 'We should eat.'

At his age, after the things he'd done, Reacher would have said there wasn't much coming, in terms of new and delightful experiences in his life. But strangely the bacon-and-egg dinner in Billy's kitchen was one of them. They felt like conspirators. Or castaways. Like a random group, stranded overnight at the airport. They didn't really know each other. Maybe the first-class cabin, taken by taxi to a country hotel. Mackenzie found candles

181

and lit them. Which then made it feel like the start of a movie. The opening scenes. An innocent group gathers. Little do they know.

Noble cooked, and talked about heroin. It was both his pay cheque and his passion. He knew its history. Once upon a time it was a legal ingredient. It was in all kinds of stuff, branded with famous names still known today. There was heroin cough syrup. There was heroin cough syrup for children. Stronger, not weaker. Doctors prescribed heroin for fussy babies and bronchitis and insomnia and nerves and hysteria and all kinds of other vapours. The patients loved it. Best health care ever. Millions got addicted. Corporations made a lot of easy money. Then folks got wise, and by the start of World War One, legal heroin was history.

But the corporations never forgot. About the easy money. At that point in the story Noble was melting butter in the egg pan, and he paused the spoon mid-air, as if to emphasize his point. He said remember, this is an active-duty DEA agent saying this stuff. We know who causes our problems.

The corporations took eighty years to get back in the heroin business. They came in the side door. By that time in history heroin itself had negative PR. Nothing more than underworld squalor and a bunch of dead rock singers. Kind of sordid. So they made a synthetic version. A chemical copy. Like an identical twin, Noble said, looking at Mackenzie. Exactly the same, but now it had a long clean name. All bright and shiny. It could have been a toothpaste. They put it in neat white pills. What were they for? Getting high, baby. Whatever you want. Except they couldn't put that on the pack. So they said they were for pain. Everyone has pain, right?

Not really. Not at first. Pain was not yet a thing. Institutes had to be funded, and scholarships endowed. Doctors had to be persuaded. Patients had to be empowered. Which all worked in the end. Pain became a thing. Self-reported and untestable, but suddenly a symptom as valid and meaningful as any other. As a result, America was flooded with hundreds of tons of heroin, in purse-size blister packs, backed with foil.

By that point of the story they were eating, and Noble was in full flow. Like he was teaching a class at the academy. He paused again, with his fork mid-air, and he said, 'Let me emphasize two very important things. First up, most of this stuff goes to the right people for the right reasons. No one could deny that. It does a lot of good. But equally, no one could deny enough has fallen out around the edges to also cause a lot of harm. Because second up, no one should ever underestimate the appeal of an opiate high. Far as I can tell, it's a beautiful thing. The way they talk about it, it's the best thing ever. For some folks it hits the spot so hard it reboots their lives.'

He paused to drink some of Billy's beer.

He said, 'These are regular folk I'm talking about. American as apple pie. They like the ball game on the radio, and country music. Not the Grateful Dead. They were seduced by the clean white pill. It made them feel real good. Maybe for the first time in their lives. These are plain people. But smart. They soon figured out ways it could make them feel even better. They got the time-release version, and broke it up, so they got the whole hit at once. Couple times a day. Maybe three. Then they discovered the patches. You stick them on your skin. Like when you're quitting smoking. A long clean name on the pack, but it's the same stuff your great-great-grandma lined up for. A nice little maintenance dose, all day long. You could wear two, if you like. Or three. But licking them was better. Or sucking them, or wadding them up and chewing them like gum. So much better, in fact, it got easy to want more than the doctor gave you. It got to where you're prepared to drop ten bucks here and there, now and then, for a couple extras. Then a hundred bucks for a whole pack, if need be. Every day, if need be. There are ways to get a hundred bucks every day, right? By that point these folks are already hopeless addicts. But not in their own minds. It's partly a pride thing. Addicts are other people, with a dirty needle in a toilet stall. What they have is a pharmaceutical product, made in a lab, by pretty girls in masks who hold test tubes up to the light, with wondrous concern radiating from their clear blue eyes. They've seen it on the television, in the breaks between innings. But in fact they're running worse risks. Those patches ain't made for licking. Fifty thousand people died last year. Regular folk. Four times as many as got killed in gun crimes.'

He paused again, to eat an egg.

He said, 'But we're winning. I would say we've already won, in my region, at least. We can track prescription pain medication from start to finish. We can take out the bent doctors, and we can train the rest to be cautious about how many days they dispense, and we can eliminate pilferage in the factories and along the transportation vectors. So right now the black market is virtually dead, and the medical market is heavily scrutinized. Total success. Except the previous bonanza left us with millions of addicts. Regular folk, remember. They thought a dirty needle in a toilet stall was not their fate. But it's a free market. When we bit down, the price of pills went up, because of supply and demand. What used to be ten bucks was suddenly fifty. It was a crisis. Suddenly regular cartel powder up from Mexico looked like an irresistible bargain. Remember, deep down it's the same chemical. These folks are canny shoppers. None of them ever paid sticker for a car. And numbers don't lie. Even when they factored in the cost to their dignity, with the dirty needles and the toilet stalls and all, hey, the powder was still a bargain. We swapped one problem for another.'

He paused again, to put his silverware together, and push his plate away. He took a long drink from his bottle.

He said, 'But overall it was good news for us. We like the new problem better. The regular cartel powder is harder to hide. We can follow it better. From our point of view it was like the system had just swallowed a barium meal. Whole networks lit up like neon. Standards got less precise. Our job got easier. But not everywhere. A certain part of Montana, for instance. Nothing lit up at all. We couldn't see incoming product. No cartel powder going there. So what happened to their addicts? Did they all cold turkey? Or die? Or is someone else supplying? That's something I would want to know. So I went out to check. I discovered nothing of value. Except one trivial thing. Anecdotally along the way, I discovered I had spooked a low-level operative, who triggered a long-standing pact with a friend, who was also a low-level operative, but in another network. The pact was both of them would immediately get the hell out the very first time either one of them heard a whisper of trouble. Which was the smart play, no question. I'm guessing this wasn't their first rodeo. These things always fall apart in the end, and they always fall hardest on the lowest-level guys. Better to get out early. Which is why Billy ain't coming home. Billy was the friend. From Mule Crossing, Wyoming. He's in the wind, with his pal from Billings, Montana.'

Mackenzie said, 'Where have they gone, do you think?'

'A new hustle,' Noble said. 'Someplace else.'

'Are you looking for them?'

'We're not about to call out the National Guard. We'll put their names and their faces in the system.'

Reacher said, 'Surely the pact implies they worked for the same network, not different. One whisper made two guys run. Maybe what looked like two different networks were really two parts of the same thing.'

'Maybe,' Noble said. 'I don't know much about them. It's an opaque network, remember. That's why I went. Odds are the guy in Montana was just a street-corner dealer. Or the rural

185

equivalent. Odds are Billy was, too. Business schools call it customer-facing. And some of those guys have been to business school. Not guys like Billy and his pal. People who own guys like Billy and his pal.'

'So what next for you?'

'I'm going to find clean sheets and make up a bed. I can't claim lodging expenses, if there's a bed in the house.'

'Then what?'

'Back to some real work. This all was a waste of time.'

'The government got a house.'

'Two houses,' Noble said. 'Don't forget Billings, Montana. I bet we won't be able to sell either one of them.'

Mackenzie said, 'Is there any way you could let us know if you find Billy?'

Noble shook his head.

He said, 'I can't help with your sister. I'm sorry, ma'am. But what have you got? A lot of guesswork and hope for the best. A federal manhunt costs a million dollars a day. They need a very good reason. Which you can't give them. You got a lot of probable and not much cause.'

Mackenzie didn't answer.

Noble said, 'But I wish you the best of luck.'

TWENTY-FOUR

They left Noble in the house, and drove back to Laramie, with Reacher sprawled across the rear seat, and Mackenzie upright in the front, and Bramall at the wheel, one-handed. They agreed on the chain hotel Reacher and Bramall had used the night before. It had proved adequate, except for no coffee. Reacher said the diner he had found was a good substitute. Bramall agreed. He had found it too. He said breakfast there was excellent.

'But then what?' Mackenzie said. 'What do we do after breakfast? What's our next move? We have nothing now.'

'Thanks to the DEA,' Bramall said. 'Trust them to start a stampede.'

'We have more than some folks,' Reacher said. 'I agree, losing Billy is an inconvenience. But it's worse for others. Like that lady up near the old homestead. Even all the way out there. She needed something bad today. She was getting scratchy. She was waiting for Billy. But he isn't coming. So what next for her? Tomorrow she'll be desperate. She'll come looking, surely. She'll come to town. They all will. If Rose is an addict, she'll come to us.'

They met in the lobby at eight in the morning. Bramall was in a fresh shirt and Mackenzie was in a fresh blouse. Reacher's clothes were a day old, but he felt OK in their company. He had used a whole bar of soap in the shower. They walked up to the diner and got a table. Mackenzie was OK with it.

She said, 'Maybe six weeks ago the price of pills had gone especially high, and that's why she had to sell her ring. To afford them.'

'Maybe,' Reacher said.

'I want it to be pills,' she said. 'Not needles in a toilet stall.'

'Of course.'

'I'm sure Special Agent Noble was speaking broadly when he said there are no pills on the black market any more. There must be some.'

Reacher said nothing.

Mackenzie said, 'Before this is over, I'll want to know why it happened.'

'Probably our fault,' Reacher said. 'Depends on the wound she got. Could have been a scratch, but if it was something serious on the battlefield, with the medics under fire and so on, then she'll have gotten a morphine jab ahead of a rough evacuation. Then maybe another morphine jab ahead of triage, and another while she was waiting for surgery. And then she got two weeks in a recovery room with a big tub of opioid pain medication by the bed. She was probably an addict before she left the hospital.'

'Depending on the wound. Maybe it's still painful. Maybe that's why she needs the pills. Or the powder, now. With the needles in the toilet stall. If Agent Noble is right.'

'Did your sister wear silver clothes?'

'Why?'

'Porterfield's neighbour might have seen her in his car. She remembers a silvery colour.'

'Was it winter?'

'A month before the start of spring.'

'You can get winter coats in silver. Almost like foil. Like a high-tech material.'

'Would she wear that colour?'

'I might,' Mackenzie said.

Reacher thought about it. The hair, the eyes, the face, with a silver foil coat. She would look like the picture on the back of a shiny magazine.

An exact replica.

They drove to the university geography department and took another look at the giant book of maps. They traced the settlements westward, from the Mule Crossing turn. First came Billy's place, south of the dirt road, and then Porterfield's, north of it, and then his neighbour's, south again. They had seen all of those. Beyond them lay twelve more places. Six each side of the road, altogether stretching forty long miles into the mountains. Then the dirt road ended. No way out, except to turn around. Not really a bowl, not really a valley. Just a chain of rising foothills, with a road that quit when the mountains came.

Mackenzie said, 'You think she's in there somewhere?'

Reacher said, 'She was either living with Porterfield, or she was visiting with him on a regular basis, yet no one ever saw her, except maybe one occasion. If she lived anywhere else, she would have to drive in and out through Mule Crossing every single time. More people would have seen her, surely. Maybe even the old guy in the post office. But no one ever did. She must have been driving there and back the other way. Deeper into the hills. A buck gets ten she's there right now. Where else would she go?'

'She doesn't own a car,' Bramall said. 'Not according to the Wyoming DMV. Or any other state.'

'She camps out in abandoned ranch houses. Either she finds cars or steals them. She doesn't care whose name is on the title. All a car has to do is start up when she needs it.'

'I want to go there,' Mackenzie said. 'Back to Mule Crossing. It's like the neck of a funnel. If she's in there, she's got to come out sooner or later. I want to be there when she does.'

'If I'm right,' Reacher said.

'If you're wrong, we'll find her in town tonight. Or tomorrow.'

They pulled over and sat in the car, near the old post office, in a spot where they would get a good head-on view of anything coming down the dirt road. Just before the turn, where everyone would slow right down, and look first one way, and then the other, carefully, before making the left or the right on the pavement. Close enough for faces. At first it was awkward. Reacher figured they were all having the same trouble, picturing exactly what it was they expected to see. They knew the theory. The lack of Billy would draw the addicts out. But what would that look like? Reacher had seen his share of movie trailers. The walking dead. All kinds of zombies. He realized he was expecting some kind of apocalyptic vision.

The first candidate approached out of the west in an ancient pick-up truck that was lurching and bouncing and trailing a dust cloud a mile long. Not Rose Sanderson. The driver turned out to be a thin-faced man, with a turned-down mouth, as disapproving as an old-time preacher. Maybe an addict, maybe not. He looked left and right and turned towards Colorado.

The dust cloud settled.

They waited.

From the back seat, Reacher asked Mackenzie, 'Where were you, when Rose was at West Point?'

She turned around.

'University of Chicago,' she said. 'Then Princeton, for postgrad.'

'Studying what?'

'English literature. Different, I know.'

'Not so different. Some of them can read at West Point now. If you take it slow and point to the letters.'

She smiled.

'I didn't mean it like that,' she said. 'I know Rose is as smart as I am. Obviously. It's a scientific fact. I meant she was prepared to kill people, and I wasn't.'

'That was the big dispute?'

'It was never a big dispute. We never fell out. But things happened so fast back then. All of a sudden Rose was in the army. And that was a serious thing. Our resources were stretched thin. She was hardly ever home for nine years. I was never told where she was. I couldn't go visit. Most of the time I couldn't even call. Meanwhile I was working. I got married. That's how it was. We had real lives. Like everyone else with a sibling.'

'Except she was prepared to kill people, and you weren't.'

'I don't mean she wanted to, or planned to. It was an ethical discussion. That's all. We were eighteen. I wasn't saying it had to be all or nothing. In fact it never is. No one says always or never. Everyone says sometimes. But her sometimes were not the same as mine. She would pull the trigger before I would. Which was OK. Maybe I was wrong. Maybe I was naïve. It wasn't the difference of opinion that bothered me. We always had different opinions. It was that she had thought about it, seriously, carefully, and decided yes, she could do it. For real. Which changed her a little. She changed herself, by deciding it. For the first time ever I felt not the same as her.'

Reacher said nothing.

She turned back.

191

They waited.

The second candidate for the apocalypse was the woman who had given the strawberry pie to Sy Porterfield. His neighbour. Second place on the left. She was in a battered Jeep SUV. She looked left and right and turned towards Laramie. Maybe heading to the market. Maybe planning to spend time in the fruit aisle.

The third vehicle they saw came from behind them. It turned in off the two-lane, and passed them by, and set out down the dirt road west.

It was a pick-up truck.

On the front it had snowplough pistons, bolted to the frame.

TWENTY-FIVE

Bramall looked a question, and Mackenzie and Reacher both nodded, so he started the engine and bumped up on the dirt road. A unanimous decision. The obvious play. It cost them nothing to follow the pick-up at least as far as Billy's place. Their eyes would be on the neck of the funnel throughout. Any random driving dead would pass right by, close enough to touch. Certainly close enough to eyeball in great detail. Then in the end if the pick-up kept on going, they could coast to a stop and turn around, and call the snowplough pistons a weird coincidence.

'What if it turns in?' Mackenzie said.

'Maybe it's a competitor just heard the news,' Reacher said. 'Maybe he wants Billy's Rolodex. Maybe snowploughing is a very competitive business.'

'Suppose it's Billy himself?'

'I'm sure the Boy Detective changed the locks. Or glued them up, or whatever they do now. Either one of which will make our boy good and mad. He'll get all cross and frustrated. He'll go get his deer rifle from his truck, to shoot the locks. He'll be standing right there on the porch with it when we show up. Finger on the trigger.'

'Only if we turn in too.'

'He hasn't heard the phone message. He'll think we're Mormons. Or whichever it is let women join in now.'

By that point they had caught up to about a hundred yards behind the pick-up. Which would be considered a very close pursuit, in such a vast landscape, but they were invisible, because of the dust cloud. The pick-up's mirrors couldn't see them.

They rolled on, in secret convoy. The pronghorn herd was grazing a new patch of pasture. Two miles gone. Less than a minute remaining, at their current speed.

The pick-up slowed. They saw it loom large and ghostlike in the cloud ahead. Bramall backed off. The pick-up braked, lights flaring, all the way down to walking speed, and then it turned a wide slow left into the mouth of Billy's driveway.

'Go for it,' Reacher said. 'Go after him.'

Bramall looked at Mackenzie.

She hesitated.

Reacher said, 'He hasn't heard the phone message. He doesn't know who we are. We're just three random people.'

Mackenzie said, 'He knows where Rose is.'

Bramall turned in. No dust on the driveway. It was a forest track, all rock and grit and gravel. Now the Toyota was plainly visible. They hung back. They saw the pick-up through the trees. Two hundred yards ahead of them, flashing through the sun and the shadows.

'Stupid to run and come right back,' Reacher said.

'Maybe he wants his money,' Mackenzie said.

They rolled on, keeping pace. The pick-up drove through the final curve and out of sight. Another fifty yards it would be out of the woods. Then the last hundred, over the beaten red dirt, to the house.

'Let me out here,' Reacher said. 'I'll walk the rest of the way, in the trees. I can cut the corner. I can get there faster.'

'Is that smart?' Bramall said.

'It's smarter than sticking together. A good squad never bunches up. Too big of a target.'

Bramall stopped the car and Reacher slid out. Bramall drove on. Reacher watched him go, and then he threaded his way into the woods, and set out on what he hoped was a straight line to the last tree before the house. He got close just in time to see the pick-up drive across the last of the dirt, and park near the house.

He waited.

A hundred yards away in the mouth of the driveway he saw Bramall roll to a stop. His Toyota was well hidden. No glint of paint, no gleam of chrome. All completely covered with thick red dust. Better than desert camouflage.

He waited.

The pick-up's engine turned off.

The driver's door opened.

A guy got out. He was young. Early twenties, maybe. Six feet tall. Couple hundred pounds. Maybe more. Most of it fat. He was a big shapeless guy. He looked slow and clumsy.

Not Billy.

Billy wore a thirty-two waist, and a thirty leg, and an eight and a half shoe.

The big guy took a ring of keys from his pocket, and stared at it like he had never seen one before. He carried it up on the porch, and walked to the door. He chose a key and bent down to the hole.

He looked puzzled.

He touched the keyhole with his fingertip.

Then he straightened up and spun around, as if he was suddenly certain someone was behind him. With a camera, maybe. For kids to watch on their phones. And laugh.

Reacher stepped out of the trees.

He walked across the dirt, and waved a come-on to Bramall. The guy by the door watched him all the way. Not reacting. Still looking puzzled. Reacher stepped up on the porch. Up close the guy looked harmless. His shape made his clothes tight and smooth. There were no unexplained lumps or bumps in his pockets. He was unarmed. He was very young. He was no kind of a physical threat.

Maybe not the smartest kid, either.

Not a whole lot going on behind his eyes.

Reacher said, 'Who are you?'

The kid said, 'I came by to get something.'

Which was technically non-responsive, but Reacher let it go. Bramall and Mackenzie stepped up on the porch. The kid looked at them. Still puzzled. Reacher looked at the keyhole. There was a bead of glue in it. The Boy Detective had changed one lock, maybe at the back, and glued all the others. Efficiency. Saving taxpayer money.

The kid said, 'Who are you?'

Reacher said, 'I asked first.'

'I'm doing nothing wrong.'

'Just tell me your first name.'

'It's Mason.'

'OK, Mason, it's good to meet you. Why are you here?'

'I came by to get something.'

'For who?'

'For me. Billy said I could have it.'

'Who is Billy?'

The kid said, 'He's my brother.'

'Is he?'

196

'Well, half.'

'Where is he now?'

'I don't know. He ran off again.'

'Has he done that before?'

'Two times that I can remember. This time he called me and told me where he left his truck. He said I could have it. And something in his house, too.'

'Where was the truck?'

'Up near Casper.'

Reacher nodded. Nearer Mule Crossing than Billings, Montana. The other guy had driven more miles than Billy. Why? Must have been their agreed-upon vector. They were planning to head southeast. Through Nebraska, and away.

He said, 'What kind of something did he leave in the house?'

'I'm not sure I should tell you.'

'Was it money in a box?'

The kid looked surprised.

'Yes,' he said. 'In a shoebox.'

'Did he want you to bring it to him?'

'No sir, it's for me. He said he's already with a guy who has plenty.'

'Where?'

'He didn't tell me. He wouldn't. No way. He used to say to me, Mason, if you ever have to run, you tell no one where you're going, not even me.'

'You completely sure he didn't tell you?'

'Yes, sir.'

'What does Billy do for a living?'

'He works the snowplough.'

'What about the summer?'

'I think he buys and sells things.'

'What kind of things does he sell?'

'Just things. Like flea-market things.'

'Where does he sell them?'

'I think all around. Wherever people are who want to buy them.'

'Do you know any of his customers?'

'No.'

'Have you ever seen a woman who looks like my friend here?'

'No.'

'Do you know what an accessory is?'

'Something you put on your truck.'

'Also a legal word,' Reacher said. 'It means if you know a secret, and you don't tell, then you go to jail too. Billy has strayed far from the narrow path of righteousness, I'm afraid. He has made some poor choices in his life. The government seized this house yesterday. A federal agent put glue in the lock. That's what they do now. So this is our last chance to help you, Mason. If you know where Billy is, you better tell us, right now.'

'I don't know where Billy is,' the brother said, kind of happily. 'But don't worry. He'll be back in a year or two. That's what happened the last two times.'

Reacher looked at Bramall, who shrugged. Then at Mackenzie, who nodded. She believed the kid.

Who said, 'How do I get in the house?'

'You don't,' Reacher said. 'No point. The money is long gone. It was in a federal evidence locker before you woke up this morning. But you can keep the truck. Get a blade for the plough, and you could set up in business.'

They watched the kid drive away. Mackenzie stayed on the porch and looked at the view. The wide empty plains on the right. The old post office, and the firework store. The pronghorns, about a mile away. The red road, still neatly scraped, still nicely cambered. On the left, the low jagged peaks, like miniature mountain ranges.

She said, 'Logically we should keep on going. She's not here.

198

She's not at Porterfield's place, which is next. She's not at the pie lady's place, which comes after that. So logically we could just keep on going, and then stop before the fourth place. We'd be closer. Nothing could happen behind us. It would still all be ahead of us.'

'If Reacher is right,' Bramall said. 'Which he might not be.'

'Then why has no one seen her?'

Bramall didn't answer.

Reacher said, 'I guess the gift of the truck was a cowboy kind of thing. Billy was making sure someone looked after his best horse, so to speak, come what may. All that kind of good stuff. But ten grand in a box is different. That's a lot of money to give away. I don't think he wanted to. I think he was out on the road when he got the call from Montana. Too far from home to come back and get it. The pact meant he had no time. He had to go to Casper immediately. And given the direction the other guy was driving from Billings, we have to assume they carried on east through Nebraska. And if we time it from Scorpio's first voice mail, this all was at least forty-eight hours ago. They're in Chicago by now. Except I don't think they went to Chicago. I don't think they would have felt at home there. My guess is they turned south for Oklahoma. They could make some kind of living there. Or the same kind of living.'

'Possible,' Bramall said.

Mackenzie said, 'But Special Agent Noble will never be able to figure that out, because he'll never know where the truck was found, because of our decision to give it to the brother.'

Bramall said, 'Our?'

'Nothing to be ashamed of. I'm sure it was done with the best of intentions. Job creation is a wonderful thing. But I want Special Agent Noble to have a shot at finding Billy. Because I think he would tell us if he does. Why wouldn't he? I think we should call him. I think we should tell him about Oklahoma.'

'It was only a guess,' Bramall said.

'Based on a fact,' she said. 'Which Noble hasn't got.'

'He might guess different.'

'At least he'll get a chance to.'

'You really want me to call him?'

'I think we should.'

Bramall looked at Reacher.

Reacher said, 'He cooked, after all. Normally we would send a note of some kind.'

Bramall took out his tortoiseshell reading glasses, and a small notebook. He opened it with his thumb.

Reacher said, 'You have Noble's number in there?'

Bramall said, 'Just the western division's switchboard.'

He dialled and played phone tag for a long minute, saying the name over and over again, with variations, Special Agent Kirk Noble, Special Agent Noble, Kirk Noble. Eventually the guy himself must have come on the line, because Bramall reminded him who he was, in terms of the bacon-and-egg dinner, and then he said now there was very strong reason to believe the fugitives had gone to Oklahoma.

Evidently Noble asked to speak to Reacher.

Bramall passed the phone.

Noble said, 'There's a problem with Porterfield.'

TWENTY-SIX

Noble said, 'I typed it up, word for word based on what you told me, and then I ran it through some software we have, which automatically checks against our existing databases, to see if we know the names already, for other reasons. And Seymour Porterfield came up blocked. I dug around and found three separate files on the guy, all locked, all needing high-level passwords.'

Reacher said, 'What kind of a guy would get a file like that?'

'A source of information,' Noble said. 'It's a security measure.'

'Interesting.'

'I need to know who Porterfield was.'

'He had an expensive kitchen.'

'I need you to tell me what you know.'

'I don't know anything about Porterfield. He wore blue jeans a lot and had an eye for décor. But I don't really care. He's not why I'm here.'

'One of the files was about Porterfield and a second person. Judging by the codes, the second person was a woman. I can't read the date on the file but the sequencing suggests it was first opened about two years ago and last looked at by someone not long before Porterfield died.'

'Interesting,' Reacher said again. 'How deep in your system are these files?'

'Very deep. But I don't think they're DEA originals. I think we got copied in as a courtesy, by someone else.'

'Who?'

'It's a weird code. Not the FBI or the ATF. It's like what we used to get when we had Special Forces deployed in Colombia. Not a remote source, you understand. Somewhere fairly near our main office.'

'OK,' Reacher said. 'I understand. Don't forget to call Oklahoma.'

He clicked off. Told the others.

Mackenzie said, 'Does this help us?'

'I don't know,' Reacher said. 'Who Porterfield was two years ago doesn't necessarily tell us where Rose is now. We shouldn't invest too much time in it. I guess we could go pull off the road ahead of the fourth place, and I could make a call from there, while we were waiting.'

They parked on the slope of the shoulder, at an angle, like a cop with a radar gun. Ahead of them were twelve more homesteads, all widely separated and out of sight, all along forty more miles of the dirt road. And then nothing. No one was coming. Reacher borrowed Bramall's phone and dialled the same ancient number from memory.

The same woman answered.

'West Point,' she said. 'Superintendent's office. How may I help you?'

'This is Reacher.'

'Hello, major.'

'I need to speak with the supe.'

'You don't know his name, do you?'

'I guess not currently.'

'It's General Simpson. He'll be happy you called. He has information for you. Wait one, major.'

There were clicks and dead air, and then the supe's voice came on the line.

It said, 'Major.'

Reacher said, 'General.'

He didn't use the name Simpson. Just in case it wasn't. West Point culture was full of practical jokes, and although he very much doubted the woman who answered the phone would set him up, he couldn't be sure.

The supe said, 'What progress are you making?'

'Some,' Reacher said. 'I think I'm close to the right location.'

'Which is where?'

'Bottom right-hand corner of Wyoming.'

'So she went home.'

'Not exactly, but not far away. I found trace evidence in a house in a place called Mule Crossing. She was there about a year and a half ago. My sense is she's still in the general neighbourhood.'

The supe said, 'There's something you need to know. It might be important. Out of curiosity I tried to take a look at Sanderson's service record and medical file. I couldn't get in. They're sealed tighter than a duck's butt on a choppy day. I think your people did it.'

'My people?'

'Military police.'

'When?'

'Hard to tell exactly. Not recently. But after she left the service, almost certainly. Two years ago, possibly.'

'OK,' Reacher said. 'Now guess what I was calling about?'

'How could I?'

'The house where I found evidence was owned by a guy who also has a sealed file in a government database. Three sealed files, in fact. One of which was first opened around two years ago, and features the guy with a woman. Apparently they are not native files. The folks at the database think the agency in question was copied in as a courtesy, by another agency.'

'Do they know which one?'

'They hinted at the Pentagon.'

'I find that interesting,' the supe said. 'As you knew I would. But you didn't call just to entertain me. You want me to do something.'

'Who do you know down there?'

'A couple of people.'

'Do they owe you?'

'How big of a risk would they be taking?'

'Not much. This thing went cold a year and a half ago. It's ancient history now. And they don't have to give us chapter and verse. Just confirm or deny if Sanderson is the woman in the file with the guy who owned the house. His name was Seymour Porterfield. Social Security should show a county sheriff's notification of death around the start of spring last year.'

'He's dead?'

'It's Wyoming. He was eaten by a bear.'

Reacher spelled Porterfield's names, first and last.

The supe repeated them back.

'Thank you, general,' Reacher said. 'You can call me back on this number. My partner Mr Bramall will answer.'

'Thank you, major.'

Reacher said, 'Sir, is your name Simpson?'

'Correct,' the supe said. 'Sean Simpson.'

'Yes, sir,' Reacher said, purely out of habit.

He clicked off, and gave the phone back to Bramall, who plugged it in to charge.

They waited an hour on the shoulder, and saw no one coming, except a small herd of elk, who came out of the trees on one side of a gulch, and into the trees on the other. Overhead, black birds of prey hovered motionless, high in the sky.

The road stayed empty.

'I'm sorry,' Mackenzie said. 'I did it again. Every idea looks like a good idea. Until it turns out wrong.'

'Neither of us had a better idea,' Reacher said.

'Maybe it's a good thing if we don't see her. It would mean she doesn't need what Billy was selling. It would mean she's OK. Someone stole her ring. You said so yourself.'

'Best case.'

'Which sometimes happens.'

'Sometimes,' Reacher said.

'How often?'

'More than never. Less than always.'

'Wait,' Bramall said.

He pointed.

There was a dust cloud on the road ahead. In the west, way far in the distance, on the rising horizon. There was a tiny dot at its head, smoothed by the haze, but coming on fast.

They waited. The dot grew bigger and the cloud spun and howled behind it, furiously and endlessly generating itself anew, exactly the shape of a parachute, but infinitely long, hanging together with some kind of internal aerodynamic constraint, before finally going limp, and succumbing to wind and gravity, and drifting back to earth.

'Stand by,' Bramall said.

He pulled his phone off the charger, ready to take a photograph.

They waited.

An SUV flashed by, moving fast, an ancient model, boxy and

battered and square, covered with rust and red dust so thick it looked baked on. The window glass was just as bad, except the front windshield, which had two smeared arcs from the wipers, where the dust was thinner. Through them they got a fractured split-second glimpse inside.

Just a dull and hazy impression.

A small figure, flinching away.

A silvery colour.

TWENTY-SEVEN

Bramall swung off the shoulder and took off in pursuit like the highway patrol. The truck up ahead was still moving fast. The road ran straight for long stretches, then dipped through hollows, and rose over knolls, and curved out of sight, but the dust cloud was always there, showing the way. The big Toyota growled along, pattering hard over the rough surface, going plenty fast itself, but their quarry wasn't slowing any. In fact it was speeding up. At times the cloud between them grew half a mile long.

And then it was gone.

The Toyota came leaning out of a long fast curve, through the last of the dust, into clear air, pure and bright and empty for miles ahead.

No truck. Nothing there.

Behind them the severed cloud swayed in the wind, and pulled off the road, and died in the scrub.

Bramall stopped.

'She turned off,' Reacher said. 'There's no dust on the ranch roads. What's back there?'

Bramall made a U-turn, shoulder to shoulder, and went back to see.

'Driveway on the left,' Mackenzie said. 'I think. It's hard to be sure.'

'The pie lady,' Reacher said. 'Porterfield's neighbour. We were here yesterday. We almost missed it then.'

'But the pie lady is out. We saw her go.'

Bramall turned in on the track and drove, the same way as the day before, but faster, twisting and rising through the trees, more than three miles, during which distance they saw nothing and no one, and then as before all of a sudden the trees opened up and the Toyota burst out on the flat acre with the long view east, and the one-storey house, with its brown boards, and its ancient millwork, and its old church pew.

Nothing there.

No battered old SUV, caked with dust.

Nothing moving.

No sound.

Mackenzie said, 'There must be other ways out of here. Like the places I showed you yesterday.'

Bramall drove on, in a wide bumpy circle, all the way around the house, around the outbuildings, always tight to the tree line. They saw three separate forest tracks running onward through the trees. One went due west, one went south, and one split the difference between. They were like trails for hikers or hunters, all worn and beaten down, all gnarled with roots and rocks, all dappled with gentle sunlight, all curving out of sight.

All narrow.

But good enough for a boxy old SUV.

It was impossible to say which one had just been used. The ground was bone dry. There were tyre tracks everywhere, sharp in the dust.

'Want to gamble?' Bramall said.

'Waste of time,' Reacher said. 'These trails have too many turns. The odds would get impossible. Plus your truck is bigger than hers. We'd get stuck.'

'If it was her,' Bramall said.

'Suppose it was.'

'Doesn't matter which way she went,' Mackenzie said. 'The question is why she went. What happened?'

'We scared her,' Reacher said. 'We were waiting on the shoulder. We could have been State Police. She didn't want us to catch her. So she pulled off the road and tracked back on some weird forest service route only she knows. Now she's laying low someplace, trying to figure out what she wants to do next.'

'Where?'

'Within about a thousand square miles of right here. In a spot we'll never find.'

Mackenzie was quiet a beat.

Then she said, 'Did you see the silver?'

Bramall said, 'An impression.'

'What did you make of it?'

'A coat,' Bramall said. 'With a hood.'

'But tight,' Reacher said. 'I thought like athletic wear. The kind of thing they peel off before the race.'

'Did it look like foil?'

'Partly,' Bramall said. 'Maybe the trim.'

Mackenzie said, 'Why didn't she want us to catch her?'

'She didn't know it was you,' Reacher said. 'She didn't see your face. Her windows were dusty, and so were ours, and when she came by head-on, she was looking the other way. It wasn't an emotional decision. It was practical. She thought we were cops. Maybe she's the kind of person who can't let a cop see the inside of her car.'

'If it was her,' Bramall said.

'Because she's an addict,' Mackenzie said.

'Worst case,' Reacher said.

'Which happens.'

'More than never, less than always.'

'Which way are you leaning?'

'Hope for the best, plan for the worst.'

'Seriously.'

'I'm thinking about Seymour Porterfield,' Reacher said. 'We're assuming Billy took over his business, whereupon that kind of thing usually triggers some kind of vigorous expansion afterwards, which seems to be the whole reason businesses get taken over in the first place, all because someone else sees missed opportunities. And this is not a type of business that ever gets smaller anyway. It only gets bigger. Therefore, long story short, on a theoretical basis, for a number of reasons, we could expect law enforcement to see Billy as a bigger proposition now than Porterfield ever was. But the Boy Detective as good as told us he isn't even interested in a person like Billy. He said he was going to put his face in the system. That's code for letting him walk away. Because he's too boring to talk to. Whereas on the other hand, the even less interesting Seymour Porterfield has his own sealed file at the Pentagon.'

Bramall said, 'Could be nothing. He might once have had small-time connections in Central America. The military wrote everything down. His file might be one word long. You know what that stuff was like. You were probably there.'

'Why would a one-word file be sealed?'

Bramall said, 'I don't know.'

'What do we actually know for sure about Porterfield?'

'Very little.'

'What impression did you get?'

'Like the neighbour said. A rich guy from out of state, come to find himself, maybe writing a novel.'

'Nice life.'

'You bet.'

'You liked his house.'

'I could live there.'

'He had everything a person could need,' Reacher said. 'Including granite countertops and his very own file at the Pentagon. In fact he had three files at the Pentagon. One of which seems to cover some kind of a joint enterprise with an unspecified woman, during the last six months of his life. On top of which is the broken window in his house. Which looked like government work. Which is ridiculous. Until it isn't. Plus the guy got eaten by a bear. Or a mountain lion. Either of which is highly unlikely. And all of which lead to wild speculations about what exactly happened during those last six months. Especially towards the end. Maybe Rose ran just now because a year and a half ago she learned not to trust expensive black vehicles full of people. So to answer Mrs Mackenzie's original question, I guess right now I'm leaning slightly away from the worst case. Worst cases are usually very banal. This thing feels more complex than that.'

Mackenzie said, 'You think Porterfield wasn't the man you thought he was?'

'He could have been ten times worse. Now I don't know for sure. Which is the interesting part. It makes it equally possible he was ten times better.'

Bramall said, 'If he was, how would Arthur Scorpio know his name?'

'Through Billy, maybe. Billy was Porterfield's neighbour, just as much as the pie lady. They all talk. Maybe Scorpio liked to hear neighbourhood gossip.'

'He had ten grand in a shoebox.'

'Maybe to live on while he wrote his novel.'

Bramall didn't answer. His phone rang. He answered, and listened, and gave the phone to Reacher.

'It's General Simpson,' he said. 'For you.'

Reacher put the phone to his ear.

The supe said, 'Porterfield was a U.S. Marine.'

TWENTY-EIGHT

The supe said, 'Anything below the surface is locked down tight, but we know from Social Security and other unclassified sources that the Seymour Porterfield who died in Wyoming last year was an Ivy League postgrad who joined the Marine Corps the day after 9/11. He was the perfect recruit. A real poster boy. He went to Iraq in the first wave as a lieutenant in a rifle company. He didn't last more than a month. He was an early casualty. The injury is unspecified. He was honourably discharged, and he returned to civilian life. Back then the Marines could still afford mental-health counselling during that type of separation. There's a note that says Porterfield seemed happy to resume academic pursuits, and had realistic expectations of a future inheritance, both cash and real estate, such that no one had to worry very much, least of all the Marine Corps. Then he dropped off the government radar for a very long time.'

'Until?' Reacher said.

'Two years ago. Some office deep in the Pentagon got a brand new case. Something to do with Porterfield. We don't know what. We think they dug up his original service file for background, and then sealed it. Which usually means something. Meanwhile they were also opening a second new file, about Porterfield and a woman. That's what we can see so far. Three files, like you said.'

'Was Sanderson the woman?'

'We don't know yet. That's below the surface.'

'Are you still looking?'

'Discreetly,' the supe said. 'I'll be in touch.'

The phone went dead. Reacher passed it back to Bramall, who plugged it in to charge.

Mackenzie said, 'Does this help us?'

Reacher said, 'It might not be her.'

'Suppose it is.'

'It gives us a wounded Marine officer and a wounded army officer in the same place for six months. Such a thing could go either way. They could have been the worst addicts in the history of the world. Or they could have been doing better, with each other's moral support. Or maybe they were never users at all. They were very impressive people, after all. Porterfield quit school and rushed to sign up. Rose was top ten at West Point and did five tours. Maybe they got together for peace and quiet with someone who understood.'

'Then where is she now?'

'That's the problem. That question is also an answer.'

'Sadly,' she said. 'It forces us to conclude that these days she's more likely to be an addict than very impressive. Or she'd still be calling me.'

'Worst case.'

'You were leaning away.'

'Still am,' Reacher said. 'Still hoping for the best. May I ask you a personal question?'

214

'I suppose,' she said.

'What kind of twins are you and Rose? Do you look exactly alike?'

She nodded. 'We're identical twins. Literally. More so than most.'

'Then we should stop by the hospital.'

'Why?'

'By now people are hurting. I guess some of them might have friends, who might be willing to share. I guess some of them will try to score in town. The rest will go to the emergency room. They'll claim a raging toothache. Or a crippling backache. Whatever can't be tested. But pain is a thing now, so the doctor has to take their word for it. He has to write a prescription for the good stuff. We should check if she's been there. You'll remind them of her. Like a human missing persons billboard.'

'I feel like I'm betraying her. I'm accepting she's a junkie.'

'It's a percentage game. We have to start somewhere.'

She was quiet a long moment.

Then she said, 'OK, let's go.'

Bramall started the big V8 motor, and steered a wide circle towards the head of the driveway. They turned their backs on the flat acre with the long view east, and the brown board house, with the ancient millwork and the old church pew. They settled in for three rough miles, and then the dirt road again.

But coming the other way out of the driveway right at that moment was the woman who had baked the strawberry pie. The woman who lived there. Home from the market, in her Jeep SUV. Bramall stopped and backed up to let her by. But she stopped too, side by side, and buzzed her window down.

Bramall buzzed his window down.

So did Reacher.

The woman recognized them, from the day before, and she nodded cautiously, and then she peered beyond them at

Mackenzie. Who she didn't recognize. No sign at all. Nothing there. The exact replica. The human billboard.

A stranger.

The woman said, 'Can I help you folks?'

Reacher said, 'We came by to check a couple of things, connected to what we spoke about yesterday. We didn't know you were out.'

'Yes you did. I passed you at the turn.'

'Perhaps we didn't notice.'

'You're private detectives. You're supposed to notice.'

'We're looking for a missing woman,' Reacher said. 'Maybe we were preoccupied.'

'What things do you want to check?'

'About when you saw Porterfield,' Reacher said. 'Was he disabled in any way?'

'I don't think so.'

'Two arms and two legs?'

'Sure.'

'Was he limping at all?'

'I don't think so.'

'Talking well and thinking straight?'

'He was very courteous and polite.'

'OK,' Reacher said. 'Now about that one time on the dirt road, and what you saw in Porterfield's car. Can you tell us about that again?'

'There was nothing in the car. I was wrong.'

'Suppose you were right. What did you see?'

She paused a beat.

'It was real quick,' she said. 'Two cars passing, that's all. The wind was up, like a dust storm.'

'Even so,' Reacher said. 'What did you see?'

She paused again.

'A girl turning away,' she said. 'And a silvery colour.'

216

'It stuck in your mind.'

'It was weird.'

'Had you ever seen such a thing before?'

'Never.'

'Did you ever see such a thing again?'

'Never.'

'Are you absolutely sure?' Reacher said. 'How about in a different car? All alone. Maybe driving in from west of here.'

'Never,' the woman said again. 'Are you making fun of me?'

'No, I promise. Now here's a different question. Do you let people use your driveway any old time they want to?'

'Apart from you?'

'Point taken,' Reacher said. 'But is it generally OK for folks to drive in and use your forest trails?'

'No it is not.'

'You never allow that?'

'Why would I?'

'You ever see it happen none the less? By trespassers, maybe?'

'Never,' she said for the fourth time. 'What's going on?'

'The real reason we're here is we followed a truck. It was kind of escaping. It drove up your driveway and out again on one of your trails. We don't know which one.'

The woman looked all around.

She said, 'It escaped through here?'

'You ever had that kind of a thing happen before?'

'Never,' the woman said again. 'How could it happen? How would anyone know where my trails go anyway?'

West Point, Reacher thought. Back when reading maps was a lifesaving skill.

He said, 'Where do your trails go, in fact?'

'All over,' she said. 'You can get to Colorado if you want. Who

217

were you chasing? They must have been panicking, to come through here.'

'We think the driver was a woman.'

'OK.'

'She looked kind of small, and she was turning away. We didn't see her face.'

The woman said nothing.

'There was a silvery colour.'

'Oh my God.'

'The same as you saw before.'

'Here?'

'We followed the truck right in.'

'You're going to give me nightmares.'

They left her there, and drove back down the driveway, to the dirt road, and the two-lane, and Laramie. The hospital was out by the university. Perhaps it was connected. The emergency room had seven patients waiting. Two of them could have been suffering from Billy's absence. They looked shaky and damp. A likely diagnosis. The other five could have been students. All seven looked up, like people do in waiting rooms. They checked out the new arrivals.

Including Mackenzie.

No hint of recognition.

Nor was there at the desk. Mackenzie asked after a patient named Rose Sanderson, and a helpful woman checked a screen, and smiled an encouraging smile, and said they had seen no one with that name, while all the time looking Mackenzie straight in the eye, in an open and frank and perfectly compassionate way.

Without a hint of recognition.

Mackenzie stepped away from the desk and said, 'OK, either she's got friends willing to share, or she's in town right now, trying to score.'

218

They drove to the corner of Third and Grand, and checked block by block for the combination they wanted, which was two bad bars and a decent place to eat, all within sight of each other. They needed a meal, but Mackenzie didn't want to burn surveillance time. She wanted to watch while she ate, at least two plausible places. So they found a café across the street from two cowboy bars, both with neon beer signs behind unwashed windows. They figured there might be business transacted in such places. Cowboys liked pain pills, the same as anyone else. Maybe more so. Because of rodeo accidents, and roping injuries, and other random falls off horses.

The café was a new-age place, with all kinds of healing juices, and sandwiches Reacher figured had been put together by a blind man. All kinds of random ingredients. Huge seeds in the bread. Like sawdust mixed with ball bearings.

Bramall went to wash up, leaving Mackenzie and Reacher alone at the table. She took off her jacket, and turned left and right to hang it on the frame of her chair. She looked back at him. Pale flawless skin, perfect bones, delicate features. Green eyes, full of sorrow.

She said, 'I apologize.'

He said, 'For what?'

'When we first met. I said you were a weird obsessive, two soldiers short of a squad.'

'I think it was me who said that.'

'Only because you knew I was thinking it.'

'You had a good reason.'

'Maybe,' she said. 'But now I'm glad you're here.'

'I'm glad to hear it.'

'I should pay you what I pay Mr Bramall. The same daily rate.'

'I don't want to be paid,' Reacher said.

219

'You think virtue is its own reward?'

'I don't know much about virtue. I just want to find out what happened. I can't charge money for a private satisfaction.'

Bramall came back, and they ate, and they watched out the window.

They saw nothing.

Mackenzie paid.

Reacher said, 'There's another bar we could look at.'

'Like these?' Bramall said.

'A little better, maybe. There might be a guy we could talk to.'

He led them a block over, towards the railroad tracks, and two blocks down, to the bar with the bullet hole in the mirror. The same guy was at the same table, with the same kind of long-neck bottle. The helpful guy, or the busybody into everyone's business, or the local expert full of specialist knowledge, or the mixture of all three. His table was only a two-top, so Mackenzie sat down across from him, and Bramall and Reacher stood behind her.

The guy said, 'You're the gentleman who asked me about Mule Crossing.'

'Correct,' Reacher said.

'Did you find it? Or did you blink and miss it?'

He was talking to Reacher, but he was looking at Mackenzie. Hard not to. The mass of hair, and the face, and the eyes, and the small slender form under the thin white blouse.

No hint of recognition.

'I found it,' Reacher said. 'In fact I heard a story down there. A year and a half ago someone got eaten by a bear.'

The guy took a long pull on his bottle.

He wiped foam off his lip.

He said, 'Seymour Porterfield.'

'You knew him?'

'My buddy's friend was the guy who fixed his roof when it leaked. Which was about every winter, because it was built all wrong. So I heard things. I know about the land from way back. Those were railroad acres, even though the track was nowhere near. Some old scam, more than a hundred years ago. Every once in a while some rich guy back east would inherit a deed, and come on out and build a cabin. In Porterfield's case it was his father. He built a modern style, which I guess is why the roof was leaking. Then later he died and Porterfield got the title in his will. I guess he decided he liked the simple life, because he moved in full time.'

'What did he do for a living?'

'He was on the phone all the time, and he drove around a lot. Doing what, no one seemed to know exactly. Maybe a hobby. He had all his daddy's money. Some kind of old fortune back east. Maybe ironworks, hence the railroad connection.'

'What kind of a guy was he?'

'He was a college boy and a former Marine. But the old-money kind of both.'

'How was his health?'

The guy paused a beat.

He said, 'Weird you should ask that.'

'Why?'

'His health looked fine from the outside. You could have put him on a movie poster. But he had economy packs of surgical dressings in his house, and also his medicine cabinet was jammed with pills.'

'Your buddy's friend would check a thing like that?'

'You know, in passing.'

'Was there ever any trouble there? Any strangers showing up unannounced? Any kind of weird shit going on?'

The guy shook his head.

'No strangers,' he said. 'No trouble, either. And nothing weird, until the secret girlfriend showed up.'

221

TWENTY-NINE

The guy with the long-neck bottle said, 'I guess it was the start of the winter before the last one. Porterfield's roof was leaking bad again. My buddy's friend was out there all the time. Sometimes he would get a look in through a window. He started seeing her stuff. More and more of it. But he never saw her. If he had to do inside work, sometimes she wasn't there, and if she was, she would hide in the bedroom. He was sure of it.'

'She wasn't always there?' Reacher said.

'Neither was he sometimes. She must have had a place of her own. I guess they were back and forth.'

'But when she was there, she didn't hide her stuff,' Reacher said.

'No, it was right out in the open.'

'Any chance of confusion? Maybe it was all Porterfield's stuff.'

The guy shook his head. He said, 'I don't think so, especially the nightwear. And you can tell by the look of a place. Men and women make a mess two different ways. This was both ways at

222

once, let me tell you, right there. Two of everything. Two people. Two plates in the sink, two books by the sofa, both sides of the bed with a dent.'

'Clearly your buddy's friend undertook an extensive investigation.'

'A roof covers the whole house, man. Supposed to, anyway.'

'But your buddy's friend never actually met her.'

'Which is why he called her the secret girlfriend.'

'Never saw her coming and going, or out on the road?'

'Never.'

'Did Porterfield ever say anything about her?'

The guy drained his bottle and set it down on the table.

He said, 'He never denied it. He never came right out and said some weird thing like hey, by the way, I don't have a girlfriend. But equally he never said, by the way, my girlfriend is taking a nap, so don't go in the bedroom. All he ever said was don't go in. Period. He never said why. All in all my buddy's friend said being there was a weird experience. Like Porterfield was hiding her away, and denying her existence, so no one would ever come looking for her. Except that made no sense, because her stuff was everywhere. I think a man with bad intentions would have taken better precautions.'

Reacher said, 'Did you believe the story about the bear?'

'The sheriff did,' the guy said. 'That's about all that matters.'

'You got doubts?'

'I wasn't there. But everyone had the same private reaction. It was automatic. Once or twice in your life you find yourself wondering what you would do, if there truly was a guy who had to go. Or you wonder what you would do if something got way out of hand, and someone ended up dead, when he wasn't supposed to. Either way, you would dump him in the high woods. Exactly the kind of place where Porterfield was found. It's a total no-brainer. Maybe you would smear him with honey. Or nick another couple of veins, to keep the smell fresh. Maybe you would get lucky with the big animals, and maybe you wouldn't, but either way you don't need them. You got hundreds of other species already lining up and licking their lips. So what I'm saying is, I promise you every guy who heard the news about Porterfield was thinking hell yeah, that's how I would do it. I know I was.'

'You think the sheriff was really?'

'Privately, sure.'

'But publicly he called it an accident.'

'No proof,' the guy said. 'That's the whole beauty of it.'

'Did Porterfield have enemies?'

'He was a rich guy from back east. I'm sure they all have enemies.'

'What happened to the woman?'

'Rumour was she stuck around. No one knew exactly where. No one knew who they were looking for, because no one knew what she looked like in the first place.'

'What happened to Porterfield's roof?'

'The sheriff told my buddy's friend to fix it good, once and for all. So he put new metal over the bad part. Which is what he had wanted to do all along, except Porterfield would never let him, because it wasn't that way in the architect's drawing.'

They bought the guy another bottle of his favourite beer, and left him there. They walked back to the Toyota, which was parked across the street from the new-age café, on the far kerb about halfway between the two bars, with their beer signs and their dirty windows. By that point the street lights were on. The sky was dark. The café was closed. There was noise in the bars, but their doors were shut.

There were three guys fanned out around the Toyota. Out in the street, casting shadows, as if ready to repel a hostile attack. They were all wiry, but also tall. They all had big blunt hands.

They were all wearing denim and boots, one of them lizard.

Bramall stopped in the shadows.

Reacher and Mackenzie stopped behind him.

Mackenzie said, 'Who are they?'

'Cowboys,' Reacher said. 'Weaned on beef jerky and fried rattlesnake.'

'What do they want?'

'My guess is to scare us off. This kind of choreography usually involves that kind of thing.'

'Scare us off what? What are we doing?'

'We're poking around. We're asking questions about a woman who may be involved in some kind of unsavoury local business. We're making them nervous.'

'What do we do?'

'I need to consult with my senior partner about who goes first.'

Bramall said, 'Do you have a preference?'

'I think we should all go together. Maybe me one step ahead. But I want you to see their faces.'

'Why?'

'If I lose you can give the cops a description, from my hospital bedside.'

'Lose what?' Mackenzie said. 'I'm sure all they want to do is talk to us. I'm sure they'll be aggressive and unpleasant and so on, but I don't see how it necessarily becomes a fight. Unless we choose to make it one.'

'Where do you live?'

'Lake Forest, Illinois.'

'OK.'

'What does that mean?'

'This is already a fight. You can tell by the way they're standing. It's win or go home.'

'Did Scorpio send them?'

'That would be a logical assumption,' Reacher said. 'Technically the unsavoury local business is his. All the way up to Montana, apparently. But it's also the opposite of logical. If Scorpio can whistle up three good-looking cowboys at the drop of a hat, why would he have told a half-assed punk like Billy to shoot me from behind a tree? He would have told these guys instead. Maybe this is some kind of distant local subcommittee. Some kind of spontaneous democracy, that Scorpio knows nothing about.'

'You worried about them?' Bramall said. 'You mentioned losing.'

'Cowboys are the worst,' Reacher said. 'Not much I can do to them that a horse already hasn't.'

He stepped out of the shadows and walked ahead through the evening gloom. His heels were loud on the concrete. Behind him Bramall and Mackenzie caught up and closed the gap. They stepped off the sidewalk and crossed the street at an angle. They headed straight for the car.

The three guys moved, flowing outward to meet them, bunching up, one guy ahead and two behind, like a mirror image. Reacher was wrestling with the brawler's eternal dilemma, which was why not just take out the point man immediately? A surprise head-butt. Don't even stop walking.

Often the smart play.

But not always.

Reacher stopped and the cowboys stopped and they ended up about eight feet apart. That close Reacher thought they looked like three useful characters. Two could have been in their early forties, and the third could have been ten years younger. He was the point man. He had the lizard boots.

'Let me guess,' Reacher said. 'You're here to give us a message. That's fine. Everyone has the right to be heard. We'll give you thirty seconds. Start now, if you like. Speak clearly. Translate any local words or phrases.'

The guy with the lizard boots said, 'The message is go back where you came from. Ain't nothing for you here.'

Reacher shook his head.

'That can't be right,' he said. 'Are you sure you heard the message correctly? Generally speaking, folks out here like to welcome a stranger.'

The guy said, 'I got the message right.'

Nothing more.

Reacher said, 'Tell me when we get to the part where you say you'll kick our ass if we don't get going.'

The guy didn't answer.

Reacher watched him. Watched all of them. They weren't backing off. But they weren't coming on forward either. They were static. They were like a rookie squad when the plan stops working. Something had derailed them. Not Mackenzie. They were looking at her way more than they should, in the middle of a tense get-out-of-town showdown, but the looking was pure animal biology. Not recognition. Mostly it showed in their mouths.

The guy with the boots said, 'No one's ass needs to get kicked.'

'I agree,' Reacher said. 'Least of all mine.'

'But you should give it up.'

'Here's a counter-offer,' Reacher said. 'You don't mess with me, I won't mess with you.'

The guy nodded. Not like he agreed, but like he understood the sentence. Reacher said, 'Look, kid,' and beckoned the guy close, as if for a private word, like two world leaders sharing a confidence.

Reacher put his hand on the guy's elbow. A friendly gesture, inclusive, intimate, maybe even conspiratorial.

He squeezed.

He whispered, 'Tell whoever sent you this won't be like the

227

FBI or the DEA or the ATF. Tell whoever sent you this time it's the U.S. Army.'

The guy reacted. Reacher felt it in his elbow. Then he let him go, and the eight-foot gap opened up again. Reacher stood square on and up straight. His old professional pose. Sooner or later everyone's thoughts turned to violence. Better to deal with that upfront. Better to say, you have got to be kidding me. So he stood chin up, his full height, shoulders back, hands loose, not a circus freak, but a little bigger all around than a normal big guy, enough so they noticed. Plus the eyes, which he found most people liked, except he could blink and come back different, like changing the channel, from a happy show to some bleak documentary about prehistoric survival a million years ago.

Then suddenly he changed the channel again and smiled and nodded, in a shared, self-deprecating kind of a way, as if obviously two guys such as them could only be kidding around, and the other four would catch on eventually.

Always offer the other guy a graceful exit.

The guy in the boots took it. He smiled back, like they were just two old boys horsing around, which could happen any time, and especially in the presence of such a pretty lady. Then he turned around and led his guys away. Reacher crossed to the opposite sidewalk and watched them around the corner. They climbed in a huge crew-cab pick-up parked head-in by a fence. It backed out and took off. It turned left at the first four-way, and was lost to sight.

'See?' Mackenzie said. 'It didn't have to be a fight.'

Reacher said nothing. He stared at her. Then he stared at the corner, where the pick-up had turned.

Something wrong.

With the wrong thing.

He said to Bramall, 'Did you take interrogation classes with us?'

Bramall said, 'Only the semester with the rubber hoses.'

'We were taught the art of interrogation is mostly about listening. His language was weird. His choice of phrase. At the end he said we should give it up. What did that mean? Give what up?'

'Our quest,' Mackenzie said. 'Our search for Rose. Obviously. I mean, to give something up, you have to be doing it in the first place, and that's about all we've been doing. There's nothing else we could give up.'

'What category of person would care either way about our search for Rose?'

'All kinds. We could be treading on a lot of different toes.'

'What category of person might care most of all?'

Mackenzie didn't answer.

Tell whoever sent you.

In his mind Reacher heard General Simpson's voice, on the phone from West Point: *She might not want to be found.*

Then he thought no, that can't be right.

THIRTY

Reacher said, 'At the beginning the guy said there's nothing for us here. Then at the end he said the thing about giving it up. It was a politely threatening opening statement, and a politely threatening closing statement. But in the middle he declined to fight. I think for one particular reason. He was unsettled. There was a new factor he hadn't been briefed on. He was still getting used to it. He had been sent to kick ass, but all of a sudden he realized we were the kind of people who might kick back. He hadn't been warned about that. Which is weird, because every question we ever asked in this town, we asked it standing up. We weren't hiding. Who would send a guy with a message without giving him our descriptions?'

Mackenzie said, 'I don't know.'

'Maybe someone who never saw us standing up. Maybe someone who never really saw us at all, except as vague shapes slumped down in a car, as she speeded past on the dirt road. Hypothetically. It would be the car she remembered, not us. A black Toyota Land Cruiser, with Illinois plates. Maybe she asked three loyal friends to track it down, and run off whoever was in it. Because she doesn't want to be found.'

Mackenzie said, 'Do you think that's who they were?'

'I did for a moment. I told him the U.S. Army was coming, and he reacted. At first I thought he was impressed. Then later I thought no, his reaction might be because the person who sent him was also U.S. Army. He might have been surprised about the weird connection. He might not have known what it meant. He might have wanted to get away and report back.'

'To Rose,' Mackenzie said. 'Those were her friends.'

'Except they weren't,' Reacher said. 'They were nothing to do with Rose. We know for sure they never even met her. We know that because they didn't recognize you. How could they be friends with your twin without knowing who you were? That's why I wanted you close enough to see their faces. So they could see yours. They would have been staring at you, full of confusion. But they weren't.'

'So who were they?'

'I don't know,' Reacher said.

They drove back to the hotel. Bramall went straight upstairs. Reacher stayed out in the parking lot. He looked up at the night sky. It was black and huge and dusted with stars. They were very bright, and there were millions of them.

The American West.

Mackenzie came out and stood beside him.

She said, 'We could be in the wrong place entirely.'

Reacher was still looking at the sky.

'In the universe?' he said.

'In this state. No one recognizes me, which means no one has seen her. All we know is six weeks ago she was in some part of Billy's very large territory. When she traded her ring. Why conclude it was this part?'

'Porterfield's house. She wasn't there full-time. The roofer said so. Yet no one ever saw her heading for the turn. Which means she came and went from the other direction.'

'Two years ago.'

'Why would she move?'

'Her boyfriend died. People move, after a thing like that. It's a shock.'

'She did five tours in Iraq and Afghanistan. She's had worse shocks. She would have assessed the situation tactically. No one had ever seen her. There was no realistic threat vector against her current billet. Presumably it was a decent place. It had been good enough for Porterfield to come over. Why give it up? Replacing it would be tough.'

'I would move.'

'She would stay.'

'You know her better?'

'I know how a person lives through five tours.'

'I hope you're right.'

'We'll find out tomorrow,' he said. 'We know roughly where she is. She can't hide for ever.'

'I wanted to buy you a drink,' she said. 'To thank you. Since you won't let me pay you. But there's no bar in this hotel.'

'No need to thank me either,' Reacher said.

'I would have enjoyed it.'

'Me too, I guess.'

She moved away a couple of steps, and sat down on a concrete bench.

He sat down beside her.

She said, 'Are you married?'

'No,' he said. 'But you are.'

She laughed, short but soft.

She said, 'It was an unconnected question. Just purely out of interest. It wasn't a Freudian slip.'

'Tell me about Mr Mackenzie.'

'He's a nice man. We're a good match.'

'Do you have children?'

'Not yet.'

'Can I ask an unconnected question of my own? Just purely out of interest?'

She said, 'I suppose.'

'It's kind of weird, and I don't want you to take it the wrong way.'

'I'll try.'

'How does it feel to be so good-looking?'

'Yes, that's weird.'

'I'm sorry.'

'How did it feel when those guys wouldn't fight you?'

'Useful.'

'For us it felt like a minimum requirement. Our father had grandiose ideas.'

'The judge.'

'He thought he was living in a storybook. Everything had to be picturesque. On sunny days we ran around the woods in white cotton dresses. At first it was mostly about the hair. All sticking out. We looked like nymphs or fairies. We got the faces later. Then he started dreaming about who we would marry. We thought it was all pretty stupid. It was almost the twenty-first century, and we lived in Wyoming. We ignored it, mostly. But if I'm truly honest, deep down it made an impression. I was aware of it. It came to be part of who I am. Deep down I guess I believe being pretty is better than being ugly. Deep down I know I would choose to look like this again. I worry all that deep down stuff makes me shallow. To answer your question, that's how it feels.'

'Did Rose feel the same way?'

Mackenzie nodded.

She said, 'Rose liked things to be perfect. She was smart, and she worked hard, and mostly she made it happen that way. How she looked was the one thing she couldn't control. But happily she turned out OK in that department. I think deep down she took a lot of satisfaction from it. She wanted to be the absolute best, from any angle. She wanted to be the total package. And she was.'

'Why did she join the army?'

'I told you.'

'You told me she would shoot a guy even before he set a foot on her porch, whereas you would wait a moment longer. She could have stayed home and done that.'

'I feel like I'm on a psychiatrist's couch.'

'Lay back and pretend you're an actress in a movie. Suppose the hotel had a bar. By now you'd have bought me a cup of coffee. Black, no sugar. Or a beer, if they didn't have coffee. Domestic, in a bottle. You would have gotten some weird kind of white wine. Because of Lake Forest, Illinois. Right now we'd be at a table, talking. I would be asking why Rose joined the army, and you would be telling me.'

'She was looking for something worth it. It turned out the storybook was a lie. He wasn't the wise man of the county. At first we told ourselves certain practices were almost traditional. He was a lawyer, after all, and lawyers always get paid something. For an opinion, perhaps, prior to the filing. But there were whispers. If they were true, it was something worse. We never found out. Rose and I went to college. They sold the place and moved out of state. We were happy about it. It was a weird place for us. We always knew we were acting in someone else's play. And then the playwright himself turned out to be made up too. We reacted in slightly different ways. It left Rose needing something real, and me needing a real storybook. And we got both of them, I guess.'

Reacher said nothing.

'I'm going to bed now,' she said. 'Thanks for talking.'

She left him there, alone in the dark, leaning back on the concrete bench, looking at the stars.

At that moment, three hundred miles away at an I-90 truck stop not far from Rapid City, South Dakota, a guy in a beat-up old pick-up truck with Wyoming plates and a vinyl camper shell on the back turned into a service road he had been told led to a covered garage. His name was Stackley, and he was thirty-eight years old, a hard worker, maybe not where he should be in life, but always willing to try his best. He had been told the covered garage was half full with idle snowploughs and other winter equipment. He had been told the other half was empty. Plenty of space. He had been told they had it all to themselves.

He had been told there would be a guard at the door.

There was.

He slowed to a stop and wound down his window.

He said, 'I'm Stackley. You should have gotten a call from Mr Scorpio. I'm taking over from Billy.'

The guard said, 'You're the new Billy?'

'As of tonight.'

'Congratulations, Stackley. Drive in and park in slot number five. Forward, on a diagonal. Get out of the truck and open the tailgate.'

Stackley did what he was told. He drove in, to an echoing corrugated space the size of an aircraft hangar. On the left were ranks of giant yellow machines, mothballed for the summer. On the right was empty space. Someone had chalked diagonal parking bays on the concrete floor. They were numbered one through ten. One was at the far end, and ten was closest. Seven and three were already occupied. Seven had an old Dodge Durango with its rear door up. Three had a rusted Silverado with a roll-up cover on the bed. Stackley stopped his own truck short of it, and nosed into slot number five. He got out and lowered his tailgate.

Then he checked his watch and waited for midnight. No way to get there faster. The drivers in three and seven were waiting just like him. They nodded, not exactly friendly, not exactly wary. More like a simple same-boat acknowledgement of life's ups and downs. They were guys not unlike himself. Then an old black four-wheel-drive rolled in, and parked in the number six slot. The driver got out, and nodded all around, and opened his rear hatch door. Then he stood next to it, and waited. He looked just like the others. Late thirties, maybe not where he should be in life.

Five minutes later all ten slots were full. Ten vehicles, all in a line, ten tailgates raised or lowered, ten drivers waiting. The guard watched from the doorway. Stackley checked the time again. It was close to the top of the hour. He saw the guard take a call on his cell, saw him listen, saw him click off, and heard him call out, 'Two minutes, guys. It's nearly here.'

Two minutes later a white panel van drove in a door at the far end of the shed. It looked fresh off the highway. Stackley was reminded of a horse, hot and blowing after a long fast gallop. It nosed in and stopped almost at once, with its rear door level with the truck in slot number one. The driver got out and walked around and opened up. He pulled crisp white boxes from the back of his van, and the driver from slot number one took them from him, and twisted away to slide them in the bed of his pick-up.

The driver got back in the panel van and rolled it forward six or eight feet and stopped again. He repeated the unloading procedure with the driver from slot number two, stacking a teetering pile of crisp white boxes in the guy's arms, who then rotated away and dumped them in his own truck. Then the van moved on to the guy in slot number three, which gave the guy from slot number one the space to back out, and get straight,

236

and drive out the same door the van had come in through.

A slick operation, Stackley thought. And very well supplied. From where he was standing he could see what the guy was getting in slot number four. High-dose time-release oxycodone, and transdermal fentanyl patches, the latter in three different strengths. The boxes were made of high-gloss card, antiseptic white, pharmaceutical grade. They had brand names. They were the real thing. Made in America, straight from the factory.

Solid gold.

The panel van moved on, and Stackley stepped up. He got what Scorpio had told him he would get, which was the same volume Billy had been moving. Which was a decent quantity, for a rural area with not many people. He put his boxes in the camper shell. He put a blanket over them. Not that anyone could see in his windows. They were vinyl, all cracked and yellow. Better than a tint from a body shop.

He waited until the panel van was serving the guy in slot number seven, and then he backed up, and got straight, and drove out the door.

At that moment Gloria Nakamura was sitting in her dark and silent car, watching the alley that ran behind Arthur Scorpio's laundromat. She could see his back door. It had a rim of light, as if it was standing open an inch. It was a warm night, but not excessive. She had approached on foot, quietly, and looked through the gap, one eye, but she had seen nothing. The angle was too extreme. She walked back to her car. She tried to list the kinds of things that could make a room warm enough to want to open the door for extra ventilation. Tumble dryers, obviously, but not at midnight, and not in the back office.

Her cell phone rang.

Her friend in Computer Crimes.

Who said, 'We've lost Scorpio again. He must have gone

237

to a big box store and bought up a different batch of phones.'

Nakamura said, 'He's in his office. Probably making calls. I'm watching him right now.'

'We caught something that might have been him. You can kind of work out the triangulation backward. You can make a guess about what a signal would look like, if it was coming from his place. In which case he made a call to somewhere north of here, but not very far north. He just got a text back from the same number. It says, all good tonight including the new Billy.'

'When was this?'

'Right now. A minute ago.'

'Wait,' she said.

The rim of light around the door grew wider. Then died altogether. Arthur Scorpio stepped out into the night-time gloom. He turned back and locked the door. Then he walked to his car.

She said, 'Should I follow him?'

'Waste of gas,' her friend said. 'He's going home. He goes home every time.'

'What did it mean, the new Billy?'

'I guess something happened to the old Billy.'

Reacher, she thought.

Billy hadn't found a big enough tree.

Reacher was not a superstitious man. Not given to flights of fancy, or sudden forebodings, or existential dread of any kind. But he woke with the dawn, and he stayed in bed. He felt unwilling to move. He propped himself on the pillow and watched his reflection in the mirror on the opposite wall. A distant figure. One of those days. Not just a military thing. Plenty of other professions felt the same way. Sometimes you woke up, and you knew for sure, from history and experience and weary intuition, that the brand new day would bring nothing good at all.

THIRTY-ONE

They met in the lobby, at eight, the same as the day before. Bramall was in another new shirt, and Mackenzie was in another new blouse. By that point Reacher's clothes were two days old, but once again he had used a whole bar of soap in the shower. They walked up to the same diner, and got the same table. They ordered, and Bramall opened the subsequent conversation by asking for a consensus on a certain legal issue, which was that if they accepted Reacher's hypothesis, then by definition they would be looking exclusively at the old ranches off the dirt road west of Porterfield's place. Which was a very specific area of investigation. It was precise enough to put in a warrant. Normally a local law enforcement official would be notified. Not required, but expected. A professional courtesy.

'Are you cautioning me again?' Reacher said. 'Explicitly and every step of the way?'

'Sometimes things bear repeating.'

'Sheriff Connelly will claim Rose's place is a potential crime scene. He'll keep us out. Better not tell him. He still wants to know where Porterfield died. He'll chase any connection.'

'Rose's place is a crime scene,' Mackenzie said. 'No potential about it. Trespass, at least. Or illegal occupation of someone else's land. Wyoming has laws about that. Plus a stolen car, it seems. Plus narcotics, we assume. Plus however she's paying for them. I don't want the sheriff to be the one to find her. I can't let him put her in the system. I might never get her out again. We have to get to her first.'

'OK,' Bramall said.

They drove south to Mule Crossing, and turned at the bottle rocket billboard, and headed west on the dirt road. The first three miles were solitary. Then not long after they passed Billy's place they saw a tiny worm of dust on the far horizon. A vehicle on the road, coming towards them. Two miles away, maybe.

It's rare to see another car.

Like the neighbour told them.

'Pull over,' Reacher said. 'Park on the shoulder. If it's her, we'll want to follow. Or her friends. If it isn't, no harm, no foul.'

Bramall made the same manoeuvre he had made the day before, which was to stop dead in the traffic lane, and then back up carefully, like he was in a city garage. He ended up at ninety degrees exactly, which put the westward view through Mackenzie's window. She buzzed it down and buzzed it up, to wipe the dust away.

The cloud got closer. It was still early in the day. The air was still cool. No thermals yet. No haze, no shimmer. They could see the oncoming vehicle clearly. It was tiny in the distance. Dark in colour. Too far away to say more. Bramall kept the engine running. Transmission in gear, foot on the brake. Ready to go, either left or right.

The cloud got closer. The vehicle got clearer. It was old or dull or both. No flash of chrome against the morning sun. No gleam of paint.

240

'It's not the friends,' Mackenzie said. 'It's too small. Their truck was a huge thing.'

The cloud got closer. The vehicle was brown. Rust or dust or sunbaked paint. Hard to say. It was hugging the road. It looked wider than it was tall.

'It's not her,' Mackenzie said. 'It's too low. Hers was way more square.'

A minute later it blew on by, juddering and bouncing. No one they had seen before. Just a beat-up old pick-up truck, with Wyoming plates and a vinyl camper shell on the back. A guy at the wheel, late thirties maybe, looking straight ahead, paying no attention.

Nothing.

'Onward,' Reacher said.

They drove on west, past Porterfield's driveway. Then eleven miles later past his neighbour's, as inconspicuous as ever. They had six more places ahead, three on the left, three on the right. The plan was to look at them all, one by one. Simple in principle. Maybe not in practice. The big book of maps had shown neat brown rectangles for houses and barns, but Mackenzie said over the years such places could have built way more than that. Maybe with the proper permissions, maybe not. There could be garages, and smaller barns, and tractor barns, and wood stores, and generator huts, and hobby huts, and staff cottages, and guest cottages, and in-law cottages. Maybe even summer houses deep in the woods. A hundred places for Rose to hide, Reacher thought. But she would have chosen somewhere civilized. Not a cellar or an attic. Reasonably big. Not up a tree. Porterfield had come by from time to time.

Hope for the best.

The first driveway opening was on the left. They took it. It led to a track like the others they had seen, uneven, full of roots and rocks and gravel. The Toyota clawed onward, but slowly, like an

241

overweight goat. There were more conifer trees than before, and aspen, because the elevation was greater, and the terrain more mountainous. The track stayed in the woods all the way, except one bare spot on the shoulder of a hairpin turn, looking east. The pie lady's place was too far away to see. The nearest neighbour. The curvature of the earth was in the way. Then the track swung back into the woods, and wound ever onward and upward.

Six miles later they came out on a scruffy five-acre compound full of the kind of buildings Mackenzie had mentioned.

There was a main house, all log, old, modest in size, nearly matched in its dimensions by a separate log cottage, newer, some distance away. In between were log barns and wood stores and storage structures, some of them big enough for a decent truck, some of them as small as garden sheds or dog houses.

First thing they did was knock on the door. No one was home. Not a surprise. Reacher figured no one had been home for a couple of years. Maybe more. Every step on the porch raised a puff of dust, from the red sand, blown as fine as talcum.

Second thing they did was check the surrounding terrain. It was crusted smooth by wind and snowmelt. Undisturbed. Certainly there were no new tyre tracks. The Toyota's own stood out crisp and fresh and vivid. A total contrast. Mackenzie felt that was game over right there. She felt it was impossible to live in Wyoming without a vehicle. Therefore no sign of a vehicle meant no sign of life. Rose wasn't there. Not camped out in any of the various buildings. Reacher agreed. Bramall agreed.

They moved on.

They drove the six miles back down the track, and turned on the dirt road, and headed west again. One down, five to go. The next driveway would most likely be on the right.

'Look,' Bramall said.

He pointed.

Up ahead, still far away, another worm of dust. At its head, another vehicle coming towards them. It was rare to see another car? Not really. It was getting like Times Square.

They drove on, closing the gap.

It was a big vehicle coming.

'That could be her friends,' Mackenzie said. 'Same size of truck.'

'Block the road,' Reacher said. 'Make them stop.'

Bramall took his foot off the gas, and steered left, and straddled the crown of the road. He put his hazard flashers on, and blinked his high beams, and coasted on slowly to a hundred-yard stretch that had a knee-high rock ledge on one side, and a drainage ditch on the other. He came to a stop halfway between them. No way around. The engine idled. The hazard flashers clicked urgently. He pulsed the headlights, fast, slow, randomly, like Morse code.

Up ahead the big truck slowed. Behind it the dust cloud caught up momentarily, and then thinned out and fell away. The truck stopped three hundred yards west, in the middle of the road itself, like a long-distance showdown.

'More than one person,' Reacher said. 'They can't agree what to do. They stopped to talk it out.'

They waited.

Up ahead the truck moved forward. Slowly. Like cruising a parking lot. It rolled on. Two hundred yards away. One hundred. Fifty yards away.

It was the same crew-cab they had seen the night before. Huge size, a rumbling exhaust. Three people in it. The same guys. Reacher was sure of it. They came to a stop fifty feet away. Bramall turned off his hazard lights. For a second the tableau was frozen, two trucks facing off, close together, engines idling, on a narrow red ribbon in the middle of a vast version of nowhere.

Mackenzie got out of the Toyota.

Bramall moved to do the same, but Reacher put a hand on his shoulder.

243

'We need to talk,' he said.

'About what?'

'Your client. She's got a tough day ahead.'

'You know what's going to happen?'

'Unfortunately,' Reacher said. 'It's the only thing that fits.'

But Mackenzie was already turned around, miming impatience, so Bramall slid out to join her, followed by Reacher, three steps behind. From the crew-cab came the guy with the lizard boots, and his two companions. Six people altogether, in two groups of three, all of them eyeing the no-man's-land between their radiator grilles, their postures subject to ancient instincts. They met in the middle, five polite feet apart, safely longer than a dagger's thrust, another ancient instinct.

The guy in the boots said, 'The message hasn't changed.'

'I thought about that,' Reacher said. 'Seemed to me, if you boiled it right down, the main takeaway from the message was we should go back where we came from. Which makes it more of a suggestion, don't you think? Call it a request, to assume good manners on your part. And hey, plenty of requests are perfectly reasonable. We all know that. I would like to request a million dollars and a dinner date with Miss Wyoming. But the point of a request is that it can be declined. Respectfully, with great regret, and so on. But declined none the less. Which is what is happening here.'

'Unacceptable.'

'Get used to it. We're going to stick around, and if any of the actual landowners out here have a problem with it, I'm sure the state has laws that would allow them to seek a remedy.'

The guy said, 'Right now we're being nice about it.'

'My advice, you should keep on being nice about it. Even if we lose, we'll do some damage. Two of you will go to the hospital. Best case. But from what I've seen, I have to say, the best case looks unlikely. I don't think we'll lose. I think all three of you will go to the hospital.'

The guy paused a beat.

Then he said, 'OK, it was a request.'

Reacher said, 'I'm glad we got that cleared up.'

'There's nothing for you here.'

'Who made the request?'

'I'm not going to tell you. This whole thing is about privacy. You don't get it, do you?'

Reacher said, 'You got a phone?'

'Who do you want to call?'

'Take a picture. Video would be better. You got video on your phone?'

The guy said, 'I guess.'

'All we'll do is say our names. Maybe add a line of background. On your phone. Then you can take it back and show it to whoever it was who made the request. That would be fair to all concerned.'

'You might follow us there.'

'We promise we won't.'

'Why would we trust you?'

'You live in there somewhere. We know that. By now it's a one-in-five chance. We'll find you sooner or later. It's only a matter of time.'

The guy didn't answer.

'But I'd rather do it this way,' Reacher said. 'This way is better.'

The guy didn't answer. But eventually he nodded. One of the back-row guys stepped up with a phone. He held it horizontal between splayed fingers, and crossed his eyes, and said, 'Go.'

Mackenzie said, 'Jane Mackenzie.'

Bramall said, 'Terry Bramall, private detective from Chicago.'

Reacher said, 'Jack Reacher, ex-army, once upon a time CO of the 110th MP.'

The back-row guy lowered the phone.

Reacher said, 'We'll wait here.'

'Could be a couple hours,' the guy with the boots said. 'You got water?'

The other back-row guy carried bottles of water from their truck to the Toyota. Then they backed up and turned around and drove away. The dust cloud picked up behind them, turning, rising, falling, hanging in the air like evidence, showing the way they had gone, like a *whoosh* in a cartoon strip.

Bramall said, 'Do we follow?'

'No,' Reacher said. 'A professional courtesy. Not required, but expected.'

Mackenzie said, 'You know, don't you?'

'I know two things,' Reacher said. 'She lives here, and no one recognizes you.'

THIRTY-TWO

Bramall backed up to where the rock ledge petered out and the ditch filled in. He parked on the shoulder, a little tilted, facing west. Reacher drank a bottle of donated water, and walked back to the ledge, and sat in the sun. The last of summer. No one talked. Mostly Bramall sat in the car, nothing on his face, a man life had taught to be patient. Mostly Mackenzie stood alone, as far from the car as Reacher, but in the other direction. High overhead ravens circled, and looked, and thought not yet, and soared away.

In the end it was less than two hours. It was ninety-three minutes, which was an hour and a half and change. Far in the distance a smudge of dust kicked up, with a black dot in front of it, which grew larger, until they could see who it was. It was the three guys in their crew-cab. Back again. Like before, they stopped fifty feet out, and they climbed down, and they walked forward.

Reacher and Bramall and Mackenzie went to meet them. They all stopped, six people, groups of three, five polite feet apart.

The guy in the boots said, 'Just Mrs Mackenzie.'

Reacher waited.

Mackenzie said, 'No, all three of us.'

The guy said nothing.

Reacher waited again. For their plan B. He knew they had one. Stupid to come without.

The guy said, 'OK.'

He turned and walked back and the three of them climbed in their crew-cab again. Bramall and Mackenzie and Reacher climbed in the Toyota. The crew-cab backed up and turned, and drove away west. Bramall followed, hanging back, drifting left, drifting right, trying to miss the worst of the dust.

The crew-cab turned in on the second track on the right. Bramall followed. The track was wide, but the surface was bad. Roots, rocks, gravel. Up ahead the crew-cab bucked and bounced. Its tyres chirped and slid on stones worn smooth by time. There were trees left and right, mostly conifers, some gnarled by the wind, some stately. There were distant blazes of gold, mostly in the gulches and the gullies, where the aspen was happiest. The track went left and right, around trees, around rocks the size of cars, some of them piled high on top of each other, some of them overhanging.

After more than four slow miles the track came to a building. It was made of logs, and looked like a vacation cabin. Livable, but not for long. Not a permanent home. Dusty windows. Unoccupied. Maybe abandoned. The crew-cab didn't stop. It churned on by, all four wheels working, and half a mile later it passed another cabin just the same. Dusty windows, unoccupied. Maybe abandoned. Reacher figured they were in a compound, laid out like an old-fashioned vacation camp, with isolated accommodations in separate woodland clearings, all connected together by winding tracks like the one they were on, which in theory might sooner or later lead to some kind of central destination.

It did. The track came around the base of a wooded slope, and opened up on what looked at first like empty blue sky, but turned out to be a small plateau on the low slopes of a mountain, with infinite views north and east. There was a sprawling log house made of massive timbers. Not a commercial enterprise. Not an office or a camp clubhouse. Just the main family home. Maybe the cabins had been for their guests. Or for children and grand-children. Maybe great-grandchildren. Some kind of patriarch's dream. Maybe the owner had been a big man in the county.

The crew-cab didn't stop.

They followed it onward, away from the big house, along another winding track, around a long artful curve through the trees, and then another in the other direction, and finally they came out in another clearing, which had a cabin set high on a rock foundation, at the head of a small fissure or ravine, which crumbled away in a southwesterly direction, and which thinned the trees enough to show a narrow view of the empty plains and the distant horizon. From the front porch the magic hour before sunset would be spectacular. The house itself was made of logs, neat and plain, like a child's drawing, with a door in the middle, and a window on the left, and a window on the right, with a green metal roof and a chimney. Civilized, Reacher thought. Reasonably big. Not up a tree. Plus far from anywhere, comfort-ably concealed, as secret as could be, but with a view from the porch.

Why give it up?

Next to the house was a barn, with an open door.

Parked in the barn was an old SUV, an ancient model, boxy and battered and square, covered with rust and red dust so thick it looked baked on.

Up ahead the crew-cab stopped.

Bramall stopped.

The guy with the boots got out. He walked around to the Toyota's front passenger door, and he pulled it open.

He said, 'Mrs Mackenzie first.'

She got out. The guy led her down a beaten-earth path, and up the porch steps, to the door. He knocked, and she waited. A small figure, her face set, her hair tumbling everywhere.

The guy got a response from inside, and he opened the door, and held it, like a bellboy in a hotel. Mackenzie stood still for a second, and then she walked past him, and into the house. The guy closed the door after her, and came down off the porch, and walked back to his truck.

No sound.

No movement.

'Rose Sanderson is in there?' Bramall said.

'Yes,' Reacher said.

'You know this because you know two things.'

'Three altogether,' Reacher said. 'I didn't mention the extra one.'

'You know Rose lives here, and you know no one in town recognizes her sister.'

'And I know she won a Purple Heart.'

Bramall was quiet a long moment.

'It was a facial wound,' he said.

Reacher nodded.

'Had to be,' he said.

'How bad?'

'Bad enough that no one recognizes her sister. Bad enough she hides all the time. Bad enough she turns her face away. Bad enough she holes up in the bedroom when the roofer works inside.'

Bramall sat in the car, but Reacher was stiff from sitting. He got out to take a stroll. To loosen up, like he had at the comfort stop in Wisconsin. He took the ring out his pocket. The gold filigree, the black stone, the tiny size. *S.R.S. 2005*. Against the vast wilderness all around it looked impossibly delicate, and intricate, and finely wrought.

He walked to the lip of the ravine, and looked at the view. He could see fifty miles. A slice of Colorado, but mostly Wyoming. Thin clear air, immense tawny plains, spiky trees, rocky out-crops, hazy mountains. Nothing moving. He felt all alone on an empty planet. He could imagine hiding out there. Seeing no one. No one seeing him. Nowhere better.

She might not want to be found.

He turned away, and walked up to the garage, and took a look at the old SUV. It was an ancient Ford Bronco, the same make and model he rode in from Casper to Laramie, with the guy who turned logs into sculptures with chainsaws. That had been a basic vehicle, but Rose Sanderson's was plainer still. It was scoured back to bare metal by wind and sand. The metal looked like it had returned to some kind of primitive ore. It was scabbed and pitted, and dented here and there by minor collisions. No panel was straight. The tyres were worn. The front end smelled of gasoline.

He walked back to the Toyota. By that point Mackenzie had been in the house an hour. Bramall had his window down. For the air, presumably. Thin and clear, warm in the sun, cold in the shadows.

Bramall said, 'One of those days.'

'I woke up knowing,' Reacher said.

'A hands-on client is always a problem. I could have prepared her. I could have cleaned things up a bit.'

'I suppose your job is done now. Don't leave without me. I need a ride back to town.'

'After you give her the ring.'

'Not important any more. Not in the scheme of things. Mrs Mackenzie can pass it on.'

251

'I won't leave right away,' Bramall said. 'Partly because I think Mrs Mackenzie is about to request an extension to my contract. She's going to need some kind of help. If not from me, then at least she'll expect a ride to the hotel. Or the airport.'

'Does your phone work from here?'

'Two bars, if you face the ravine.'

'Which the house does. She could have called from here. When she said, shut up, Sy, I'm on the phone. It was either here or Porterfield's place. Had to be one or the other.'

'You plan on asking her much about Porterfield? I'm with the majority here. The thing with the bear is most likely bullshit.'

'That plan has changed. Because of the hands-on client. The story skipped straight to the big reunion. Rose won't talk to us now. It won't occur to her. Why would it? When your long-lost twin sister shows up at your door, you don't necessarily invite the cab driver in the house. You don't make small talk.'

'You wanted to know the story.'

'I got most of it,' Reacher said. 'I got to the part where it ends about twenty miles before the road runs out.'

Twenty minutes later the front door opened and Mackenzie stepped out on the porch. She turned and closed the door. She stood still, more than a minute, visibly breathing, deep and slow, in and out. Then she stepped down on the scrub path. She started walking. Bramall and Reacher got out of the car to meet her. She had been crying. That was clear.

At first she said nothing. It was as if she had lost the power of speech. Her lips moved and she made sounds, but no words came out.

'Take it easy,' Bramall said.

She took a breath.

She said, 'My sister would like to speak with Mr Reacher now.'

Reacher looked at her, first in surprise, then as if about to ask a question, which he didn't, because what could he say? Is she a mess? Was it worse than you expected?

She looked back at him, defeated, and she half shrugged and half nodded, as if saying yes and no to everything.

He walked down the scrub path and stepped up on the porch.

THIRTY-THREE

Reacher turned the knob, and opened the door, and stepped inside. He realized in his mind he was expecting some kind of an elaborate gothic vision, involving shrouded windows and darkness, with maybe a lone candle burning somewhere, and a vague figure talking softly behind a heavy veil. The reality was a bright sun-filled house made of shiny logs the colour of wildflower honey. The front door opened directly into the living room. It was small and neat and clean, but mostly empty. Nothing in it but two large armchairs, placed one either side of the fireplace, at comfortable and companionable angles.

Rose Sanderson was in the left-hand chair.

Below the neck she was her sister's double. No mistake. She sat in a chair the exact same way. Her resting posture was identical. The angle of her wrist. The spread of her fingers. The tilt of her waist. A replica.

Above the neck, not so much. Not any more. She was wearing a silver track suit top, with a tight hood, which was pulled up around her head. She had tightened the drawstring in front until only an oval of face was showing. On the left was a web of scar tissue, random and uneven, and on the right was a sheet of aluminium foil, oozing with some kind of thick ointment. She had pressed the foil to the shape of her head. Like half a mask.

A silvery colour.

She wasn't sweating. She wasn't trembling. Her eyes looked OK. Better than OK. Her eyes were the eyes of a person who felt deeply serene and contented.

She said, 'I want to ask you about something my sister said.'

Her voice was the same. Same note, same pitch, same volume. Reacher shook her hand and sat down in the empty chair. Up close he could see the left-hand part of her face was somehow reconstructed. It was stitched together from small fragments. The right-hand part was hidden under the home-made tinfoil poultice.

He said, 'What do you want to ask me?'

'My sister says you found my class ring in a pawn shop.'

'I did.'

'Therefore your involvement here was completely accidental.'

'It was.'

'But it strikes me you would say that anyway, whether or not it was true. And it strikes me my sister is the type of person who might believe it.'

'Where else would I find your ring?'

'A police evidence locker, maybe.'

'Who do you think I am really?'

'Maybe still the 110th MP.'

'That was a long time ago.'

'Then why did you mention it on the video?'

'So you would know I wasn't bullshitting about being in the army. No one would claim the 110th if they didn't have to.'

She nodded inside her hood. The foil on her face rustled and clicked.

Reacher said, 'Are you expecting a visit from the 110th MP?'

'Not specifically,' she said. 'Maybe someone like that.'

'Why?'

'A number of things.'

'Not me,' Reacher said. 'I'm just a guy, passing through. Nothing more.'

'You sure?'

'Promise.'

She nodded again, as if the matter was settled.

He took the ring from his pocket, one last time, and he handed it over. She rolled it in her palm, and looked at it from every direction. She smiled. The foil clicked, and a jagged hollow crease appeared in her left cheek, as if the structure of her face had collapsed. Maybe a weak suture.

She said, 'Thank you.'

He said, 'You're welcome.'

She said, 'I honestly thought I would never see it again.'

Then she gave it back.

'I would owe you forty dollars,' she said. 'Haven't got it right now.'

'It's a gift,' he said.

'Then I accept. Thank you. But not now. Would you hold it for me? Just a month or so. I could call when I'm ready.'

'You're worried you'll trade it away again.'

'Just recently everything has gotten so damn expensive.'

'Must be difficult making ends meet.'

'It is.'

'Is that why you're worried about meeting someone like the 110th MP?'

She shook her head.

'I'm not worried about what I do,' she said. 'No one is interested in my situation. They've given up on people like me.'

'Then why expect a visit?'

'Something different. I had a friend whose case is still open. Back burner I'm sure, but some work must get done. One day they'll have enough.'

'For what?'

'To take another look, I suppose. My working assumption is one day they'll send a guy. For a moment I hoped you were him, equipped with my ring as a stage prop. But apparently you're not him. That's OK. I just wanted to check. Would you ask my sister to come by again?'

Mackenzie was in the front seat of the Toyota. Her skin was pale. Her flawless face looked hyper-vivid, impossibly smooth, impossibly perfect. Reacher told her Rose wanted to see her again. She looked a question at him. He didn't know what she was asking. Maybe she was looking for some kind of general agreement it could have been worse. Some kind of optimistic thinking. Or not. He couldn't tell. He made an all-purpose don't-know expression, and she nodded, as if she understood. She got out the car and walked up the path to the house. She went inside again.

She closed the door.

Reacher took her place in the car.

He closed the door.

Bramall said, 'How was it?'

'Pretty bad,' he said. 'It hasn't healed.'

'What state was she in?'

'High as a kite.'

'On what?'

'Something she claims has just gotten very expensive. I guess she's still holding out for the good stuff. She's not in the toilet stall yet.'

'Agent Noble implied she would have to be by now. He claims he tracks every shipment.'

'Maybe he was out sick the day they taught real life. Nothing works a hundred per cent.'

'What did she want to speak with you about?'

'She's expecting some kind of investigator to show up one day, asking questions about Porterfield. She was disappointed I wasn't him. She thinks it's still an open case.'

Bramall didn't reply.

Reacher asked him, 'What did Mrs Mackenzie have to say?'

'Nothing good.'

'I woke up knowing.'

'Rose Sanderson got hit in the face by five pieces of shrapnel from an improvised explosive device concealed at the side of a road outside a small town in Afghanistan. The shrapnel appeared to be mostly small fragments of metal, probably off-cuts from a village-style engineering shop. The five pieces that hit her peeled her face off in chunks, and what stayed on was then badly abraded by smaller particles in the blast. But these days battlefield medicine is a miracle. They found most of the missing parts in her helmet and they sewed her back together again. Big name plastic surgeons, the whole nine yards.'

'But?' Reacher said.

'Two main problems,' Bramall said. 'I mean, OK, this was amazing work, no question. This was a definite KIA in Vietnam, and probably any other time in history, until the last few years. It was a virtuoso performance by the doctors. But great as it was, it was actually pretty lousy. It just can't be done. She was left with scars like a jigsaw puzzle. Nothing fits right. Nothing works right. She looks like a horror movie. And that's the good news.'

'What's the bad news?'

'The concealed explosive device was concealed in a dead dog. That's something they do out there. This one was maybe four days old. Getting ripe. The weather was hot. The blast drove rotting tissue and necrotic pathogens and all kinds of bad bacteria deep under the skin of her head. This all was four years ago, and she still can't get rid of the infection. She leaks pus. She looks like a monster twice over. She's in pain all the time.'

Reacher was quiet a long moment.

Then he said, 'No wonder she didn't tell her sister.'

'It's a subject they plan to discuss.'

'Why did she stop calling a year and a half ago?'

'They haven't gotten to that yet. But something to do with Porterfield, surely. What else could it be?'

Reacher got out of the car again. He wanted the air. He walked back to the edge of the ravine, and watched the distant view. It was like looking out through a narrow window. Behind him the house was cradled by wooded hills. He wondered who it belonged to.

He walked back to the crew-cab truck. All the windows were down. The three guys inside were laying back. Patient. Saving energy. They knew it was all going to take as long as it took. Maybe a cowboy thing.

The guy in the boots looked up.

Reacher said, 'You told me you were being nice about it. I agree. You're being very nice about the whole thing. That should be placed in the record.'

The guy moved his head, as if accepting the compliment.

Reacher said, 'How did it start?'

'We needed a place to live. We stumbled on this compound. Rose had already claimed it. But she let us stay. She helped us settle in. We helped her with a couple of things. We got kind of protective, I guess. She doesn't like people to see her.'

'How long ago was this?'

'Three years. Rose was just out of the army. She was just moving in.'

'Who owns this place?'

259

'Someone who hasn't cared to visit in three years at least.'

'You must have known Sy Porterfield.'

'I guess we met him a bunch of times.'

'What did you make of the story with the bear?'

'I guess we thought it was what anyone would do.'

'What did Porterfield do for a living?'

'We never enquired. All we knew is he seemed to make her happy.'

'She's high as a kite right now.'

'Do you blame her?'

'Not one little bit. But I worry about her supplies holding up.'

'We can't discuss that with you. We don't know who you are.'

'I'm with her sister.'

'Not really. The other guy is the detective she hired. No one understands who you are.'

'I'm not a cop,' Reacher said. 'That's all that matters. I don't care about that stuff. But she could have a problem, now Billy is gone. That's all I'm thinking.'

'You know who Billy was?'

'Snowplough driver. Especially good in powdery conditions.'

'You were a cop back in the day.'

'Everyone was something back in the day. I'm sure you can walk past a cow without feeling the need to drive it to the rail-head. Billy ain't coming back. I hope Rose will be OK. That's all I'm saying.'

The guy said, 'They already got a replacement for Billy. He was by here this morning. His name is Stackley. Seemed like a nice enough guy. Reminded me of a cousin I got in insurance. So all is right with the world again. It's back to business as usual.'

Reacher said, 'What is she buying?'

'Oxy and fentanyl patches.'

'We talked to a guy who said that's a thing of the past.'

'It's getting expensive.'

'He said it should be getting impossible. Where is it coming from?'

'It's the regular stuff. Same as always. In the white boxes, with the brand names. Made in America, right out the factory door. You get to where you can tell the difference.'

'You guys like it too?'

'A little bit, now and then. To take the edge off, time to time.'

'I heard that kind of thing was hard to get now. Maybe I was misinformed.'

'You weren't,' the guy said. 'Matter of fact it is hard to get now. Most places very hard. But not here. Which gives you all a big problem. I don't know what your plans are now, but you need to get one thing straight from the get-go. Rose won't move from here. Not an inch, not in a million years. How could she? She's hooked up here. You don't know what that means to a person. Look at it from her point of view.'

THIRTY-FOUR

The magic hour was the last part of the sun's daily travel, like a sixty-minute farewell performance, when it was low in the sky, shining sideways through the atmosphere, which reddened its colours and lengthened its shadows. Reacher sat on the porch step and watched the tawny plain go gold, then ochre, then chili-pepper red. Bramall was below him, on a rock at the edge of the ravine. The guys from the crew-cab were sitting in the dirt, leaning their backs on trees.

The door opened and Mackenzie stepped out.

Reacher stood up, and she came down the steps past him, on to the path through the scrub. Meanwhile the guys from the crew-cab all got up and dusted themselves off. Mackenzie met them at the end of the path. She shook their hands, one by one, and thanked them for caring about her sister.

Then she said to Bramall, 'Back to the hotel.'

Mackenzie felt weird, she said, leaving her sister where she was, but Rose would have it no other way. She liked it there, she said,

262

and she had everything she needed. She refused to leave, categorically, even for one night, even to see a doctor. She refused even to consider going to the hospital, or the Veterans' Administration, or looking at a clinic, or a rehab centre, or living in Lake Forest, Illinois.

'Give her time,' Bramall said.

They made the turn at the old Mule Crossing post office, and drove back to Laramie on the two-lane. They ate in town, and drove back out to the hotel, where Bramall parked and said goodnight. Reacher stayed out in the lot again. The night sky was still there. Still huge and black and dusted with millions of bright stars. Microscopically changed, he supposed, since the night before. But not because of his tiny dramas. It was completely indifferent.

Mackenzie came out and sat down on the bench.

He sat down beside her.

She said, 'She's only halfway addicted.'

He said, 'I had a brother. Not a twin, but we were close growing up. Now I'm asking myself, if this was him, what would I want from people? Something polite, or something uncomfortable? I'm not making a point here. I really don't know. Help me out.'

'I want the truth,' she said.

'She looked a lot more than halfway addicted to me.'

'I meant her reasons. She's in pain. Partly she needs it. She's not doing it just for fun.'

'What's with the aluminium foil?'

'The infection. She scrounges up antibiotics if she can, and grinds them down, and mixes them with antiseptic salve from the first-aid aisle. She spreads it on the foil like butter. If she can spare one, she mixes in an oxycodone pill.'

'Not the life she expected.'

'You knew last night. When you asked how we felt about being pretty.'

'It was the only thing that fit.'

'She's doing OK, I think.'

'Me too.'

'I even liked the house, in a way. I was surprised. For some reason I thought it would be dark inside.'

'Me too,' he said again.

'Now tell me what happens next.'

'I wish I knew.'

'Seriously,' she said. 'I need to figure out how to handle this.'

'She's doing OK because she gets high every day. You could give her money, I suppose, and most likely she would continue to do OK, as long as this new guy Stackley keeps on showing up on time, and as long as the Boy Detective doesn't plug the last leak and put everyone out of business.'

'Which could happen.'

'Nothing lasts for ever,' Reacher said. 'Her situation out there is not as secure as she thinks it is.'

'Even if it was, I couldn't leave her there.'

'How are you going to move her out?'

'That's what I'm asking. I'm open to ideas.'

Reacher said, 'Is she getting no treatment at all?'

'At the beginning she was in the hospital a whole year. She ran out of patience. She hasn't seen anyone since. She won't. She refuses to.'

'Instead she lives quietly and self-medicates. She does it well enough we both just agreed she's doing OK. We should respect that. The only way to get her out of there is promise her the exact same thing someplace else. Or even better. As many pills and patches as she wants. You would have to find the right kind of doctor. You would have to find her a quiet place to live. You would have to promise her no hassle. And you would have to mean it. Nothing for a year at least. Which is OK. This kind of thing is a very long game.'

'She doesn't like people to see her.'

'Then she's better off here than Illinois.'

'They don't have the right kind of doctors here.'

'How big is your yard?'

'I think six acres.'

'You could build her a cabin. With a high fence. You could throw her prescriptions over. Leave her alone for a year. See what happens.'

'So the only way to help her is to be a better pusher.'

'The Boy Detective said we shouldn't underestimate the appeal of an opiate high. I'm sure she's real pleased to see you, but you should assume getting what she needs right now feels more important to her.'

'That's tough to accept. Not about me. That she's so far gone.'

'She needs you on her side right now. Proving that is your job one. Don't disapprove of her. What choice does she have? Just bite your lip and shovel pills down her throat. Don't forget she's tough underneath. She's a combat veteran. Sooner or later she'll realize she needs to shape up or ship out, and then she'll want to talk. To you especially, because you were the one who treated her right. That's when you can help her.'

'I hope I can.'

'There are books about it. You can spend the first year reading.'

'Did you take classes?'

'Not enough curriculum time,' Reacher said. 'In the MPs it was all rubber hoses and nightsticks. But the medics had good people. Psychiatrists in uniform. The weirdest thing you ever saw. Always some inflated rank. I knew a couple. They would tell you a bunch of things.'

'Like what?'

'They would tell you to figure out what's upsetting her deep down.'

265

'That's obvious, surely.'

'But they're shrinks, and they're in the army. They would say a person can have two things wrong at once. They would say they know what infantry officers are like. They would want more detail on the incident with the roadside bomb.'

'Why?'

'Specifically they would want to know if there were other American casualties. If so, they would assume Rose is taking it hard. She was an infantry officer. She got her people killed. The facts don't count. She could have been already wounded and unconscious before anything else even happened. Doesn't matter. They're her people. It's her fault. That's how infantry officers think. Small words, but they mean a lot to those guys. The top boy at West Point said she led her soldiers well. That's the hall of fame right there. You could put that on your tombstone. She led her soldiers well. An infantry officer couldn't hear finer words than those. Because it's hard to do. Ultimately it works because you make an unspoken promise not to get them killed. It becomes a thing in your head.'

Mackenzie said, 'She won't talk about it.'

Reacher said, 'The shrinks would also want to know the status of the mission. Was it a routine kind of thing ordered from above? Or was there an element of initiative involved? In which case, they would assume she was taking it even harder. She led her soldiers into harm's way, literally.'

'They're shrinks. You said so yourself. They overcomplicate things. If you hear hoof beats, you look for horses, not zebras. Rose is upset deep down because someone stuck her face in a blender and smeared it with dog shit.'

Reacher said nothing.

Mackenzie said, 'What?'

'I'm sure that's most of it. How could it not be?'

'But?'

'I think like a cop. I can't help it. Her final rank was major. The guy at West Point told me on her last tour she was doing a pretty big job. Which for a major means desk time and briefings. She had limited opportunities to get out and about. Why would she choose to go look at the side of a road outside a small town? She wouldn't. She was bored with that kind of stuff four tours ago. She went because her command presence was required. She had some kind of operation running. She had captains below her, and lieutenants below them, all covering their own ass, so we can be certain the protective detail around her was thick on the ground. We can be certain lots of people were involved. Was she the only one hurt? Unlikely, but we don't know for sure. The files are sealed. Which means most likely her operation was a failure. Perhaps with multiple U.S. casualties. So her face may not be all of it.'

Mackenzie said, 'I don't know if you're trying to cheer me up, or bring me down.'

'It's all bad,' Reacher said. 'Whichever way around. Let's not be Pollyanna. But she had a boyfriend. Sy Porterfield. There were two dents in the bed. That says something about how she sees herself. It's a glimmer of what might be possible.'

'She won't talk about him. I told her about the comb you found, and she didn't deny it. She said it was safer I didn't know. Whatever that means.'

'She thought I was an investigator come to ask questions about him.'

'No one believes the bear story.'

'Which could be an additional traumatizing factor. She really doesn't know what happened to her boyfriend. She really isn't sure which would be worse, the bear or not. The shrinks would throw a party. They would tell you it's a whole big mixture of things.'

'In other words it could be worse than just her face.'

'That would be a glass half empty type of interpretation. But it's why I asked if you wanted polite or uncomfortable.'

'I said truth. You're speculating.'

'Agreed,' Reacher said. 'And I sincerely hope I'm wrong about all of it.'

She was quiet a beat.

Then she said, 'You're a kind man.'

'Not a word that gets used often.'

'Thank you for being here.'

'My pleasure,' he said, and it was. It was a concrete bench in a blacktop lot, but a yard above the ground it was spectacular. The stars were better than he had ever seen. The air was cool and soft and hummed with silence. Beside him on the bench was a woman who looked like the back of a shiny magazine. He figured she would feel firm and lithe and cool to the touch, except maybe the small of her back, which might be damp.

She asked him, 'Do you remember what I said about my husband?'

'You said he's a nice man and you're a good match.'

'You have a very precise memory.'

'It was yesterday.'

'I should have told you he keeps a mistress and ignores me.'

Reacher smiled.

He said, 'Good night, Mrs Mackenzie.'

She left him there, the same as the night before, alone in the dark, on the concrete bench, looking at the stars.

At that moment a mile away, Stackley clicked off a phone call and parked his beat-up old pick-up truck in a lot behind an out-of-business retail enterprise three blocks from the centre of town. Earlier in his life he had favoured expensive haircuts, and one time when waiting in the salon he had read a magazine that said success in business depended entirely on ruthless control of costs. Thus wherever possible he slept in his truck. Hence the camper shell. A motel would take what he made on two pills. Why give it away?

The old gal across the Snowy Range had bought a box of fentanyl patches, but he had given her one he had already opened, an hour before, very carefully, so he could skim out a patch all his own, for his pocket, for later. The old gal would never notice. If she did, she would assume she was too stoned to count right. A natural reaction. Addicts learned to blame themselves. The same the world over.

He took scissors from his glove box, and he cut a quarter-inch strip off the patch, and he slipped it under his tongue. Sublingual, it was called. Another magazine in the same salon said it was the best method of all.

Stackley couldn't argue.

At that moment sixty miles away, in the low hills west of town, Rose Sanderson was putting herself to bed. She had pulled down her hood, and taken off her silver track suit top. Under it was a T-shirt, which she took off, and a bra, likewise. She peeled the foil off her face. She used her toothbrush handle to scrape excess ointment off her skin. She buttered it back on the foil. With luck she might get one more day out of it.

She ran her sink full of cool water. She took a breath, and held her face under the surface. Her record was four minutes. She came up and shook her head. Her hair had grown back in. She had cut it the week before West Point. She had to get a hat on. There were regulations. She had kept it short for thirteen years. Now it was back. With coarse threads of grey. Like barbed wire in a hay bale.

The least of her problems.

She took scissors from her cabinet, and she cut a quarter-inch strip off her patch, and she stuck it behind her bottom lip. A maintenance dose. It would keep her asleep all night. It would keep her warm, and gentle, and relaxed, and at peace, and cradled, and happy.

At that moment three hundred miles away, in Rapid City, South Dakota, Gloria Nakamura was sitting in her car, watching Arthur Scorpio's back door. Once again it was showing a rim of light. It was propped open an inch. Another warm night. He had been in there more than two hours. She had been working on her list of what might make a room hot enough for extra ventilation. Electronic equipment, maybe. She knew a guy with a home cinema. He had a closet full of black boxes, that gave out a penetrating kind of heat. It was thin and fierce and smelled faintly of grease and silicon. The guy had a fan in there, whirring all the time.

Her cell phone rang.

Her friend in Computer Crimes.

Who said, 'Give me a yes or no answer. Do we assume it was Scorpio who got the text message about the new Billy?'

She said, 'We couldn't take it to court.'

'That wasn't a yes or no answer.'

'Yes, we can assume it was Scorpio.'

'The same signal just got a voice mail from a tower in Laramie, Wyoming. From someone by the name of Stackley. He called Scorpio Mr Scorpio. He said all was well, but there were stories about two men and a woman poking around, asking questions. One of the men was a very big guy and they were in a black Toyota.'

Reacher, she thought.

Her friend said, 'Then Scorpio called back and left a voice mail in return. He told this guy Stackley the same thing he told Billy. He wants the big guy out of the picture. He was ordering a homicide again.'

'Wait,' Nakamura said.

Scorpio's door was opening. He stepped out to the alley and turned back and locked up. Then he headed for his car.

'I'm going to follow him,' she said.

'Waste of gas,' her friend said.

She clicked off and started her motor.

Scorpio went home.

He went home every time.

At that moment six hundred miles away, in a small town named Sullivan, in the Oklahoma panhandle, Billy ran a red light. He was in a six-hundred-dollar Ford Ranger pick-up truck, more than twenty years old. He was out to get a second six-pack. He was mildly buzzed from the first. His pal from Montana was back at the motel, waiting in the room. The next day in the afternoon they were due to meet a guy who had connections in Amarillo, Texas. The employment situation was looking good.

The light he ran had a cop parked on it. The guy lit up his roof bar and yelped his siren once. Billy froze and kept on rolling. Dumb. He had nothing to hide. The buzz, maybe, but hey, this was the panhandle. A couple of beers was probably a minimum requirement to get behind the wheel. Apart from that he was respectable. He couldn't run anyway. Not in a six-hundred-dollar piece of shit.

He hit the brake and pulled in at the kerb.

Like all humans the cop was prey to small subliminal emotions. Billy's failure to stop right away kind of pissed him off. He found it cocky and disrespectful. Normally he might just have pulled alongside and dropped his far window and told the guy to take it easy. But now he felt a hot bite of annoyance, and it kind of puffed him up and set his jaw, and he found himself launching into the whole big performance.

He pulled up behind the pick-up, and left his lights flashing.

271

He put on his hat. He counted to twenty and got out the car. He unlatched his holster and put his hand on his gun. He walked forward slowly, and stopped level with the old Ford's load bed, and he called out loud and clear, 'Sir, please step out of the vehicle.'

The door opened.

Billy got out.

'I'm sorry, sir,' he said. 'I guess I was daydreaming. I guess it was a good thing no one else was around.'

The cop was pretty sure the air coming off the guy smelled like beer.

He said, 'Licence.'

Billy dug in his pocket and handed it over.

The cop said, 'Sir, please wait there.'

He walked back to his car, as slowly as he could. He got in. He had a computer terminal on a swan neck, bolted to the tunnel near the shifter. Courtesy of the last new mayor. All kinds of budget promises.

He typed in Billy's details.

Up came a code from the western division of the federal DEA.

He got out of the car again. He walked back to Billy, as slowly as he could, and when he got there he spun him around, and banged his head on the old Ford's roof, and cuffed his hands behind his back.

THIRTY-FIVE

They met in the lobby at eight in the morning. After the diner they drove to the grocery store, where they bought stuff for Rose. Food, mostly, some of it wholesome, some of it not, but also soap, and a pair of pink socks, and a new comb with wide-spaced teeth, and a paperback book. The kind of little thing that got left out, when a household budget came under pressure.

They bought two of every type of antiseptic cream.

Bramall's phone rang in the checkout line. He looked at the screen and said, 'It's Special Agent Noble, from the DEA.' He answered and listened, and made appreciative but non-committal noises. At one point he left a split-second gap, as if he should be saying something, but wasn't. As if he was choosing not to. One federal guy playing chess with another. Reacher knew the signs.

Bramall clicked off and said, 'Billy was arrested last night in a small town in Oklahoma. Noble questioned him by phone. So far he's denying everything. Including he claims he doesn't know anyone named Rose Sanderson, or where she's located.'

'Yesterday's news,' Mackenzie said. 'We don't need Billy any more.'

The drive back to Rose's place was a typical Wyoming time warp journey. In their minds they didn't have far to go. It was a purely local trip. Mule Crossing was just down the road, and Rose lived just west of the turn. But in reality it took two whole hours to get there. The long, long two-lane, and then the dirt road, slower than they wanted through the infinite space, and then the rutted four-mile driveway. The sky was the colour of steel. Not a threat, but a reminder. Winter was on its way.

The three cowboys met them where the track came out of the woods in the final clearing. They were doing nothing. Just waiting and watching, strung out in a ragged line thirty yards short of the house. Like a defensive perimeter. *We got kind of protective.* Bramall slowed down, in a no-threat kind of way, and eased around to where he had parked before. Reacher unloaded the groceries and stacked them on the porch. Mackenzie carried them into the house. She closed the door behind her.

The clearing went quiet.

Reacher saw Bramall at the edge of the ravine. A small neat man, in a dark suit, with a collar and a tie. He should have looked out of place in the wilderness. But he didn't. He looked perfectly at home. He was that kind of guy. He was thinking about something. Reacher could see it in his face. A problem. A struggle. Some kind of an ethical dilemma.

Reacher was pretty sure what it was.

Billy.

Not yesterday's news.

Tomorrow's news.

Reacher walked over to where Bramall was standing.

He said, 'I know,' in what he hoped was a sympathetic way.

274

'You know what?' Bramall said back.

'You feel bad you didn't tell the Boy Detective we found Rose without Billy's help.'

'Would you have?'

'No,' Reacher said. 'Too much information. What happened in Oklahoma?'

'He ran a red light. The system kicked out his name and his face. Noble called him and tried to get some answers out of him. The question is why he did that. It could have been purely a courtesy on our behalf, because he was sympathetic to Mrs Mackenzie's situation. She asked him if he could let her know, after all. Maybe he was just going through the motions for her. Or maybe not. Maybe he was getting real. Maybe he figured since he got handed Billy on a plate anyway, he might as well write up a comprehensive report. It would scratch an itch, after all. He doesn't like the ghost network. In which case, if he knew where Rose was, the book says his first logical move should be question her as a witness, or arrest her for buying illegal narcotics, or both. This is not the time for me to risk either outcome. Not right now. For many reasons. One of which is my client's stated preference to keep her sister out of the system. So I didn't tell him. And yes, I feel a little bad about it. I prefer not to conceal things from people like him.'

'Was your contract extended?'

'For the duration of the current crisis.'

'How long will that be?'

Bramall glanced up at the house.

He said, 'I'm not an expert.'

'How long will Billy hold out?'

'If Noble gets real?'

'Even if he doesn't, I guess. Billy could say something stupid at any time. Some little slip. The Boy Detective might prick up his ears. There's a big prize, don't forget. Folks who can tell the difference say what they're getting out here is the real deal. Made in America. Straight out the factory door. Whole shipments of it, in the proper boxes. Which the Boy Detective thinks is impossible. He'll take it personally. He'll hunt it down. He'll plug the last leak. This is not the time to risk cold turkey either. I'm sure your client's other stated preference is to keep her sister out of the locked ward in the hospital.'

Bramall glanced up at the house again.

He said, 'I assume the kind of decisions they're making can't be made fast.'

'Normally I guess not,' Reacher said. 'But this time they can't be made slow, either.'

'How long have we got?'

'My instinct would be get out of here within two or three days.'

'Until then we should say nothing to Noble.'

'Easy for me,' Reacher said. 'But you have a licence from the state of Illinois.'

'Tell me about it. While simultaneously having credible evidence a man named Arthur Scorpio, in Rapid City, South Dakota, which is presumably comfortably inside the western division, is currently coordinating a network invisible to the DEA, but that extends at least into Wyoming and Montana, and that uses some kind of last-surviving loophole source, like El Dorado, the discovery of which would be hailed as a major triumph and the capstone of an outstanding regional success story. I could hand it over on a plate. In fact I have a professional obligation to do exactly that. If and when I believe a crime has been or is about to be committed. And on top of all that I have obvious ethical obligations. I should tell Noble everything I know.'

'But not yet,' Reacher said.

'Because the illegal supply must be allowed to continue. At

276

least until my client arranges an alternative semi-legal supply somewhere else.'

'Relax,' Reacher said. 'You're retired.'

'Second career.'

'Fewer rules than the first.'

'But more rules than you.'

'I have rules,' Reacher said. 'I have plenty of rules. One of which says a wounded veteran gets the benefit of the doubt. But another of which says always be gone before the government arrives. So I agree. We need to thread the needle.'

The house stayed quiet and the door stayed closed. Reacher borrowed Bramall's phone, and carried it to the head of the ravine, where it could soak up maximum signal.

He dialled the number he remembered.

The same woman answered.

'West Point,' she said. 'Superintendent's office. How may I help you?'

'This is Reacher,' he said.

'Hello, major.'

'I need to speak with General Simpson.'

'Wait one, major.'

The supe came on and said, 'Developments?'

'We found her,' Reacher said.

'Condition?'

'We have concerns,' Reacher said. 'The Purple Heart was a severe facial wound. She has dependency issues with the pain-killers we gave her in the hospital. She has no visible means of support.'

'Can I help?'

'At this point only with information. I need to know which boxes she checks. In terms of her mental state. Might help us with what happens next.'

'What information?'

'It was a roadside IED. I want to know more about it. Specifically why she was there, and who else was hurt or killed.'

'I'll try.'

'And I want to know more about Porterfield. She said it's safer if we don't. I'm not sure what that means. Who was this guy? All we know is fourteen years ago he was a brand new butter-bar lieutenant who didn't make the first cut. What part of that twelve years later got him so much attention?'

'Sanderson must know.'

'I can't push for an answer. The emotional situation here is delicate.'

'Did you give back the ring?'

'She asked for a layaway. Until happier times ahead.'

'Will they come?'

'Maybe,' Reacher said. 'The first part will be hardest.'

He gave the phone back to Bramall. Then they waited, ending up in the same places as the day before, Reacher on the porch step, Bramall on a rock at the edge of the ravine. The cowboys were all grouped together in the mouth of the track, standing around, as if they were expecting someone to show up, sometime soon.

Stackley was a man who believed data and information should be put to work at once. It was rule one in the modern business environment. Or maybe rule two, after ruthless control of costs. Different magazines didn't always agree. He played it safe by working both ends. Every morning, right there in his truck, before he got up, he read his overnight texts and played his voice mails. Therefore right away that day he knew the big guy was supposed to exit the picture. He spent his early calls working out how to do it. He was a man who believed delegation was the hallmark of a successful executive. It was rule one in the modern environment. Or two, or three. Or whatever. But it was definitely up there.

By the time he turned at Mule Crossing, Stackley had decided on his strategy. By the time he passed what he had learned was his predecessor Billy's place, he had decided on the bait. By the time he passed what he had learned used to be a guy named Porterfield's place, he had decided on exactly where to offer it.

He drove on, many miles, and turned in on the next-but-one track on the right, ahead of what he knew from the morning before was a slow four miles over roots and rocks. Not good for his truck. But he was a man who believed productivity depended on the maximum use of all fixed assets. It was the number one rule in the new environment.

Behind him Reacher heard the front door open, and he stood up and turned in time to see Mackenzie step out of the house. In the shadows behind her was a small vague figure. A silvery colour. Mackenzie closed the door on it and came down the path. She glanced at the cowboys, still all the way over at the mouth of the track. She headed for Bramall, and Reacher followed. She chose a rock and sat down on it. Reacher chose one six feet away. Bramall used the one he had used before. They looked like three castaways on a rocky shore, making a plan. The endless plain behind them looked as wide as an ocean.

Mackenzie said, 'We're making progress, I think. More than I thought we would so soon. That is, if in fact she means what she's saying. Sometimes I think she's agreeing to things far too easily. Because they're about the future. She knows nothing will change today. That seems to be the limit of her horizon. But every day becomes today when you get there. She needs to take this seriously. She needs to understand the day will come when I have to move her.'

'When will that be?' Bramall asked.

'New accommodations and the right kind of doctor are the essential components. We can get those searches started immediately, while we're still waiting here. As soon as tomorrow, if we want. By the way, I decided to move in. I think we all should. There are empty houses here. The drive back and forth to the hotel is ridiculous.'

Bramall said, 'Move in?'

'More efficient, don't you think? If I'm close by all the time, I can look after her all the time. Maybe in the end we might get this done faster.'

Bramall said, 'We don't know who owns this place.'

'Someone who hasn't shown up for three years. Why would they show up now? We won't be here very long.'

Bramall said, 'How long, do you think?'

'Depends entirely on the accommodations and the doctor.'

'Best guess?'

'Mentally I'm allowing a month,' she said. 'Worst case two.'

Up at the head of the driveway there was engine noise and tyre scrub and the cowboys stood back. Reacher saw a beat-up old pick-up truck drive out of the woods. It had a plastic camper shell in the bed. He had seen it before. On the dirt road. Driving by, with a guy at the wheel, late thirties maybe, looking straight ahead, paying no attention.

Mackenzie turned to see.

'This must be Stackley,' she said. 'Rose hoped he would come by again today.'

THIRTY-SIX

Stackley saw the cowboys step back. He recognized them from the day before. The same three guys. Partly they were moving to get out of his way, and partly to form up like a welcoming committee. Or like a guard of honour. Deep down Stackley enjoyed dealing dope. Customers were so grateful and enthusiastic. Not like some jobs he had worked.

Then beyond the cowboys he saw the dusty black Toyota. Right there. The actual truck he had called Scorpio about. He had described it, parked on the shoulder of the dirt road, like a cop, with the two men and the woman in it, who folks said had been asking questions. One of the men was big.

Stackley had called it in, and had he gotten his reply.

He looked at the house. All quiet. The door was closed.

He looked right, at the far tree line.

Nothing there.

He looked left, at the rocks near the edge of the ravine.

Three people sitting on them.

An old man in a suit.

A pretty woman.

And a very big guy.

Stackley stopped his truck in the mouth of the driveway. He paused a second, and then shut it down. He got out and led the eager cowboys back to the camper door. Where he did something he never did. He let them see inside. He pulled back his blanket a little too far, as if carelessly, and he exposed the boxes, dozens of them, most still shrink-wrapped, some opened but still mostly full, all white and clean and printed with American writing. Behind his shoulder he felt the hum of desire. Which was good. He needed his new pals to feel what he had to offer.

He huddled them close, and he told them what they could do for him, and what he could do for them. Delegation. Rule one in the modern environment. Especially against a guy so big.

Reacher saw them cluster at the back of the truck. They all looked inside. Inspecting the merchandise, maybe. They seemed happy with the quality, or the quantity, or both. They reminded Reacher of his mother, a lifetime ago, on a foreign base somewhere, huddling on the kerb with the other army wives, when the fish truck came to call. Then Stackley moved in close, and started on a big discussion. The price, maybe. Important to them all, in different ways.

Mackenzie said, 'Rose isn't coming out of the house. I guess her friends are buying for her. Maybe they always do. Which would mean Billy never saw her. He couldn't have helped us anyway.'

Reacher said, 'We need to talk about Billy.'

'Why?'

'He's in the system now. The Boy Detective has already talked to him once.'

'He's denying everything.'

'Will he for ever?'

'I assume you guys were kidding about the rubber hoses and the nightsticks.'

'He'll take a deal. Or he'll cough it up by accident. He doesn't know which pieces they're missing. Sooner or later he'll say the wrong thing. It would be prudent to assume the clock is already ticking. We might want to revisit the timescale for getting out of here. No point still being around when the supply cuts off. Definitely no point still being around when the Feds show up. I know how hard this is for both of you, but those kind of problems would make it much worse.'

'You don't think a month is possible?'

Reacher saw money change hands, behind the truck at the mouth of the driveway.

He said, 'I think we should aim for a little faster.'

He saw small white boxes change hands in the other direction.

'How much faster?' Mackenzie asked.

'I told Mr Bramall my instinct would be get out of here within two or three days.'

'Impossible.'

'How fast can you do it?'

The truck started up and turned around, and headed back down the driveway. The cowboys carried the small white boxes towards the house. They stacked half of them on the porch, outside the front door, and they took the rest away with them, down a path that curved through the trees, and out of sight.

'It's about finding the right doctor,' Mackenzie said. 'She can't live without this stuff.'

'Ask your neighbours back home.'

'They go to rehab. We need a pusher.'

'We're sitting ducks here,' Reacher said. 'Some kind of trouble is coming.'

*

Mackenzie spent another hour with her sister, and then she came out and said she was ready to go check out of the hotel. Back in four hours, she had promised. With her bags. Ready to stay as long as it took. Bramall shrugged, and finally agreed to do the same. Outside his comfort zone, but hey, second career. Reacher said he was already checked out. He never paid for more than a night at a time. His toothbrush was in his pocket. He had no other luggage. All in all he would prefer to stay in the peace and quiet, and see them later. Mackenzie went back in to tell her sister the updated arrangement, and then she and Bramall drove away.

Reacher sat on the porch step. Already his accustomed spot. Ahead of him the ravine widened and fell away. Beyond it the horizon was dusty orange, with ghostly blue mountains behind it. The air was clear and silent. He watched birds of prey riding thermals, and condensation trails eight miles up, and a chipmunk on a rock ten feet away.

Then behind him the front door opened.

The chipmunk disappeared.

The shared voice said, 'Major Reacher?'

He stood up and turned around. She was in the doorway, in her silver track suit top. The hood was pulled forward. She was peering out from deep inside. Shadowy scars, and aluminium foil. Steady eyes.

She said, 'I would like to continue yesterday's conversation.'

'Which part?'

'When I thought you were here on business.'

'I'm not.'

'I accept that. All I want is your opinion. You might know things I don't.'

'Come sit down here,' he said. 'It's a beautiful day.'

She paused a beat, and then stepped out and crossed the porch. She was lithe and petite and moved like an athlete. Which she was. The infantry was an athletic discipline. She sat on the same step as Reacher, maybe a yard apart. She smelled of soap, and something astringent. The stuff on her face, he figured. Under the foil. Sideways on all he could see was the hood, pulled forward like a tunnel.

The chipmunk came out again.

She said, 'I told you I had a friend whose case is still open.'

'Sy Porterfield,' he said.

'You are here on business.'

'No, but I picked things up along the way.'

'How much do you know about him?'

'Very little,' Reacher said. 'Except he was your friend for a spell, and a rich Ivy Leaguer, and a Marine, and wounded, and he liked authenticity so much he would rather catch drips in a bucket than replace his leaky roof.'

'That's a fair summary.'

'Also he had three sealed files in the Pentagon.'

'I can't talk about those.'

'Then how can I give an opinion?'

'In theory,' she said. 'Why would an investigation just die away?'

'All kinds of reasons. Maybe it wasn't what they hoped it was. Maybe it dead-ended. Maybe it was too hard all along. I would need to know more.'

'I can't tell you.'

'Then let me make an educated guess. Maybe it fell between two stools. The Pentagon seems to have the original file. Let's say two years ago Porterfield had something on his mind. Why would he call the Pentagon? That was not a natural reflex. Twelve years before he had been a combat lieutenant in the Marines. The Pentagon was never a part of his life. I bet he never even saw the place. I bet he didn't have the phone number. But he found it out and dropped a dime. Which means the thing on his mind must have had some kind of high-level military aspect. Then the Pentagon copied in the DEA, which means it must also have had some kind of high-level narcotics aspect. Maybe there was miscommunication. Maybe the Pentagon thought the DEA was dealing with it, and the DEA thought the Pentagon was dealing with it. So in the end no one dealt with it.'

'I can't talk about the details.'

'We know his house was broken into after he died.'

'Yes, I saw that. I went back a few times, just to walk around.'

'Looked like an old-fashioned black-bag job to me.'

'I agree it was neat.'

'You know who it was.'

'I can't talk about it.'

'You know what was taken.'

'Yes.'

'Will you answer one question?'

'Depends what it is.'

'Just a yes or no answer. That's all I need. No details, no background. Nothing more than you want to say.'

'Promise?'

'Just a yes or no. To put my mind at rest about something.'

'About what?'

'Do you know how Porterfield died?'

'Yes,' she said. 'I was there.'

Special Agent Kirk Noble's division was based in Denver, Colorado. His office was a bland beige space temporarily brightened up by the gold from the shoebox he had taken from Billy's house in Wyoming. It was all laid out on his desk, all in an orderly fashion. All the gold trinkets. The crosses on the chains, the earrings, the bracelets, the charms, the chokers, the fashion rings, the wedding rings, the class rings. He had to fill out an inventory form. Description and value.

Some of it was junk. Some of it was pressed out of thin alloys no jeweller would have recognized. Twenty cents, literally, for some of the items. Others were merely mediocre. Seven bucks by weight for this, nine if you were lucky for that. Other items were better. There was an eighteen-carat wedding band, thick and heavy. A handsome piece. Fifty bucks in a pawn shop, easy. Same for a pair of earrings. Eighteen carat, solid and heavy. Two of them. Maybe sixty bucks together.

When he was finished he looked at his list. The right-hand column. The values. They made no sense. They were completely random. From practically zero all the way to a decent wad of cash. Stopping, crucially, at every price point along the way. Two bucks, three bucks, four bucks, all the way to more than sixty. Which was not how the business worked. It was not like a boutique delicatessen, where you bought a pinch of this and a twist of that. You bought a ten-dollar bag of brown powder for ten dollars. Or you didn't. Or you bought two for twenty dollars. Or three for thirty. What an economist would have called stair-step pricing.

Whereas Billy's pricing was notably granular. As if he was selling five-dollar bags, and six-dollar bags, and thirteen-dollar bags, and seventeen-dollar, and nine-dollar. Full service. Whatever the customer wanted. Filled there and then, and weighed on a scale.

Highly unlikely.

Therefore perhaps he wasn't selling bags of powder at all. Perhaps his product came in bulk. Perhaps for retail purposes the large quantities could be broken down, all the way to individual items if necessary, for folks with limited resources. Or cut with scissors into halves and quarters, for the truly broke.

Just like the old days.

Impossible.

He picked up his desk phone and called down to the jail.

He said, 'I'm expecting a transfer from Oklahoma. Name of Billy something.'

The voice on the phone said, 'We just processed him in.'

'Take him straight to an interview room. Tell him I have questions. I'll come down in a couple hours. Let him sweat till then.'

Nothing more than you want to say, Reacher had promised, and it turned out Rose Sanderson wanted to say nothing more. Not on the subject of Porterfield, at least. She just nodded to herself, inside her hood, as if the matter was settled.

Then she said, 'My sister told me you asked how it felt to be pretty.'

'Yes,' he said.

'You knew about me by then.'

'It made sense.'

'I'm sure she gave a conflicted answer. She's still pretty. Deep down pretty people know other people feel they're getting something for nothing. They have to be aw-shucks about it. They have to say it makes them feel shallow. But now I can tell you. It makes them feel great. It's like bringing a gun to a knife fight. Sometimes I would dial it up and just mow them down, one by one, bam, bam, bam. It's a superpower. Like clicking the phasers from stun to kill. There's no point denying it. It's a significant evolutionary advantage. Like being as big as you are.'

'We should have children,' he said.

He heard a click of foil inside the hood. A smile, he hoped.

She said, 'Those days are over.'

'Apparently Porterfield didn't agree.'

'We were friends, that's all.'

'There were two dents in the bed.'

'How do you know?'

'The guy who fixed his roof told a guy who told a guy who told us in a bar.'

'The roofer was looking at my bed?'

'Your bed? Sounds like you agree with him.'

She said, 'Sy was different.'

He said, 'What would it take to fix the infection?'

'A long course of IV antibiotics. It's a common thing. Most wounds get infected. The bacteria wall themselves off. It's hard to get rid of.'

'And you don't want to go to the hospital.'

'I didn't like it. I was an embarrassment. I was every soldier's worst fear. A disfiguring wound. The glamour was with the arms and legs. All that scientific technology. Titanium and carbon fibre. Some of those legs cost a million bucks. They looked better than new. Guys would wear shorts to show them off. Not me. I would have been a PR disaster.'

'You can get IVs at home,' Reacher said. 'With a certain kind of doctor. Your sister will find one. The kind who will also advocate a very long slow glide path, when it comes to dependency issues. The kind who might want to maintain your current habit for at least another year, while you settle in.'

'I don't believe her.'

'That she wants to?'

'That she can.'

'She has money. This is the civilian health care system we're talking about here. She can get what she wants.'

'People will see me. It's a suburb.'

'It's Lake Forest, Illinois. You could wear a bag on your head. They'll think it's performance art. A year from now you'll have your own show.'

'I like it here better.'

'Because of what Stackley brings. Before that what Billy brought. Which is a freak aberration. That trade was closed down. You're on the end of the very last leak. They're hunting for it right now. They have Billy in a cell. They're two steps away

289

from cutting you off. Think about it tactically. We need immediate action.'

She didn't reply. She just breathed a bit harder, and stiffened. He felt it from a yard away. A low vibration, through the wood of the step.

She said, 'I'm going inside now.'

He said, 'I'm sorry I upset you.'

'I'll be fine ten minutes from now.'

She stood up, and stepped up on the porch, and then he heard her turn around again and wait. He looked up at her. She looked back at him from deep inside the hood. In the movies her eyes would have lit up red.

She said, 'This is the problem. It will need to be seamless. Unfortunately I find I need this stuff. Like right now the most important thing in the world to me is a new fentanyl patch. Right now that's worth a hundred rings or a dozen sisters. But fortunately I have a new fentanyl patch. I already decided to lick it. I already made that choice. Does all that upset you?'

'Yes,' Reacher said. 'A little bit.'

'Me too,' she said.

He waited ten minutes for the hit to click in, but she didn't come out again. So he took a walk, around the tree line, until he saw the cowboys coming along their path towards him. The three guys, as always with the one in the lizard-skin boots a step in front. They said hello to Reacher in a way that made him feel they were surprised to see him. He told them he had stayed behind.

The guy in the boots said, 'The others aren't here?'

'For a couple more hours,' Reacher said.

'Were you talking to Rose?'

'I was,' Reacher said. 'As a matter of fact.'

'How's she doing?'

'She said she was there when Porterfield died.'

'I believe that's true.'

'Where were you?'

'We were in Colorado. Spring was late down there. We got work hauling hay.'

'What did she say about it when you got back?'

'She never talks about things like that.'

Reacher said nothing. The three guys looked at each other, a little hesitant, a little momentous, as if they had just gotten a weird idea.

The guy in the boots said, 'We could show you the place where he was found, if you want.'

'Is it near here?' Reacher said.

'About an hour on foot. Mostly uphill.'

'Is it interesting?'

'The walk is interesting. As far as the argument goes. You get to judge what kind of person could have carried a body that far.'

'You said anyone could have.'

'I said anyone would have. There's a difference. The people who could have are a subset of the population.'

'OK,' Reacher said. 'Show me.'

They crossed the clearing near the corner of the house, and headed towards another gap in the trees, but first the guy in the boots detoured to the crew-cab, and came back with a rifle. He said right or wrong, remember why they were going. It was bear country.

THIRTY-SEVEN

The path rose through the woods, which thinned a little as the slope got steeper. Some trunks were scored by elk antlers. There were moose prints on the ground. No sign of bear. Not yet. Which Reacher was happy about. The guy's rifle was an ancient M14 Garand. A U.S. soldier's main squeeze sixty years before. A clumsy weapon. But competent. Except it was chambered for the NATO round. Which was a slim little thing compared to a bear. Maybe it was all the guy had left. Maybe he had traded the rest away, to pay for something that had suddenly gotten expensive.

Better than nothing, Reacher thought.

They walked on. The air felt thin. Reacher felt he was breathing hard. Not the three cowboys. They looked normal. They were used to it. At sea level they would be dizzy with excess oxygen. Maybe better than licking a patch. The hike itself was no big deal. Roots and rocks and gravel, the same as the tracks they had been driving, but narrower. The gradient was modest. Occasionally there were big steps up. Carrying a heavy weight would have been slow and awkward, but possible. For a subset of the population. Like the guy had said.

Five minutes later they came out on an open area where a young tree had been pushed down by a moose. There were animal tracks in and out, some of them large.

The guy with the rifle said, 'It was a place like this.'

'Like this?' Reacher said. 'Or this place?'

'It's further on. But you get the picture. In case you want to turn back now.'

Reacher looked left and right and onward, into the trees. He wasn't sure what he expected to see. He felt a bear was unlikely. What were the odds?

'I'm OK,' he said. 'Let's keep going.'

They did. The woods changed around them as they walked. The clearings stopped coming, because the trees themselves thinned out, to the point where the whole vista became a kind of low-density mixed-up half-woods, half-clearing type of land-scape. Low scrub on the ground. Access lanes were clear and straight. Lines of sight were long. It was good predator country.

The guy with the rifle said, 'Still OK?'

Reacher looked all around. The back part of his brain was stirring. It was telling him that kind of terrain was best gotten out of, and quickly. Some kind of a primitive instinct. The front part was thinking about bears. Unlikely, it was telling him. But a reality at some low level of probability. A factor. Worth taking into account. Worth preparing for.

In his mind he heard General Simpson's voice, on the phone from West Point: *Off post she would have been armed at all times.*

He looked all around again.

There were no bears.

Not there.

He said, 'Let's go back.'

The guy said, 'Why?'

Because I want to get back in the trees, he thought.

Out loud he said, 'I get the picture now.'

And he felt he did. Stackley was the new Billy. Inheritor of the whole local empire. Including the periodic voice mail instructions. Stackley must have gotten a new one. Shoot the Incredible Hulk from behind a tree. All over again. Or whichever cartoon character he was by then. Message received and understood. Except Stackley hadn't tried to execute the mission himself. He had bought in mercenary services from the outside. During the big discussion behind the camper shell. The pitch, the offer, the bait, the acceptance. Maybe handshakes.

He knew because of the weapon. And culture, and habit, and plain common sense. How likely was it a Wyoming cowboy would venture into legitimate bear territory without a rifle capable of shooting a bear? It was like getting dressed in the morning. Therefore it became a logical sequence. The wrong gun meant there were no bears, which meant they were not close to where Porterfield had been found, where bears had been plausible, which meant the three guys had brought him to the wrong place for a completely different purpose. With an M14, which for sure was capable of shooting a person. Or gut-shooting a person. After that they wouldn't need bears. What had the guy said, in the bar, with the long-neck bottle? *You got hundreds of other species already lining up and licking their lips.*

He looked all around. Not good. Wide gaps, slender trunks.

The middle of nowhere.

No witnesses.

No proof. That's the whole beauty of it.

For a second he wondered how much they were getting paid, but then he dismissed the question, partly because it was inherently vain, and partly because the answer was obvious. *Far as I can tell, it's a beautiful thing. The way they talk about it, it's the best thing ever.* They were getting a couple boxes of oxycodone and fentanyl patches. Like getting offed in prison for a carton of cigarettes. Life was cheap. Then for another second he felt betrayed. He felt they had gotten along well so far. He had made an effort. He had been polite. Then he got real. He looked at it from their point of view. Some things were more important to a person. More important than family and friends and any kind of a regular trustworthy life.

No one should ever underestimate the appeal of an opiate high.

He hoped they were getting a couple boxes each.

They would have to earn them.

He turned and walked back, keeping the guy in the corner of his eye. He wasn't too worried about the first cold shot. It would miss. Snatched at, unaimed. The second shot might get complicated. And the third. And the rest. There were twenty rounds in an M14 magazine. He slowed down, to keep the guy in front of him. He intended to keep him there all the way. A shot low in the back would work just as well. The round would go through and through, and bury its smeared and bloody self deep in the grit ten feet away. It would never be found. How could it? The round that killed him would be a random singularity a quarter-inch wide in an uninhabited state bigger than some foreign nations.

No proof. That's the whole beauty of it.

He slowed again, a wordless shepherding, a polite *after you*. The guy with the rifle walked on ahead. He could afford to. They were heading back to the first clearing they had seen. Where the young tree had been pushed down by the moose. *It was a place like this.* Their preferred location, presumably. Why else had they stopped there?

They walked a minute downhill, some places single file, as the trees thickened up again. Reacher stayed last in line. Where he wanted to be.

He scanned ahead, and picked a spot.

Just in case.

295

He said, 'Let's go back a different route. I already saw this view.'

Which was a tactical risk. They didn't know he knew. Not yet. The time for making waves came later, not sooner. But it was a much smaller risk than arriving exactly where they wanted him. That was for damn sure. Open ground, that they knew, and he didn't.

The guy with the rifle stopped and turned around.

He said, 'I don't think there is another route.'

'Must be,' Reacher said.

'You wouldn't want to get lost out here.'

'I have a pretty good sense of direction. Most days I can tell which way is up.'

The guy took a step. Now he was maybe ten feet from Reacher, face to face on a narrow section of path, with the rifle held easy down by his side. The other two guys were closer, maybe five feet away, standing apart, so the guy with the rifle could see through the gap between. Underfoot were roots and rocks and gravel. Either side were trees.

As good a place as any.

Reacher took a step.

He said, 'This land is not where Porterfield was found.'

'You're the big expert now?' the guy with the rifle said.

'Sheriff Connelly conducted a thorough investigation. At a minimum we can expect he searched every building on the land where the corpse was found. As it turns out the only building he searched was Porterfield's. Therefore Porterfield was found on his own land. Which is about forty miles from here. With some kind of different ecology. They have bears there.'

The M14's safety was a small manual catch tight in front of the trigger guard. Clicked back, it was set to safe. Flicked forward, it was set to fire.

Reacher watched it carefully.

So far it was set to safe.

But all four of the guy's fingers were near it.

Reacher said, 'Put the weapon down, and we'll talk about it. It doesn't have to be like this. Maybe we can all find a way out together.'

The guy said, 'How?'

'Put the weapon down, and we'll talk about it.'

The guy didn't.

Reacher said, 'You need to look ahead. Stackley is your best friend today, but tomorrow he could be out of business. Rose's sister is taking her to Chicago. A suburb, not the city. A nice place. She could make it a charitable foundation. You could go with her.'

'We're fine here.'

'They have Billy in a cell,' Reacher said. 'They're two steps from cutting you off.'

As soon as he said it he knew it was dumb. They reacted like Rose Sanderson had. Sudden breathing, and stiffened postures. The low hum of instant panic. Plus in their case some kind of instant urgency, about what to do next. As if the glittering payday they had been promised could be snatched away. Reacher saw in their faces his words *cutting you off* translate instantly into a howling voice in their heads screaming *get more now now now*.

The guy raised the rifle, right hand to left hand to right hand, a clumsy old thing, nearly twelve pounds in weight, nearly four feet long.

His trigger finger detoured ahead of the guard.

It flicked the safety catch forward.

Reacher crashed into the guy nearest him and used the bounce to hurl himself against a tree. Not really diving out of the way of a bullet, for such a thing was surely impossible, but it was easy enough to estimate a bullet's likely future trajectory comparatively far ahead of time, and then avoid it, not forgetting that

Newton's Laws of Motion said the same bounce that helped him also helped the other guy, but in the opposite direction, towards the gun, action and reaction, which in his case got him killed. The rifle fired and the guy got hit and went down like he had walked into a clothesline. The roar of the shot died away to an immense cracking mountain echo, then a whisper, then nothing. The guy with the rifle stared. Reacher peeled off his tree and smacked him in the head and took his rifle away.

The guy staggered and dropped to his knees.

The third guy was frozen in place.

Reacher said, 'Check your friend.'

But even from there he could see it was hopeless. The guy had fired high and the round had gone through his buddy's throat. Just as good as a gut shot, from the point of view of the prevailing theory. Maybe even better. The bullet would fall to earth a hundred yards away. The soft tissue of the neck would be quickly consumed. Damaged vertebrae would be carried away and crushed, for the spinal cord inside. No proof at all.

The guy kneeling down looked up and shook his head. Reacher pointed the rifle at him, and then at where he wanted him to go. Which was next to the guy with the boots, who was struggling to his feet, steadying himself with a palm on the ground, then finally making it.

'Lead on,' Reacher said. 'We'll go this way after all.'

They stumbled ahead of him, and he followed behind, carrying the rifle one-handed. They offered no resistance. They were completely passive, as if resigned to their fate. Maybe in shock. Maybe an addict thing. Maybe a cowboy thing.

They got back two minutes after Bramall and Mackenzie got back from checking out of the hotel. Rose Sanderson was out on the porch, greeting her sister. Bramall was over by his car, giving them space. The two guys and Reacher came out of the woods right in the middle. And stopped. Centre stage. No need to tell the story. It was all right there. Two guys, not three, both of them sheepish and beaten, driven from behind by Reacher with a rifle.

Rose Sanderson seemed to recognize the rifle. Her head turned. The cuff of her hood traversed like a periscope. She stared at the scene. At the two guys. At the rifle. At Reacher. He knew she was thinking. Like an infantry officer. She was running war games through her head, like a chess computer. Like a West Point graduate.

She found one that fit.

She said, 'Was it freebies from Stackley?'

He said, 'Yes.'

'I guess that's really bad.'

'I'm not loving it so far.'

'What does Stackley have against you?'

'His boss doesn't like me.'

'But you're not here on business.'

'I picked things up along the way.'

'What happened up there?'

'One KIA,' he said. 'Friendly fire. Hasty aim, a moving target, confusion in front of him.'

'Let them go,' she said. 'Keep the rifle. It's their only remaining weapon.'

The two guys shuffled off down their own path, and the sisters moved to meet Reacher and Bramall at the porch step, where they all sat down to talk. Sanderson had her hood pulled forward again. It was moulded into a narrow vertical aperture. It turned and lined up with Reacher's face, and she said, 'I apologize for them.'

'No need,' he said. 'No harm, no foul. Tactical sophistication and superior skill in manoeuvring overcame an initial material deficit.'

'When did you know?'

'First sign was we stopped in a clearing and they got a bit weird. But I guess the guy couldn't pull the trigger. I guess he had never done it before.'

'I apologize for them,' she said again. 'They were my friends.'

'No need,' he said again.

'But I can't condemn them. You have no idea of the magnitude of what they were offered.'

'I'm getting an idea. From cause and effect alone. I'm taking it seriously, believe me. I'm not judging it, either. It is what it is. You got to do what you got to do. Right?'

'Yes.'

'Right now what you got to do is go inside and get a brand new patch, because after that the next thing you got to do is make a choice.'

'Between what?'

'You can have a sensible conversation about what comes next.'

'Or?'

'I'm moving on without you.'

THIRTY-EIGHT

R ose Sanderson went inside to get a brand new patch, and
as the door closed behind her Bramall's cell phone rang.
He checked the screen and said, 'It's Special Agent
Noble, from his office in Denver.'

'Don't answer,' Reacher said. 'He's going to ask if you found
Rose. Either as a pleasantry in passing, or because he wants her
for a witness. You can't tell him where she is. Not now. You'll feel
bad holding out on him.'

'He might have something for us.'

'He hasn't retired yet. He's all take and no give. Don't answer.'

Bramall didn't. The call timed out and voice mail clicked in.
Bramall retrieved it immediately. He listened, and he said, 'He
wants to know if we found Rose.'

Behind them the door opened again and Rose stepped out.
Small, lithe, graceful. With the hem of her hood leading the way.
She sat down on the step.

She turned her hood Reacher's way.

She said, 'Obviously it's your own decision when to move on.'

He said, 'I'm not looking to save the world. All I wanted was to know the story. Which I do now. Not a happy ending. I don't want to be here when it turns even worse. I don't want to be here while you go cold turkey in federal lock-up. With no medical supervision. Not even antiseptic cream. While your sister gets busted as some kind of an accessory, all because the Boy Detective thinks a rich white woman would balance the books on the TV news. While she goes bankrupt, fighting the bullshit charges. While Mr Bramall loses his licence and has to find a third career. I want to be gone before all that happens.'

She said, 'You make it sound certain to happen.'

'They have Billy in a cell. And you have a dead cowboy on your land. Someone will find him, like someone found Porterfield. Sheriff Connelly will search your place. Unless the Boy Detective has already gotten here first, thanks to Billy drawing a hand-lettered map. Unless the supply cuts off before either one of them arrives, in which case you'll be in the ER five times a day with a toothache. One of those things is certain to happen.'

'How long before the supply cuts off, do you think?'

The thing that mattered most.

'That's a circular argument,' Reacher said. 'If I move on without you, my first stop will be Rapid City, South Dakota. I need to pay Arthur Scorpio a visit. He lied to me about Porterfield, and he told two separate people to shoot me from behind a tree. He crossed the line. It's not going to end well for him. He's going in the tumble dryer. Two days for me to get there, and one day to do it. I would say the supply cuts off about three days from now.'

'You're forcing my hand. Either I agree to go now, or you'll make me go anyway. It's a unilateral three-day deadline.'

'It's an unintended consequence. Look at it from my point of view. Obviously I don't want to be here when it goes from bad to worse. And obviously when I leave here I have no choice except go straight to Rapid City. What else could I do? The guy is messing with me. What would you do if you were taking rounds from a distant building?'

'I would call in an air strike.'

'This is my version.'

'So I have three more days here.'

'But only as an unintended consequence. I'm not looking to save the world.'

She didn't reply.

Jane Mackenzie said, 'Reacher, three days is not possible.'

'Let's challenge that assumption,' he said. 'Let's make it possible.'

They moved inside. Bramall took a chair, and Mackenzie took the other. Sanderson said she was happy sitting cross-legged on the floor. Reacher laid out on his back, with his arm behind his head, and he stared at the ceiling, and listened. They started out by making a list of what Rose would need, which was easiest done by making a list of what she already had, which was quiet and isolated accommodations, and access to pharmaceutical-grade opioid medications in daily doses wildly in excess of what any responsible physician could even contemplate.

Mackenzie said in the long term the accommodations were no problem at all. But in the short term they didn't exist yet. She and her husband owned no beach houses or hunting cabins. There was an original staff apartment over their stable block, but it would need new heat and a new bathroom.

Reacher said, 'Do you have a guest suite?'

'Two, but they're in the house.'

'With you and Mr Mackenzie, a nice man and a good match. Is he going to be a problem with all of this?'

'No, he's going to be totally on board.'

'Are you sure?'

'Completely.'

'OK,' Reacher said. 'How about Rose lives in a guest suite until further notice. Put her in the east wing, facing the lake. You've got a six-acre yard and I'm sure it's a quiet leafy street. Not like living in the middle of Times Square. We need to take fast decisions here. We can't let the perfect be the enemy of the good.'

Mackenzie looked at Rose, who nodded. She agreed. She could afford to. It was about the future. Which wasn't coming. The second item on the list meant they could never get there.

Mackenzie said, 'We need to be realistic about the doctor. We haven't even started looking yet. I'm sure they're thin on the ground. I suppose the internet will help. But we might have to wait for an appointment. And I'm sure they at least go through the motions. They'll want an initial consultation. Or else right now the right guy is on Anguilla playing golf. You know what this crap is like.'

'I don't,' Reacher said.

'Two weeks,' she said. 'I live in that world. Trust me. This feels like a two-week thing, absolute bare minimum.'

No one answered.

From deep in her hood Rose said, 'You're all very polite people. So I'll say it myself. I'm the big problem. How are you going to bridge the gap? How are you going to hook me up every day for two weeks? Some of which will be spent on the road. A different town every night. You can't do it.'

Again no one answered. The questions hung in the air. *How are you going to bridge the gap? How are you going to hook me up?* It was the snag in every plan. Like a splinter in a banister rail. The rest was easy. Reacher could picture it all. Except for that. The quantities were staggering. It would be a full-time job.

To fill the silence Mackenzie talked for a spell about Lake Forest, Illinois. It sounded like a very nice place. Their house was a grand old Tudor, with ancient bricks and leaded windows, and a long sloping lawn, and a stone dock, with a small boat, and the glittering lake beyond, as big as an ocean. Then Reacher realized she wasn't just filling the silence. Or bragging on her real estate. She was spinning some kind of shared twin fantasy from long ago, about the lives they were going to have, and what would be in them, like an ideal dream. He could understand how girls in landlocked Wyoming would want a waterfront. Now Mackenzie was saying she had made it happen. It was right there for the taking. She was saying come live in your dream for the rest of your life. With its damp lawns and its mossy bricks. It was a masterpiece of gauzy seduction. Reacher could only imagine how much more power it had, from one twin to another, down on some unknown level of intimacy. It was enticing. Irresistible. Worth sacrificing for. Great psy-ops. Except he was left with a couple of questions.

How are you going to bridge the gap? How are you going to hook her up?

Down in Denver Kirk Noble had gotten caught up in some other thing, and then he had gotten dragged into a meeting about something else entirely, so in the end he left Billy to sweat way longer than two hours. Closer to four. He stopped and looked in the one-way window. Good and carefully. He prided himself on reading the signs. Right away he saw Billy was a hardscrabble country boy, maybe forty years old, lean and furtive, like a fox and a squirrel had a kid, and spent half the time baking it in the sun, and the other half beating it with a stick. He wasn't sweating and he wasn't shaking. He wasn't drumming his toe or picking a nail. Not a user. Not even a smoker.

Such a guy would give nothing up. Except by accident. Foxes and squirrels had numerous admirable qualities, but they didn't get college degrees. There would be some kind of side door. Some kind of trigger. Maybe approval. Billy was the type of guy who most likely never had much. Maybe he could be stroked into prideful reminiscences, about the deals he had done. Maybe using the granular-priced jewellery as a show-and-tell example. He could recall how he came by each item. He could say, yeah, some chick had no money so she gave me this.

In exchange for what, Billy?

Noble sent a runner to his office for the shoebox of jewellery.

The impromptu conference broke up, and Reacher went out on the porch. Then Bramall came out. Reacher imagined Sanderson would replace him in the armchair. He imagined the sisters would talk. Not too long, he hoped.

Bramall said, 'We can't fix this.'

'There must be a way,' Reacher said.

'When you figure it out, be sure to let me know.'

'You sure you want me to? You have more rules than me.'

'One of which makes me delinquent if I don't prepare a plan B on behalf of my client. At least a mental sketch. In this case it would have to start with hospitalization privileges for Rose. No federal lock-up. A private facility of our own choice. Secured, if they want, at our expense. Obviously the guy to talk to would be Noble, down in Denver. He has the discretion. We already have a relationship. I should maintain it. I should have answered his call. I'll have to answer the next one. I might need him in the future.'

'We don't need plan B yet.'

'Better to lay the ground.'

'If you answer the phone to him now, you'll have to tell him where Rose is. Which will lead straight to plan C, which is the whole thing falls apart. Or you'll have to lie to him, which is technically a felony.'

Bramall didn't answer.

Reacher said, 'Will you do me a favour?'

'Depends what it is.'

'Go ask Mrs Mackenzie if her sister mentioned whether Stackley is coming by again tomorrow.'

'Why?'

'I want to know.'

Bramall went in, but a minute later it was Rose Sanderson herself who came out. She sat where she had before, on the step, hooded, a yard away.

She said, 'My sister gave me money. I told Stackley to come back every day until it's gone. Or until he runs out of product.'

Reacher said, 'What happens when he does?'

'Sometimes they miss a day. I guess they go somewhere and get more. We're real happy to see them come back.'

'I can imagine.'

'I'm sorry.'

'Don't be. We both took the same history class.'

She nodded, inside her hood.

She said, 'Morphine dates from 1805. The hypodermic syringe dates from 1851. A great combination, just in time for the Civil War, which left hundreds of thousands of addicts. Then World War One, same thing. Literally millions of addicts in the 1920s.'

'The army likes tradition.'

'World War One was also the start of large-scale facial injuries. Millions of them, by the end. The French called them the *mutilés*. The mutilated. Which is a good word, because that's how it feels, and because it sounds like mutated, which is also how it feels. You feel yourself become a different person. There was an early type of plastic surgery back then, but mostly they wore tin masks. Artists would match them to their skin colour. But nothing really worked. City parks had benches painted blue, where the public was trained to look away. That's where they sat. But most of them never went out. Most of them never saw daylight, ever again. Most of them died of infections or killed themselves.'

'You don't have to convince me,' Reacher said. 'I don't care what you chew.'

'But you can't get it for me. Not fourteen days straight.'

'Suppose I could. Suppose you could get it for ever. What would you do?'

'Seriously?'

'Give me an honest analysis. You like the truth.'

She paused a beat.

'I would party at first,' she said. 'Big time. No more rationing. No more cutting patches. I would bathe in the stuff.'

'Dangerous.'

'God, I hope so. It's a world you don't understand until you're in it. There is no feeling better than tiptoeing all the way up to the gates of death. All the way up to the big black door, and then knocking on it. It's a whole different zone. If I hear a news story about some other user dying, due to some batch of something showing up unexpectedly strong, I'm not feeling sorry for the guy. I'm thinking, where can I get some of *that* good stuff? Not because I want to kill myself. Far from it. I want the exact opposite. I want to live for ever, so I can get high every day. I'm sorry, Reacher. I'm not the person I was. I mutated. You should have found someone else's ring.'

'What next, after you're done partying?'

'Eventually I guess I would have to tone it down. Probably get the IV, if I can have it at home.'

'You think you can tone it down?'

She nodded, inside her hood. 'I love it like crazy, but there's enough of the old me still in there. I know that. I made it through West Point and nine years in the infantry. I could make it through this. As long as I knew I didn't have to quit entirely. As long as I knew the promise was always there. Maybe Saturday night, if

I was good all week. I think I could get myself to that level.'

'And then what?'

'Then I'll hide out in my sister's house until I'm a hundred years old. By which time we'll all be ugly and I won't stand out so much. Until then let's not be Pollyanna. There won't be any then-what going on. I don't see how it could.'

'You could get a job.'

'You must have missed that memo.'

He smiled.

'I work now and then,' he said. 'Labouring, or nightclub bouncer. One time I dug a swimming pool in Key West, Florida. By hand. I bet it's still there.'

'The psychiatrists came to see me in the hospital. There was a new school of thought, about confronting issues head-on. No false comfort. I was an O-4, don't forget. All grown up. I was supposed to be able to take it. They showed me the data. Employees with facial disfigurements upset customers and co-workers so badly that virtually a hundred per cent of them end up working alone in a back office.'

'OK, don't get a job.'

'Then we had long conversations about how much our person-alities are tied up with our faces. About subliminal cues and nuances. Something very fundamental. Later I realized the head-on stuff went only so far. Now they were being subtle. They were dropping hints. They were telling me my romantic life was over.'

'Porterfield didn't agree.'

'He was different.'

'Was he blind?'

'He had problems of his own.'

Behind them the door opened, and Mackenzie came out on the porch, followed by Bramall. Mackenzie looked like she had something to say, but Bramall's cell phone rang. He took it out and checked the screen.

He said, 'It's Special Agent Noble, from his office in Denver.'

He looked at Rose.

Then he looked at Reacher.

Asking for something.

Reacher said, 'You want me to be the bad guy?'

He took the phone. He hit the green button. He put the phone to his ear.

He said, 'Hello?'

THIRTY-NINE

Noble asked why Reacher was answering Bramall's phone, and Reacher gave him a vague reply, about Bramall taking a walk, maybe out of range, therefore leaving his phone behind.

Noble said, 'Mrs Mackenzie hired Bramall, right? For actual money.'

Reacher said, 'Yes.'

'But not you.'

'No.'

'Then it's better I talk to you anyway. Can Mrs Mackenzie hear what you're saying right now?'

'Yes.'

'Move away.'

Reacher held the phone up toward the ravine, and mimed heading that way for better reception. When he got there he stood on a rock, and said, 'What's going on?'

In his ear Noble said, 'I think you found the sister.'

'Why?'

'Are you saying you didn't?'

'I'm asking how you think we could have.'

'How hard could it be? She was in there somewhere.'

'It's a very large area.'

'That's a description,' Noble said. 'Not a denial.'

'Finding an entrenched individual in an unlimited acreage of forested land peppered with abandoned cabins is virtually impossible.'

'That's also a description.'

'I can do this all day long,' Reacher said. 'I was in the army.'

Noble said, 'I need Rose Sanderson.'

'Why?'

'For information. I need to close a file.'

'You have Billy for that.'

'Billy is why I need Sanderson now. I think Billy is lying to me. He's boasting. Either for fun, to tempt me into wasting time chasing rainbows, or just for the sake of his ego. Some dealers love to lie about how they can get the good stuff. It makes them look cool. They're the man, and so on. But before I can close the file I need corroborating testimony from a customer. Just in case. It's a cover-your-ass thing.'

'What did Billy tell you?'

'That he was still selling what he always sold. Domestic oxycodone and fentanyl, branded and packaged inside the United States.'

'Obviously that's a boast,' Reacher said. 'You told us it's impossible.'

'It is impossible. I can prove it. Literally everything is barcoded every step of the way. Literally every pill. We have access to their data. There is zero leakage now.'

'So he's boasting.'

'Except he knows things he shouldn't. There have been packaging changes. He knows the new promotional message on the inside of the hospital pack. No one ever sees that.'

'So he's not boasting.'

'Of course he's boasting. They track every conveyor belt, and every package, and every carton as it goes out the door, and they have GPS on the trucks, and they match the orders with the payments received, and if there's a mismatch anywhere all kind of red lights start flashing. Which isn't happening. Nothing is going astray.'

'So which is it? Boasting or not?'

'I would like to put my mind at rest. Either way I need to ask Rose Sanderson exactly what she was buying.'

'Why not go up the chain? Surely a wholesaler's testimony would carry more weight than a customer's.'

'I don't know these people. It's an opaque network.'

'Won't Billy name names?'

'So far he's playing the good soldier. I only got what I got by tricking it out of him sideways. I would need to start a whole new investigation. I don't have time. We can do it quicker this way. We don't need much. We're only closing a file. All she has to say is Billy is a lying asshole and he was selling regular Mexican powder all along.'

Up at the house Sanderson and her sister and Bramall were still on the porch. They were talking a lot. Some kind of a big discussion.

Reacher said, 'OK, if I ever get the opportunity, I'll be sure to tell her what you need.'

Noble said, 'Where are you now?'

'It's a very large area.'

'Are you at her place?'

'It's hard to pin down an exact spot.'

'You're talking on a cell phone.'

'On an omnidirectional antenna somewhere inside a giant circle the size of New Jersey.'

Noble said, 'Certain laws apply when a citizen talks to a federal agent.'

Reacher said, 'Sorry, I was waiting for the dramatic music.'

'Do you know Rose Sanderson's current location?'

'Certain other laws apply when this citizen talks to a federal agent. Mostly the ones about saving breath by skipping bullshit. I know how these things go. And I know you know. Usually worse than expected. Therefore you always have a plan B, so the main office sees a notch on your bedpost anyway. Anyone will do. You want Rose Sanderson on the record buying Mexican powder. Just in case. She's your plan B.'

'She breaks the law every day.'

'You should forget her right now. Seriously. She would be a very serious blunder on your part. She was wounded in the face in Afghanistan. You met her twin sister. Think about it. Their photographs will be printed side by side in every newspaper in the world. The movie star and the monster. Before and after serving her country. Now you're busting her for pain medication? The backlash would be ferocious. The DEA would be ridiculed. I'm saving you from a PR disaster.'

'Do you know where she is?'

'In the state of Wyoming.'

'Are you refusing to answer my question?'

'No,' Reacher said. 'I'll answer all your questions. Including the ones you haven't thought of yet. Let's set up a call about three days from now. On two conditions. You butt out till then, and you forget you ever heard Rose Sanderson's name.'

'Why three days?'

'That kind of question would fall under the butting-out part of the deal.'

'I'm not going to negotiate with you.'

'Then suggest an alternative approach. Oh yeah, there isn't one. So let's try to get along. I was an MP, remember. The same

314

as you, except different clothes. I'm not out to screw you. I'm trying to do you a favour. This is one of those lucky things that happen from time to time. I take the tiny slice I want, which is Rose Sanderson, and you get all the rest. It's a big deal, I promise you. It will win you a medal and make you a hero. Even Mr Bramall thinks it will be hailed as a major triumph and the capstone of an outstanding regional success story. It's something for nothing, Noble. The opposite of collateral damage. The Boy Detective would take that offer, I think, in the comic books. He knows it's how government business gets done.'

'You're not the government.'

'You never really leave,' Reacher said. 'Not if you're the right kind of person.'

Noble said nothing. Checkmate again. He couldn't argue. Not without saying yeah, all our lives are bullshit.

'Three days,' Reacher said. 'Relax. Maybe take in a show.'

He clicked off the phone. He walked back to the house. Bramall met him halfway. Reacher gave back the phone.

'Three days,' he said. 'Plus he forgets about Rose.'

'Nice work.'

'Thank you.'

'In exchange for what?'

'We let him pick up the pieces.'

'What pieces?'

'I'm sure there will be pieces.'

'You saying you got an idea now?'

'More like a mental sketch,' Reacher said. 'I need to ask you a question.'

'What question?'

'When you were in Rapid City, why were you eyeballing Scorpio's laundromat? What did you expect to see there?'

'Customers, initially. According to phone records Rose called there once. Who else would call a laundromat? Only a customer, surely. Maybe she lost something there. Maybe she wanted to know the opening time. I wondered if it meant she lived nearby. Or had, at one time.'

'But there were no customers.'

'Only one or two.'

'Any other traffic?'

'None at all.'

'Did you watch the back?'

'A couple of bikes.'

'But no loading or unloading.'

'None at all,' Bramall said again. 'It's not a loading dock. Just a regular door.'

'OK,' Reacher said.

Then Mackenzie came by, and said she wanted to go find the cabins they would be sleeping in that night. Apparently Rose had told her there was a nearby clearing with four small houses all in a square. They were aired out and habitable. Apparently Rose kept them like that all the time, because she felt it was a shame to see good things go to ruin.

They found the right path, which was like all the other paths Reacher had seen, including most recently the path where the guy with the boots had aimed the rifle. Apart from that it was easy going. After a hundred yards they came out on a clearing, exactly as promised, with four one-room houses built around a space about the size of a tennis court. Like a tiny village. The houses were made of log, each one different, each one built like a serious structure, each one no bigger than a single-car garage. All four doors were unlocked. Bramall claimed one at random. Mackenzie moved in opposite. Reacher split the difference, facing south.

In a city the place would have been called a studio apartment. A living room with a bed in it, or a bedroom with a sofa in it, plus a token kitchenette, and a tiny bathroom. Overspill accommodation for house parties, he figured. They ate and drank and made merry at the big house, but came out there to sleep. Maybe four couples, who all knew each other.

He put his toothbrush in the bathroom glass and came out to find Mackenzie watching him from the doorway.

She said, 'My husband has started the search for a doctor. He's taking vacation days from work. He understands the parameters. The housekeeper is preparing the suite. Mr Bramall is ready to drive us all to Illinois. I'm sure his vehicle will be comfortable.'

'I agree,' Reacher said. 'It's a fine truck.'

'I guess what I'm saying is the rest is up to you now.'

'The rest?'

'Bridging the gap.'

'OK,' Reacher said. 'That seems fair.'

'If you can.'

'I'm working on it.'

'Will it be possible?'

'It might feel a little hand to mouth at first. A little insecure. Rose will need to hang tough. I hope she can. She told me there's some of her old self still in there. She was smart enough to ask me to hold her ring. Or self-aware enough. To some extent she knows what she's doing. She can still think the old way. At some point she'll have to trust us and we'll have to trust her.'

'When will we leave?'

'Tomorrow,' he said.

They ate dinner together, out of what they had brought from the grocery store. Rose was high as a kite and happy. She was mobile and animated. Under her hood and her foil she laughed and smiled and turned from person to person, and talked and listened and answered. Mackenzie laughed with her, half the time projecting boundless energy and support, like a tractor beam in a science fiction movie, something solid for her sister to lean on,

317

and the other half of the time projecting hopeless bewilderment at her new situation. She was adrift. There were old-time fairy tales where the beautiful sister came home scarred, and all kinds of hidden anger and resentment was revealed, ahead of a warm and tearful resolution. But this was different. There was no narrative template. They were both the beautiful sister. They started level. There was no anger or resentment. There were no issues. They were the same person. Almost. Reacher saw the air between them ebb and flow, sometimes making them a single organism, like an aspen grove, sometimes making them separate, but never completely. They were a unit. They were a they. Always had been, always would be. But neither one knew how the current version worked. Or even what it looked like, from the outside. How would they describe themselves now? Would it have to be I and she? No longer we? These were not questions they had asked before.

Then Reacher told them how he thought the next day might go. Bare bones, a rough outline, three steps, plenty of holes still to fill. Mackenzie was horrified. Bramall looked away, as if to say, is that all you've got? Rose quieted down and Reacher felt her eyes on him, under her hood. He felt careful appraisal. She was his main audience. She had the most to lose. She was a professional soldier. She knew no plan survives first contact with the enemy. After that it was about luck, or not. She knew that for sure.

Afterwards Reacher asked Bramall to move his truck behind the house, out of sight from the mouth of the driveway. Then he walked up the cowboys' path, to where he figured their quarters must be. He found them on the porch of a low log building made to look like an old-time bunkhouse. Two guys, not three, sipping from cans of beer. He thought they looked uneasy, with shock and guilt, presumably, and a more ancient humbling, the guy in the boots especially, where you fail to kill a man, and then you

318

look up and see him walking towards you. Some kind of an atavistic feeling, deep in the back of your brain, about your place on the ladder, from back when the only ladders were trees.

Reacher said, 'We live in crazy times.'

Neither guy answered. Perhaps they thought he had earned the right to speak uninterrupted. Like giving a lecture. Maybe a cowboy thing. He wanted to tell them no hard feelings. That he understood the pressure. How it distorted judgement. But in the end he didn't. Too complicated. Instead he told them what they had to do for him. He spelled it out, step by step, and he walked them through it, and he gave them what they needed. He saw it was better than forgiveness. Their heads came up an inch, with new resolve in their eyes, as if they were subject to an older legal system, where through labour or forfeit they could buy back their freedom.

Reacher walked back to Sanderson's place. It had a light on inside. He checked where Bramall had left the Toyota. It was safely out of sight. Not bad for the FBI. He walked back to his one-room cabin. The little village. Mackenzie's place had a light on, and so did Bramall's. All kinds of people, going to bed. All kinds of preparations and rituals. Maybe lengthy. Maybe Bramall brushed his suit, like a valet. No doubt Mackenzie had a complicated routine, involving potions and unguents.

For sure Sanderson did.

Reacher got into bed. Log walls, log ceiling. He understood the appeal. They were solid and massive. They made him feel safe.

FORTY

The cowboys were up at dawn, drinking coffee from tin mugs, in rocking chairs, on their bunkhouse porch. The sun came up behind the hills, and threw a flat shadow across the plain. In her house Rose Sanderson slept on. She was not a dawn riser. Fentanyl saw to that. Bramall was up, already showered, and dressed, with his hair brushed, and his necktie knotted. Mackenzie stirred, and woke, and lived a happy oblivious moment where nothing had ever happened. Then she remembered, and half wanted to go back to sleep again, and half wanted to get up and do something, anything, for as long as it felt like progress. In the end going back to sleep won the contest. For a short time. Outside the air was cold. Early on a late summer morning, high in the mountains.

An hour later the cowboys walked down to the mouth of the driveway. They waited there, the same as they had the morning before, and the morning before that, except now they were two, not three. They stood around, not talking, like part of the landscape, infinitely patient. In her house Rose stirred, and woke.

She put her hand on her night table. Two patches. Still there. She breathed out and sagged back on her pillow. It was safe to get up. Bramall had made coffee in his token kitchenette, and was out on his porch drinking the last of it. Mackenzie was in the shower, hosing water through her hair.

An hour later the cowboys still waited. The sun climbed higher and came up over the ridge behind them. It dappled the trees where they stood, and warmed the air. In her house Rose was showering. Bramall was still on his porch, his coffee long gone, just passing the time. He was a man life had taught to be patient. Mackenzie was in her cabin, in an armchair, on the phone with her husband, talking about doctors.

An hour later the cowboys were still waiting. Waiting for the man, for their connection, for their hook-up. Wasted hours. Part of a user's life. They leaned on trees and breathed the air, soft and piney. In her house Rose Sanderson was dressed, in her silver top, with the hood pulled forward. She had cut a new piece of aluminium foil, and smeared it with new lotion, and smoothed it into place. She was in her living room, with the window open. In position. Ready. As was Bramall, fifty yards away in the woods. He was sitting on a log. Mackenzie was fifty yards the other way, leaning on the trunk of a fir, with filtered sunlight playing in her hair.

A minute later at the mouth of the driveway there was the sound of a straining engine, and the scratch and patter of struggling tyres, and the cowboys stood aside. The beat-up old pick-up truck came out of the woods, carrying its camper shell on its back like a turtle. At the wheel Stackley scanned ahead. He saw no black Toyota. No big guy. No one else.

He eased to a stop.

The guy with the boots walked over.

Stackley got out.

He said, 'How's it going?'

The guy said, 'You owe us.'

'For what?'

'The big guy.'

'You got it done?'

'Yesterday in the afternoon.'

'How did you do it?'

'Lured him in the woods and shot him with a rifle.'

'Want to show me?'

'Sure,' the guy said. 'But he's an hour uphill. We didn't want him found too soon.'

'Then how do I know you did it?'

'We're telling you.'

'I need proof. This is a very large fee we're talking about here.'

'Two boxes each.'

'Between you,' Stackley said.

Then he looked again and said, 'There were three of you yesterday.'

The guy said, 'Indisposed.'

'With what?'

'Sore throat.'

'I need proof about the big guy,' Stackley said. 'This is a business deal we got going here.'

The guy with the boots put his hand in his pocket and came out with a slim blue booklet. Silver printing. A passport, maybe three years old, a little curled and bent. He handed it over. Stackley opened it up. The big guy's photo was right there. A face like a stone. His name was Jack Reacher. No middle initial.

'From his pocket,' the guy said. 'Less messy than his scalp.'

Stackley put the passport in his own pocket.

He said, 'I'll keep it as a souvenir.'

'Sure.'

'Nice work.'

'We aim to please.'

'But you caught me out,' Stackley said. 'Business is too good. I'm running low.'

'What does that mean?'

'You'll have to wait.'

'That wasn't the deal.'

'What do you want me to do? Say no to someone else, just in case you got it done, which frankly I didn't expect so soon? I can't hold stuff back on a theoretical basis.'

'So you got nothing left?'

'Not much.'

The guy said, 'Want to show me?'

'Sure,' Stackley said. He wasn't averse. A dwindling stock was a kind of advertisement all its own. The modern environment. Business was all about velocity now. It was rule one. He turned towards the camper door.

And came face to face with the guy from the passport.

Reacher eased out of the trees, and crept up within a yard of the guy. He was about to tap him in the kidney, but right then the guy turned around towards the camper door, so he tapped him in the stomach instead, just enough to fold him over. He used the same hand on the guy's shoulder to force him face-down in the dirt, where he searched him. He came up with his own passport from one coat pocket, and a nine-millimetre from another, and a .22 jammed in one boot, and a switchblade jammed in the other. The nine-mil was an old Smith & Wesson Model 39, with handsome grips made of polished wood. The .22 was a Ruger, not a vest pocket gun, but it fit in the boot. The switchblade was a piece of junk, made in China, maybe in a toy factory.

Stackley was huffing and puffing in the dirt, and squirming a little, which Reacher thought was excessive for a guy barely hurt.

He checked the pick-up's cab. Nothing in the glove compartment. But under the lip of the driver's seat there was a mounting clip, where a fire extinguisher might have been, except in this case the clip had been modified, and was currently full of another elderly nine-millimetre with wooden grips, in this case an old Springfield P9. Apart from that there was nothing but drifts of old gas receipts and sandwich wrappers.

Reacher stepped back to where Stackley was lying, and he held the old Smith out at arm's length. He clicked the button and dropped the mag from five feet up. It hit Stackley in the head. Stackley yelped. Reacher dropped the gun itself. Stackley yelped again. Reacher did the same thing with the Ruger, mag and frame, and then the Springfield, mag and frame. A total of six separate yelps.

Reacher said, 'Get up now, Stackley.'

Stackley forced himself upright, a little bent over, a little pale in the face. All shook up. Rubbing his painful head. Facing the same kind of animal issues the two cowboys had, the night before. You fail to kill a man, and then you look up and see him right there. Does he own you now?

Reacher said, 'Open up the back of the truck.'

The doors were flimsy plastic. Stackley got them propped wide. Then he stood back. Reacher pulled a blanket aside. One forlorn box, mostly empty. It had just three patches left in it, each one individually wrapped, all of them sliding around in a space made for more.

Not much.

Reacher stepped away.

'Stocks seem to be running low,' he said. 'What do you do about that, in the normal course of business?'

'I'm sorry, man,' Stackley said. 'About the other thing. I had no choice. I was told to do it. It wasn't personal.'

'We'll discuss it later,' Reacher said.

'There's a guy. I have to do what he says. He told me to. It wasn't like I wanted to. You have to believe that.'

'Later.'

'I really didn't think these guys would do it. I thought I was going through the motions, that's all. So at least I could say I tried. It's their fault really.'

'I asked you a question.'

'I don't remember what it was.'

'Your stock is low,' Reacher said. 'What happens next?'

Stackley got a look in his eye, like some kind of a thought process was taking place back there. He looked up, and then down. A junction, Reacher thought, or a transition. A change from one thing to another. From winning to losing, from hope to despair.

To surrender.

Stackley breathed out, like a sigh of defeat.

He said, 'When I run out I go get more.'

'Where from?'

'It's a kind of warehouse, where you drive in and line up. You wait until midnight.'

'Where is the warehouse?'

Stackley paused a beat.

'We have a special burner phone,' he said. 'We get a text message.'

'Where is your special burner phone?'

Stackley pointed at the camper shell.

He said, 'In a locker in back.'

Reacher said, 'Get it for me.'

Stackley stepped up and leaned inside. Reacher heard the snap of a catch. Afterwards he recalled a split second of fast chaotic thought, like his whole life was flashing in front of his eyes, except it wasn't his whole life, merely his mistakes of the last thirty seconds, explained and analysed and ridiculed and exaggerated to a ludicrous degree. To the point where in his mind he saw his name as a footnote in a psychology textbook about bias confirmation, in a famous case where a guy saw a movement in another guy's eyes, and took it to mean exactly what he wanted it to mean all along.

Stackley hadn't surrendered. Instead he had thought hard and fast and seen a way out. A lifeline. The guy was no dummy. The change in his eyes had been a movement away from losing and back to winning. From despair back to hope. Reacher had read it completely wrong. Completely ass-backward. Too optimistic. Too willing to look on the bright side of life. Which also screwed up his conclusion about the weapons. He had instinctively assumed once you had taken a Springfield, and a Smith, and a Ruger .22 from a guy, then you were pretty much done with finding more firearms. Which had made it fun to take them apart and drop them on the guy's head.

Whereas the psychology textbooks would say a guy with three could have four, dead easy. Especially a dope dealer, who took things in trade.

Dumb.

Stackley straightened up and turned around.

He had a gun in his hand.

From the locker in the camper shell.

The gun was an old Colt .45, worn steel, rock steady. Maybe nine feet away. Eight, if Stackley braced forward for the shot. Hard to miss from there. The downside of being a big guy. A sudden evolutionary disadvantage. Too much centre mass.

Reacher watched Stackley's eyes. The guy was still thinking hard. Cost, benefit, advantages, disadvantages. All the reels were coming up cherries. In the short term he could solve his immediate this-minute problem. In the long term he could impress Arthur Scorpio as a reliable guy who got things done. All by pulling the trigger. Right there, right then. Just once. The only negative was location. Couldn't leave a corpse in the mouth of the driveway. It would need to be moved a mile into the woods. But he had the cowboys for that. They would trade labour for a free patch. For two, they would carry a corpse to Nebraska.

Reacher said, 'Don't point the gun at me.'

Stackley said, 'Why the hell not?'

'It would be a serious mistake.'

'How would it, man?'

Stackley raised the Colt.

Two-handed.

He pointed it at the centre of Reacher's chest.

Like aiming at a barn door.

He said, 'How exactly is this a mistake?'

'Wait and see,' Reacher said. 'Nothing personal.'

Stackley's head exploded.

There was a wet thump like a watermelon rolling off a table, and then immediately the flat crack of a supersonic NATO round in the air, and the antique bark of an M14 firing. Stackley's head came apart in an instant cloud of red mist, and fragments of it followed his body down, vertically, like a disappearing trick, into a puddle of clothes and limbs and lifeless flesh. Reacher looked back at the house, and saw Rose Sanderson at her window, checking downrange, assessing her aim. Which was pretty damn good, he thought. From a hundred yards out she had put a round through the gap between himself and the cowboys, and she had hit Stackley right above the ear. All with a rifle dumped by the army twenty years before she was born.

Impressive.

She came out of the house and walked down towards them, hood forward, carrying the rifle one-handed. From the right Bramall came hurrying in, and from the left came Mackenzie, who had the most trouble with what she found. Theoretically she might have been happy with what turned out, in pragmatic terms, and maybe even moral terms, but a human head shattered by a high-velocity rifle bullet was far from theoretical. It was a purple mess, steaming slightly in the cold mountain air. She turned and looked at her sister. *She was prepared to kill people, and I wasn't.* One thing to talk about it. A whole different thing to watch it happen.

Reacher said, 'Thank you, major.'

Rose said, 'How much did he have?'

The thing that mattered most.

'Not much,' he said.

'Shit.'

She stepped around Stackley and looked in the back of the truck. She twitched the blanket aside and poked around. Her shoulders slumped. Not exactly surprise, but certainly disappointment. *No plan survives first contact with the enemy.* She looked back at Reacher, as if to say, *this one went south pretty damn quick, didn't it?*

She said, 'Where does he go to get more?'

He said, 'The conversation didn't get that far.'

'Arthur Scorpio's place, right?'

'No,' Reacher said. 'There's no traffic at Scorpio's place. No loading or unloading. Whatever Scorpio does, he does it by remote control.'

'What exactly did Stackley tell you?'

'He said there's a warehouse, where they drive in and line up and wait until midnight.'

'Where?'

'He said he gets a text message on a burner phone. He said the phone is in there.'

He heard the click of catches and the muted thump of compartment doors being opened and shut. Maybe twelve of them. The camper shell had lockers all over it. Like living on a boat.

'There's no phone in here,' she said.

'There never was,' he said. 'It was a decoy. It was a way to get to his gun.'

'So how do we know where to go?'

'We don't.'

She just stood there. Tiny, slumped, defeated. She was a drug addict. She had just shot and killed her dealer. Catastrophe. Like jumping off a building. Right then she was in mid-air, falling fast, the hiss of terror loud in her ears.

She was going to panic.

Reacher said, 'Forget the phone. The phone was a trick. He invented it. They couldn't possibly work it that way. A warehouse big enough to drive in and line up can't be a moveable feast. It can't be a last-minute arrangement. It must be a permanent location. Fixed and secure. Hidden away somewhere.'

Rose said, 'But where?'

Bramall said, 'Where is his regular phone?'

He ducked down, a small meticulous figure amid the gore. He dug through Stackley's crumpled pockets. He came out with a Samsung smartphone about the size of a paperback book. It had a cracked screen. No password. Bramall dabbed and swiped.

'He replaced Billy three days ago,' he said. 'Obviously he would have had to pick up supplies.'

There were no text messages from three days before. No emails. But there was a voice mail. Bramall played it, and listened, and narrated as he went.

He said, 'There's a service road leading to a covered garage. The covered garage is for snowploughs and other winter equipment. There's plenty of space and they have it all to themselves. There will be a guard at the door.'

Reacher said, 'Where?'

'It doesn't say.'

'It must. Stackley was new.'

329

'It doesn't. Maybe it's somewhere he was already familiar with. Maybe they already told him the general area.'

'Who left the message?'

'Sounds like a transportation captain. He's all about the details.'

'Is there an area code?'

'Blocked number.'

'Terrific.'

Rose Sanderson went back to the camper shell. She leaned in and came out with the three wrapped patches. She gave one each to the cowboys. For old times' sake, Reacher figured. A parting gift. And like a good officer. Always make sure your men are OK. She kept one patch for herself. She took another from her pocket. The last of yesterday's purchase. She butted them together, and then fanned them out, like a tiny hand of cards. She counted them. One, two. Then again, in case something had magically changed. One, two. Then again, obsessively. Same result.

She said, 'This is not good.'

Reacher said, 'How long?'

'I'll be getting sick by tonight.'

'Where would we find snowploughs?'

'Are you kidding? Everywhere. Billy had a snowplough.'

'At his house. I mean big machines stored in a covered garage.'

'An airport?' Bramall said. 'Denver, maybe.'

Reacher said nothing.

Then he said, 'Three days ago.'

He stepped over the leaking body and leaned in the pick-up's cab. Sandwich wrappers. Gas receipts. He threw the wrappers on the driver's seat and piled the gas receipts on the passenger seat. He checked the floor and emptied the door cubbies.

He said, 'What was the date three days ago?'

Mackenzie told him. He riffed through the flimsy paper,

checking dates. Some receipts were a year old. Some were brittle and yellowed. He learned to look at the crisp items first.

Bramall said, 'Let me help.'

In the end they split the drift of paper four separate ways. They all stood around the pick-up's hood, and licked their thumbs, and speeded through the piles, like bank tellers with dollar bills around a counting table.

'Got one,' Mackenzie said. 'Three days ago, in the evening. Not a gas station. I think it's a diner or a restaurant.'

'I got gas here,' Bramall said. 'Three days ago, also in the evening.'

They clipped them under the pick-up's windshield wiper, like parking tickets. They scanned through the rest. They found nothing more.

'OK,' Reacher said. 'Let's take a look.'

The diner check was for thirteen dollars and change, paid in cash at 10.57 p.m., three days before. The gas receipt was for forty bucks even. Most likely prepaid in cash before lifting the nozzle, two twenties on the greasy counter. At 11.23 the same night.

Reacher said, 'He had a late dinner, and was done by eleven. He drove twenty minutes and got gas. Done by eleven-thirty. Then he drove to the secret warehouse and waited for midnight.'

The gas receipt had Exxon Mobil at the top, but no address except a location code. The diner was called Klinger's, and it had a phone number. The area code was 605.

'South Dakota,' Bramall said.

He walked away to the head of the ravine, where his cell worked better. He called the number. He came back and said, 'It's a mom-and-pop on a four-lane coming north out of Rapid City.'

*

331

Mackenzie and Bramall and Sanderson went to pack their stuff in the Toyota. Reacher's toothbrush was already in his pocket, and his passport was back where it belonged. He found Stackley's Colt and picked up the other three disassembled guns. He told the cowboys to put Stackley in the camper shell and drive the truck somewhere remote. An abandoned ranch, maybe. He told them to park it in a barn and leave it there. He pictured Stackley ten years from then, all dried up and mummified, discovered by chance with the remains of his head in an empty fentanyl box. The whole story, right there. A cold case that would stay cold for ever.

The cowboys drove away, leaving no trace behind except blood and small flecks of bone and brain tissue on the gravel. Reacher figured they would be gone an hour after the clearing went quiet. *You got hundreds of other species already lining up and licking their lips.*

Bramall brought the Toyota around. The women had taken the rear seat. Mackenzie had her travelling bags in the trunk next to Bramall's. Sanderson had nothing to bring with her except a canvas tote bag. She was looking around, already separated from her home of three years by the thick tinted glass in the Toyota's windows. Not that she cared. Nothing to stay for. Her dealer wouldn't be stopping by any time soon. That was for sure.

She settled back and faced forward, breathing shallow.

Reacher got in the front next to Bramall, who put the car in gear and set out down the driveway. Four miles of roots and rocks, and then the dirt road out of there.

FORTY-ONE

Gloria Nakamura walked the length of the corridor to her lieutenant's corner suite. She had been summoned. She didn't know why. When she got there the guy was looking at his computer screen. Not email. A law enforcement database.

He said, 'The federal DEA have custody of a guy with the first name Billy and a home address in Mule Crossing, Wyoming. He was arrested in Oklahoma for running a light. He is thought to have fled Wyoming because of a warning from a friend about a DEA operation in Montana. So no need to call the two men or the county dog. Billy's days of shooting people from behind a tree are over.'

Not Reacher after all, she thought.

For some reason she felt disappointed.

'But here's the thing,' her lieutenant said. 'The feds don't know about Scorpio. The report makes that clear. They're asking us all to cross-check Billy's name against our open files, to help them figure out who's running him. They don't know.'

'Are you going to tell them?'

'Hell no. I don't want a bunch of fancy-pants federal agents swooping in here to grab the glory. Scorpio belongs to the Rapid City Police Department. He always has. We're going to get him.'

'Yes, sir,' Nakamura said. 'We know Scorpio already replaced Billy. Inadmissible evidence, but there's a new guy out there.'

Her lieutenant said, 'There's another DEA request on the system. Looks completely separate, but I don't think it is. It was posted just afterwards. They're asking if anyone in the western region is seeing domestic packaged prescription oxycodone or fentanyl. Lots of it, like in the old days.'

'I thought that was over.'

'It is over. Every truck that leaves the factory is logged in the computer, and followed on GPS, plus they know exactly what was in it to start with, so in theory if they wanted to they could track down every single separate pill.'

'So why are they worried?'

'Something must not be working right. Or Scorpio is smarter than we thought. Either way, we can't let the feds get him first. So whatever you're doing now, I want you to do it ten times harder. Put your other cases on the back burner. I don't want federal agents coming in here.'

Bramall's navigation screen showed their best route would be Laramie to Cheyenne on the highway, and then straight north on a state road, all the way. So they turned at Mule Crossing, off the dirt road, on to the two-lane, past the post office, past the firework store, past the bottle rocket billboard, and all the way up to the highway, where they turned east. Mackenzie looked anxious all the way. She had jumped off the same building as her sister. They had jumped hand in hand. They had committed to the same problems, one from the inside and one from the outside. Sanderson herself was sitting with her head turned, watching out her window. Her hands were clasped together. To keep them from shaking, Reacher thought. She was pushing herself hard. She was rationing. Maybe she had set a target. A hundred miles, maybe. Before the next quarter inch. Or five red trucks, or a rest area, or a hybrid car.

Reacher checked the guns. The Smith & Wesson 39, the Ruger .22, the Springfield P9, and the Colt .45. All four were scratched and battered. But they probably all worked. All were only part loaded. The Smith had four Parabellum rounds in it, and the Springfield had five. He liked the Smith better, so he put all nine rounds in it, eight in the mag and one in the chamber. He dumped the empty Springfield in the door cubby. He put the Smith in his coat pocket. The Ruger was an ancient thing, a Standard, maybe dating all the way back to 1949, when it was the company's first product. It had just two rounds in it, .22 Long Rifle rimfires. Not Reacher's favourite calibre, so he dumped it in the door cubby along with the empty Springfield. The Colt was a military M1911, and judging by the style of its engravings and markings it could have been even older than the Ruger. It had three rounds in it. He held it by the barrel and half turned in his seat and offered it to Sanderson.

She was sitting behind Bramall, at that moment turned towards him at an angle where he saw more of the left side of her face than the right. Amazing work, Bramall had said. A virtuoso performance. But actually pretty lousy. Reacher thought all three things were true. She was sewn together from pieces the size of a postage stamp on a regular first-class letter. He could only imagine the immense skill and care employed in the surgery. Hours and hours of precision work. Reattaching nerves and muscles. But some hadn't taken. There were dead spots. And each postage-stamp piece was thickened and scarred at the edges, and lumpy with sutures. There had been some guesswork about what went where. Her nostril was stitched to her cheek at an odd angle. He couldn't compare it to the other side, because of the foil.

She said no to the gun. Not in words, but by unclasping her hands and holding them up. He saw a faint tremor. Nothing terrible. But it was still early. He turned back and offered the gun to Bramall. Who had different problems. More rules than Reacher, and a licence from the state of Illinois. He thought for a moment, and then he took the gun, but he put it in the door cubby, not his coat pocket. Some kind of an ethical compromise.

Nakamura saw Scorpio go in his back door just as late morning turned into lunchtime. She was parked on the cross street, at just the right angle. Scorpio left the door open again. Just an inch. Another warm day. A cloudless sky, above the tangle of cables on their leaning poles. Power lines and phone wires. Some thick, some thin. Some old, some new. Some very new. Maybe fibre optics, for the internet.

She took out her phone and dialled her friend.

She said, 'Look out for that signal again. Scorpio just went in his office.'

Her friend said, 'It's not an exact science.'

'You got it right last time, about the new Billy. There was a DEA bulletin.'

'I saw it.'

'Plus another one, posted just afterwards, about prescription medication. Which is weird, because they already track that stuff. They log the trucks as they leave the factory, and they log their routes by GPS, and they match invoices to payments. So where's the leakage?'

'That's your job. I'm just a humble tech.'

'Which is why I call you all the time. So I don't make a fool of myself.'

'What's the wild idea this time?'

336

'The computer guys at the factory could erase a whole truck, right? They could just delete it completely. They could erase its inventory and its GPS track. Like the departure never existed. Like that particular truck was in the shop that day. Or parked in the lot.'

'That suggests corruption among computer guys. I may not be the person to ask.'

'Is it possible?' she said.

'They would have to erase the invoice too. Also the original order. They would have to amend the factory production records, otherwise it would look like they were making more pills than went out the door. If they did all that, then everything would balance. The unrecorded surplus would be a kind of ghost quantity, floating out there somewhere.'

'Could they do all that?' she said.

'Of course they could,' her friend said. 'A computer does what it's told. The result depends on who's doing the telling.'

'What about someone not in the factory? Could they do it by remote control?'

'A hacker, you mean? Sure, if they breached security. Which would be tough, since we're talking pharmaceuticals and the DEA. But not impossible. You can buy software from Russia.'

'What kind of equipment would he need?'

'In the end nothing more than a laptop. But getting there would involve a lot of high-speed number crunching. There would be a lot of stuff running at once. He would have a couple of racks at least. Like his own server.'

'Hot, right?'

'We use max AC down here.'

'Thanks,' she said.

She clicked off, and looked at the wires overhead, and Scorpio's open door.

*

Bramall's cell phone rang just north of a place named Defiant, which had a John Deere dealership and not much else. Bramall fumbled the phone up out of his pocket and checked the screen. He offered it to Reacher, the same way Reacher had offered him the Colt.

The screen said *West Point Superintendent's Office.*

Reacher said, 'How does it know?'

'I programmed it,' Bramall said. 'When he called the first time.'

'You can take the boy out of the FBI,' Reacher said.

He answered the phone.

The same woman.

She said, 'Major Reacher, please.'

'Ma'am, this is Reacher.'

'Please hold for General Simpson.'

The supe came on and said, 'Major.'

Reacher said, 'General.'

'Progress report?'

'We're in the car.'

'Can she hear what you're saying?'

'Loud and clear.'

'Is she OK?'

'So far.'

'We're still working on the roadside bomb. Those files are sealed up pretty tight. But we got something new on Porterfield. Through the Marine Corps side. They had a stray copy classified at a lower level.'

'What did you get?'

'There was an arrest warrant out on him. Sworn a week before he died.'

'By who?'

'Defense Intelligence Agency.'

'Have you seen it?'

'No point. The DIA never says why.'

'Did it feel like a big deal?'

'It was DIA. That's always a big deal.'

'Do you know anyone there?'

'Forget it,' Simpson said. 'I want to retire in Florida, not Leavenworth.'

'Understood,' Reacher said. 'Thank you, general.'

He clicked off and passed the phone back to Bramall. As he turned he saw Sanderson's eyes on him, from under her hood. She knew something was up. He had asked, what did you get? She wasn't dumb. She knew what was out there.

He said nothing.

She said, 'Let's talk later.'

Then she turned away to look out the window. Reacher faced front. Bramall drove on.

FORTY-TWO

An hour later they stopped late for lunch in a one-light town. There was a Shell station and a family restaurant. Reacher saw that Sanderson wanted to stay outside, on the smokers' benches, to take care of business. But she forced herself inside, and ate first, fast and dirty, and then she excused herself and ducked back out again.

Reacher went with her. He sat beside her, a yard away. A concrete bench in a blacktop lot. With almost the same person. She had a ready-cut quarter-inch, rolled tight and set to go. The size of a wad of gum. She slipped it in, and chewed a little, and sucked a little. She clicked her neck and leaned back and looked up at the sky.

She said, 'I can't believe you talk to the supe on the phone.'

He said, 'Someone has to.'

'What did he tell you?'

'There was an arrest warrant out on Porterfield.'

She breathed out, a deep sigh of release and contentment. The fentanyl, Reacher guessed, not memories of her boyfriend's demise.

She said, 'Arrest warrants lapse when the suspect dies. Obviously. So that's ancient history now. You should forget all about it. Although I'm sure you won't. My sister says you still think like a cop. You won't let things go. Probably you think I killed him. You have to, really. We were domestic partners at the time. Statistics don't lie.'

'Did you kill him?'

'In a way.'

'What way?'

'Better that you don't know. Or you'll want to do something about it.'

'That's not a smart thing to say to someone who won't let things go.'

She didn't answer. She just breathed. Deep, long, slow, in and out. All was well with the world. Reacher had read a report that called it a euphoria users swore had no equal.

She said, 'Sy was wounded in the groin.'

Reacher said, 'I'm sorry.'

'Not a glamorous location,' she said. 'The second most feared, as a matter of fact, after a disfiguring facial wound. But they sewed him back together again. It all worked. He could have sex. Except one of the sutures always leaked. Under certain circumstances. It could get messy.'

Reacher said nothing.

'Apparently there's a lot of blood pressure involved,' she said.

'I hope,' Reacher said.

'And he had an infection. From the day he was wounded. His uniform pants were filthy dirty. He had been wearing them every day since California. The bullet punched tiny shreds of dirty cloth way deep inside. Happened all the time. The bugs take hold, and then you can't move them. They must be smarter than we are.'

'That was twelve years before.'

'He started out seeing doctors. But he didn't like them. In the end he looked after himself.'

'Like you did,' he said.

'I was like him,' she said. 'He showed me how to do it. He showed me how to do everything. He showed me the gates of death. The doctor said the leaky suture was equally likely to burst. Every night he could have bled to death. He said he learned to live with it. Then to love it. In the end I did too. Mostly.'

'Sounds like an interesting way to live.'

'He told me he felt secure with me. But I was never sure why. Did he think it was because I was a nice person? Or did he think I owed him for his attentions, because I was even more hideous? I couldn't let him think that. Or I would have to think it too. I would have to accept I needed special favours. Which I never took before. Why should I start now?'

Reacher didn't answer. She was quiet a long moment. She sighed again. A deep low shudder of pure contentment. She spread her arms along the back of the bench. Her right hand came near Reacher's shoulder. She laid back and looked up at the sky.

She said, 'How important is a woman's face?'

'To me?'

'For example.'

'A little bit, I guess. But for me it's mostly the eyes. Either there's someone home or there isn't. Either you want to knock on that door or you don't.'

She sat up and half turned on the bench. To face him, full on. She dropped the zipper on her silver top, maybe three inches down, and she eased her hood back, all the way, and off. Her hair spilled out and down and forward. Like her sister's, but shorter. Maybe greyer. But it fell the same way. It framed her face the same way.

Her eyes were green, and they were warm and liquid with

some kind of deep dreamy satisfaction. There was sparkle, muted, like winking sunlight on a woodland stream. And bitter amusement. She was mocking him, and herself, and the whole wide world.

He said, 'We're of equal rank, so I'm allowed to say it. Discouraged, but permitted. I would knock on your door.'

'That's nice of you.'

'For real. I'm sure Porterfield was for real too. He won't be the only one. People react in different ways.'

She pulled her hood back in place and tucked in her hair.

He said, 'You should get the IV. It's the foil that looks weird.'

'First I have to live through the night.'

'Sheriff Connelly found ten grand in a box.'

'Sy didn't trust banks. He preferred cash. What was in the box was all he had left. The banks lost the rest, back when I was overseas. Maybe that's why he didn't trust them.'

'How long would ten grand have lasted?'

She sighed again, deeply contented.

'Not long,' she said. 'Not the way we were going at it. And sometimes we had to buy food. And he was for ever paying the guy who fixed his roof.'

'Why did you stop calling your sister after he died?'

'That's easy,' she said. 'Reduced circumstances. I had to sell my phone.'

'Was it DIA who burgled his house?'

She nodded. 'They were late to the party. The circus was over by the time they arrived. But they got what they wanted.'

'Which was?'

She didn't answer. She just waved the question away, like it didn't matter.

Nakamura's cell phone rang. Her friend from Computer Crimes. He said, 'Scorpio is making calls. Or at least the signal we think

343

is Scorpio. The traffic feels about the same as three days ago. And he called the same number again. The one that texted back about the new Billy.'

She said, 'He's still in his office.'

'He's doing it by remote control. It's happening a little ways north of here. I assume the guy who texted is his man on the spot.'

'Can we tap his computer wires?'

'We already are. It's called the internet. But he has a firewall. We could hack him but it would take us days.'

She said, 'The driver must be his. Of the ghost truck that never leaves the factory. Except it does. The guy must know where to drive it.'

Her friend said, 'I wonder if they remembered about employment records. They would need to amend the guy's hours and miles. That might be a way in.'

'We don't have the records.'

'Then there's nothing you can do.'

'Maybe there is. Only half of this thing is records and computers. The other half is a physical reality. It's a real truck, driving on a real road, with physical stuff in it. How would it get here?'

'From where?'

'New Jersey, I think.'

'I-90.'

'And what's a little ways north of here, where the text came from?'

'I-90.'

'Where could he stop?'

'Lots of places. A lonely gas station ten miles out from an exit. Or some old industrial park somewhere, full of empty sheds with roll-up doors.'

She said, 'Scorpio is not going to leave his office tonight, right?'

'He never does,' her friend said. 'Except to go home.'

344

'OK, I'm heading up to the highway to take a look.'

She clicked off and started her motor.

They had already driven as far as New York to Boston, but they were still in Wyoming, and so far barely halfway through their trip. The big Toyota kept on rolling. Mackenzie and Sanderson talked together in the back, in quiet murmurs, in the kind of fast, unfinished shorthand Reacher guessed must be second nature to twins. Sanderson stayed in the good zone for most of an hour. Then she started to fade. Pretty fast. She withdrew into herself, as if she was preparing for a hard internal battle. She seemed to cramp up and get uncomfortable. She stared out the window. Maybe she was setting herself a new target. Different from on the highway. Maybe three herds of antelope, or two of mule deer, or a break in the snow fence.

Nakamura drove north out of town on the four-lane, past Klinger's family restaurant, where she ate sometimes, if work brought her out in that direction. She kept on going, through the empty miles before the I-90 ramps, looking left and right, seeing what there was to see. Which wasn't much. In fact nothing at all, from the truck driver's point of view. Not exactly a stolen vehicle, but hot none the less. Or in fact cold. Zero degrees. It wasn't there. It didn't exist. Which put a lot of pressure on the driver. Attention had to be avoided. No speeding tickets, no weird manoeuvres, no traffic cameras, no exposure at all. South of the highway felt wrong. He wouldn't go there.

North of the highway was worse. She carried on under the bridge and came out amid no density whatsoever. No cover, no concealment. Mostly open prairie. Flat land. Distant horizons. She drove ten minutes, and pulled over on the shoulder. There was nothing ahead of her.

South of the highway felt wrong.

North of the highway felt wrong.

Therefore the guy stayed on the highway. Had to. No other choice. He never got off. There was a rest area six miles east. It was a big place. She had been there before. Food, fuel, a state trooper building, a motel in back, some highway department stuff. All kinds of nooks and crannies.

She U-turned ditch to ditch and headed back to the highway. She hit the ramp and hit the gas.

They stopped again, at a gas station that had a two-table coffee shop next to the car wash machine. Mackenzie used the bathroom. Sanderson popped another quarter-inch strip. She sat on a bench outside, and nursed a go-cup of coffee, with the smell of unleaded coming from one direction, and auto shampoo from the other. Reacher came out and she scooted over, as if to offer him room, plus a yard of space between.

An invitation.

He sat down.

He said, 'You OK?'

'Right now,' she said.

'Tell me about the gates of death.'

She was quiet a long moment.

Then she said, 'You build up a tolerance. You need to use more and more, just to get to the same place. Pretty soon you're taking what is technically a fatal dose. One sniff would kill a straight person stone dead. And then you want more. Now you're taking literally higher than a fatal dose. Are you brave enough for the next step?'

'Were you?'

'I felt the same way when I was overseas. The only way to get through was never back down. Always step up. Always take it on. You had to be scornful. Like, is that all you got? So sure, I took the next step. And the next.'

She sighed. The new quarter-inch strip was kicking in.

She said, 'That's the beautiful thing about next steps. There's always another one coming.'

Reacher said, 'Logically there must be a last one.'

She didn't answer.

He said, 'What did Porterfield do for a living?'

'Didn't the roofer tell you?'

'He said he talked a lot on the phone. Sheriff Connelly said he drove a lot of miles in his car.'

'Sy was a disabled veteran. He didn't work.'

'Apparently he filled his time somehow. Was it a hobby?'

'Why do you care about Sy so much?'

'Just a professional thing. Either he was killed somewhere else and dumped in the woods, or he got eaten by a bear. I never had a situation where getting eaten by a bear was a genuine possibility.'

'There's a third possibility.'

'I know. And I know you were there. You told me.'

She was quiet another moment.

'I'll make a deal,' she said. 'I'll tell you the story if we win tonight.'

'That's a hard bargain,' he said. 'Could be tough. Is the story worth it?'

'It's not exciting,' she said. 'But it's sad.'

'Then we need more of a prize. I would want to hear your story too.'

'About the roadside bomb? My sister told me your theories. A failed operation with multiple U.S. casualties.'

'Worst case,' he said.

She sighed again, long, hard, deeply, happily.

Almost like purring.

She said, 'It was way worse than worst case. It was a catastrophe. But it wasn't my operation. I was representing the

347

support effort, but the whole thing was a much bigger deal than that. It was devised at a much higher level. The town was in hilly country, compact in size, not walled but well defended. The road looped in on the right and out on the left. Long story short, we needed to take the town, but the pointy-heads said we had to do it without unprovoked civilian casualties. Which at the time was code for no air strikes. So we planned approaches by armoured infantry on the road from both directions at once. But the same pointy-heads had some clever analysis that said the enemy would expect that, and be capable of defending it, so we should mount a third approach up the open hillside, halfway in between, so we could come up in the middle of the town and isolate both sets of defenders at once.'

Reacher said, 'How bad was the terrain?'

'That was everyone's first question. It was the kind of place you had to get eyes-on. The pointy-heads worked out a spot where we could see the whole rise at once. They said in terms of seeing one contour in particular it was where we had to be. They were very precise. But they said not to worry, because it was outside RPG range. So we went there. The dead dog was on the exact same spot. Three of us died, and eleven were hurt.'

'Any of yours?'

'Happily no. Only upward, which isn't the same. But that was the problem. That's why the files were sealed. Some big names went down. It was a failure of intelligence. With a small letter, not a capital. Ours was less than theirs. Once again we under-estimated them. These unshaven guys wearing dresses had predicted exactly how we were going to attack, and even exactly where we would stand to plan it out, and exactly when we would show up to do it. A day either way on that, maybe. But four-day dogs are what they like best, and that's what we got. The umpires would have to call it one-zip for them. We had fourteen down. Cost them nothing except a cell phone and someone else's dog.'

'OK,' Reacher said.

'You were worried I got my people killed.'

'I thought it would upset you.'

'I wouldn't be here if I had,' she said. 'I wouldn't have made it through.'

Then Mackenzie came out, and next Bramall, and they both stood around in let's-go poses, so eventually Sanderson got up, and Reacher followed her back to the car.

They hit Rapid City's southern limit just as the sun was setting.

FORTY-THREE

They drove through town, straight south to north in the dark. Reacher recognized some of what he saw. He recognized the street with the chain hotels. He recognized the all-day Chinese restaurant, where Scorpio's guy had picked him up, in the battered old Lincoln. They kept on going and came out the other side of town on what Bramall's phone said was the four-lane that led up to Klinger's diner. And it did, as promised. Klinger's turned out to be more of a family restaurant, all lit up, floating alone in a vast dark parking lot, somehow both faded and majestic all at once.

They went in, and ate, because it was dinnertime. Eat when you can, Reacher said. You don't know when the next chance will come. Sanderson endorsed the theory. For a small guy Bramall was always hungry. Mackenzie said she didn't really feel like eating, but in the end she ordered a meal. Afterwards she said it was good. Reacher agreed.

They asked the waitress if she knew an Exxon station about a twenty-minute drive away. The woman screwed up her face, like she knew, like it was on the tip of her tongue. Then like she knew once, but she didn't know any more. One of those questions so everyday it couldn't be answered.

Then something came to her.

'The highway gas is Exxon,' she said. 'Up at the rest area.'

Back in the car Bramall looked at his navigation screen. The closest rest area was six miles east of the closest on-ramp. The electronic brain said it was twenty minutes away. Bramall said the pharmaceutical factories were mostly in New Jersey. Trucks would come west. A secret warehouse inside an I-90 rest area would be a very convenient thing to have. It could be stocked and re-stocked at any time of night or day. Equally it could stock and re-stock incoming visitors at any time of night or day.

'But it didn't,' Reacher said. 'Stackley told us they had to wait until midnight. It sounded like the opposite of a warehouse to me. Nothing was stored there for people to show up and get. It was the other way around. People got in line and waited for stuff to show up. Maybe it arrives there at midnight. So I agree, the rest area is the obvious place. But as a meeting point only. As a rendezvous. With a lot of moving parts. One rogue westbound truck comes in, and six or ten guys like Billy and Stackley load up and move out. It must be a real fast hustle. Right in the middle of an I-90 rest area, but under the cover of a shed half full of snowploughs. The voice mail said they've got it all to themselves. I guess that's correct. It's summertime.'

Bramall said, 'So after eating dinner at Klinger's, Stackley drove twenty minutes to the rest area, where he bought gas, and then he rolled a hundred yards around a corner and waited till midnight. All we have to do is figure out which corner. Which won't be difficult. The rest area is a finite size. We're looking for a service road leading to the snowploughs. How many can there be?'

'Is it always this easy?' Mackenzie said.

'Mr Bramall makes it look easy,' Reacher said.

Sanderson said nothing. She was infantry. She knew about pointy-heads and their best laid plans.

Bramall started up and headed north on the four-lane, through the night-time darkness, all the way to the highway ramps, where he made the right to head east towards the rest stop, which the machine told him was just six minutes away.

The machine was correct. Exactly six minutes later Bramall coasted off into a giant central facility. The eastbound and west-bound lanes skirted it in mile-wide loops through the prairie. It was like a town all by itself. It had lit-up acres of Exxon gas and diesel, and half a dozen bright neon fast food franchises, and a highway patrol building, and a chain motel, and a highway depart-ment office with a weighbridge.

What it didn't have was snowploughs. At least not within easy view. Reacher felt red-hot infantry scepticism coming out from under Sanderson's hood. Mackenzie looked disappointed. Maybe not so easy after all.

They gave it one more go-round. After which they were con-fident there were no snowploughs stored anywhere within the bounds of the facility. There were no service roads leading to covered garages half full of any kind of winter equipment.

Which raised an obvious question. If not there, then where? There had to be winter equipment stored somewhere. A lot of it. Winter was a serious issue in South Dakota. Mackenzie said maybe so serious they used a whole separate depot for it. She knew the west.

But where was the depot? Who could they ask? It was a weird question. Do you know where the state stores its snowploughs? No one would know. Most folk would take it for some kind of a weird political stunt, to make a point, or to expose their igno-rance, like asking if they knew their congressperson's name.

The only people who would know the answer were people who were currently somewhere else. Wherever the state stored its snowploughs.

Reacher said, 'He prepaid his gas at eleven twenty-three. Right here, very close to where we're sitting now. Let's say it took him two minutes to walk back from the kiosk and get set. Let's say he started pumping at eleven twenty-five. How long does forty bucks last?'

Mackenzie said, 'Out here you could fill a big tank.'

'So it took a few minutes. It could have been well after eleven-thirty before he was back on the road. But he was the new boy there. He didn't want to screw up. He needed a big margin of error. He must have been going somewhere real close by. Three-minute maximum, literally. He would want to make sure he got there on time. Or early. He would want to be comfortable.'

'What's three minutes from here?'

'Maybe the separate depot. For the snowploughs. A central facility. Access from both sides. On the same land as this, before eastbound and westbound narrow down again. Right next door to here, maybe. It's a wedge of wasted space otherwise. There could be an inconspicuous little off-ramp, with a sign, saying highway department only. Plenty of trees all around. No one notices a thing like that.'

'Then it could be in either direction. We might have already passed it. There must be wedges of space both sides. We don't know which way to go now.'

'We didn't already pass it,' Sanderson said. 'There were no inconspicuous little ramps. I notice a thing like that. It means for the moment we're trapped on this road. But neither can the enemy reinforce an ambush up ahead. So on balance I'm happy. The tail gunner can relax for a second. If you're right about a separate facility, then it must be east of here. And if Reacher is right about how anxious Stackley was, it must be close by. Close enough to get back on the highway and then get off again immediately. If he's wrong about how nervous Stackley was, it could be farther away. But it's within fifteen or twenty miles maximum, because even if the guy was cool as ice, he had to get where he was going by midnight latest. And he couldn't drive a hundred miles an hour to do it. Those guys can't get away with things like that. They must never stand out. So I would recon to the east. If we don't find anything, we still have time to come back and think again.'

Bramall looked over his shoulder at Mackenzie.

His employer.

'Want to try it?' he said.

'Yes,' Mackenzie said.

Bramall circled the parking lot, under sodium lights high on poles, looking for the way back to the travel lanes. In the corner of his eye Reacher thought he saw a pale blue car, circling the other way. A domestic product. A Chevrolet, possibly. Nothing fancy. A plain specification.

He looked again.

It was gone.

Bramall found the exit and followed the arrow marked Sioux Falls, which was east. He watched the road ahead, like a good driver should. Sanderson and her sister and Reacher all watched the left shoulder. They watched the narrowing space between the eastbound and the westbound lanes.

It turned out Stackley had been anxious, but not quite as anxious as Reacher thought he should be. It was more than three minutes out. Closer to four and a half. They saw an inconspicuous off-ramp. They saw a small bland sign, that said *Authorized Personnel Only.*

'Don't take it,' Reacher said. 'Not yet. We need to make a better plan.'

354

FORTY-FOUR

G loria Nakamura drove every inch of the rest area. Night had fallen, but it was all lit up. She pictured a truck pulling in. Maybe not a semi. Maybe not an eighteen-wheeler. Maybe just a panel van, loaded with smaller orders from mom-and-pop pharmacies and suburban clinics. A Ford Econoline, or some such. Probably painted white. Probably a shiny high-gloss finish, to suggest health and cleanliness and antiseptic pharmaceutical wholesomeness. Probably a bland brand name in a friendly font, pale green like grass, or blue like the sky.

Where would it park?

Nowhere near the State Police building, for obvious reasons. Not near the gas pumps, either. Even in the dark. The oil company had cameras, in case of drive-away no-pays. Not near the entrance or the exit either, because the highway department had cameras too, for traffic flow. The truck couldn't afford to show up on video. Not in South Dakota, when the mothership's computer had it idle in a factory lot in New Jersey. There was a big parking area shared between the restroom block and the fast food franchises.

It was lit up bright. But it had cameras too. For liability, she supposed. In case someone got in a fender bender, and blamed it on the burger stand. Probably an insurance requirement.

There was a weighbridge, with a highway department office, all tan brick and metal windows. Closed up and dark. But it was way out in the open. Too exposed. She pictured the panel van, with its rear doors open, feeding a cluster of smaller vehicles. An anxious crowd, waiting. People like Billy, and the new Billy, and all the other guys like Billy, in pick-up trucks and SUVs and old sedans. Loading up, before taking off.

Where would they do that?

Nowhere. The rest area felt wrong.

She circled the parking lot one more time. In the corner of her eye she saw a black SUV, circling the lot the other way. It had blue plates, she thought. Illinois, maybe. She looked again, but it was gone.

Bramall pulled over on the shoulder, in the dark, a mile further on, where the eastbound and the westbound lanes came back together again, either side of a standard grass median. Safe enough. If a trooper came by, they could say they had an engine light, or a worry about a tyre. There wasn't much traffic. Cars blew by, one by one. Then a semi truck, in a howl of noise and wind. The Toyota rocked on its springs.

Reacher said, 'How far is the next exit?'

Bramall checked his screen.

'About thirty miles,' he said.

'Waste of gas. Do a U-turn across the median. Rose and I will get out at the depot ramp. You and Mrs Mackenzie can go park in the rest area and walk back through the trees from the west. You can meet us there. We can take a look around and figure out how we do it.'

'You want me with you?' Sanderson said.

356

'Why not?'

'I can't,' she said. 'I don't feel so good.'

'You can fix that.'

'I can't,' she said again. 'I only have one strip left.'

'We're about to get more.'

'We don't know that.'

'You have to use your last strip some time.'

'I want to know I still have it.'

'Shape up, major. I need you with me, and I need you in good condition at midnight. I'll leave you to work out the timings.'

The car went quiet.

Then Mackenzie said, 'Let's go.'

Bramall waited until he saw no headlights coming either way. He turned the wheel and drove across all three traffic lanes. He bumped down onto the median, which was dished in the middle, like a wide drainage channel. For snowmelt, Reacher figured. The ploughs had to dump it somewhere. The Toyota drove down one slope and up the other, where it bumped up into the west-bound lanes and turned and took off, in the direction it had come from. Now they were heading the same way the truck would be later. Coming west from New Jersey. It was already rolling. It had been rolling for hours. It was somewhere behind them, past Sioux Falls by then, doing the long miles Reacher had done in the huge red truck with the sleeper cab. With the old man at the wheel. *My wife would say you feel guilty about something. She reads books. She thinks about things.* They were seeing what the truck would see later. Which was nothing much for a mile, and then at the edge of the left-hand headlight beam an unannounced off-ramp, and a sign that said *Authorized Personnel Only*.

Bramall stopped on the shoulder a hundred yards later. Reacher got out and walked around to Sanderson's door. She got out. Boots, jeans, silver jacket zipped to the neck. But this time

357

the hem of her hood was folded back. For peripheral vision. For situational awareness. She was ready for action. Her face was exposed from her cheek bones forward. The foil on the right, and the scars on the left. The misshapen mouth. One eyebrow terminated halfway through, for no good reason, except it was sewed to something that wasn't an eyebrow.

'It's dark,' she said. 'It's OK.'

Bramall drove away.

They waited on the shoulder. No traffic came by. She was chewing hard. Not gum, he thought. Her last quarter-inch. Or maybe half of it. She could have torn it in two, thumbnail to thumbnail. *I'll leave you to work out the timings.* He hoped she knew what she was doing. It wasn't working like it had before. She wasn't calm. Maybe the last quarter-inch never was. How could it be? It was like swinging on a trapeze, letting go, flying through the air towards nobody, hoping somebody would get there and catch you before you fell. Maybe the new gold standard for insecurity. An addict with an empty pocket. Suspended above the abyss. Nothing in reserve.

They walked back the hundred yards and stopped level with the sign. *Authorized Personnel Only.* Nothing coming.

Reacher said, 'Ready?'

They ran across the traffic lanes, and around the sign, and into the ramp. Where they stopped and got their breath and looked ahead. They were on a heavy-duty engineered road, good for heavy-duty trucks. It was long enough to disappear into the darkness. There were trees planted both sides, to pretty it up, but it was industrial access, nothing more.

Sanderson said, 'Do you have a flashlight?'

Reacher said, 'No.'

'I'm sure Mr Bramall would have lent us one. I'm sure he has several.'

'Do you like him?'

'I think my sister chose well.'

They set off walking through the dark. There was enough moon to get by, helped by occasional spill from distant headlights, which flashed on things like camera strobes, so they could be fixed in time and space, and accounted for. Beginning to end the ramp was half a mile long, and it led to a drive-in, drive-out garage big enough for heavy equipment. They stayed in the trees and scoped it out. There were four roads in total, an on-ramp and an off-ramp each side, like four long legs on a skinny insect, all meeting at the garage, which had a door each end. Both of which were closed. There was no one around. No vehicles. No sound. It was a snowplough shed at the end of summer.

Deserted.

'What time is it?' Sanderson asked.

'Ten o'clock,' Reacher said. 'Two hours to go.'

'Is this going to work?'

'It looks right. It's what the voice mail said. There's a service road leading to a covered garage.'

'That was then. They might have a different place for tonight.'

'As good as this? I doubt it. This place is solid gold.'

'There's no sign of life.'

'Not yet. I think that's the point. They get in and out real fast. It's a totally hidden location. Who pays attention to these places? Someone drives in here, they're invisible.'

He turned and looked back. The truck from Jersey would come in from the east, the same way they had walked. Then it would loop around the garage and head back the other direction, for the empty run home. Stackley would have headed west. The other guys like him could have headed either way. It was a secret rendezvous and a hidden highway interchange all in one. Solid gold.

They walked up to where they thought Bramall and Mackenzie would come through the trees, and found them just arriving. They did the tour again.

Mackenzie said, 'Obviously I'm not the person to ask how we play this.'

Sanderson said, 'Operationally the soundest plan would be ambush the incoming vehicle halfway along the service road. After it leaves the highway but before it gets to the garage. One operation, maximum one round fired, maximum one enemy killed. Focused and efficient.'

'How would we ambush the vehicle?'

'I don't know if we should.'

'I don't follow.'

Reacher said, 'We don't know what kind of vehicle it is. But it came out the factory gate, so it's probably an official pharmaceutical truck. I'm sure the Boy Detective discussed the matter with them. Lots of meetings and memos. The truck is probably locked. Maybe only the driver can open it. A combination or a special key. Your sister doesn't want to run the risk of having to beat it out of him.'

'Would you?'

'The guy already took money to deliver to the wrong address. Clearly he's open to a negotiation. Fair exchange is no robbery.'

'So which?'

Bramall said, 'There could be ten or twelve guys picking up here. To get what they got we would have to rob them all, one by one. On their way out of here. Like the ticket booth in a parking lot. Twelve robberies, one after the other. Maybe a minute apart. I don't think we could do it. We have no choice.'

'Rose?'

'Like I said, the ambush chooses itself. Let's hope the truck is not locked.'

'There's a third way,' Reacher said. 'The best of both worlds.'

360

FORTY-FIVE

Nakamura returned to the rest area, because she ran out of options. It was a bad location, but maybe better than anywhere else. She pictured a panel van, shiny white. Where would it park, to conduct its business? As far away as possible, surely. Which meant somewhere on the far edges of the lot. Late in the evening there were many empty rows. Folks liked to park as close as possible to the buildings. Why not? Why give themselves an extra walk?

She cruised by, in her pale blue car. She was right. The western edge of the lot was completely deserted. Row after empty row. The eastern edge had just one lone car. It was parked with its grille tight up against the trees.

It was a black SUV, with a blue licence plate.

Illinois.

She dialled her phone.

She said, 'Expedite a request for an out-of-state plate.'

In reply she got a burst of static and a verbal OK.

She read out the number. She kept the phone to her ear, and

parked next to the black SUV. It was a Toyota. She got out and checked it over. It was dusty. It had done some miles out west. It was hard to see inside, because the windows were high and she was short. But it looked like folk were travelling. There were bags in the trunk. But why park there?

She looked ahead at the trees and concluded a person could walk through them. But what for? Illicit activity was safe enough in the last row of the parking lot. No one needed to hide out in the woods. There was nothing on the other side, until eventually the trees thinned out and the regular median started up again. Technically a person could walk from there to the next rest area with grass under his feet all the way. Or was there a highway department maintenance depot in the way? She couldn't remember. There was one somewhere. They were the kind of places you never really paid attention to.

There was static in her ear, and a voice on her phone.

It said, 'Illinois DMV lists that plate as a black Toyota Land Cruiser, registered to Terrence Bramall, at a Chicago business address. He describes himself as a private detective.'

Sanderson walked to her starting position, and Reacher went with her. He wanted to know she was still chewing. Or if not, whether that was a good thing or bad. She was still chewing. Doing OK. He hoped she wasn't peaking too early. She had the Ruger Standard. The .22. Two rounds in it. It was all she would take. Bramall had the Colt .45. Three rounds in it. Mackenzie had the empty Springfield. Better than nothing. Like the man said, ninety per cent of everything was striking a pose.

Reacher said, 'Get the story ready for me.'

Sanderson said, 'A hundred things could go wrong.'

'Not a hundred,' he said. 'Couple dozen, maybe.'

'The arrest warrant was bullshit. I want you to know that, whatever. They were trying to shut him up.'

'You want me to know part of the story, but not all of it?'

'I want you to know that part at least.'

'What was he trying to say?'

'Something he shouldn't.'

'OK,' Reacher said. 'Stay on the ball and tell me the rest later. You doing OK?'

'So far.'

'Good until when?'

'What time is it now?'

'Close to ten-thirty.'

She did the math in her head, and she didn't answer.

Reacher walked back to his own starting position. But before he got there Bramall walked up with his phone, which was glowing green, with what was apparently a call in progress with the West Point Superintendent's Office.

'For you,' Bramall said.

Reacher took the phone.

He said, 'General.'

The supe said, 'Major.'

'We're currently manoeuvring. Success or failure within two hours from now.'

'Do I want to know the details?'

'Probably not.'

'What are your chances?'

'Uncertain. It's a rules of engagement issue.'

'She got more scruples than you?'

'She could hardly have fewer. But there are things I won't do. And we have civilians with us.'

'Welcome to the modern army. You could come back and take a class.'

'She told me Porterfield's arrest warrant was bullshit.'

'What was your reaction to that?'

'She would say that, wouldn't she.'

363

'Mine too. But she appears to be right. My friends to the south got into the file, and there's nothing in it. It has to be phony. No one knows the guy who swore it out. We looked him up, and the only match on the name was a guy in the press office in a Marine Corps medical battalion.'

'The way she talks, I think she feels Porterfield had some kind of a just cause going on. In which case there must be a lot of files. He was an unemployed veteran who had to change a dressing every day. If a guy like that gets a bug up his ass he tells everyone about it. He writes letters to the newspaper and calls his congressman every day. And then the White House and the talk shows and every law enforcement agency he can think of. His name must crop up everywhere. I want to know. She might never tell me.'

'How is she doing?'

'Pretty good, all things considered.'

'Is her attitude OK?'

'In what way?'

'Are you free to talk?'

'Sure,' Reacher said.

'Why I wanted to call. We found a sideways reference to a document in a medical ethics case. An army psychiatrist had published a paper. The charge was he had failed to adequately conceal the identity of his subject. The paper was about a woman officer who had been grievously wounded in the face. During an on-site inspection she wasn't required to attend. She was standing in for another officer. Purely as a personal favour. The operation was nothing to do with her. She was there because some other asshole had another appointment. Which upon investigation turned out to be extremely unworthy. The guy killed himself when the questions started. Turned out he was getting jacked off by some Afghan whore, while the most beautiful woman in the army was getting maimed. The paper was about her psychological struggle to see herself as wounded in the line of duty.'

'The woman was Rose Sanderson?'

'It was while she was still in the hospital. She said the publicity upset her.'

'She hasn't mentioned it,' Reacher said.

'It's a factor,' the supe said. 'She feels betrayed.'

At eleven o'clock the compound was still pitch dark and silent. Which Reacher expected. His theory allowed for maybe twenty minutes of furtive gathering, and then frantic action at midnight. And then nothing again. So he wasn't worried. Not yet. Not unless he was completely wrong, and a bunch of guys was assembling somewhere else entirely, miles away, right then, slapping each other on the shoulder, opening their trunk lids and their tailgates wide, exposing hungry space inside.

Possible.

He waited.

Eleven-thirty was just the same. Pitch dark and silent. Still OK. Still consistent, still logical, still expected. But getting close. All the well-known sayings. The crunch was coming. The money shot. The rubber was about to meet the road. For the first time in his life he paid close attention to what his body was doing. He felt stress building inside him, and he felt an automatic response, some kind of a primitive biological leftover, that converted it to focus and strength and aggression. He felt his scalp tingle, and an electric flow pass through his hands to his fingers. He felt his eyesight grow vivid. He felt himself get physically larger, and harder, and faster, and stronger.

He knew Sanderson would be feeling the same things. He wondered how they mixed with fentanyl. He hoped she was doing OK.

Then he saw headlights on the service road.

FORTY-SIX

The headlights were dim and yellow, which meant it was an old vehicle, and they were at a modest height and a regular width apart, which meant the old vehicle was normal size. Not a giant pick-up truck. Not a huge SUV. It drove up to the building and the wash from its lights on the siding showed it to be a sedan maybe twenty years old. Shaped like a slug. Dull paint, an indeterminate dark colour. No hubcaps. A snapped-off antenna.

It backed up and parked neatly, out of the way, and a guy got out. He could have been fifty. Thick around the waist, hair plastered to his scalp with oil. He was wearing blue jeans and a grey sweatshirt with a word on it. A brand name, perhaps. He walked over to the roll-up door, and did something with a key. Then he squatted like a weightlifter and hauled on the bottom lip, and the door came clattering up, getting faster, as if a counter-balance was kicking in.

The guy walked into the garage and a minute later there was a muted repeat of the same noise, as the far door clattered up.

Inside on the left were ranks of huge yellow snowploughs. On the right was empty space. Someone had chalked diagonal parking bays on the concrete floor. They were numbered one through ten. One was at the far end. Ten was at the near end.

The guy in the sweatshirt walked back to his car. He leaned in and got a clipboard from the passenger seat. It had a pen on a string. Some kind of a list. The guy walked back to the garage and took up station near the entrance.

There will be a guard at the door.

The guy took out a handgun and checked the chamber.

Eleven forty-one in the evening.

Four minutes later there were more headlights on the service road. Higher, wider and brighter than the guy's old sedan. It was a Dodge Durango SUV. It drove towards the garage door. It stopped next to the guy. The window came down. Something was said. The guy checked his clipboard, and waved the truck inside. It parked at an angle, in a chalked-out bay.

A minute later a rusted Silverado drove up the road. No better condition than Stackley's old thing. But no camper shell. It had a flat vinyl cover on the bed. Then an old black four-wheel-drive showed up. Both parked inside.

By five minutes to midnight nine of the ten chalk bays were occupied. Only number five was empty. The guy in the sweatshirt looked relaxed about it. Rules were rules. The other nine guys waiting next to their trucks looked happy about it. More to go around.

The guy in the sweatshirt checked his watch.

His phone rang.

He listened.

He called out, 'Two minutes, guys. It's nearly here.'

Two minutes later a white panel van came charging up the road, going fast, then braking hard. It stopped and waited. It had New Jersey plates. The guy in the sweatshirt gave it a sign, and then he ran inside the building. The van turned and drove along the outside of the garage, all the way, front to back. It turned again, tight and awkward, and nosed in through the rear door. The opposite way from everyone else. It stopped level with the truck in bay number one. The guard ran up inside and met it there. The driver got out.

Which all changed the plan. Afterwards Reacher was mad he hadn't read more into the chalk numbers on the floor. At first he thought they might represent geographical regions, or length of service. Some tradition or perk of the job. Or nothing at all. Maybe they were there just for the fun of it. You chalk some bays, you might as well chalk some numbers. To make it look professional.

But they were a priority order. Some kind of a status ladder. Maybe number one was the guy with the best volume. Like salesman of the week. Like a prize. Part of which was the right to a fast getaway. First served, first out of there. A decent incentive.

There were a dozen different mechanical ways to make that happen. All kinds of manoeuvres. But by far the simplest was to bring the panel van in through the rear door.

Reacher was at the front door.

He had foreseen that the guard and the driver from the panel van would be side by side at the start of the process. The plan was, as soon as the driver opened the van, unsuspectingly, voluntarily, without having been beaten or coerced in any way at all, so that everyone's conscience was entirely clear, then Reacher would fire a nine-millimetre round over their heads, into the booming space beyond, to freeze them, to claim possession of the panel van, whereupon Sanderson would announce her presence from behind, and they would all glance back and see a mysterious figure pointing a handgun, and any spark of early trouble would snuff out right then. Only an expert would spot the

Ruger for a .22. Only an expert with X-ray vision would know it was nearly empty. He thought the plan would work. First the guard and the driver, and then the other guys. Two different categories of people. He felt the sequence was important.

He was at the wrong end of the garage.

Everything was turned around.

He was now Sanderson.

She was now him.

With adrenalin, and fight hormones, and fentanyl, or maybe half fentanyl and half withdrawal, and pain and discomfort, and the sweats and the shakes. Right then she would be watching the driver. Waiting for him to open up. A combination or a special key. Or maybe not. Maybe just a regular door. In which case it would all happen faster. The .22 was quiet for a firearm, but still a lot louder than anything else in life. In the echoing space a .22 would do the job just fine.

If she took over.

If she did it.

Nothing yet.

Still nothing. Maybe it was a long combination. Like a computer. All kinds of characters, upper case, lower case. Numbers and symbols.

Nothing.

Then a colossal gunshot explosion, and a brutal *bang* as a bullet hit a beam overhead.

Everyone froze.

Up ahead she stepped out and said, 'Stay where you are.'

Like he would have.

Behind them he stepped out and said, 'Nobody move.'

Like she would have.

They glanced his way. He had the Smith aimed low, at their waists. He had learned that angle worried people. Some kind of an old animal instinct.

369

Up ahead she shook her head. They were turned around. The next lines were his.

He used his MP voice.

He said, 'Remove all cell phones and firearms from pockets, holsters, and other places of concealment. Place them on the floor at your feet. Do not get cute with me. In a moment I will search you. If I find a further firearm I will shoot you through the back of the knee with it. If I find a cell phone I will shoot you through the back of the knee with my own firearm. These are promises as solemn as government debt. Please take a moment to think about it. We're not cops or federal agents. This is purely private business. For you, just a temporary nuisance. So weigh it up. You can walk the rest of your life, or you can use a wheel-chair. Figure out what works best for you.'

Eleven guys, eleven phones, twelve guns. The guard had a small .38 on his ankle. Mackenzie stepped out to collect them. She was pointing the empty Springfield. She looked like an after-noon movie. The beautiful queen of the underworld. They all stared. Reacher told them to kick their guns and their phones towards her. She picked them all up, one by one, and she put them in a bag she found in the panel van. It had a cheerful logo, in greens and blues, like the grass and the sky.

Reacher and Sanderson herded all eleven guys into bay number five. A tight fit. Like on the stairs, getting out of the ball game. Trapped between two slab-sided trucks. Reacher and Sanderson stood off at forty-five degree angles, face on, guns levelled. Not operationally necessary. Either one of them would have been effective. But two had a calming effect. It kept unwise thoughts to a minimum. And therefore casualties. It was a humanitarian deployment of resources. The modern army.

At first he thought it was working. The eleven guys were unusually subdued. They were stunned, quiet, defeated, some-how shaken. Somehow demoralized.

Somehow sickened.

Then he realized.

Sanderson's hood was still peeled back.

Behind them in the corner of his eye he saw Bramall reverse the Toyota through the same door the van had used, and manoeuvre it backward straight in line with the panel van, the tailgate close to the van's rear doors. He saw Mackenzie start shovelling boxes across, from one vehicle to the other. White and crisp and shiny. Lots of them. Bramall lent a hand. They worked hard together. Box after box. Space became an issue. He saw them tossing bags out of the trunk, over into the back seat.

He stepped back a pace and looked left and right along the row of vehicles. He liked the look of the Dodge Durango best. It was a regular shape. It looked like it would have familiar controls.

He pointed at it.

He said, 'Whose is that?'

Some guy shuffled.

Reacher said, 'Are the keys in it?'

The guy nodded.

'Gas?'

The guy nodded.

'Good to go here,' Bramall called out, from behind.

'OK,' Reacher said. 'We know what we're doing. By the numbers now. One, two, three, and out of here.'

Step one was Mackenzie visiting every vehicle except the Durango, including the guard's old car outside, and adding all the keys to her bag. Most of the cars were old enough to hot-wire, but the pharmaceutical van was a brand new Mercedes, with a chip in the key. It was going nowhere. Which was good. The Boy Detective needed to see it, sitting there stranded, inert, caught out and shamefaced. It explained everything, all by itself. It was the master clue.

Step two was Mackenzie and Bramall getting in the Toyota and driving away.

Which they did.

Step three was Reacher coming close and central, with the Smith aimed two-handed, low, at their waists, or lower, and then Sanderson backing off, step by cautious step, toward the Durango, feeling one-handed behind her for the handle, getting in, starting up. She backed out of the angled slot, and then couldn't go forward because of the panel van in the way, so she reversed all the way out through the front door.

And was gone.

Reacher waited. On his own. Eleven guys penned up. He felt them stir. A flicker of anger. At themselves, at first. Eleven to one. Ridiculous. What were they, pussies? Which was a bad kind of thing to think. They were going to make trouble for themselves. He had seen it before. Sooner or later he would have to shoot one of them in the leg. To get their attention. It would be their own fault.

Behind him in the corner of his eye he saw Sanderson back the Durango in through the same door the panel van had used. Now she was on the right side of it, and facing in the right direction. Ten yards from him. He heard the transmission clunk. From reverse back to drive. Engine idling. Foot on the brake. Ready to go.

He backed away, raising his aim a little as he went, but not much, randomly scouting side to side, to the guy on the left, to the guy on the right. Then back to centre mass, getting farther away, step by backward step, hearing the Durango's passenger door squeal open behind him, no doubt Sanderson leaning across inside. He got there and backed into the seat, still with the Smith held level, but the guys had given up. No weapons, no phones, no transportation. They were already thinking ahead, about how to get the hell out before the hammer came down.

'Go,' Reacher said.

Sanderson hit the gas, and she jinked the wheel twice, first right, then left, and she met the start of the westbound ramp doing about sixty miles an hour.

FORTY-SEVEN

Sanderson eased off a beat, to let a guy one lane over get well out the way, and then she merged on the highway, and crept back to sixty. Four and a half minutes to the rest area. The car felt rough and noisy. Not up to Bramall's standards. But possibly better than her ancient Bronco.

She said, 'How much did we get?'

The thing that mattered most.

'More than two weeks' worth,' he said. 'That's for damn sure. You owe me the story now.'

'I did all the hard work.'

'Doesn't matter. You said you would tell me the story if we won tonight. No difference who did the work.'

'When I've seen it,' she said. 'When I've seen more than two weeks' worth.'

'It's way more.'

'I want to bathe in it.'

'You should. You did well tonight.'

'Thank you.'

'Are you still doing well?'

'Did you see the way those guys looked at my sister?'

'Yes,' Reacher said.

'Did you see the way they looked at me?'

'Yes,' Reacher said. 'I saw.'

'That's how I'm doing.'

They pulled off again, just a short hop, into the rest area. They rolled past the gas and the diesel, and the fast food, and the highway patrol, and the highway department weighbridge. All the way to the chain motel. Where Bramall had scouted two main advantages. It had private parking in back, so the Toyota would be hidden from casual view. And it was so absurdly close to the scene of the crime that no one would think to look there. They were in South Dakota. There was infinite space all around. Every instinct would be to search the far end of a radius that was growing by sixty miles every hour. No one would look close to home.

Sanderson drove around the back and found the Toyota waiting. Bramall and Mackenzie were standing one either side of the tailgate. Which was open. They had been tidying the load.

Which was spectacular.

There were dozens and dozens of boxes. They were stacked in a block a yard high and a yard wide and a yard deep. There were brand names and pictures. There were quantities. There were tens, and twenties, and fifties, and hundreds. Over and over again. One box had twenty packs of twenty patches. Some kind of pharmacy size. Four hundred items right there.

'More than two weeks,' Sanderson said.

She leaned in and pulled out a box. She opened it up and took out a foil pack the size of a fat playing card. Twenty patches. She put it in her pocket. The richest woman in the world. The new gold standard for affluence. An addict with more than one hit.

She turned to Reacher and said, 'Now I'll tell you the story.'

'Later,' he said. 'First I'm going to pay Arthur Scorpio a visit.'

'I'm coming with you,' she said. 'Scorpio has a place in the story.'

They trawled through Mackenzie's bag and found the phone they had taken from the guard at the door. There was an old batch of text messages from three days before, ending with the guard telling Scorpio *All good tonight including the new Billy.* The current batch was not as happy, and it was very one-sided. Since a quarter past midnight Scorpio had been sending increasingly frequent and urgent demands for information. *What is going on? Must hear back from you immediately.*

Reacher said, 'Tell him there was a delay. Tell him the guy will come over to the laundromat and explain in person as soon as he can. Write it so it sounds like him.'

Mackenzie did the texting. She seemed most at home with it.

Sanderson traded her last-round Ruger for Bramall's three-round Colt.

Then she got back in the Durango with Reacher, and they drove away.

Gloria Nakamura saw the whole thing through the trees. In the end she had figured the Toyota was parked where it was for the same reason everyone else was parked where they were. *Why give themselves an extra walk?* The folks from the Toyota had wanted to hike the other way. Not towards the restrooms, but into the trees. Towards nothing, unless the maintenance depot was there. Which it had to be, or else who would want to hike in that direction? Circular logic, but it made sense to her.

She followed.

She stopped ten feet short.

She saw Bigfoot. She saw Terrence Bramall from Chicago. The private investigator. Who had taken her table in the breakfast place. Two times. She saw a pretty woman. She saw a second woman, horribly disfigured. Immediately she knew this was the owner of the ring. She sensed it. The ring she had worn herself, just briefly. *West Point 2005*. The black stone.

She watched. Bramall and the normal woman walked back through the trees. They passed twenty feet from her, but they didn't notice. Then nothing happened for nearly an hour. Then vehicles started to show up, and finally the white panel van, New Jersey plates, fast and furious, just as she had predicted. Running wild, technically not there at all, erased from the record.

Then there was a gunshot, and the black Toyota showed up again, and drove in and drove out, and then a Dodge Durango, and then it all went quiet again, until about a dozen different guys crept out and started milling around.

They looked sheepish.

She stepped out of the trees, with her badge in one hand and her gun in the other.

They ran, hard and fast, in eleven different directions.

She called it in, but she knew it was hopeless. The highway belonged to the state troopers, not the PD's traffic division, plus late at night any number of guys could run across all three lanes undetected, and then they could disappear beyond the shoulder to either the north or the south, into space so big it was effectively infinite.

They were gone.

She looked at the empty panel van, and the eight parked vehicles, and the old sedan outside, and then she walked back through the trees, and drove back to town. She wanted to see what Scorpio was doing.

Sanderson and Reacher took the four-lane south past Klinger's restaurant. She was chewing steadily all the way. Not partying or bathing yet. She was maintaining. She was getting herself where she wanted to be, and she was keeping herself there. He thought the huge quantity they had gotten from the panel van had changed her. He guessed part of being an addict was always being anxious. The next buck, the next hit, the next day, the next hour. She was no longer anxious. She would not be anxious for a very long time. Maybe ever again, if it worked out with the sister. So was she still an addict? Not the same way. Now it was all upside. The highs, literally, and none of the lows.

He could see the highs were worth having. Her face was not expressive. It didn't work that way. But her eyes were alive. And her body. She looked like she was having the best day of her life. Without a near-fatal dose. Once necessary, maybe, to obliterate how bad it was for the other twelve hours of the day. But not any more. Now she could take it easy. Maybe she would be OK.

Not his area of expertise.

He said, 'The supe told me why you were on the road outside the small town.'

She said, 'I told you.'

'You told me you were representing the support operation. Representing is a real five-dollar word. Maybe you could use it, if you were asked to stand in by a senior officer. But you were already a major. We didn't need a colonel to figure out how to haul ass up a hill. So there was no senior officer, which makes it a weird choice of word.'

She was quiet for a moment.

Then she said, 'How did the supe know?'

'A shrink wrote a paper.'

'He saw it?'

'He's been looking for you.'

'Bullshit.'

'He's calling in favours.'

'For me?'

'He said you felt betrayed.'

'By the shrink.'

'He meant by the situation.'

Again she was quiet.

She said, 'I was in the hospital a long time, and I got to know a lot of people. Missing an arm or a leg. Believe me, no one had it easy. But I hated those guys. They wore shorts. They could make the best of it. I would have been OK with a leg. Even for doing a favour. I was overseas five times. Some shit was going to happen. Even an arm. But not my face. You saw how those guys looked at me.'

Reacher said nothing.

She said, 'They wrote it down wrong. All they did was check a box. I never felt betrayed. Truth is I felt unlucky. Literally for the first time ever. At first I didn't even know what it was. It was new to me. It was like getting a lifetime of bad luck all in one day. Every rotten thing. Of course the guy who asked me to go for him was out catching a disease. He had to be. It was inevitable. I'm surprised he wasn't doing something worse.'

He said, 'Now tell me Porterfield's story.'

She ducked her head and looked up at the street signs.

She said, 'Do you know where we are?'

He said, 'We make a right up ahead. Then a left somewhere.'

'I'm going to pull over.'

'Why?'

'To tell you the story. Before we get there.'

Nakamura eased to a stop on the cross street, and then rolled forward until her view was perfect. Scorpio's back door was open. She could see the rim of light.

She turned the engine off.

She got out of the car, and walked halfway there. The Supreme Court said if she was reasonably sure a crime was afoot in a public place, then she could intervene without a warrant. But

Scorpio's back office was not a public place. The Court said therefore she would need evidence tantamount to an emergency. Gunshots or screams or cries for help.

The alley was silent.

She crept closer.

She heard Scorpio's voice, talking low. A composed sentence. A monologue. He was leaving a message. He sounded worried. He wanted answers. The guard at the gate, no doubt. His man on the spot. Who couldn't answer. Reacher had taken their phones. She had heard him, even in the trees. She had absolutely believed he would shoot them through the back of the knee.

She crept closer.

Now Scorpio was off the phone. There was no discernible sound at all. Maybe a low hum. Maybe the noise of a fan. Certainly no gunshots or screams or cries for help.

She crept closer.

She put her eye to the gap.

No angle.

She put her fingertips on the door and pushed it open.

Sanderson pulled over in a strip mall lot. She put the lever in park, but she kept the engine running. The Durango was full of gas. It was ready for a long trip somewhere. A sales trip. Idaho, maybe, or Washington state.

She said, 'Turns out there are a lot of nerves in the groin.'

'Who knew?' Reacher said.

'Sy was in pain all the time. Also addicted, of course. At first he got treatment direct from the Marine Corps. Then they stopped prescribing. No reason was given. At first he thought it was medical caution. These were powerful opiates, after all. But he needed them. He argued about it, but it got him nowhere. So he started doctor shopping. He drove all over. Then he started buying. Which was easy enough. Back then there was plenty to go around. Which made him mad. Every other faucet was wide open. Why was the Corps being cautious? He got back to them. They let something slip. Turned out it wasn't caution about prescribing. Their inventory was all screwed up. They were running out.'

'Someone was stealing.'

'Sy made it his life's work to find out who. On behalf of himself and his brother Marines. He was made for the job. He was already buying, after all. He was already in the network. All he had to do was poke around a little. Eventually he figured it out and wrote it up and sent it to the Defense Intelligence Agency.'

'Why them?'

'He had a theory. DIA spanned all the services. Better than sending it direct to the Marine Corps. They might bury it.'

'What happened?'

'We waited. We figured five or six days. The mails are slow from here. But he was sure they would get back to us immediately. What actually happened was we heard nothing for six months. Then he got the arrest warrant.'

'Someone was covering his ass.'

'That's what Sy thought. He gave it up, there and then. You win some, you lose some. You can't fight city hall. We went up to the high woods, because it was the start of spring. The first tiny shoots were out. He was happy as can be. He was an east coast guy, really, quite reserved in his nature, but he was messing around that day and chewing on a stick and pretending to be a mountain man. We lay down on the ground. We had stuff in our pockets. A day like that, we both knew we were going to chase it. We were going to hit it hard. We were a couple who shared a hobby. We wanted to make it epic together.'

'What happened?'

'He died.'

*

Nakamura pushed the door. Six inches, eight, ten, twelve. She leaned in the room. Scorpio had his back to her. He was sitting alone at a long bench covered with humming computers. Tower units, screens, keyboards, mice. The room was hot. A fan was running. She took out her badge and her gun. She pushed the door all the way open.

Scorpio heard it. Or felt the air, or sensed her presence.

He turned around.

'Stay where you are,' she said. 'Let me see your hands.'

He said, 'You're trespassing.'

'You're committing a crime.'

'You're harassing me.'

She took a step and raised her gun.

She said, 'Face down on the floor.'

He said, 'You're making a fool of yourself. I'm doing my accounts after a long hard day. So I can pay my taxes to pay your wages. One of the many burdens a small businessman bears.'

'You're hacking pharmaceutical industry security. Which is supervised by the federal government. Are they going to find Russian software? In which case you're in a lot of trouble.'

'I run a laundromat.'

'The laundromat of the future. It looks like IBM in here. But your system just crashed. Check your GPS. Your panel van is stuck in a snowplough shed. Reacher took the key. And everything else.'

Scorpio went quiet.

She put her badge away and took out her handcuffs.

Then it all fell apart.

Behind her a guy walked through the open door with two go-cups of coffee from the convenience store. Black coat, black sweater, black pants, black shoes. More than six feet tall. A bruise on his neck. She had seen him before.

Scorpio hit her in the back of her head, and she sprawled on the floor, and her gun went clattering away. She was dazed for a second, and felt herself being mauled and manhandled, and then she came to sitting on the floor, cuffed to a table leg. With her own handcuffs. Her skirt was up. She pulled it down, one-handed. Her bag was gone. With her phone.

Scorpio asked her, 'What did you mean, everything else?'

She said, 'All of it.'

The guy in black said, 'Want me to go check it out?'

'We'll both go,' Scorpio said.

He looked at the alley door, at the inner door, at Nakamura.

'Bring the car to the front,' he said. 'I'll go out that way. We'll leave her right here.'

The guy in black hustled out. Scorpio locked the alley door. He sat down and stared at a screen.

Nakamura said, 'You're out of business.'

'No,' he said. 'I'll never be out of business. It's about moving on, that's all. One door closes, another door opens. Nothing lasts for ever. I'll get what I need somewhere else. I always did before.'

He left her there, sitting on the floor, handcuffed to the table. He turned out the lights. He stepped through the inner door to the laundromat. He closed the door behind him. The office went pitch dark. She heard the door lock from the other side. Then immediately she heard the street door open. Not Scorpio going out. Too soon. He was still thirty feet away. It was someone else coming in. The guy in black, presumably. With the car.

But then she heard a muffled voice.

Familiar.

She thought it said, 'What have you got in your pockets?'

Sanderson said, 'Afterwards I realized he wasn't chewing on a stick. Or just a stick. It was to hide himself chewing on something else too. He had started the party early. He was going for the big OD. One fatal dose on the walk up the hill, and another when we got there. He hated his life. The thing with the DIA kept him going. But that was over now. They had closed ranks against him. He gave up. He decided this time, when he knocked on the gates, if they opened for him, he would go in.'

Reacher said nothing.

'And why not?' she said. 'It was the end of everything. He had no money. Which was different for him. Like me being unlucky. I watched him go. He started out good. He was happy as could be. I guess he knew what was coming. He was lying on his back, with the smell of pine all around. His breathing got slower and slower. Then it stopped. That's how it was.'

'I'm sorry.'

'I was too. For myself. For him, I was happy. It was for the best. Like people say. I left him there. He loved those hillsides. He loved the animals there. I packed my stuff and drove home.'

'What was the black-bag burglary for?'

'His copy of the report. In the desk drawer. The first place anyone would look.'

'What was in the report?'

'Old-fashioned cash at the supply depot door. A colonel in a Marine Corps medical battalion was selling stuff to Arthur Scorpio. That's how Scorpio did it two years ago. Different now. But back then Sy was buying the stuff he should have been getting all along. It was weird. I guess the colonel saw the file and took care of the problem behind the scenes.'

'Scorpio knew Sy's name too,' Reacher said. 'He gave it to me as a decoy.'

'Maybe the colonel told him.'

'Or maybe he told the colonel. If the roofer saw things, then Billy did too. Maybe Billy told Scorpio, and Scorpio told the colonel. The investigation hadn't started yet. Now it never would.

The guy shut it down with the phony warrant. I think that's the only way the timing works.'

'You're saying Scorpio sold him out.'

'We should get going,' Reacher said. 'Time to pay him a visit.'

FORTY-EIGHT

Sanderson and Reacher rolled through dark tomb-quiet streets, slow but never stopping, to the corner with the convenience store, where up ahead they saw a black sedan slowing at the kerb. Arthur Scorpio's car. The same car that had picked him up outside the restaurant with the chromium phone. The same guy in it. Last seen gasping for breath on the laundromat floor.

Sanderson stopped tight behind the Lincoln, and Reacher caught the guy on the sidewalk, halfway to the laundromat door. He hit him once, just a loosener, and the guy took a knee on the concrete, and flapped a hand in surrender. Turned out he had been sent to bring the car around, ahead of a trip to a highway department maintenance depot, where there was a problem of some kind. Mr Scorpio would be out in a moment.

Reacher put the guy in the Lincoln's trunk, which was big enough for two of him. The old square design. Then he headed for the laundromat door and got there just as Scorpio came out from the office. Tall and bony, maybe fifty, grey hair, black suit, white shirt, no tie. He closed the door behind him, and locked it, and turned back around.

Reacher stepped inside.

He said, 'What have you got in your pockets?'

Scorpio stared.

Didn't answer.

'You told Billy to shoot me,' Reacher said. 'And then the new guy, same thing.'

No answer.

'They didn't get the job done,' Reacher said. 'As you can see. So what happens next?'

Scorpio said, 'It was nothing personal.'

Then he glanced at the street.

'Your boy ain't coming,' Reacher said. 'It's just you and me now.'

'It was business. What would you have done?'

'You sold out Sy Porterfield, too.'

'He was a nuisance. He had to go.'

Reacher heard a faint metallic sound. In the office. Maybe a machine, counting quarters.

He said, 'What was the colonel's name?'

Scorpio didn't answer.

Reacher went to hit him.

Scorpio yelped, 'Bateman.'

Like a sneeze.

'Thank you,' Reacher said.

Nakamura heard Scorpio say Porterfield was a nuisance and had to go. Which was a confession of some sort. It had legal gravity. She was torn between shouting out and keeping quiet. In the end she compromised by clinking her handcuff against the table leg. To no effect. No one bust down the door. Then Scorpio shrieked what could have been *Bite me*, and then she heard

387

nothing more, except grunts and gasps, and the scrape of heels on the floor.

And then the slow roar of a tumble dryer, growling and droning, around and around, with a heavy load, thumping and bouncing.

Sanderson parked alongside the black Toyota, to further shield it from view. Her room was next to Reacher's. She said goodnight and went in. He went into his. He sat on the bed. He heard her through the wall. Moving around. Then he heard her go out again.

There was a knock at his door.

He opened up.

Her hood was still back.

She said, 'I guess things have changed about what I'm likely to do. You could give me my ring now. It would be safe.'

'Come in,' he said.

She sat on the bed, where he had. He took the ring from his pocket. The gold filigree, the black stone, the tiny size. A long journey, for a small item.

She took it.

She said, 'Thank you again.'

'You're welcome again.'

She was quiet a long moment.

She said, 'You know the weirdest thing about this situation?'

He said, 'What?'

'I'm on the inside looking out. I can't see myself. Sometimes I forget.'

'What did the shrinks say?'

'What would the 110th say?'

'Deal with it,' Reacher said. 'It happened. It can't un-happen. Most folks aren't going to like it. Deep down humans haven't been modern very long. But some won't care. You'll find them.'

'Are you one of them?'

'I told you,' Reacher said. 'I'm all about the eyes.'

She pushed down her hood. Her hair spilled out.

She said, 'Would you like to see me with the foil taken off?'

'Honest answer?'

'The truth.'

'You sure?'

'Don't be polite.'

'I would like to see you with everything taken off.'

'Does that line work often?'

'Now and then.'

'There's a lot of ointment.'

'I hope,' he said.

'The best way to get it off is take a shower.'

'We could do that. It's a motel. We could use a whole bar of soap. They always bring more.'

She closed his door. She stood on the bed to kiss him. She was fifteen inches shorter. Much less than half his weight. She felt impossibly delicate. The foil crinkled and the ointment oozed.

'Shower,' she said.

He unzipped her silver coat, and she shrugged it off. He pulled off her T-shirt and unhooked her bra. She felt like he had imagined her sister would feel, firm and lithe and cool to the touch, except the small of her back, which was damp. She peeled off the foil. It slid off her skin. Underneath were different shapes. Entry wounds, maybe, not exit wounds. Easier to stitch. But red with infection.

They spent twenty minutes in the shower. Then four hours in bed. Most of it sleeping. But not all. At first he was cautious. Not because of her face. Because of her size. She was tiny. He thought he might break her. Then he figured hey, she survived the army. How much worse could it be? After that they got in the same groove together. Not better than fentanyl, he was sure. But better than aspirin. He could testify to that.

Before seven the next morning Reacher was carrying coffee back to the room, when Bramall cut him off, with the phone. Another call in progress with the West Point Superintendent's Office.

But first Bramall said, 'I already called Special Agent Noble. DEA is on its way to pick up the pieces. We need to get out of here right now.'

'Works for me,' Reacher said.

He took the phone.

He said, 'General.'

The supe said, 'Major.'

'We're about to exfiltrate. The mission succeeded. We resupplied and we're good to go.'

'Do I want to know the details?'

'Probably not,' Reacher said.

'We found out about Porterfield's crusade. It was a colonel named Bateman who killed it. But DIA didn't like him. They left Porterfield's copy of the report in his house for a month. They hoped the sheriff would find it. Outside pressure would have given them cover. But the guy didn't bite. Eventually they had to go get it back. But they got Bateman later, for something else. He went down hard.'

'Thank you, general.'

'Thank you, major.'

Reacher walked the phone back to Bramall. He was fussing around the Toyota, moving stuff, trying to make more space. Mackenzie was helping him.

Reacher said, 'Relax.'

He walked back to the room. Sanderson had new foil in place. Her hood was forward, and the drawstring was tight.

He said, 'The supe told me Colonel Bateman went down later. So that's two for two. Him and Scorpio.'

'Would that make you feel better?'

'A little,' he said.

'Me too, I guess.'

'I'm not coming with you.'

'I figured you wouldn't.'

'Get the IV.'

'I will.'

'Good luck.'

'You too.'

They didn't kiss, because the foil was new. Instead they stepped outside and Sanderson got in the car. Reacher shook hands with Bramall, and Mackenzie, and he watched them drive away. He walked up to the gas and the diesel. He found another homeless guy running another hitchhiking market. A dollar to play. Like Sioux Falls. Maybe a South Dakota thing. There were only three choices. Because of the way the lanes were laid out.

You could bid for south on a state road.

Or east on the highway towards Chicago.

Or west on the highway towards Seattle.

Reacher paid his dollar and chose south on the state road. Ten minutes later he was in a carpenter's truck, with a guy who was heading to Kansas, looking for tornado work.

Lee Child is one of the world's leading thriller writers. He was born in Coventry, raised in Birmingham, and now lives in New York. It is said one of his novels featuring his hero Jack Reacher is sold somewhere in the world every nine seconds. His books consistently achieve the number-one slot on bestseller lists around the world, are published in over one hundred territories, and two blockbusting Jack Reacher movies have been made so far.

He is the recipient of many awards, most recently the CWA's Diamond Dagger for a writer of an outstanding body of crime fiction, the International Thriller Writers' ThrillerMaster, and the Theakston Old Peculier Outstanding Contribution to Crime Fiction Award.